MW01128767

THE CARMEL SHEEHAN STORY

JEAN GRAINGER

Copyright © 2020 by Jean Grainger

All rights reserved.

No part of this book may be reproduced in any form or by any electronic or mechanical means, including information storage and retrieval systems, without written permission from the author, except for the use of brief quotations in a book review.

❀ Created with Vellum

This book is dedicated to all of the women and children who found themselves at the mercy of the institutions of the Irish church and state.

CHAPTER 1

*C*armel dusted the mantelpiece with the ridiculous-looking purple feather duster the twins gave her for Christmas. She came to the photo, just as she did every day. She didn't dare lift the large silver frame, dusting around it so carefully, afraid she would drop it. Bill and Gretta beamed out at her as they had done every day of her seventeen-year marriage. Her husband was dressed in his best suit standing proudly beside the now deceased Gretta looking so young and innocent in floor-length white lace. The veil on her head looked old-fashioned now, but it was all the go back when she and Bill got married. They looked so in love, so full of hope. She frequently caught him staring at it as he shoveled his dinner wordlessly down his throat every evening after milking. The pain of his grief was still there in his eyes. The initial agony had dulled to an empty unfillable void, but Carmel knew that Bill missed his first wife every single day. She was no substitute, and never would be.

She tried so hard in the early years, making nice dinners, keeping the house spotless, she even tried to 'spice things up in the bedroom', following to the letter the instructions in *Cosmo*, but nothing worked. She would take to her grave the look of perplexed horror on his face the night in the first year of their marriage, when he came upstairs to

1

find the bed scattered with rose petals, candles burning everywhere, and Carmel reclining, in what she hoped was a provocative way, in a new cream silk nightie. He just stood there for a second, looking appalled, and then muttered something about a sick calf in the shed that he needed to check on. By the time he got wordlessly into bed beside her an hour later, she was in flannel pyjamas buttoned to the neck and all traces of flowers and candles gone. It was never mentioned again. She burned with shame whenever she thought of it, another failure. That side of the marriage never existed. She had been dreading it, and in the first nights she was relieved when he put out the light and simply fell asleep, but as time went on she knew they should be doing *something*. The years passed and apart from that one incident, the subject was never raised again.

She fleetingly played with the idea of asking him, once or twice, if she was doing something wrong. She wondered why on earth he wanted to marry her in the first place, but she never had the courage to speak up. He didn't confide in her about anything, he never had, it would only embarrass them both. She didn't think it was because of the age difference, even though she was only forty to his fifty-four, it was more that they were totally incompatible. She loved people and chatting and Bill was so quiet, he rarely spoke, and when he did his words were economical, delivering information only.

'The spuds are going to be ready in around ten days so I'll have some sent up,' had been this morning's only communication.

'Do you think it will be a good crop this year?' she asked, trying to extend the only conversation with another human apart from Julia that she would have all day.

Bill made a sound which she took to mean 'I don't know', and left for the farm. No 'have a nice day dear' or 'What do you plan to do today, Carmel?' or even 'Thanks' for the creamy porridge, grilled rasher and home baked soda bread he had eaten for breakfast.

The Bill she woke beside every morning bore very little resemblance to the man in the wedding photo. Certainly, three decades had passed, his dark curly hair was grey now, and the lean young farm-hand had become a paunchy middle-aged farmer. But it wasn't just the time that had changed him. People in the town had said to her that the day Gretta died a bit of Bill died as well. She'd had to listen to how charming he was as a young man, how chatty and genial. It was hard to believe they were not in some way blaming her for the transformation.

SHE HAD no idea what he was like before but for the seventeen long years that she knew him he was undoubtedly the most monosyllabic man in Ireland. Julia was the worst for reminiscing about the old Bill. She exclaimed, as often as she could, as loudly as she could, to as many people as she could, how Bill was so much happier before. The before, of course, referred to 'before Carmel'.

As feelings of bitter hatred for her sister-in-law threatened to rise up within her, Carmel tried to think good thoughts,

'Challenging interpersonal relationships are a great opportunity to practice your mindfulness,' she quoted her self-help CD through gritted teeth. Bill never saw her Wayne Dyer or Deepak Chopra books and CDs, she kept them out of sight. Not that he'd say anything, but he'd get that look, the one that spoke volumes, the one that said, 'Gretta wouldn't be sucked in by all that nonsense.'

The look of disappointment on Bill's face was such a regular feature of her life. So, she kept her interest in mindfulness and gratitude and trying to live her best life, to herself. At night she listened to Dr Wayne Dyer's lovely deep voice podcast about drawing positive energy to you, as Bill snored rhythmically beside her. If he saw her, listening on her headphones, he never once asked what she was listening to. In a way she was glad, it was her thing. Louise Hay, Dr Dyer, and so many others made her feel less alone. She had the internet on her phone and she was in lots of Facebook groups. One in particular she really enjoyed, set up to discuss the teachings of Dr Dyer. It was based in the UK, and the people on it were so nice and they talked so much about positivity and love and service to mankind, she felt good being around them, even if it was only virtually. They were her only friends and her name on there was CarmelIreland.

3

She'd log in most mornings and instantly someone in the group would send her a smiley face or a wink, or a 'good morning Carmel-Ireland!' post.

Whatever about Bill, he didn't care what she did, she could never let Julia see what she was up to. She'd have her committed to the county home as a nutcase, or bring her down to the priest to be exorcised. As far as Julia was concerned, there was only one place for faith or spirituality and that was up at mass every Sunday morning, anything else was heresy.

She tried so hard with Julia. Well, at the start she did anyway. Growing up in the children's home, Carmel always thought of sisters, and by association sisters-in-law, as lovely, benevolent forces for good in a person's life. She devoured novels where sisters and brothers and cousins solved mysteries or went on adventures, and longed, more than anything, for a family herself, one of her very own. When she married Bill, a handsome if quiet widower with nine-year-old twins, Sinead and Niamh, she thought she was getting just that, but from the very first day when Bill brought her to this house, meeting her step-children and sister-in-law, Carmel knew something was very wrong. It was not like any book she'd ever read. The children were not timid exactly, more standoffish, like they didn't want her there, and Julia was openly hostile.

Carmel was not a welcome addition to the sad little household of Bill Sheehan and his lost-looking girls.

Julia talked constantly about Gretta, about how nice she was, how kind, how funny, how well- dressed, and when she really wanted to put the boot in, how much Bill and the twins adored her. Carmel knew perfectly well that her husband didn't love her, he probably didn't even like her very much, and while she had sadly come to accept that fact, it wasn't nice to have her nose rubbed in it almost daily when Julia found a reason to 'pop in'.

CHAPTER 2

*C*armel started as the clock struck the hour. She tried to breathe, berating herself for her jumpiness. Nothing bad was going to happen. Julia was at work; as principal of the local National school she never left before four pm, so the chances of her 'popping' in before then were zero.

She glanced around the familiar house. Even if anyone did call, nothing was amiss. Everything was exactly as it should be, exactly as it was since the day Bill and Greta first decorated it. Carmel remembered the first time she saw Bill's house, surrounded by a little flower bed and a neatly clipped lawn. She remembered her heart soaring as Bill pointed it out to her on the drive up the hill out of the town of Birr. She would never forget the sensation of relief and sheer joy, a home of her very own at long last. It was short lived happiness but she still remembered that feeling, like everything was going to be ok. In the beginning, she imagined adding her own little touches, but very early on Bill said he wanted nothing changed, and he meant nothing at all. The same yellow and orange flowery curtains hung in the windows, the same Tupperware, the same brown patterned crockery, it was like a time warp, stuck in the eighties. She cleaned it, cooked in it, she even did the garden, but it was Bill and Gretta's house, not Bill and Carmel's.

Julia pointed that fact out frequently.

Carmel sighed, thinking of her witchy sister in law. She was all pointy and thin, exactly like a witch in a story, and her dark hair was pulled back into a severe bun. She was terrifying in every way. Carmel's heart went out to the little kids who had to have her as head-mistress.

Julia claimed she never had time for marriage, and then when poor Gretta passed away so young, she knew that Bill and the twins needed her. She spun this story so often to anyone who'd listen, Carmel could almost recite it by heart. Subtext, they still need her, as his new wife turned out to be such a disappointment.

The twins' graduation photo stood proudly beside their parent's wedding one. Sinead and Niamh were identical and even after all these years Carmel regularly let herself down by calling Sinead Niamh or vice versa. Only their mother and Bill could tell them apart; another jibe from Julia. They were nice enough girls, Carmel tried to be fair, but they missed Gretta and they didn't want a new mother, that much was very clear. She'd lost count of the number of times she tried to engage the girls in activities or outings so that they could get to know each other, as all the parenting books she bought insisted was vital. Each time she tried though, her offers were rebuffed, and Julia swept in, suggesting something much more *appropriate,* as if Carmel wanted to take them to a lap dancing club or to a rave.

She gave up eventually, another failure. They were both up in Dublin now, Sinead working as Administration Manager in Dublin Airport, while Niamh was expecting her first child, a honeymoon baby after the wedding of the century.

Carmel's cheeks blazed at the memory of Bill's speech the day Niamh married Cillian, about how proud Gretta would have been, how lucky they were to have her for the years that they had, how tragic was her loss for the whole family. He never referred to Carmel, or even looked in her direction. Sinead, the chief bridesmaid, wiped her eye, not wanting to smudge her carefully applied make-up, while Niamh's new husband squeezed his bride's hand reassuringly.

Bill raised a toast, 'To Gretta' he said, his voice choked with emotion. At least the guests had the good grace to look mortified, some throwing her a pitying glance. Carmel got no mention in any other speeches either, even though she made the cake and the flower girl dresses. The bride and bridesmaid and their Auntie Julia went to New York wedding gown shopping. It never occurred to them to ask Carmel. She remembered how foolish she felt because she'd got a passport specially, having never left Ireland before she didn't have one, but she used the special service in the Post Office so everyone in Birr knew she got a passport, thanks to Betty Big-Mouth the post-mistress, so further embarrassment ensued when she wasn't asked to go on the big trip.

Ronan Collins came on the radio. He was her favourite DJ and she loved his programme, he played all the songs she loved, and not the really old stuff that Bill liked, but songs from the seventies and eighties. Sometimes she talked back to Ronan when he spoke, if Bill heard her he'd be horrified. He'd think she was bonkers as well as unlovable, but it was nice to have someone to talk to, even if he was on the radio and had no idea that Carmel Sheehan existed quietly in the town of Birr, Co Offaly.

She used to dream that one day she'd hear Ronan's voice say, 'And now I have a request here for Carmel whose birthday it is today from her loving husband Bill and her daughters Sinead and Niamh', but she never dreamed of that anymore. She even thought once about sending in a text to the show on her birthday to wish herself a happy birthday, but she stopped herself. That really would be barking mad.

She finished dusting and checked the fire surround for any specks of ash. It was set with paper and sticks with the coal strategically placed on top 'for maximum chance of combustion'. She smiled at the phrase, Sister Kevin used to say that, when they were lighting fires in Trinity House, the children's home where Carmel grew up.

She wondered how things were there now. In the seventeen years since she left, there must have been a lot of changes. The older nuns probably died or retired, just as well, she thought. They were of a different time. There were so many rules and regulations now about children in state care. It was necessary of course, awful things happened to kids over the years in homes just like Trinity House, but she hated hearing stories of how horrific things were for people in institutions. She switched off when such tales came on the radio, not because she didn't care, but because she wanted to say that not everywhere was like that.

Julia popped in last week and more or less asked her straight out if she was abused.

'I'm so tired of all this whining on the radio, these so-called victims,' the witch announced as she made herself at home. 'I mean, look at you for example, were you abused? Your mother, the misfortunate wretch had you in a home for fallen women, and you ended up in an orphanage and nothing happened to you did it?'

Carmel was mortified, she mumbled an agreement and gave Julia her cup of tea.

Trinity House was good, not as good as a home and a family of your own of course, but good enough. The nuns who ran it were kind and they did their best. The day she left there to get married she was happy and sad at the same time, she was leaving the only home she ever knew. She remembered Sister Margaret saying,

'Your mother would have been proud of you Carmel,' as she walked with the nuns to the chapel down the street from Trinity House in the beige skirt and jacket she had found in a charity shop and altered herself to fit.

Sister Margaret was just being nice, nobody had the faintest clue who her mother was, and whether or not she would have been proud of her daughter on her wedding day was a mystery, but it made Carmel feel a bit happier anyway. The wedding was nice, the mass said by Father Tobin and he was so kind and funny, and afterwards the nuns put on a nice spread in a room off the community hall. Nobody was there from Bill's side, Julia stayed in Birr to mind the girls, and the witnesses were Sister Kevin and the sacristan, Mr. O'Neill. She remembered poor Sister Margaret and Sister Bonaventure trying to keep the conversation going over tea and sandwiches, they even made a little wedding cake, but Bill agreed with everything they said and contributed little else. After an hour, he put Carmel's small suitcase in the boot of his car and off they drove to Birr, to begin their married life. Not a word passed between them on the journey. She knew from the few meetings they had before the wedding he wasn't what you'd call chatty, but she supposed it must have been hard for him to remarry and he would need time to adjust. She had been so wrong though, he never did adjust.

CHAPTER 3

*S*he considered running around with the Hoover one more time but there was no need, the place was spotless. She looked around at the dated furniture and carpet, the décor picked out by Gretta. All Laura Ashley flowery cushions and pastel borders. It was probably lovely at the time, but now it looked awful. She would have loved to go up to Dublin and go into Hickey's Fabrics and buy material and make curtains and covers for the couch. She was very good with a needle and thread and made most of her own clothes in Trinity House from other people's hand-me-downs. The nuns said she had a gift for needlework.

Not that the interior design of the house mattered really, she supposed. Nobody ever saw it except Bill, Julia and the girls. She had tried to make a few friends in Birr at the start, joining a book club and the church flower committee, but Bill didn't encourage it.

'I don't want the whole parish traipsing through here, nosing at what I've got.' He decreed, giving her that disappointed look again, at the stupidity of someone even suggesting such a thing.

She learned from Julia that Gretta used to do the church flowers as well, she was gifted at arranging apparently, so Carmel bowed out, not wanting to look like she was trying to replace Saint Gretta. Soon after she stopped attending the book club because the deal was the members had to take turns to host it. Bill would have had a fit if she had anyone in to sit around drinking tea and talking about books. So, nobody dropped in except Julia.

She checked the clock again. Bill was meeting somebody from the Irish Farming Association today to discuss compensation for the flooded fields of last winter, so he wouldn't be needing his dinner at one like he usually did. She had until at least six before he'd be home.

She took the page furtively out of her apron pocket though she was alone. It was getting worn on the creases she had read it so often, but it was like a drug to her, like that bar of chocolate in the fridge calling you. Once you knew it was there, resistance was impossible, no matter how hard you tried. She had printed out the Facebook message she had received on Bill's printer which he used for farm business. The terror of logging into her Facebook account on his computer, then using his printer, had nearly given her a heart attack. She slipped the single sheet out of its envelope and sat down on the kitchen chair. Carefully she read it again, though by now the words were etched on her mind.

Dear Mrs. Sheehan,

I hope this message finds you well. I also hope it doesn't come as too much of a shock to you. I have been trying to find you for many years and eventually I believe I was lucky in my search, I will explain how when we hopefully meet. I believe your mother, your birth mother I mean, was a lady called Dolly Mullane. She passed away two years ago, I'm sorry to tell you, but she asked me to help her to find you. She spent years looking for you, and I can't tell you how sad I am that she didn't live to see you again.

My name is Sharif Khan and I run a nursing home called Aashna House in Bedfordshire, England, where your mother spent her final years. She was my mother's closest friend so I knew Dolly very well, long before she came to stay at Aashna House.

I do not know if you would like to meet me, or if I have anything to offer except to tell you of your mother but if you would like to, I will be in Dublin on the 9th of April. I will stay at the Gresham Hotel and I will be in the lobby at 2pm. I will wait until 2.30 and if you do not arrive I will assume you do not wish to have any contact with me. I bear no bad news Mrs. Sheehan, but I have some photographs and some correspondence from your mother that I feel it is my duty to deliver to you.

I hope to see you on the 9th then,
Yours sincerely,
Sharif M. Khan.

She folded the page carefully and slipped it back into her apron pocket, her heart thumping. She glanced at the clock again. It was noon now and the bus was at 12.35. It would arrive into Dublin at 1.40 and if she jumped in a taxi she would be at the Gresham on O'Connell Street by two.

* * *

SHE SAT IN THE LOBBY, trying not to pull at her dark green V-necked jumper that she now realized was too tight across the bust. It looked fine, nice even, when she was standing up in her black jeans and ankle boots but sitting down she felt like the Michelin man, her spare tyre bulging over her waistband. She should have had her hair done, but if she wandered nonchalantly into Clipz in Birr for a blow dry, Julia would be sure to hear of it, so she didn't risk it. She tried to straighten her mid brown bob herself with a brush and the blow-dryer but it ended up a bit wonky. At least she had managed to put the boxed dye in her hair to cover her blonde roots. Julia said natural blonde hair was a bit trashy looking, and brown was a better colour, more low key. She put on a little make-up but felt uncomfortable since she so rarely wore any. She never had any occasion to get glammed up as they said in the magazines. She knew her eyes were nice, dark blue, her friend Kit in Trinity House always said Carmel's mother must have been beautiful.

Kit was killed in a car accident in Australia, only a month after she got there, determined to make something of herself. She was so brave, she wanted Carmel to go with her, to take a job in Dunnes Stores and save up enough for the fare, and just take off, chance their luck and be someone, not a pair of orphans but young women with their whole

futures ahead of them. But Carmel had been too scared, too institu-
tionalised to follow her friend. She regretted that now. Maybe Kit
would never have been in that taxi if Carmel was with her. They had
written religiously every month, telling each other everything. Carmel
remembered reading bits of her letters out to the nuns in the
evenings, heavily censored of course, and their genuine distress when
they got the word from the man from the Department of Foreign
Affairs that Kit was dead. Carmel had been inconsolable, especially
because the last letter she sent was full of hurt and anger. Kit had
written to say she was mad to marry Bill, that she could do better than
him, and Carmel reacted badly. Kit had been right of course, not that
she could have done better probably, but that she should never have
married Bill Sheehan.

She dismissed the sad thoughts, they were not serving her well
when she was jittery anyway. She ordered a cup of tea but realized
when she sat down that nobody else was drinking tea in the lobby,
they were in the bar or the coffee shop so she felt a bit foolish. The
waitress looked none too pleased at having to carry it out and she
almost slammed the teapot down, spilling some on the marble-topped
coffee table. She thought about just walking away from it but decided
that would look even more daft, so she sat on the overstuffed sofa and
tried to look like it was a perfectly normal thing to do. She wished she
wasn't here before this Sharif Khan, the nerves were threatening to
get the better of her.

Dolly Mullane, she thought, rolling the name around in her head,
she'd even said it aloud a few times to see how it sounded. Her mother
was called Dolly. She tried to picture a Dolly, lots of make-up and
fancy clothes, a 'good time girl' as they might have said long ago. No
wonder she got pregnant. Carmel never allowed herself to dwell on
her birth mother. In the home it was a source of regular speculation
with the others, the children inventing such amazing people to be
their real parents. She never bothered with that. One day she was
baking with Sister Margaret in the kitchen of Trinity House when
someone came on the radio, looking to meet their child given up for
adoption years earlier. The nun snapped it off immediately.

'No good ever comes of that kind of thing. You're a sensible girl not to be dwelling on it.'

Carmel nodded. She would have loved parents of her own, but it wasn't to be. She was given up into the care of the state as an infant. Her mother had not been married, and as a result she had been abandoned. Her mother was never heard from again, and an opportunity for adoption never presented itself. That was as much as she knew.

'Mrs. Sheehan?'

Carmel started as the man touched her shoulder, interrupting her daydream.

'Ye...yes, that is she, me, that is me... I mean I'm Carmel,' she finished weakly.

'Sharif Khan.' The tall Indian looking man stretched out his hand to shake hers. 'May I?' he asked, indicating the sofa opposite her, placing a leather briefcase on the seat beside him. He sat down elegantly, looking perfectly at ease. He was wearing a biscuit-coloured jacket with a dark shirt and dark trousers, and what surely must be handmade shoes. They didn't look like shoes any Irish man would wear, slip-on, tan-coloured, in a sort of soft leather that shone. On anyone else they would have looked a bit feminine, she certainly couldn't picture the outfit on Bill but on this man, it looked incredible.

'Yes..yes of course.' She was tongue-tied. He was so striking looking. She wasn't the only one to notice either. Several women's eyes were on him she noticed as she glanced around the lobby. He had short silver hair, a clipped silver beard and caramel skin, but it was his eyes that mesmerized her. They were perfectly almond shaped and almost black in colour, with long thick lashes.

He smiled at her, revealing even white teeth. Saying nothing.

Carmel felt uncomfortable under his gaze. She shifted awkwardly on the stupid sofa, wishing the coffee table was high enough to hide behind instead of the height of her knees.

'I am sorry for staring, but it is quite remarkable. You look just like your mother. For a moment, it was as if she had returned.' His voice purred, and his accent was very posh sounding, like someone out of Downton Abbey, but with a hint of foreign as well.

He clearly didn't do small talk, no chat about the weather, no endlessly dodging around the issue as Irish people would do. Carmel realized he was the first foreigner she'd ever spoken to properly. There was the Polish girl in the shop in Birr of course, but that was just 'Good morning' or 'Thank you', and there once was a missionary nun who came from Ghana to visit Trinity House a few times, but she was Irish.

'It's nice to meet you Mr. Khan,' she began, trying to sound normal.

'Sharif, please. May I call you Carmel?' That smile again.

'Of course, yes,' she swallowed. Her heart was thumping in her chest, she was sure he could hear it. She was definitely nervous about what he might tell her, but there was something else. There was something very unsettling about him.

He reached into his briefcase and took out a big padded envelope. He held the envelope in both hands and smiled down at it, nodding slowly.

'I have waited for a long time to deliver these to you Carmel, and I feared it would never happen. I wish Dolly was here, I really do..'

He handed the envelope over to her. It contained something bulky.

'There are forty letters in there, one for each of your birthdays, and several photographs. There is also a box containing a piece of jewellery. Your mother made me learn who each person in each photo is so I could tell you, if I ever got the opportunity.'

'Can I get you something sir?' The same waitress approached, looking the picture of sweetness and light this time.

'Ah, a cup of tea like my friend here would be very nice, thank you.' He smiled quickly and the girl beamed.

'Certainly sir, just a moment.' And off she tripped.

Carmel's hands were shaking, she couldn't open the envelope. Why did the nuns say her mother had never tried to contact her? Was it true that she wasn't just dumped on the state, never given a second thought? That was her story, that was who she was, and now this man turns up out of the blue telling a very different story? Could she believe him?

Maybe it would be better if she never opened this envelope. Her life was what it was, she had a roof over her head, food to eat, what good could any of this do now? Thoughts raced round her mind, a myriad of feelings threatening to overwhelm her. Regret, fear, curiosity, resentment, anger, all vying with each other for supremacy to bubble to the surface. Suddenly she couldn't stay there, in this public place with the whole of Dublin watching on and this man... she had to get away. She stood up, not caring if she looked rude or ridiculous.

'I'm sorry. I need to go, I can't...I'm sorry.' She held the envelope to her chest and grabbed her jacket in the other hand. Almost stumbling in her haste to escape, Sharif put out his hand to steady her.

'Carmel, please wait.' He placed his hand on her arm. 'This is overwhelming, I understand. Please, take the key of my room, it is on the third floor, 353. I will be busy for the afternoon, you may use it in privacy to read your letters.'

Carmel looked at him, then down at his brown hand on her arm, suspicion and panic were all she felt.

'I can't imagine what this must be like, but please, trust me, I mean you no harm.'

'I just can't...I'm sorry.' She began, barely coherent. She felt her throat constrict, sweat beading on her forehead.

'Breathe Carmel, deep breaths...' he said quietly.

She tried, her breathing was shallow and panicked.

'Slowly, empty your mind, just focus on your breath. Breath in cool clear air, expel the feelings of fear.'

She looked at him, her eyes fixed on his. She felt trapped.

'Breathe.' He said again. 'Breathe in blue, breathe out red.'

Slowly her breath returned to normal as she followed his instruction, her eyes never leaving his.

Once she was calm again, he handed her the room key and smiled.

'Take your time, my mobile number is written on the envelope. You can call me or send a text whenever you want to talk. If you are hungry or need anything have room service deliver it.'

He placed her bag over her shoulder.

'It is going to be fine. Dolly loved you so much, and to all who knew her, you were a real person, she talked about you all the time. It must feel strange, of course, I feel like I know you and you have never heard of any of us, but it is all good I promise you. Read your letters and you'll see.'

Carmel had so many questions but now was not the time. She nodded and took the key.

She couldn't even start thinking about what it must look like to take a hotel room key from a man she had only just met in the lobby of the Gresham while her husband discussed flood plains and water pumps in Birr with some civil servant, oblivious to it all. She didn't care. She wanted to read these letters, in peace, by herself, and maybe fill in the parts of her that were missing all her life. Parts she never even really realized were not there.

CHAPTER 4

She walked quickly towards the lift, feeling that everyone was watching her. Of course, they weren't, people only care about their own drama, she told herself. In the lift she looked at the handwriting on the envelope again. 'To Whom it May Concern' in copperplate cursive. It looked vulnerable though, as if the writer was trying to sound official, not her real self. On the back, was Sharif's number.

She inserted the credit card style key in the slot of room number 353 and to her relief the lock clicked, and the little light went green. She pushed the door and walked in. It looked just like any hotel room, she supposed. Well, she'd never actually been in a hotel room before, but she'd seen them on TV. There was a small leather suitcase on wheels standing in the corner of the room but other than that there was no evidence of Sharif Kahn or anyone else. The room was immaculate, decorated in muted shades of cream, terracotta and red and Carmel thought it was beautiful.

She sat at the little table beside the window that had two upholstered tub seats either side, perfectly coordinated with the décor, and placed the envelope on the table. Outside the busy thoroughfare of O'Connell Street, traffic and people went about their business, having no idea that something momentous was happening in room 353. She took a deep breath, trying to imagine what Dr. Dyer would advise at this exact moment.

'Breathe, be still, understand that everything is as it should be, everything happens at exactly the right time.' She could hear his voice stilling her fluttering emotions. Sharif reminded her of Dr .Dyer she realized, he was calm and warm and had a lovely deep voice as well.

She peeled open the seal and put her hand inside.

Extracting each item slowly, she placed them on the table. There was a bundle of letters, tied up with a gold ribbon, all addressed to Carmel. There was also one of those little photo albums, the kind that only fits a few 6x4 inch prints, with a wood-effect plastic cover, and finally a small jewellery box. The box was heavy and encrusted with coloured stones.

What to look at first? She fumbled with the ribbon on the letters, eventually freeing them. There were several, all written on Basildon Bond unlined blue paper. She picked one up.

My dear daughter Carmel,

Happy Birthday to you, my darling daughter. It is 2013 and you are now thirty-seven years old. I can't believe I haven't seen you for thirty-seven years. I've written to you every year on your birthday and it is my dearest wish that someday you will read my letters. Writing them makes me feel a little closer to you. I used to write you so many letters in the early days, letters full of regrets and tears and pain, but I'll never send you those. I hope you are happy and loved, wherever you are. I'm sixty years old, twenty-three years older than you, but I have cancer so I don't know if I'll see your birthday next year. It's my own fault, the cigarettes did for me. I hope you don't smoke my love, lung cancer is a horrible way to go. I'll never stop looking for you, not while I have breath in my body, and even if I fail or run out of time, Sharif is determined to succeed. If you are reading this, you'll have met him. He is a special man, my love, trust him.

With all my love today and every day,
Your loving Mum, Dolly.

It wasn't until Carmel saw the tear drop on the page in front of her, smudging the ink, that she realised she was crying. Her mother loved her, she really loved her and regretted giving her up. Nobody had ever said those words to Carmel before. Some of the nuns had been fond of her, she knew that, but to hear someone say that they loved you after all these years, it was overwhelming. She read all of the letters, forty in all. She managed to build up a story of what had happened to her mother. It wasn't anything she hadn't heard a hundred times before but when it was her own story, the story of how she got to be in the world, it was fascinating. Some were short, the pain of loss palpable through the decades, others were long and newsy as if catching up with an old friend. She said she had to give Carmel up. She was young and unmarried and was forced into a Magdalen Laundry, a workhouse for women who found themselves pregnant out of wedlock. She wasn't given a choice in the matter. She never wanted to, but she was forced to leave her baby once she was ten days old. Her plan had been to go to England, make some money, and come back for Carmel once she was set up, but when she came back to the laundry where she gave birth, they said the child had been adopted. They slammed the door in her face.

Carmel had to stop reading then, panic setting in again. She assumed she came out of a Madelene Laundry, but she had no memory of it. All she knew was Trinity House.

Dolly never married, she never had any more children, she lived and worked quietly in England, in a variety of dress shops, and ladies' tailors. She loved clothes and she eventually earned enough to buy a small house in the village of Barton le Clay. She had a little business, dressmaking, and she loved it.

Every single year, sometimes twice or three times, as often as funds permitted, she would come to Ireland, looking for her daughter, but she was never given any information apart from the fact that her child had been adopted and that there was no way to know anything further.

The last few letters tell of her sadness to sell her little cottage and to move into Aashna House, the nursing home run by the son of her friend Nadia. Carmel learned how close to the Pakistani community her mother became through her career as a seamstress and how, when the time came when she could no longer take care of herself, the welcoming embrace of Aashna House run by Sharif was the obvious choice. Carmel tried to remember if she'd ever met a Pakistani person before Sharif Khan, but she was sure she hadn't.

When she finished reading she held the letters up to her face and maybe she was imagining it, but she thought she could smell a sweet scent, lavender maybe. Just to hold in her hands, letters written to her from her own mother was astounding. Her eye rested on the photo album; she was reticent, not wanting to shatter the illusion that she'd built up in her head of her mother. As she read the letters she imagined Dolly as small, slim and kind-faced, with white coiffed hair and a smart skirt and jacket. She put the letter down and opened the album.

The first photo was of a baby, in black and white but a fair-haired baby, wrapped in a shawl of some kind. She flipped the photo page and read on the back.

'Carmel, five days old, April 1976'

Carmel flicked it back again and stared at the child in the photo. It was her. Carmel as a baby. She never pictured herself as a baby before. The nuns had no pictures, there was never a reason to take any.

The next photo was of a couple walking on a beach, the man was long-haired and bearded, wearing a kind of loose flowing shirt and jeans. The woman, or girl really, she couldn't have been more than eighteen or nineteen, had long brown hair, hanging loose down her back and a yellow and mustard patterned maxi dress. Both were laughing happily into the camera.

Carmel flipped it over, 'Me and Joe, Dollymount, 1973.'

So that was Dolly. She was pretty, and slender. Carmel tried to see a likeness to her own in the face but failed. She looked at the man more closely, he had blond, what the nuns called dirty blond, hair and a kind of straggly beard. He looked like a hippie, but he had lovely straight teeth. Was Joe her father?

There were only two other pictures. The first was a group shot of a dark-skinned woman wearing a bright pink sari, a tall, handsome man, clearly her husband, with one arm around her shoulder, and in front of them a little boy with almond shaped black eyes, smiling shyly for the camera. She turned it over.

Nadia, Khalid and Sharif, 1975.

The last one was a recent photo, based on the fashion. In it there was a large group of people, twenty or more, and in the middle of them a slight, smiling woman, in a wheelchair. She was very thin, and her skin had a yellow pallor. The woman was wearing a bright turquoise scarf on her head, tied behind, pirate style and was dressed in an elegant white shirt tucked into jeans. She wore long silver earrings, and around her neck was a necklace with a bright blue stone. The only person Carmel recognised in the picture was Sharif, he had a stethoscope around his neck and was smiling brightly at the woman in the wheelchair.

Carmel flicked it over.

'Me after Chemo at my birthday party in Aashna House. Sharif said I needed to take this one with him in it so you'll believe him if he ever finds you.'

Carmel felt a lump in her throat, the 'if' was scribbled out and 'when' was written over it.

'The earrings and necklace are yours now darling. I got them in Karachi, from my friend Nadia when we went to visit her family, and I love them.'

Carmel opened the box, it definitely looked foreign, in Ireland, boxes for jewellery wouldn't be that colourful, and there, sitting on the blue satin lining, were the earrings and the necklace.

Her phone beeped and she jumped.

'Customers please note bin collections will be on Saturday due to bank holiday.'

She dismissed the automated text from the council but noticed the time.

It was 4pm, Bill would be home in two hours, looking for his dinner, and Julia was finished school, she could call in at any moment. Panic gripped her, where had the last two hours gone? She had to get back. She couldn't bear answering their questions about where she'd been all day.

She gathered the letters and album into the envelope and was just about to place the box in beside them when she stopped. She opened the jeweled box again and took out the earrings and the necklace and slowly put them on. She stood up and looked in the mirror. She looked dreadful, eyes red from crying, mascara smudged all over her face, make-up blotchy.

A knock on the door. She started in shock. Maybe it was the hotel management, knowing she shouldn't be in there, coming to throw her out.

'Carmel?' She heard her name through the door.

Sharif! She hadn't time to fix her face, she'd have to open it.

'Just a minute!' she called, running to the bathroom to splash her face. She patted her face with tissue, afraid to use the lovely white towels in case she left make-up on them. Looking marginally better, she opened the door.

'Hello. Thanks for letting me use the room...' she began, anxiously trying to fill in the silence.

'It was my pleasure.' He smiled, and she noticed how his eyes crinkled.

'I was just going...' she said, making for the door.

'Please,' he laid a hand on her arm once more. 'Please let us order some tea, perhaps some refreshments for you, you have not eaten I assume?'

Carmel was flustered. 'No. No thanks, I've to get back, my husband...and his sister...they will be wondering where I am and...'

'Please,' he repeated. 'I have some things I want to tell you, things about your mother, I would like to talk to you about her.' His measured and serene manner was in direct contrast to Carmel's disquiet. She looked at him and remembered what her mother had written. 'He is a special man, trust him.'

'Ok. I'd like to hear it...I'm sorry, this is just all so unexpected. And I'm sorry for running off earlier, I just got overwhelmed.' She allowed herself to be led back to the chair by the table. Once she was seated, he went to the hotel phone.

'Hello, this is Dr. Khan in 353, could you please send up tea for two, an extra big pot if you can, as well as a selection of sandwiches? Thank you.'

'So, you're a doctor,' Carmel blurted, instantly realising how gauche that sounded. She was just like Julia, who would manage to put aside her hatred of everything foreign for a doctor.

'Yes I am, an oncologist. The home I run in Bedfordshire is a care home for those in the last stages of life. That is how your mother came to me, though I have known her for years of course, she was a wonderful friend to my mother. We all miss Dolly very much, we were very close.'

CHAPTER 5

*H*e sat down opposite her.

'So you saw the pictures? Those pieces are lovely on you by the way. She would have been so proud to see her daughter wearing her precious things. Did you read all of the letters?'

Now that she knew he was a doctor his manner made more sense, reassuring and kind. He was comfortable asking delicate questions. Carmel felt when he looked at her he was gazing into her mind.

'Shall I tell you about her?' he asked, his dark eyes never leaving hers.

Carmel's face must have registered her dilemma. She'd buried her curiosity about her mother all her life, as a way to save herself from the emotional rollercoaster that meeting birth parents inevitably seemed to cause. Sharif misinterpreted the reason for her hesitation however.

'I'm sure he'll understand.' Sharif spoke quietly, sitting still, almost aware that any sudden movements on his part would send her scurrying out the door.

'Ha!' Carmel was aware how loud her reaction was, and how inappropriate it must seem. She felt her cheeks redden and she rushed to explain,

'Sorry, you must think I'm awful. It's just that he wouldn't, understand I mean.'

Sharif looked perplexed. 'But he does know of your circumstances, the fact that you were adopted?'

'I wasn't.' The pain of years of rejection weighed heavily in those two words.

'But I assumed, that you were placed into care and adopted. That's what your mother thought as well.'

Sharif lost a little of his assurance and composure.

'No. I never was, I was born in a laundry, that's where they put women like my mother, you know, who were pregnant. I don't know how long I was there, there are no records. I must have been moved to Trinity House at some stage, that's a children's home out in Drumcondra run by the Sisters of Charity, I spent all of my childhood there. Then, when I was eighteen, the nuns told me it was time for me to move on, the state wouldn't pay for my care anymore, but I had nowhere to go. Because I'd been there the longest, they allowed me to stay on, as a helper. I didn't earn anything, but I got room and board in return for taking care of the little ones and things like that. I used to help in the convent as well with some of the older nuns. I liked it actually, they were lovely mostly.'

Sharif looked at her in admiration.

'I'm amazed at how you can be so calm. I, we, always thought you had been adopted.' He paused. 'But please, I'm sorry for interrupting. Please go on.'

'Well, I suppose I always knew I couldn't stay there forever. The nuns never put pressure on me or anything, but the authorities used to visit, and the sisters were in breach of the regulations by keeping me there, and I hated the idea of them getting in trouble. But I had no proper skills, I was okay at school, but not brilliant or anything, and anyway further education wasn't available for kids in care. Then one day, they got a letter, from a widower, asking if there were any young women interested in meeting him and his children, with a view to marriage. I suppose it must sound like a story from the fifties rather than the nineties, the nuns even remarked on how ludicrous a suggestion it was in that day and age, but I said I thought he sounded nice and I'd be happy to meet him.'

If Sharif thought that it was a mad or tragic story, his face gave no indication of it. 'Go on.'

'And so I met Bill one day in Trinity House and he was quiet but nice, at least I thought he was. He took me out for a cup of tea, told me about his home and the farm and his little twin daughters. And so, after about three or four meetings, he proposed and I said yes. I felt like I was getting a home and a family at long last.'

The silence filled the space between them, then there was a knock on the door, her heart leapt, her nerves jangling.

'That will be the tea.' He got up and walked over to the door, had a brief word with the porter, tipped him and returned bearing a tray, laden with tea and sandwiches.

'So, shall I pour?'

She smiled and nodded. Glad that the interruption had diffused the atmosphere created by her revelations.

She took a sip of tea and one of the sandwiches he offered.

'So, did you live happily ever after?' Sharif asked.

Puzzled by the question, she thought for a moment. Nobody had ever asked her that before.

'I suppose I was grateful that he wanted me, that he was willing to marry someone with no past, no family to claim her, and he is kind, in his own way. He doesn't say much, and he's out a lot and now that the girls are gone, well there's not much to do around the house, but he's never cruel or mean. The problem is, that he loves his first wife, he still does and I'm no match for her. I tried to be, to be a good wife and mother but it never really worked out. To be honest, we never talk, I...I...' she struggled to find the right words, 'I disappoint him.'

Carmel flushed red. She'd said too much. Suddenly the room seemed stuffy and she needed to get out. What was she thinking? Sitting in a hotel room telling a blank stranger her deepest secrets? She must be losing the plot.

Sharif put his hands together and tapped his mouth with his joined index fingers, deep in thought. Carmel noticed the length of his

27

fingers, the perfect cream-coloured crescents on the nails. So different to Bill's calloused hands, his gnarly fingernails.

'I have a proposition,' he said with enthusiasm. 'Let us walk, you telephone your husband to reassure him there is nothing untoward about your tardiness in returning home, and we will get out into the fine Irish sunshine. There is a park I believe not far from here, we can walk and talk and it may not seem so…intense…as it now does.'

Noting Carmel's reticence he added, 'Carmel, we have so much to say to each other. So far, I am in shock. Your life is nothing like we imagined. Your mother waited for this day all of her life, how happy she would be to be here with you now, back in Ireland. I want to hear your story, and I want to tell you hers. But sitting here, in a hotel room with a man you have only just met, well it must seem a little… awkward, especially in the light of the revelations you have had to absorb today. So, I propose that we walk, we chat and perhaps we can stop for tea, or a drink if you prefer?'

The simplicity of the plan made her smile. He struck her as a man who just did things, he didn't over think it. Unlike her, who over-thought absolutely everything. Perhaps an afternoon wandering around Dublin with him, learning about her mother, wasn't the end of the world. She both longed for and dreaded to hear the story of how it came to be that she spent her life as a child of the state, and this might be her only opportunity. Neither Bill nor Julia would ever understand, not in a million years. They thought they knew her background and while Bill never mentioned it, Julia did get in the odd poisoned barb. She was beneath them, that much was made very clear. Her birth family or her past was never going to be dinner table chat.

'I'd like that,' she heard herself say, 'I won't ring him, I'll explain when I see him, it would only…complicate things.'

'Very well Carmel, as you wish.' He stood up, gave her a grin and taking three of the little sandwiches, he went around the room gathering his umbrella, hat and coat. It was a knee-length camel wool coat and his hat was one of those you'd see in films about the war, did they call them Trilbys? Anyway she thought he looked the picture of elegance. She judged him to be in his early forties, but the way he moved fascinated her. Like one of those big cats you'd see on nature programmes sometimes. Confident, unflappable, self-assured.

The weak May sunshine bathed O'Connell Street in thin yellow light as they ambled along. They stopped to look in a window of a shop advertising Irish paraphernalia and she noted Sharif looking at her reflection in the glass. She caught his eye.

He smiled, 'I'm sorry, it's just you look so much like her. Dolly was a unique person, a free spirit, a lover of risks and jokes and she had a hatred for conventions or rules.'

'Like the rule that said, don't give away your baby you mean?' Carmel shocked herself with the bitterness she heard in her voice. They were walking again.

'You're angry, and I don't blame you. What happened to you, and what your mother *thought* happened were two very different things, but this is what you must understand Carmel, she was not allowed to keep you. She would have loved nothing more, but the father, your father, was a married man and even though she went to her grave believing that he loved her, he never left his wife. She could not go home, her father was a very strict man and her mother died when she was young, just eight years old. She explained to me how powerful the nuns were, they said she couldn't have you, she was a young girl alone with no support, no job or money, the nuns insisted she leave you and there was no fighting those nuns. She gave in and her plan was for you to be taken into care, just for a little while, until she got herself sorted out with a job and a home, and then she would come back for you.'

'So, what happened?' she asked, skirting around a bunch of giggling teenage girls.

'When she came back to the baby home to get you, by now she had a good job. She and my mother set up a dressmaking business in London, she had a little flat and she felt she could offer you something more than a life of drudgery and poverty.'

'If all this is true, why didn't she come and get me if it was what she wanted?' Carmel willed herself not to cry.

'She did. When she went back, they said you had been adopted and that they couldn't give her any details. She was devastated but they just threw her out onto the street and refused to engage with her about it at all. So, after trying and trying, and getting nowhere, she returned to England. I remember her in our living room over the years, my mother comforting her when I was just a boy, she cried she railed against the system. Over and back she went to Ireland, several times, she got legal help, saying she never gave permission, but the mother and baby home claimed that she did and that it was all done legally and above board. Eventually it went to court and the judge ruled against your mother. She always said that was the second worst day of her life, the first was the day she gave you up. My mother was with her, and for months Dolly could neither work nor communicate properly, she stopped eating, she refused to go out. My parents, together, helped her to find a way to live again. Not the life she wanted, nothing like it, but a life nonetheless.'

Carmel tried to absorb what he was saying. None of this made any sense but she knew instinctively he was telling the truth.

Sharif went on, 'She never married, though she had many admirers, but she never paid them any attention. She only had one goal, and that was to find you. She wrote to you frequently and told me that she would never give up. The authorities told her that your name had been changed and refused to tell her what it was, so it was as if you vanished into thin air. They told her that her only hope was if you tried to make contact with her when you were an adult. She waited, hoping every day for some contact. She wrote to the adoption board, to charities, to support groups, giving her details, in case you ever tried.

She heard about using the internet to trace people from a patient and so she went off to the local community college and learned how to use a laptop and I helped her to buy one. She searched and searched again, asking everyone, anyone who had been in care, adopted, fostered, if they ever came into contact with you, but to no avail. Social media, of recent years, has been wonderful, she was in so many Facebook groups set up for people trying to reunite.'

They had walked across the city to Stephen's Green park where the after work crowd was beginning to appear. People pushed babies in strollers, toddlers and children ran to the ducks with bags of stale bread and Carmel marveled again at how ordinary everything was when she felt like her world was being turned on its head. Sharif suggested they sit on a bench.

'Did you ever look for her?' he asked gently.

'No,' Carmel answered truthfully. 'I didn't see the point. I just thought I was abandoned. Not adopted, not fostered, just dumped on the state. I thought she didn't want me then, so why would she want me now? I used to fantasise when I was very young, six maybe, that she would come for me, that it had all been some big mix-up and we would go off and live happily ever after, but I grew out of that.' Carmel's voice cracked.

'Why were you not adopted?' Sharif asked gently. 'Do you know?'

'No.' Carmel shook her head. 'Not cute enough I suppose. If you don't get taken by two or three there isn't much hope. People want babies.' She shrugged.

'That could not be why. I've seen your baby picture. You were a beautiful baby and you are a beautiful woman. There must have been another reason.'

Carmel blushed to the roots of her hair. Nobody had ever called her beautiful. A nun once said she had good bones but that was as close to a compliment as she had ever received.

'Well,' she said, praying her voice wouldn't betray her discomfort, 'if there was, we will never know. I have no paperwork it seems. When Bill married me, I needed a birth certificate and there was no file in existence. I was, still am I suppose, a nobody.'

Carmel didn't mean for her tone to sound self pitying, it was just how she saw it.

'You are not a nobody, you shouldn't think of yourself that way. You were loved by your mother, so much. If she was here now she's ask you, what do you plan to do with your life?' Sharif asked.

Carmel chuckled. 'I don't have any plan. Bill will probably put up with me, he'd hate the idea of divorce.'

Sharif did not return her smile.

'Do you work outside of the home?' Sharif asked, and Carmel struggled to answer. It was embarrassing.

'no, no I don't, I would like to have a job, but Bill wouldn't like me to work. He'd feel like people might say he couldn't provide for me.'

'But what if it wasn't up to Bill? What would you like to do? Where would you like to go? What's your dream?' Sharif probed.

Carmel looked at him, deep into his eyes. She sighed,

'I know I must seem pathetic to you, and I probably am, but people like me, we don't get to have a dream you know? We're lucky if thigs work out ok, that the best case scenario. Take for example, my friend Kit, she was in Trinity House as well, grew up there, just like me. She left care and went to Australia and she begged me to go with her. I was too afraid, but she ended up being killed in a car accident. I don't mean that it was good to be scared, but because she was a kid like me, nobody cried, except me, and one or two of the nuns. I went from being a ward of the state to being Bill's wife. I never even had a proper job, I've never been anywhere, I don't have any skills. Not everyone can be like you.'

Despite her efforts to stop, her eyes brimmed with tears. She tried to pull herself together, but it was as if a dam had opened and nothing she could do would stop the deluge now.

Sharif handed her a chocolate-coloured silk handkerchief. She was afraid to use it, but he took it from her hands and wiped her face. Then he put his arms around her and held her to his chest. She could hear the beat of his heart, and though every fibre of her being told her that sobbing in the arms of this handsome but total stranger was absurd, a little part of her felt safe. It was a new feeling, that someone was on her side, that she wasn't alone.

She fought the urge to break free, to apologise for her outburst, to run frantically to the bus. Instead she stayed there, breathing in the smell of him, a citrusy, spicy smell, and soaked up the comfort of his embrace, as he rubbed her head, and let her weep for her mother, for herself, for the lost little girl, the bitter teenager, and for the bride that felt she deserved no better than a broken-hearted man's hospitality.

CHAPTER 6

The evening chill was settling in, the heat of the sun gone as it set over the Dublin skyline. Everyone was back in coats and scarves again. Carmel shivered in her thin jacket, despite the heat of Sharif.

'You're cold. No wonder, you've hardly eaten all day. Let's go for dinner, and perhaps a little champagne?' His eyes twinkled as he took off his scarf and wrapped it around her neck. It was cashmere and smelled of him.

She smiled. 'I've never had it.'

'Not even on your wedding day?'

'It wasn't that kind of wedding,' Carmel said with a sad smile.

Sharif stood up and tucked Carmel's arm in his as they left the park.

'There are so many stories to tell you,' he began, 'It's hard to know where to begin.'

'Why did she never marry?' Carmel asked.

Sharif paused, then spoke. 'She had lots of offers, One time, I remember this man wanted to take your mother out. She told me often about him. He was a good man, kind, steady, with a good job and a nice house and car. He tried every way he could think of to get her to marry him, but nothing worked. She told me she wished she could have fallen in love with him, he was on paper, perfect, but she couldn't. She had only had one great love in her life and it didn't work out, and that was your father. And she could never then consign herself to a loveless marriage, no matter how convenient or suitable. She told me one day, as we were sitting in the garden having tea, my mother, Dolly and I, that she hoped you were in love with someone who was yours to love and that he loved you in return.'

Carmel said nothing, no words were needed.

They ate at the Shelbourne, in a secluded corner, lit by candlelight. Carmel had never been anywhere as luxurious. She drank champagne and ate crab and steak that Sharif ordered, and they talked as if they had known each other for years. Once or twice Julia and Bill crossed her mind, but she dismissed them. They wouldn't be worried, they would just resent the fact that she had the audacity to go off without clearing it with them first.

She told Sharif funny stories about Trinity House. She had never considered herself as funny before, but Sharif was wiping his eyes with mirth at her tales of the nuns and their idiosyncrasies. Like how Sister Josephine was addicted to building programmes on the TV and was always telling people where they should put two-by-fours and lintels and RSJs, though the chance of *her* actually doing any construction were zero. Or Sister Finbarr who couldn't abide Sister Clare so she deliberately made her porridge with sour milk at least four times a month. As Sister Clare would retch, Finbarr would apologise profusely but would drop Carmel a sly little wink. Or how Sister Margaret had a bit of a crush on Father Lennon and was like a giddy schoolgirl when he came in for his scone and tea after ten o clock mass in the church next door.

'Oh Carmel,' Sharif laughed, 'you are as your mother was fond of saying 'an out-and-out scream'. You have just her sense of humour, she made all the residents and staff at Aashna House laugh every day. They would have the same experiences as she did, but she had a unique ability to see the funny side of everything, and especially of herself. She was one of a kind, or at least I believed so, until today.'

'I wish she'd found me,' Carmel said quietly. 'Maybe I'd have a great life in England now, making clothes just like my mother, maybe even have a little shop. Happy as Larry, with my own money and a little flat, and a car.' She sighed wistfully.

Then something occurred to her.

'How did you find me in the end?' she asked.

'Did I not tell you? I am in a Facebook group, relating to Dr. Wayne Dyer, and so I regularly 'like' people on that page, or their posts and so on. There are lots of alternative therapists, spiritual people, things I am interested in. Well, you must have posted something or liked something I liked, because on your birthday a reminder popped up. 'Its CarmelIreland's birthday today, help her celebrate!' You know the way they do? And so I did a little digging, my friend's daughter calls it Facebook stalking, and as soon as I saw your picture, I knew you were the Carmel we were looking for all these years. The rest was easy, finding out where you lived, you liked SuperValu in Birr, County Offaly, and the hairdressers, and a few other businesses, then using the electoral register online I found you. Simple!' he grinned.

'Amazing.' Carmel shook her head. 'Dr Dyer helped you find me. That probably sounds crazy to you, but I really like him and I think there's something in what he says. I don't have many friends around Birr, so Facebook keeps me sane. Imagine, it led you to me. It's just such a pity that it was too late for Dolly.'

'I DON'T THINK you're crazy at all, quite the opposite. I want to show you something,' Sharif said suddenly. He pulled his sleek-looking smart phone out of his pocket and tapped a few buttons, then he handed her the phone. The image on the screen was of a paused video, dated two years earlier.

'What is it?' Carmel asked.

'I made this video on Dolly's birthday. My mother threw her a party, she invited all the staff and of course the residents of Aashna, some of her's and Dolly's loyal customers, a few old neighbours.

Everyone, including Dolly, knew it was going to be her last, the cancer was ravaging her entire system. We were just keeping her comfortable.'

He nodded encouragingly and she pressed play. There she was, her mother, in a wheelchair just like in the photo, the bright scarf round her head as she blew out the candle on her cake.

'Speech, speech!' called several voices in the crowd.

Her mother laughed and looked around,

'Alrigh' alrigh', she said. 'I'm dying. D'yez not know tha'? I'n supposed ta be lyin' surrounded be candles and mickey dodgers rustlin' their habits and rattlin' the rosaries!'

The crowd laughed. Carmel was surprised at Dolly's strong Dublin accent. After all the years in England you'd think it would be gone or at least diluted, but she sounded like the women who sell the fruit and flowers on Moore Street.

'Seriously though, thanks to yez all for comin', tis great ta see ye. I won't see most of yez again, in this life anyway, but thanks for everythin', for makin' me welcome, for bein' me friends. I havta say a special word though, to me adopted family, the Khans. I honestly don't know how I'd a survived without them. Nadia, my best friend, Khalid, her late husband, and such a rock of support to me, and their darlin' boy, Sharif. I wanted to dance at your weddin', I said I would, but time is runnin' out so I'll havta be there in spirit. Hold on though, for the right one, d'ya hear me?' she grabbed Sharif's hand and he bent down beside her. Dolly addressed the crowd once more, 'Though he's no spring chicken, he's still a catch!' She grinned as the audience chuckled. She took a sip from a glass, the effort of talking taking it out of her.

'I don't believe in regrets, not really, you make your decisions and that's all there is to it, but if there was one thing I'd change, it would be that I'd never have left me beautiful baby girl all those years ago. As yez all know I've spent years tryin' to find her, but she's out there somewhere, and I hope she's happy and tha' somewhere deep inside her, she knows tha' her mother loved her then, and still loves her now.

So if yez don't mind I'd like to raise a toast, To Carmel, wherever you are my love.'

'To Carmel,' the crowd echoed.

'A song!' shouted someone.

Dolly laughed, a wheezing laboured sound.

'Well, yez did ask for it, me swan song I suppose you'd call it... though I'm more like an auld duck croakin' and wheezin' but I'll give it a go...' Her thin reedy voice struggled to be heard but she persevered.

'When I was just a little girl, I asked my mother what will I be. Will I be handsome? Will I be rich? Here's what she said to me...' the whole crowd sang along; 'Que sera, sera. Whatever will be will be, the future's not ours to see, Que será será.'

CHAPTER 7

The video ended and Carmel closed her eyes. Sharif leaned over and held her hand in his, saying nothing, until the waiter came to clear the table.

'she loved me.' She whispered.

'More than anyone or anything.' Sharif confirmed, his hands never leaving hers.

After lingering over coffee, they eventually walked in the direction of the bus station. The last bus was at eleven so she would make that. They walked in silence, darkness enveloping the city, each lost in their own thoughts. Eventually Sharif spoke.

'I was married once, to a beautiful girl called Jamilla, she got cancer, it was diagnosed too late and she died. It was then I decided to be an oncologist.' He kept looking right ahead as they walked. 'I never thought I could feel about anyone like I did about her but I realise I was only a child then, we were so young, twenty-four and twenty-two, a lifetime ago. I buried myself in work, in my friends, my family, and it was enough, it was fine. Aashna House is such a special place, we are a hospice, but we are so much more. We hold retreats, meditations, mindfulness courses; we even had Dr. Wayne Dyer there two years ago, he had heard about us and came to visit. He spent a long

38

time talking to Dolly; she made him laugh so hard.' He chuckled at the memory.

Carmel stopped walking. 'Wait a minute, are you telling me my mother actually met Wayne Dyer? In person?' She was totally stunned.

'Yes, they got along famously.' Sharif smiled at her incredulous expression.

'I love him. I have all his books, his CDs, I listen to his guided meditations all the time, I just can't believe my own mother actually met him. This day is getting crazier and crazier. I could never have imagined when I woke up this morning that today would turn out like this, it's all been just wonderful. As if my life in Birr just faded away and this new me has emerged or something.' she smiled. 'Knowing what I know now, I'm going to find it so hard to go back to the old me.'

He stopped and seemed to be thinking, as if weighing up what to say next. Taking a deep breath, he started, 'I am not a rash person; I am cautious and need to be in possession of all of the facts before I make decisions. I don't know what is happening here, but I know this. I think you are the funniest, sweetest, most beautiful woman I've ever met, and I don't want you to get on a bus to go back to a man who doesn't love you. He loves a ghost; there is no room for you. Jamilla is gone, and she will always have a little place in my heart, but I am here, and so are you. We are alive, and we can feel and who knows what happens after this, but I just know I don't want to say goodbye.' The calm composure seemed to be gone and he sounded so vulnerable.

Carmel couldn't believe what she was hearing. Was this real?

'Come back to England with me tomorrow, we'll take it from there. You could work at Aashna House, I just know our residents would be overjoyed to meet long-lost baby Carmel and you'd cheer them, just as your mother did before you. You could do that, or maybe start up our mothers' dressmaking business again. There are some little apartments in the grounds where some staff, and residents who are still able to care for themselves live. You could stay, until you decide what to do next. What do you say?'

His eyes burned with hope and trepidation. Carmel wanted to hug him. It was like a film or a novel, but she never for even one second thought it happened to real people, people like her. But yet, this gorgeous, funny, kind man, who knew her real mother, was standing in front of her in a Dublin street asking her to leave everything, leave Bill and Julia and all rest of it and start again. A new life, one of her very own, there because she wanted to be, and more importantly because someone else wanted her to be there too. It was exhilarating. She'd never made an emotional decision before, in fact she'd made very few decisions, she was the kind of person where things were decided for her, but maybe she could grasp this chance. The chance to be happy, to have her time here mean something.

They were standing outside a busy pub, and judging by the singing coming from inside, there was a party in full swing.

Carmel looked up into the face of the man she had met eight and a half hours previously. Nothing about any of her life made sense until this moment. She was always the outsider, someone to be endured because there was nowhere else for her to go. With Sharif she felt like she had come home at last.

'Are you sure? I mean you don't have to…just because you promised Dolly….' Carmel wanted to be clear.

'I know I don't have to. I want to. I want to have you in my life Carmel. It seems rushed, I know that. And if you knew me better you'd realise how out of character this is for me, but something is telling me to hold on to you and never let you go.'

Someone emerged from the pub, talking on his phone. As he opened the door, they heard the crowd singing…

'Qué será será, whatever will be will be. The future's not ours to see, Qué será será.'

The End

The Future's not ours to see

CHAPTER 8

*C*armel switched on the small, battery-powered transistor to the tinny sound of the news jingle. Bill was gone into town, and any sound was better than her own thoughts racing around in pointless circles. She could settle to nothing. Yesterday, she cleared out the hot press, discarding ancient pillowcases and frayed sheets, and this morning she was determined to give the cupboards in the sitting room a good going over, but nothing could take her mind off what had happened in Dublin.

She could have done it, gone off with Sharif when he asked her, made the new, amazing life he talked about. When he suggested it over a delicious dinner and wine, it all seemed so possible, so enticing. But the cold reality of the morning after, as she lay awake, alone in the hotel room he'd booked for her, was that, of course, she couldn't just up and leave. That was fine on TV shows or in romantic novels but for ordinary women, living ordinary lives, running away with handsome strangers was just not an option, no matter how tempting the offer. She left Sharif a note, thanking him for such a lovely night, for the photos and letters from her birth mother, for finding her, but explaining she had to go back to Bill.

On the bus back to Birr, she'd googled Aashna House about fifty times; it looked every bit as beautiful and peaceful as he said it was. Sharif was there as well, on the staff page in his suit and white coat, a gentle smile playing around his lips. She gazed at him, with his caramel-coloured skin, brown eyes, and silver hair.

As she washed up the breakfast dishes in the sink, the details of their day together, what it felt like to be with him, crowded into her mind. Did she dream it? Did this man really find her on Facebook? Offer her a better life, with him, and all the memories of the mother she never knew? And, if this magical thing really happened, what on earth was she doing back in the kitchen of Bill Sheehan's farmhouse in County Offaly?

She cursed her cowardice and her sense of duty. She just couldn't do it when push came to shove, as Sr Dympna was fond of saying. The nuns who reared her would have been so disappointed if she had chosen to leave her marriage, to run away with another man to England. The fact that the stranger was the most attractive man she'd ever seen would surely only compound what would have been already a mortal sin. Bill had no idea of the life-altering events of recent weeks. She told him that she'd gone to Dublin to visit an old nun who was dying in Trinity House; he always almost winced when she mentioned the orphanage where she was brought up as if he didn't want reminding of his wife's humble beginnings.

He accepted the story unquestioningly, in fact, he'd not even asked about her overnight disappearing act, she had to volunteer an excuse. Julia, of course, on the other hand, was all questions. Which Nun? Surely, they were all dead now, the ones that were there when Carmel was a child, she'd been gone from Trinity House for seventeen years? How come this was the first they'd heard of it? On and on she went, like an old terrier at a bone, determined to extract every little last scrap of information. Trying to catch her out. Julia had a nose for lies, all her years as a teacher and then principal of the local primary school made her super sensitive to untruths.

If she ever wanted to scream the truth, it was during these grillings by her sister-in-law. Julia always struck when Bill was out farming, but Carmel kept her opinions to herself like she always did. If she ever

43

did get the nerve to answer Julia back, she would be reminded sharply that she was little Carmel Murphy from a home for fallen women, and in no way the equal of the Sheehans with their big farm going back generations.

'No,' she thought as she wiped down the countertops for the fifth time, 'she'd stay no matter how awful it was. To do anything else would be sheer madness, and on top of it all, she was married in a Catholic Church, in the eyes of God, where she promised to love Bill for better or worse. Well, she mused, she didn't know about better, there were few if any, of those days in all the years, but there were certainly worse days.

She thought all the time about her mother Dolly and the letters she left with Sharif. The idea that her mother spent a lifetime searching for her, to no avail, both cheered and saddened her. So, her birth mother had not, in fact, dumped her in an orphanage and forgotten about her. The letters she wrote and entrusted to her doctor and friend Sharif were secreted away in a small biscuit tin at the back of Carmel's underwear drawer where neither Bill nor Julia would ever find them. Bill couldn't care less, she was sure, but Carmel knew Julia regularly let herself in when there was nobody at home for a good poke around, though she had no idea what the other woman was trying to find.

All these new feelings flooded her mind. Carmel never had anyone to love her, even all these years with Bill were totally devoid of emotion and yet, Sharif told her that Dolly tried everything to find the baby girl she had been forced to leave in the care of the state but met blank walls of opposition from the church authorities each time. It was so much to take in. She replayed the impending conversation in her mind once more. She was going to have it out with Bill. Never once in all these years did she question him, ask him why they were here together, living out this charade of a life. Sharif had asked her why and she couldn't answer him. Maybe it was because she thought she didn't deserve any better or something, but she owed it to herself to at least have one proper conversation, even if the thought of it made her nauseous with nerves.

The crunch of tyres on the gravel outside brought her back to reality; Bill was home early for lunch. She swallowed down the panic; she could do this. He'd been visiting his solicitor in town. She only knew that because she'd overheard him on the phone to one of the twins; apparently, he was giving each of them a site on which to build a house. He imagined, in his foolishness, they'd come back and live in Birr, but Carmel thought they would do no such thing. The girls hated Birr and its provincial ways; they were city slickers through and through. They would build the huge fancy mansions alright, but as soon as they were ready, the girls would say they couldn't move jobs or whatever, and they'd sell the houses and buy even grander places for themselves in Dublin, miles away from County Offaly. Julia had dropped several heavy hints about how a few sites for herself would be ideal as well, but Bill either didn't hear it or was choosing to ignore it.

Bill, being the only boy of the Sheehan family, got the farm, and his sister Julia got the college education. That was how it was back in the day. But even though she draws a fine salary from the Department of Education, has a nice house of her own in the village, and will get a big fat pension when she retires, Julia wanted more. Carmel never understood it, she never went anywhere, she had been wearing the same clothes for years, just greed she supposed. She felt very put out that Bill got the farm in the first place and always acted as if they owned it together. Bill, she knew, felt no such thing.

The back door opened and in he came. Dressed in his good suit, he looked so uncomfortable.

He said nothing, no greeting, but went to the bedroom to change into his working clothes.

Emerging a few moments later, she thought his face registered a bit of surprise that his lunch wasn't on the table.

She snapped off the radio, and the silence in the big old-fashioned kitchen was deafening.

'I'd like to talk to you, Bill.' She heard herself say, her voice sounding strangely formal to her own ears.

'I'm late with the milking...' he began but she interrupted him.

45

'I'm sorry but this is important.' Her voice was stronger than she ever imagined it could be.

'What is it?' he sighed, as if she bored him with demands every day of the week when quite the opposite was the case.

'Why did you marry me?' There. It was out. The question that had plagued her for seventeen years.

'What?' Bill's face wrinkled into confused distaste and he went to the back of the door for his jacket, he clearly wasn't staying around for this.

Carmel knew she'd never get the guts to do this again, so she ran to the door, barring his exit.

'Please, Bill, I really want to know. Why? You came to Dublin, looking for a wife, and someone to be a mother to your two daughters and I agreed, but from that day to this, we've hardly spoken to each other. We don't have a...' she felt her face redden, 'normal marriage, in any sense. You don't seem to need or want me for anything but cooking and cleaning, so what did you do it for?'

Her voice was raised now, and she felt less in control but she needed to say it. She was blushing furiously and she could feel her cheeks burning with the shame of it, but she had to plough on. It was now or never.

Bill stood in front of her, his eyes downcast, and it was impossible to know what he was thinking.

Long seconds passed.

'Please, Bill, I just don't understand...' she knew she sounded pathetic but maybe pity for her would make him speak.

He sighed. 'For God's sake, Carmel, I've work to do, I don't have time for this...' He made to pass her.

'No!' she almost shouted. 'I've done everything you asked of me for seventeen years but we've never had a proper conversation, not once in all that time, and I just don't even know what I'm doing here.'

He looked at her as if she had taken leave of her senses. This was not the Carmel he was used to. He realized there was no getting away from her, so he blurted, 'Right. Fine. Gretta was gone, and I thought it would be a good idea. It turns out it wasn't. The girls didn't take to you, and I don't need another wife. I had one and she died.'

Each cruel and heartless word fell like a rock on her head. He didn't mean to be horrible, it was just how he saw things.

'I tried with the girls, but Julia…' she began.

'I know, she took over. Look, 'twas either marry someone and have them in here, or have Julia, and I didn't want that. She was angling for it the minute Gretta died, but it's more the land she's after and she can go and whistle for it, this is my farm, not hers, no matter what she may think.'

She heard that hard determination in his voice. Being reared with nothing meant this deep feeling Bill and Julia had about land and ownership was lost on her, but Carmel had lived in rural Ireland long enough to know that people would do anything, literally anything, to protect their land.

'So, I was brought in just to stop your sister moving in here and taking control of the farm?' She tried to keep the raw pain out of her voice; she needed to be as matter of fact as Bill was.

'Well, I didn't consider how Julia would turn the girls against you; she never thought I should have taken someone out of a place for unmarried mothers.' He shrugged.

The term unmarried mothers jarred with her, it was such a judgmental name, and yet it was what places like Trinity House were called for a long time. And anyway, she wasn't any kind of a mother, married or otherwise. She was just the child of one of these unfortunate women, who fell afoul of the Irish church and state in less enlightened times.

'And you? What did you think? That someone like me would do?' Carmel fixed him with a stare despite trembling inside.

He thought again before he spoke. Each word delivered with painful slowness.

'Well, not that. If I thought like that I wouldn't have married you, 't'wasn't your fault. You can't be blamed for, well, whatever your mother was. But you're right. It was a mistake, but here we are, and there's nothing either of us can do about it now.'

Carmel tried to ignore the slight against her mother, as if becoming pregnant was some kind of awful sign of her character.

'But if you saw Julia trying to undermine me with the girls, why didn't you say something?'

He shrugged. 'That's women's business, rearing kids, girls especially. I just thought ye'd work it out.' He shrugged on his working jacket. 'I've got to go milking.'

Before she had time to react, to say anything, he was gone out the door. She stood in the kitchen, trying not to cry.

She went upstairs, took her biscuit tin of letters and locked herself in the bathroom, put the lid down and sat on the toilet.

One by one, she re-read her mother's letters, taking comfort from them. Somebody loved her. Someone she hadn't seen since she was a baby, someone she couldn't remember, someone who spent her life searching for her daughter.

As she was reading, she heard the back door open once more. Like a thief caught in the act, her heart thumped wildly as she stuffed the letters back into the tin and buried it under the newly organised blankets and sheets in the hot press. She stood up and examined her tear-stained face in the mirror.

'Carmel? Carmel!' Julia's sharp voice rang out in the empty house.

Carmel splashed water on her face but she knew it wasn't going to help to disguise the fact that she'd been crying.

She tried calling, 'I'm in the bathroom.'

No response.

Eventually, she had to come out. Julia was on the landing.

'What were you and Bill talking about?' she barked.

'What? ...nothing...I...' Carmel knew she must look like a rabbit caught in the headlights.

'Don't lie to me. Bill was parked up outside his solicitor's office this morning, then, as I was coming in, he nearly blew me off the road. So, something is going on and I want you to tell me.'

Carmel hated it when Julia spoke to her as if she was one of the misfortunate kids under her command in the primary school. Julia resented her, she never wanted Bill to marry again and she used every opportunity to run his wife down. Carmel thought in the early days it was because she was twenty-eight years younger than him but she was wrong. Bill's admission only confirmed what she always suspected. Julia had it all worked out when Gretta died, she'd move in, take over the girls and the running of the house and when Bill died she'd get everything. The girls had no interest in the farm, a financial settlement would do them fine, but Julia would own the land. Bill's marriage to Carmel ruined all her plans.

Carmel thought about her mother, imagining her as Sharif described her. Brave, and impossible to intimidate. She tried to channel Dolly's strength and tenacity. Julia was livid, her dark hair scraped back off her head, her pointy features and rake-thin body almost quivering with temper. She was only in her mid-forties but looked much older.

'If you have a question for your brother, you should ask him, not me.' She spoke quietly.

'What? Don't you tell me what to do,' Julia sneered. 'He's up to something, and by the way, lady, so are you. I don't believe that fairy story about the dead nun above in Dublin for a moment. If something is happening with this land then I have a right to know.'

Julia moved closer, her face only inches from Carmel's.

Sounding much more confident than she felt, Carmel responded.

'No, you don't. This land is not yours, it is Bill's and mine, and one day it will belong to Niamh and Sinead. You don't feature anywhere.' She had no idea where all this strength was coming from, first challenging Bill, and now Julia. It had taken seventeen years but it felt good. She had hit a nerve with her sister-in-law.

'You! You don't own anything!' Julia's cheeks reddened and her eyes flashed with fury at Carmel's audacity. 'You're forgetting something, I know full well what you are. A nobody, whose dirty tramp of a mother, off, no doubt with every Tom, Dick or Harry that wanted her, dumped her child to be a burden on the Irish taxpayer. How dare you place yourself above me.'

Carmel could feel the spittle from Julia's lips on her face.

Carmel wiped her face and took a step back. All the insults, slights, and cruel remarks made by her sister-in-law over almost two decades crowded her mind. Carmel had never in her whole life spoken out, she was a background person, but Dolly was not a tramp, and her daughter was not worthless.

She smiled serenely, knowing it would drive Julia mad. 'Why does anyone have to be above or below anyone else? You decide who goes where in your stupid, mad, bigoted head, why? What does that do for you? Does it make you feel superior or something? Because if you need to run others down in order to think well of yourself then you have a serious problem. Why does the farm matter so much to you, Julia? You have a fine house, and all the money you could want and yet you drive yourself crazy about this bit of land? Bill won't leave it to you, he'll leave it to me and his daughters, legally he has to, and even if he didn't, he'd rather leave it to the Dog's Home than leave it to you. You constantly sniffing around, looking to see what you can get, it's pathetic. He can't stand you, by the way, he only married me to make sure you didn't move in. Why do you think that was, Julia?' Carmel was enjoying herself.

'You turned Niamh and Sinead against me, and they were only little girls. I could have loved them, I wanted to, but you had to spread your poison like you always do. The kids in the school hate you too, did you know that? Every kid in Birr dreads going into third class because you're the teacher. What a waste of a life.'

'How dare you!' Julia screamed, slapping Carmel hard across the face. Carmel was stunned, her face stung, but Julia grabbed her and she lurched forward, sending Julia off balance, causing the other woman to lose her footing on the bit of loose carpet at the top of the stairs. She fell backwards down the stairs, landing in an undignified heap below. She managed to get herself up, as Carmel froze on the top step.

Once she was upright, she spat, 'You will pay for this, you mark my words, you illegitimate slut.' Julia smoothed down her skirt and tried to fix her hair. 'You should have been left to skivvy for your betters above in Dublin instead of my brother giving you a respectable home, you've bad blood in you, no wonder you're the way you are,' she hissed.

'Get out, Julia. Just get out.' Carmel was suddenly resolute and weary of it all.

Julia's car sent a spray of gravel as she reversed in temper. Carmel went quietly to her bedroom and packed her bags. There was nothing for her here anymore.

CHAPTER 9

She only had a few Euros in her purse and no bank card, even if she had one she'd have been too terrified to use it. Another wave of panic washed over her, the thousandth such wave since she left Ireland two days ago. The journey over to England had been okay, she had taken the bus and boat as that was the cheapest way to England. She'd never travelled anywhere before, so it was terrifying and exhilarating at the same time. Arriving to the reception of Aashna House, with her bag in her hand and no plan, had been the most terrifying moment of her life, but Sharif's welcome dispelled any fears instantly. He was genuinely thrilled to see her. She assured him that she wanted to work, she wasn't a freeloader and he smiled.

'Of course you're not, I never thought you were, but let's get you settled first, shall we?' his smile made her melt inside. He took her bag and put it behind the desk at reception.

'Can you get this sent down to 201 please and also have some supplies sent from the kitchen please, Marlena?' he asked the receptionist.

When Sharif gave her a tour of the clinic, she glanced sideways as they walked, admiring him. He was wearing a charcoal grey suit and a pale pink shirt under his white coat and Carmel thought he looked amazing.

'I look different in my doctor outfit.' He grinned, catching her looking at him. When they met in Dublin, he was dressed more casually. He'd joked with Carmel that there was absolutely no clinical reason whatsoever for it but that the residents felt more reassured when Dr Khan appeared in his white coat and hung a stethoscope around his neck.

There was a variety of other staff too, who stopped to greet Sharif as they wandered round the exquisite house and grounds, and she was struck by how familiar and relaxed they all seemed around him. In her limited experience, doctors were to be revered, along with priests, but they joked with him and it seemed such a happy place, despite the fact that people came here to die. She met Zane, a care assistant, Oscar the Yoga teacher, Ivanka who was an occupational therapist, though Carmel hadn't the faintest idea what that might be, and a cleaning lady called Ivy, who smoked like a chimney despite Sharif's admonishments.

Now that he was back in his own environment, she felt intimidated by his position. She didn't know anyone who'd been to university except Julia and Bill's girls, so the idea that someone as highly educated and successful as Sharif would want to associate with her made her feel anxious.

The main house, the hospice itself, was housed in an old manor house but while it maintained the grand facades of nineteenth-century opulence outside, inside it was transformed into bright airy spaces and cosy, exquisitely decorated private rooms. Each room was different and while the medical technology employed was the most advanced, it was cleverly disguised so each patient's room felt very homey. She had remarked how it didn't smell like an institution. Sharif laughed and said every effort was made to use natural products for cleaning so there should be no offensively strong odours of disinfectant, and the cooking was done in a separate building on the grounds. Where possible, patients were encouraged to eat in the large bright glass-ceilinged Atrium, designed for that purpose, but for those unable to, food was brought to them.

As well as various treatment rooms, there was a large multipurpose building as well, called Kaivalya, the Sanskrit word for unity, which was used for lectures, concerts, and a variety of social events, and it was often used by local community groups. It overlooked the gardens with the lake in the middle and a fountain. Sharif told her he was happy to have people come in and use it, the small fee they paid helped with the upkeep but more importantly, it made the patients feel part of the outside community. Palliative care, he explained, was as much about mental health as about physical well-being. He'd visited several hospices all around the world before deciding on the format for Aashna House, and there was nowhere like it.

'Of course, I've had to beg and borrow for years to get it going but people are kind. Death is a universal reality, so perhaps people feel happy to donate in life with the hope that it is storing some kind of karma for their own inevitable end.' He chuckled. 'A kind of insurance policy.'

'Well, a dumb priest never got a parish,' Carmel remarked and Sharif gave a peal of laughter.

'What?' she asked, glad she had made him laugh.

'You're just like Dolly, so funny. She had the funniest sayings as well...she cracked me up and so do you.'

Just like when they met in Dublin, her Irishisms seemed to cause him no end of hilarity and Carmel basked in his admiration.

As they walked through the gardens in the early spring sunshine, there was an outdoor Yoga class going on, people of varying physical ability saluting the sun. The accommodation section was mainly for resident staff, and some patients who, while ill and in need of medical support, wanted to live out as much as possible of their time independently. There was also a family support section, where family members of very ill people could stay, cook a meal, or watch TV. It really was a remarkable place.

'I don't know what I was expecting, but it's nothing like I imagined,' Carmel admitted as they sipped coffee in the restaurant.

'I know. I think people expect candles and hushed voices and a smell of boiled cabbage when they think of hospices. To be fair, very few are like that, but I do like to think Aashna is one of a kind. It's been my whole life's work. This place means the world to me.'

After the tour, he opened the door to a lovely apartment.

'This is yours for as long as you want it,' he said, handing her the keys.

'But I can't...' she began. She had no money for rent and this place must cost a fortune.

'Carmel, I thought I'd never see you again. And now, here you are. Please, let me do this, for you and for Dolly.'

The two-bedroomed apartment was the loveliest living space she'd ever seen and Sharif assured her that she wasn't inconveniencing anyone by being there. There was a bright sunny master bedroom with a double bed and fitted wardrobes and even a bathroom off it, with a huge shower and a deep Jacuzzi bath. The second bedroom was smaller but really cosy and decorated so nicely, the whole place was like something she'd seen on those makeover programmes on TV. In awe, she wandered round touching surfaces, the lovely French doors opening onto a courtyard full of plants and shrubs, the glittering black marble worktops, the entertainment unit on one wall, which held the largest TV she'd ever seen. The living area was open plan, with a kitchen, a sitting room with a big squashy leather sofa, and a dining table with four chairs. It was gorgeous, all creams and whites and a few splashes of colour here and there in rugs and prints.

Carmel had never in her whole life had a place of her own. She'd taken Sharif when they were in Dublin to see Trinity House, just to see it from the outside, and she had to admit that it looked quite dreary and forbidding. When she saw the dismay on his face, that she had spent half of her life there, she'd tried to convince him that it wasn't that bad, not in comparison to some of the stuff you hear about children who grew up in the care of the Catholic Church in Ireland, but she knew he was horrified. Despite her best efforts to make it sound less Orphan Annie, she knew her life story was pathetic, a life not lived, just endured year after year, with no hopes, plans, or dreams. She tried to explain to him that she didn't feel so hopeless when she was in Trinity House, it just was what it was, and she knew no better. Some kids got parents, and dogs and holidays and big extended families and others didn't, and she was one of the ones that didn't. She didn't feel self-pitying about it; it was how things were. Wishing for different was like wishing for a white blackbird.

When he came to find her in Ireland, he assumed that she had been adopted. Sharif explained to her how Dolly had come back to get her, years before when she was still a baby but Carmel wasn't given back. Nobody ever explained why she wasn't adopted, she just wasn't, but for some reason, Dolly was told she had been, and that contact would be impossible. Carmel told Sharif how she wished so hard as a child to be picked by some family, taken home and loved like their own. It happened on TV but it never seemed to be an option for her. As the years went on, the prospect became less and less likely. Other children left the home to go to families but nobody ever showed the slightest interest in Carmel.

The reality of her new situation as she wandered around her new home crashed over her like an icy wave. Panic threatened to engulf her. She'd only ever lived in two places, Trinity House and with Bill in County Offaly. What on earth had she been thinking? Leaving everything she ever knew to just up sticks and land over here in England with a total stranger. She was worried that people would look at her askance, wondering why the very eligible Dr Khan, who could have anyone he wanted, who owned and ran Aashna House, was showing a woman with no obvious skills around, and moving her into this amazing apartment.

As he showed her around, his bleeper went. He read it and apologized.

'I'm sorry, a patient needs me. Can I leave you here to settle in? I'll come and find you when I'm free. Please feel free to wander around.'

'Of...of course...sure.' She tried not to panic.

He went to the door and then turned back, standing in front of her, his hands on her shoulders.

'I can't tell you how happy I am to see you. Please don't worry, everything is going to be fine now.' He kissed her cheek and was gone.

She sat down and tried to focus on her breathing. Calm, she told herself, just try to be calm. In and out, in and out. Gradually, her heartbeat returned to normal.

She looked out on the large lawn in front of the apartment block, filled with patients and their families on such a sunny day. The residents, all of whom were terminally ill, were not all in bed as she imagined they would be. Sharif explained how the ethos of Aashna was that people should suck the marrow out of life, enjoy it, experience new things as much as they were able, and not just sit around waiting to die. Most were busy with various activities, painting, even brewing beer, and those that were very ill were in bright rooms that looked nothing like hospital wards.

She moved tentatively to the sofa in her very own apartment, the sun streaming through the glass doors but was afraid to relax, full sure someone would appear any moment and demand to know who on earth she thought she was. The glass-topped table had a vase of yellow crocuses on it and Carmel tried to imagine a future where she would cook in her little kitchen and she would have friends sit at the table and eat a meal as her guests. She'd have to find a few friends first, she reminded herself ruefully.

There was a large glass and enamel mirror over the fireplace and she stood to assess the woman looking back at her. She thought she looked every one of her forty years, crow's feet radiated from her big blue eyes. The reflection confirmed what she suspected, that her dark shoulder-length hair made her look like a ghost. The stress of the last few weeks had caused her to lose weight and her spare tyre had just melted away. In fact, she thought she looked kind of gaunt. She was naturally blonde but she had allowed Julia to convince her to dye it dark last year. She could hear her sharp voice in her head, 'Less conspicuous, the dark. Blonde can look very trashy, a nice brown colour to hide the grays, that's much better.' She hated it the moment she saw it, but to go against Julia once she'd issued a decree took more strength than she ever possessed.

She wondered what was happening back in Birr. She was afraid to look at her phone.

She thought back to the conversation with Sharif earlier in the hospice café. The whole sorry tale of the confrontations with Julia and Bill came out in a torrent and she was mortified when the tears started up again. He reached over the table and held both her hands, not caring who saw them.

'Carmel, let me tell you something. In the early days when I was setting up Aashna House, everyone said I was mad, the place was costing too much, the furnishings and facilities were so top-end I'd never make my money back. They said that people wouldn't be able to afford to live there and I'd bankrupt myself. Dolly used to ask me, "What would you do if the fear was gone?" It is a great question to ask yourself because once we remove the element of fear from our decisions, then we find our true heart's desire. Fear takes us over if we let it, allowing people to only live half of the life they choose, or sometimes none of it because they are crippled by terror and what ifs. So, all over the world, people are staying in terrible marriages, awful jobs, living places they don't want to live because they are afraid of what will happen if they take a leap of faith, they are afraid of their own instinct, they lack trust in themselves. The old Carmel was like that, but you know who wasn't? Your mother, Dolly. She wasn't afraid of anyone or anything. She tried lots of things, never backed down when she knew she was right, and she would want this for you. A new start, a chance to live your life on your terms, not somebody else's. I know she's gone, and it's so sad that you've never met her, but in a way, you have. Through me. So, let her into your life, let her guide you. I've never met anyone I've been so attracted to as you, Carmel, maybe it's because of Dolly or something, I don't know, but I'm offering you a no strings escape. If something works out between us, then wonderful, but if it doesn't, well, then, that's as it may be. The offer is not subject to you and I having a relationship; the offer stands alone. You've done the hardest part, leaving that place, those people. It will be easy from now on.'

Though the words sounded stupid, she heard herself say, 'But he is my husband, I took a vow...'

'Carmel, you are never going back to Bill. Not because I say so, obviously, but because there is nothing to go back to. He doesn't love you; you tried your best but you don't love him. You told me yourself, you were just a housekeeper. But let's just speculate for a moment, just say you hate it here, you don't want me or Aashna or any of it, you leave here and get a job and then would you be any worse off? Of course not, in fact, you'd still be much better off. You'd earn your own money, you'd have your own place, where you could just watch TV or have friends over or cook or whatever you want. So really, this feels like a huge leap, I know it does, but it's not, not in any real way.'

Her reverie was interrupted by Zane giving her a wave as he passed the window. He was funny and spoke with a real East End London accent when she met him earlier. He was so stylish, with his skinny jeans and skin-tight shirt showing off his well-toned body. His hair was shaved on both sides and sporting a full afro on the top and as Sharif introduced them she tried not to stare. It was the first conversation she'd ever had with a black person and he certainly was exotic. He would have looked like a mysterious tropical bird in Birr but over here, he was just part of the wonderfully colourful tapestry of life.

Everything in England was so different. The faces of the people for a start. The bus station at Waterloo was like a sensory assault, the costumes, hairstyles, the myriad of skin colours of the people. Sure, in Ireland there were more and more immigrants, but nothing like the huge crossroads of the entire world she experienced as she tried to find the right bus to get her to Aashna. Sharif had laughed when he caught her gazing in amazement at a group of Hasidic Jews having a loud argument in the garden as they passed. One of them was in a wheelchair but several others were crowded around him, clearly in disagreement over something. She'd never seen anyone like them with their long black coats and tall hats, their hair in plaits hanging from their temples.

She waved back and smiled. Maybe everything was going to be okay.

Her phone beeped. With trembling hands, she opened it.

It was from Niamh, Bill's daughter.

'Carmel, what the hell do you think you are doing? Dad is devastated. I can't believe U R being so selfish after all we've done for you. N'

The next text was from his other daughter, Niamh's twin Sinead, who had always been the nicer of the two, though Carmel never really got close to either girl despite her very best efforts.

'Carmel, are you okay? Please ring, we're all worried about you. Dad especially.'

One from Julia. 'You are a ridiculous woman, you came from nothing and you'll go back to nothing. Bill foolishly thought he could normalize you, but it proved impossible, we are all better off without you.'

And the one just a moment ago from Niamh again. 'Carmel, do not attempt to enter our home again, you're no longer welcome there. You have broken my father's heart, you horrible ungrateful cow.'

She could hear Julia on the phone, weaving her tale of woe to the girls. Painting Carmel as the villain of the piece, no doubt.

Carmel sighed and deleted each text in turn. Nothing from Bill; he hadn't tried to phone or send a text. He didn't have a mobile phone, possibly the last person on earth to hold out against the newfangled technology, and she knew he'd never lift the receiver on the phone on the wall in the kitchen and punch in the number. The fact that he would have no idea of her phone number said enough really. He didn't speak when they were face to face, so he would certainly never consider a phone chat. Carmel knew that, despite what Julia and the girls were saying, she had not broken his heart, and he most certainly was not devastated.

She wondered if anyone in Birr would miss her, or even notice she was gone. The gossip machine would start up soon, and Bill would be embarrassed but the people would reassure him that he was better off and that Carmel was damaged goods and that nobody that ever came out of an institution was right in the head. 'Just listen to the radio any day,' she could hear them say in the pub and the post office, 'all those people who came out of homes and industrial schools, it's very sad, but they all have drink and drugs problems and they can't make relationships work, 'tis not their fault, God knows, but they aren't suitable matches for normal people.'

Someone had placed milk and tea and some groceries in the fridge, so she made a cup of tea. Did she really do that? Just pack a bag, walk into Birr, get the bus to Dublin, and from there across the Irish Sea to here?

She wondered if Bill just got up and went out to the farm the next morning. Did he make his own breakfast? What did he think about her sudden and unprecedented disappearing act? Did Julia tell him about the fight?

She was so grateful she'd had a passport; she didn't have one for years. Even getting a passport with the birth certificate supplied by the home was such a sad experience. Her father was marked as unknown, and her mother just as D Murphy. Carmel often wondered who D was and if Murphy even was her real name. She remembered when her friend Kit got hers, her mother was listed as Murphy as well. Maybe for anonymity, the nuns listed all unmarried mothers as Murphy, it being one of the most common names in Ireland. She had applied for it secretly, hoping she'd be invited along to New York when Niamh went there with her sister and Aunt Julia to buy a wedding dress, but no invitation had been forthcoming and so the little wine-coloured book with the gold harp on the front remained pristine in the drawer beside her bed. She liked to read the message inside, where the Minister for Foreign Affairs asks that the bearer, a citizen of the Republic of Ireland, be offered all assistance necessary to travel within other countries. She knew it was silly, but it made her feel part of something. She wasn't in a family really, and she didn't have any real friends but she was an Irish citizen and the Minister cared about her.

She didn't have any cards, Bill took care of everything; there was an account at the local shop so she got what she needed and he settled up the bill at the end of the month; she didn't drive, so there was nothing else really. She had her phone, which she loved, it kept her connected to her friends on Facebook, people from groups that she'd never met, but who were more alive to her than the people in her so-called real life. She bought the smartphone with the voucher for the local electrical shop Bill had given her for Christmas. She would have loved an iPhone but it was too dear.

He assumed she'd buy a new iron or something for the house, but she bought the phone and for twenty Euros a month she could send and receive texts, though she had nobody to text, but more importantly, she could surf the net. She learned it all quickly and joined lots of groups online, all on the themes of mindfulness, and spirituality; she loved Wayne Dyer, Oprah Winfrey, Dr Phil, and all those American gurus who told you to go out and live your best life. She never acted on any of that advice of course, which led her to beating herself up even more.

She relived her departure so often, amazed at how calm she was. Once she was sure she had everything, she went to the jar beside the clock on the mantelpiece. In there, Bill kept some cash for the coal man, who was due to call to be paid. One hundred and eight euro exactly. Feeling a twinge of guilt, she stuffed the money into the pocket of her jeans and as she replaced the lid on the jar, she caught sight of the framed wedding photo of Bill and Gretta, in pride of place where it always was. How often had she dusted round it, afraid of cracking it or even touching it?

'Well,' she whispered, 'he's all yours again now, Gretta, not that he ever wasn't.' She took one more glance around, slipped her wedding ring off, and placed it beside the photo.

CHAPTER 10

She felt a bit silly setting the table for herself, just to have a cup of tea and a cheese sandwich but she tried to channel her inner Oprah who would tell her to enjoy the drink and sandwich, focus on it, really taste it, and experience it. All of that sounded like a load of old rubbish to her at the start but the more she got into the whole mindfulness thing the more it made sense to her. She sat at the table in this beautiful peaceful place and counted her blessings, she was healthy and had an envelope full of letters her birth mother had written to her over the years, she was wearing a necklace and earrings her mother had left for her, and she now had Dr Sharif Khan in her corner. Initially, he was fulfilling a promise he made to Dolly, her mother who died right here in Aashna House, but when they met in Dublin that day, something happened. It was as if he saw her, really saw her like nobody else had ever done before.

That night over dinner in a fancy place in Dublin, and later on back at the hotel, he told her more about her mother, about what a character she was. He told her about his own parents, how Nadia his mother and Dolly were best friends all their lives, he listened to her stories about growing up in Trinity House, she even told him about her best friend Kit who was so much braver than Carmel and had struck out for Australia, only to be killed in a road accident. Sr Bonaventure used to say Carmel must have been Wednesday's child, full of woe.

Bill's letter to Trinity came at the perfect time, she was too old for the children's home, she should have been gone a good few years earlier but the nuns took pity on her and allowed her to work for bed and board. If the health board or the Church authorities got wind of it, they would have been in right trouble, so when Bill wrote wondering if there was anyone eligible who would like to meet an older well-to-do farmer who was a widower with two young daughters with a view to marriage, she decided to give it a go. It was mad, certainly, and when Kit heard about it, she wrote from Australia asking if she was in a John B Keane play. He was ancient, a staggering forty-nine to her twenty-three and Kit said it was more like something from the fifties than the nineties, but it was an offer and Carmel hadn't had any of those.

It was the bravest thing she'd ever done, agreeing to marry Bill. Nobody was interested, though, and even the nuns thought she was mad, but she couldn't stay at Trinity House forever and she spent the weeks before the wedding imagining a life where she had a husband and two adorable little girls calling her Mammy. She would have friends who also had families and they'd talk about how their husband's snoring was driving them crazy or how their little one was getting on at piano lessons. In truth, Carmel hadn't a clue what married people talked about but she imagined it was something along those lines. She couldn't wait. But, it turned out that the nuns were right, that it was a mad idea, a gamble that most certainly did not pay off. Year after dreary year passed and while Bill wasn't cruel, he was just, absent. She saw him every single day, slept in the same bed, but they were strangers.

As she finished off her delicious sandwich and drank her tea gratefully, there was a gentle knock on the door.

She jumped as if she had no right to be there, but opened the door, and tried not to look like a rabbit caught in the headlights.

'Hello, you. Settled in okay?' Sharif stood outside. 'May I come in?'

She stood back to allow him in, which she knew was ridiculous, he owned the whole place for God's sake. As with every time she looked at him, the breath caught in her throat. He really was beautiful. She knew that wasn't a word usually attributed to men but Sharif Khan was beautiful. His dark almond-shaped eyes, and silver hair, which was longer on top so it was brushed back from his high brow, made him look like one of those models for coffee or expensive aftershave you'd see in the magazines at the hairdresser's. She blushed pink at the thought that he could read her mind, and tried to cover it up with a discreet cough, which turned into a wheezing fit. She really had to pull herself together.

He handed her a glass of water and waited for her to recover her composure.

'Do you have an inhaler? For your asthma?' he asked, suddenly the doctor not the rescuer.

'No,' she wheezed, 'It's not too bad. Much better than when I was a kid; I can manage.' She spoke, trying to have her breathing sound less laboured. She had had trouble with wheezing since she was a child, but nobody had ever diagnosed it as asthma before.

'Sit,' he commanded, leading her to the chair. Removing his stethoscope from his neck, he put it in his ears and raised up her jumper, placing the cold part on her back. He located it in several spots and did the same on her chest. 'Are you seriously telling me that you have had this condition since childhood and you have never used medication? Carmel, do you have any idea what damage you have done to your lungs? Each asthma attack scars your lungs and puts your heart under undue pressure, and really there is no need. I'll write you a prescription for a preventative and an inhaler for when you are having an attack. Take it to Rosa over at the pharmacy, it's beside the reception, you take the preventative morning and evening and the other as you need it.'

'Yes, Doctor,' she grinned.

'I can see you are not going to be a good patient,' he chuckled, 'just like your mother. She was impossible, smoked cigarettes to the day she died, had gin and tonics every night, loved Kentucky Fried Chicken, and organized a take-out night here every Friday where the residents had too much alcohol and a fairly savage poker school. I'm going to have my work cut out for me, as she would say.'

'Thank you,' she spoke quietly. The way Sharif drew her mother into the conversation so regularly and so unselfconsciously had made her squirm at first. It raised uncomfortable truths for her but he kept on doing it and, as each day passed, Dolly Mullane was becoming a real person. She and Kit had been right, Murphy was a default name put on birth certs of Ireland's unwanted babies. The photos her mother had left her, one of her and a man called Joe, another of Sharif's family, another of her at her birthday party, the last one before she died, were tucked into Carmel's wallet; she must have examined them a hundred times.

'What for?' he asked, as he hung his stethoscope round his neck once more.

'Everything.' Carmel spread her arms around, 'This apartment, offering me a job, finding me. All of it.'

'No regrets?' he spoke quietly. They had kissed on that first night in Dublin and Carmel thought nothing like that could ever happen to someone like her. In the intervening weeks, she convinced herself she imagined it but now that he was here in front of her, it seemed possible again.

'No, no regrets. Terror at the future, yes. Worry about well...everything, definitely. But regrets, no. That life is gone now, for better or worse. They texted me, his daughters, Julia, accusing me of breaking his heart; the reality, though, is I doubt he even noticed I was gone. Julia has probably moved in, she wanted that when Gretta died, or maybe all those years ago she still harboured hopes for Donald Wooton, the local landowning bigwig. He never looked twice at her, but everyone in the place had it that she was carrying a torch for him. At least she was until he up and married some English one he met at the races in Leopardstown, with a big farm of land and a plummy accent. Maybe she thinks if she gets her hands on Bill's farm, she'll have men queuing up for her, though I doubt it. Anyway, to answer your question, how could I have second thoughts about this place? It's so beautiful.'

Sharif pulled her gently to her feet, encircling her waist with his arms.

'And me? Any second thoughts about that?' Suddenly, all the self-assuredness disappeared, he wasn't the very wealthy, capable doctor, but just a vulnerable man. She hadn't imagined it. He liked her. She put her arms around his waist and looked up into his face.

'You're the one who should be running a mile. Seriously, Sharif, I've nothing, I've no skills, I don't know anyone or anything. I don't know what on earth you'd want to hitch your very fancy wagon to me for, honest to God, I don't. I'm about as useful as an ashtray on a motorbike, and for all I know, I could be a wanted criminal for shoving that angular old bat down the stairs.' She was convinced he was making a mistake.

He threw back his head and laughed, and the sight of it never ceased to delight her.

'I can just picture it. Well done, anyway, you said she got up again, she's fine. And as for you being useful, well, just leave that to me, okay? You forget, to me, you are someone very special indeed, not just because I've met you and know you to be a funny, charming, beautiful woman, but because in some ways I feel like I've always known you. Dolly talked about you all the time, spent hours speculating how you would be. She would look at pictures in the Irish papers, of people at parties or the races or even on the Irish news, she would scan the street crowds when they did outside broadcasts. I've lost count of the amount of times she'd pause it and call me, asking if I thought this woman or that one was you.'

Carmel grinned at the thought, it elated her. 'You're making her real for me, not just a memory, but an actual person.'

'Oh, she was real alright, larger than life…and you're her daughter.'

She laid her head on his chest and could hear his heart beating. He held her tightly and together they stood as the sun streamed in the window.

CHAPTER 11

*S*he glanced at her watch. Ten to nine. The meeting was at
nine and she didn't want to arrive too early in case she was
left standing alone, feeling awkward. He wanted her to relax and take
it easy for a few days at least, but she wanted to get busy. Eventually,
she pestered him, pleaded with him to find her something useful to do
until he gave in. She had been stunned when he suggested a role for
her. She imagined a cleaning job or something. But instead, she was
now the official events coordinator at Aashna House. He offered her
the position, explaining that the woman that used to do it called from
Portugal last week, where she was on holiday, to say she was staying
there with the love of her life, a twenty-four-year-old Syrian waiter
she'd met in a disco. Sharif explained that this development had
caused a few raised eyebrows from the other staff, given the fact that
Maureen was fifty if she was a day, but they had a whip-round and
wished her well. Sharif was more understanding than most employers
would have been, and when Carmel asked him about it, he just said
that Maureen had not always had things easy, so if this man gave her
some joy, then who was he to stand in the way?

'But what if he's just using her to get a passport?' Carmel asked. It
felt so relaxed, the two of them, chatting happily. Sharif had kicked his

shoes off and was sitting cross-legged on the floor. At first, she had smiled at the peculiar pose, but he explained that he spent most of his downtime sitting like that, it was a Pakistani thing, and it was his most comfortable position. He was a yogi as well, she discovered, and he explained how sitting cross-legged on the floor, was, in fact, an asana known as sukhasana, which aids digestion and encourages mindfulness. He reminded her of a leopard sometimes, he was so supple and flexible.

That first night they spent together and it felt like the most natural thing in the world. Carmel never imagined lovemaking to be like it was with Sharif. Gentle, passionate, and fun. She was in love, for the first time. She couldn't imagine ever being happier than this.

The conversation when she had to tell Sharif that she'd never actually had sex before was one of the most awkward she'd ever had to endure, but she was terrified he'd freak out if she didn't tell him. She knew the mechanics, obviously, but what you were actually supposed to do was a bit vague. He was incredulous at first, but when she explained about how that side of the marriage to Bill was nonexistent, he understood. She even told him about her botched attempt at seduction one time when she followed the instructions to the letter from a magazine, with candles and flower petals and sexy lingerie, but Bill had been mortified and almost bolted back down the stairs to his cattle. Sharif let her talk and then he held her tight and assured her that if she'd gone to that much trouble for him, then he would have had a very different reaction. After that, it was easy.

'Well, if he is, he is. But from what she said, he's a refugee, lost all his family in the flight from the war, and Maureen is not only remarkably good looking and well presented for her age, but there's an inherent kindness in her. Maybe he sees that too and needs her as

71

much as she needs him. She seems convinced he's genuine and I'd trust her judgement.'

'You're lovely,' she said and kissed him on the nose as she placed the plate of crackers and a glass of wine down in front of him.

'You are quite lovely yourself,' he grinned as he pulled her down to sit with him, kissing her neck as she leaned back against him.

She had taken the job gladly and tried to figure out what exactly an events coordinator did. Sharif said not to worry too much, that Maureen had left a filing cabinet full of contacts and a schedule of events on her desk in the office that Carmel now inherited. It all happened so quickly. She had been here only a few short days but it felt much longer.

Eventually, she took a deep breath to steady herself, pushed the door of the Kaivalya and entered, trying to look approachable, friendly, and competent. The more mobile of the residents shuffled into the sunny dayroom, some were pushed on wheelchairs by staff and others were assisted by visiting relatives. Everyone settled in to hear her first address as coordinator. She was quaking but determined to do her best. Sharif offered to come but she said it might be best just to go it alone. He couldn't hold her hand forever and she wanted people to see her as a member of the staff, not Sharif's girlfriend.

'G...good morning everyone and thanks for coming...'

Oh, God, she sounded like a rubbish comedian.

'I...I don't mean thanks for coming here, obviously, you are here already, but for coming to listen to me, though this is where you all come every day...'

She was babbling and she knew it, her nerves were getting the better of her. She stopped and took a deep breath.

'I'm sorry, I'll start again. I'm not used to speaking to people like this. I think I've met some of you already, but just to introduce myself, my name is Carmel, Carmel Mullane, and some of you may remember my mother Dolly.'

There was excited nudging and whispering. She was still getting used to introducing herself as Carmel Mullane rather than Sheehan. Since she never felt like part of Bill's family anyway, it seemed stupid to keep his name. This time, her name meant something to her; she was her mother's daughter and she had the name she gave her.

'So, it's true, Dr Khan found you? You're baby Carmel.' A very elderly lady spoke up in a strong Cockney accent.

'Yes, I suppose I am. Though that was forty years ago. I never knew she was looking for me; I wish I had, and maybe we would have found each other before it was too late.' Carmel heard her voice crack with emotion.

Seeing her vulnerability seemed to melt the crowd and, within moments, they had moved forward and were welcoming her warmly.

'Well, we're glad you're here, Carmel, and I know it would have meant the world to Dolly, you were all she talked about,' an old man spoke up from a motorized wheelchair. 'Most of the people here will have heard of Dolly, even if they didn't meet her. She was a good sort, old Dolly, always up to some kind of mischief.' He chuckled.

That comment seemed to bring general agreement from the gathered crowd of more than twenty-five people. Encouraged by their welcome, Carmel went on, 'So, Dr Khan has asked me to take over for Maureen and I'm really happy to do it, but I must tell you that I'm new to all of this. I understand that I am responsible for organizing activities, speakers, trips out, classes, and so on, for anyone who is interested. I have the regular schedule, but if I miss out on anything, or there is something you'd like added, please let me know and I'll try to organize it.'

The rest of the morning flew by as she spoke to people individually, asking them what things they were interested in. Some people were too ill to even consider activities, but a surprising number of people were able and wanted something to fill the days. One lady called Claire confided in Carmel that she had no idea that she had any aptitude for landscape painting until she came to the hospice, 'Imagine,' she smiled, 'I might have made a fortune had I known sooner.'

Two old ladies called Sheila and Kate took her to the window to show her the bird feeders they had built for the garden, each one with different sized apertures to attract different birds. Sharif had explained when they spotted them sitting together in the garden on

the day Carmel arrived that the women were gay and lifelong partners. When Sheila was diagnosed with stage three lung cancer, Kate
cared for her at home until her needs became too complex. They
visited Aashna House and decided it was the best place for her. It
broke their hearts to be separated and, for the first few months, Kate
would appear before breakfast and not leave until after Sheila had
gone to bed. One night, the weather outside was treacherous, Sharif
suggested a bed be put in Sheila's room and Kate stay over. She stayed
that night and every night since, nobody mentioned it and since
everyone had a private room, many patients never even noticed. They
were so happy to be reunited and their chat entertained the residents
that had few visitors.

She spoke to Oscar about the yoga classes he held every day at ten-
thirty and four-thirty and was amazed at how many residents
attended, even though many were very ill indeed. She had to concentrate hard to understand, he had a very strong Scottish accent.

'Sometimes, it might be as simple as facing the wheel chair to the
sun and the person raising their arms or even just their hands in a sun
salute, while others who are able, do stretches and poses. Yoga isn't
about how much you can do, how far you can stretch, and it's
certainly not a competition, but everyone that does it benefits from it,
I really believe that. On sunny days, we try to do it outside, it can take
some organizing with mats and chairs and all of that but it's lovely to
hear the birds.' Carmel instantly warmed to the man, he was wiry and
thin with a long grey ponytail and rimless glasses. He smelled of
sandalwood and wore loose fitting clothes. She judged him to be in
his fifties but his face was unlined and he looked so fit and flexible it
was hard to be sure.

'How long have you been teaching yoga?' she asked.

'Oh, not that long, I'm a late bloomer. I started doing it to de-
stress, that's where I met Sharif, actually. He's been practicing for
years, but we got talking one day. I used to be an investment banker,
then a deal I arranged went sour, a lot of people lost a lot of money. I
had a nervous breakdown from the stress of it all and ended up in a
psychiatric unit after I went crazy and broke up the house. My wife at

the time had to call the police; I was out of control. I spent a full year in therapy and part of that was practicing yoga every day, that was nine years ago.' He smiled, clearly at peace with his past. 'You should come along to a class, you'd be more than welcome.'

Carmel longed to try yoga, there had been an ad up in the shop for classes starting in the community centre in Birr a year or so ago, but when she mentioned it to Bill, he said they were probably all drug taking hippies and she'd be better not to be seen mixing with them. She wished now she could have stood up to him but she hadn't.

'Well, I'm actually supposed to be working, so I don't know...' she began.

'Oh, don't worry about that, a lot of the staff join in, it's something we encourage for everyone, often Sharif joins us or his mum Nadia, have you met her yet?'

'Er...no, she's away, visiting some relatives in Pakistan.' Carmel tried to hide the trepidation in her voice. She was dreading meeting Nadia; she would most likely be horrified that her eligible, successful son had hooked up with someone like her.

'Oh, that's right, she'll be back soon though, you'll like her, she's great. Anyway, I best crack on, we are going to try downward dog today with a man who has had extensive surgery, but he's determined to try. See you around and welcome to the team, Carmel.'

Everyone was so nice. When she'd finished meeting the patients, Ivy told her over a cup of tea some more stories of Dolly. Like the time she arranged a kissogram for the birthday of an old retired school teacher who was very uptight and straight-laced, but when the kissogram turned up, it was one of the young teachers on the staff of his former school making a few extra pounds at the weekends. Both of them were horrified but locked in a code of silence. Nobody in the staff knew the elderly man was sick and he certainly didn't want it known, so they both had to keep schtum. Ivy's laughter at the antics of Dolly caused her to go into a coughing fit.

CHAPTER 12

*T*he weeks flew by and she really got into the swing of the job. London blew her away. It was so gorgeous, the architecture and the history just astounded her. She loved the anonymity, people just accepting all the diversity of mankind and getting on with their own lives. Sharif really enjoyed showing his city to her; he loved London and he knew so much about it. In Brick Lane, they ate curries so hot they blew the top of your head off, and one Saturday morning they took a walking tour to see the street art of the city. She saw paintings by the famous but enigmatic Banksy and was mesmerized by the skill of these graffiti artists.

Carmel couldn't believe she was actually there, in places she'd only seen on TV, and here she was looking up at St Paul's, crossing over Tower Bridge, seeing the changing of the guard at Buckingham Palace. One time, she and Sharif were sitting outside a café at Piccadilly Circus and Prince Charles and Camilla passed by in their car. Carmel nearly squealed with excitement. Slowly, London was feeling like home and she just loved it. Bill and Julia and Birr felt like a lifetime ago.

Her first month's salary seemed a gigantic amount of money, but Sharif assured her it was the same salary as Maureen had been on before she left. She had never earned any money before and was totally ill-equipped to deal with spending it. The day Sharif took her to open a bank account, he waited outside while she went in and she didn't want to seem like a total eejit, having never had a bank account before. She refused all cards, remembering how Bill always said, 'cash is king,' and plastic cards were the slippery slope to ruination. When Sharif heard that, he gently sent her back into the branch to ask for a debit card. They'd thought it odd that she didn't want one in the first place, and assured her it would be in the post in a few days. Her heart almost burst with pride when they asked her for her address. To have an apartment number, one of her very own, and a place to call hers meant so much to her, in a way that nobody could understand.

The one hundred and eight euro meant for the coal back in Birr lasted her the entire month. Sharif offered, on more than one occasion, to give her an advance, but she refused. Once she got paid, she went into the bank and changed that exact amount from Sterling to Euros and posted it back to Bill. She considered writing a note, or a card or something, but there was nothing to say, so she just posted the cash.

She did a bit of shopping for the apartment and purchased two blouses for work, she wore black trousers every day that she washed and dried each night on the radiators. There was a tumble dryer, but she didn't want to run up the bill. The nuns had instilled a terrible fear in her of the electricity bill, so Trinity House was always chilly and damp with wet clothes hung all over the place, and Bill Sheehan would have had a stroke if she suggested getting a dryer when there was a perfectly good line in the garden. Sharif, in desperation one evening, cleared the radiators of clothes, stuffed everything in the dryer, telling her she was making her asthma worse by having excessive moisture in the air and explaining that he didn't give a monkey's about the electricity bill.

One evening, as they sat cuddled up on the sofa watching *Planet Earth 2* by David Attenborough on the huge flat screen TV, Sharif casually mentioned that his mother was coming back in two days' time. Carmel sat up straight, releasing herself from the comfort of his arms.

'Why didn't you say?' she asked.

'I'm saying it now. What's the problem? She's looking forward to meeting you.' He tried to draw her back into his embrace.

'But you probably haven't told her the full story, that I have a husband back in Ireland that I deserted, that I was in care all my life, that I haven't a bean to my name, and that I'm living here free gratis and for nothing, and that I'm the wrong side of forty...' Carmel was really getting worked up. Everyone said how close Nadia and Sharif were and she was sure the older woman would have wanted better for her only boy.

Sharif zapped the TV with the remote and the room went quiet. He sat up and faced Carmel.

'What are you freaking out for? Seriously? Why? She is my mother, I love her and she loves me. All we want for each other is happiness. When my father died, I thought she would fall apart. She might have if it hadn't been for Dolly. She came to our house every day, made my mother get up, wash, dress, do her hair and makeup, and they walked. Miles and miles and miles every day, sometimes they talked about him, sometimes it was general chat, other times total silence. Dolly knew what she needed. She made her eat, even poured a glass or two of wine down her neck, despite my mother being a teetotaller. At least she was then, now she loves a social drink. Seeing how Dolly managed her life alone made my mother realize she could do it too. It broke Ammi's heart when Dolly died. As bad, if not worse than the loss of my father, and she wanted her to find you. Over the years, my parents threw a lot of resources into tracking you down, by then they were wealthy, but with no success. She knew I was going to Dublin to meet you, but she had to leave for Pakistan to attend my cousin's wedding in Karachi. Otherwise, she would have gone to Dublin with me. Her sister's only daughter was the bride, so she felt she had to go, but she wished me well and demanded daily updates. The idea that we might feel something for each other never occurred to me, and I hate talking on the phone, that's a conversation for when I see her face to face. But she will be happy; I know she will. She will see that I love you and that you love me and that will be all that she will need.'

Carmel paled. Sharif said he loved her. He'd never said that to her before and she had never said it to him. Actually, she had never said those words to anyone.

He blushed slightly and gave a small lopsided smile. 'You do love me? Don't you?' When her eyes filled with tears, he was instantly apologetic. 'I'm so sorry, I shouldn't have rushed you, it's only been a few weeks and it's been such an upheaval for you; I'm sorry, Carmel. Forget I said anything...'

She shook her head, not trusting herself to speak.

'What? No, you don't? No, you do?' Sharif was confused.

'I do...love you, I mean. I just never heard those words before, never, from anyone. I've never heard them nor have I ever said them. I...' she was too choked up to speak.

Sharif gathered her to his chest and held her tightly. 'My darling girl, it's all over now, I swear to you. The misery is over, it's all good from here on. You have my word. I love you so much, and I will take care of you, we'll take care of each other, and this is your happy ever after.'

Two days later, after spending a huge amount of money in the local Waitrose, Carmel was cooking a welcome dinner for Nadia in her very own kitchen. She decided to cook something Irish, mainly because she had no clue what went into Pakistani dishes. The food tasted delicious whenever Sharif took her out to dinner, but it was so exotic she was sure she'd mess it up. She checked and double checked that Nadia wasn't allergic to anything and she made home-made vegetable soup from scratch with a freshly baked loaf of soda bread to start, followed by roast lamb with all the trimmings, stuffing, gravy, mashed and roast spuds, carrots and parsnips creamed together, and steamed broccoli. For dessert, she was just putting the finishing touches on an apple sponge cake that she was going to serve with custard. Sharif mentioned that his mother enjoyed a glass of white wine, so she bought an expensive bottle; she had no idea what it would taste like, she'd only ever had wine herself a few times with

Sharif. Bill used to go down to Seano's pub for a pint three nights a week, but he never invited her, and she never went to social occasions where the possibility of having a drink would present itself.

She got the meat from the Halal butcher on the high street, even though Sharif assured her that neither he nor his mother was a strict Muslim. He teased her gently about the elaborate preparations but admitted he was touched she was going to so much trouble and, before going off on his rounds, assured her that his mother was as nervous as she was. She was due to arrive at six and Carmel wanted the place spotless and everything ready by then. Luckily, she had spent her entire life catering for people, so it didn't faze her and she was confident it would taste nice. She had bought some lilies for the hall table, and they were filling the apartment with their lovely fragrance as she set the table. It gave her a thrill of sheer unadulterated glee to prepare her little home for her first guest.

It was ten to six. Sharif had assured her he'd be back in time, but she knew how he got waylaid frequently by patients or their families, so was praying he'd make it. She desperately wanted him there when Nadia arrived.

At three minutes past six, with still no sign of Sharif, the doorbell rang. Carmel quickly untied her apron and hung it behind the broom closet door. She wanted everything looking perfect. She smoothed down her hair and checked her reflection in the big mirror, a bit hot and bothered looking, but there was nothing she could do about that.

She opened the door to a small, female version of Sharif. The same dark, dark eyes, the same caramel-coloured skin, black hair cut in an elegant style that just stopped short of her shoulders. She had a smooth unlined face, and though she knew she must be at least seventy, she certainly didn't look it. She was so polished and glamorous looking, Carmel felt dowdy and thrown together by comparison.

'Oh, my word. I can't believe it. You are the image of your mother, the absolute image.' She beamed with delight as she entered the apartment, all the time gazing at Carmel. 'I'm sorry for staring, you must think me so rude but honestly, the resemblance, it's quite remarkable.

It's as if Dolly is standing in front of me again, all these years later. Oh, how she would have loved to have been reunited with you.'

Carmel was a little taken aback by the effusive nature of the greeting, but at least Nadia seemed pleased to meet her.

'Thank you, it's lovely to meet you, Mrs Khan, Sharif has told me a lot about you,' Carmel managed.

'Nadia, please, and I'm sure that he has, like when the old battle axe is coming back!' She laughed and it seemed to come from her toes. Her whole body shook and Carmel knew instinctively she was a person she would like, but Nadia had yet to learn the nature of the relationship between her and Sharif, would she be so pleased then, she wondered?

'Now, let's sit down and have a drink together before my son comes back, get to know each other a little?' She proffered a gift bag containing two bottles of Champagne and an elaborately wrapped box of chocolates.

'Thanks,' Carmel said, accepting the gift. 'I mean, thank you very much, you shouldn't have.' She had never entertained anyone before and prayed she wasn't making a total mess of it. Her education on all matters social came from the television.

'Not at all, just a small thing.' Nadia dismissed the gift with a wave of her small jewelled hand. 'I got it in duty-free, such a gruelling flight from Karachi, we had a three-hour layover in Charles De Gaulle, a wretched place, so I had nothing to do but shop for a few hours. It dragged, as I was so excited to get home and to see you. Sharif told me you looked like her, but honestly, I can't stop staring, I must dig out some of the old photos of her at your age, you'll be astounded.'

Unlike Sharif who sounded completely English, Nadia had a strong Pakistani accent, despite many years living in the UK.

'My late Husband, Khalid, oh, how he loved your mother! They would laugh for hours, she delighted him, as she did all of us. Even in his last days, and I was only able to keep him at home because of your mother, she helped with everything, she could make him chuckle and forget the pain for a moment at least.' She looked wistful then, as the pain of his loss shadowed her face for a second. 'But listen to me blathering on, I'm nervous you see, of meeting you, and when I'm nervous, I babble. Tell me all about you.'

She patted the seat beside her and Carmel reluctantly sat down. She hated being in the spotlight of anyone's attention, she was more of a background person but Nadia was insistent.

Her eyes were so dark it was almost impossible to distinguish between the iris and the pupil and she had Sharif's long curling lashes. It was clear who he took after, though his father must have been a tall man because he was over six feet and Nadia barely five.

'Well, there's nothing much to tell really,' she began.

'Oh, that accent! So lyrical and musical I always think. Dolly sounded the exact same way from the time I first met her in 1977 to the day she left us.'

'I saw a video of her, on Sharif's phone, of her birthday. She had a strong Dublin accent alright,' Carmel agreed.

'And how did you feel, watching it?' Nadia asked her. She was so direct and open, it could have been disconcerting, but Sharif's mother's warmth softened it.

'Er...well, he didn't show it to me at first, he gave me her letters to read and these...' she touched the necklace she hadn't taken off since Sharif had given them to her.

'Ah, yes, and how lovely they are on you. She bought them at a place in Karachi, you know? She visited there with Khalid and me and Sharif, of course, he was just a boy then, for a family occasion. Oh, she was all agog at the sights and sounds of Pakistan. She never really went anywhere, you see, apart from here and back to Ireland to try to find you. Have you travelled much?'

'Never. The first time I was out of Ireland was when I came here a few weeks back,' she admitted. There was no point in pretending she was anything other than what she was. If she was to be a permanent fixture in Sharif's life, then Nadia might as well know the truth.

Compassion gleamed from her eyes. 'Did you have a happy life? Were you loved?'

Carmel inhaled. 'It was okay. I was never adopted, even though they told my mother I had been. I don't know why they would have done that. So, I lived in a children's home run by nuns, and it was fine. They weren't mean to us or I wasn't ever well…you know…it was okay. To answer your question, no I wasn't loved. I was just there. I had a friend, Kit, and we loved each other, but she went to Australia and now she's dead.'

Tears shone in Nadia's eyes and Carmel wondered if she should have made it sound a bit better.

'Oh, Carmel, I'm so sorry. We tried so hard, honestly; I swear to you on my best friend's memory, we tried everything. At one stage, Khalid employed a private investigator, but the church authorities there were like clams. They would reveal nothing. Dolly used to say, 'At least some well-to-do family has her, only the wealthy can afford to adopt, the church knows how to turn a few bob.' And after each failed attempt, she would retreat to her little flat and we wouldn't see her for days. I learned that she just needed to be alone, and I didn't bother her, and then she would re-emerge, ready to try again. I remember, on one occasion, when we took her on holiday with us, Spain or the Canary Islands or someplace, it doesn't matter anyway, Sharif was about seven I think, anyway he wanted to go to an aquarium, so we went. There was one of those places where you walk underneath a glass tunnel and the fish all swim above you, you know the thing I mean?'

Carmel nodded, she'd seen them on TV.

'Well, there was an old shark there, all cuts and scrapes and scars, I don't know how it got there, but it was wild at some point, and Dolly looked at him, with his bright black eye just on the other side of the glass and she said to me, 'That's me, Nad, battered and bruised, but I'll keep on swimming.'

'As we walked back to the car park that day, Khalid was up ahead with Sharif, she asked me, "Do you think I'll ever find her? Really?" We were always honest with each other, and Khalid was convinced there was nowhere else to look. I didn't want to be negative, but I felt I owed her the truth. I told her that I thought the chances were slim, but that miracles do happen. And now, here you are.'

'Too late,' Carmel said ruefully

'For her, yes, but not for you. What happened after you left the home?'

'I got married.' She had no idea how to proceed with this. Sharif said she wasn't particularly religious, but even so, she might be horrified.

'And was it a good marriage?'

'No. No, it wasn't. He wanted a cook and a cleaner and a maid to take care of his daughters. We weren't in love, I don't think he even liked me much and his sister made sure I never bonded with the little girls; I left him.' Carmel exhaled, at least that part was over with.

'Good for you! You deserve so much more than that. How long ago did you split up?'

'Almost four weeks ago, I left when Sharif found me.'

Both women turned then to the sound of Sharif's key in the lock.

Nadia leapt up and ran to greet him, throwing her arms around him, 'Ah *mere laal*! My darling boy, how wonderful to see you again!'

'Hello, Ammi, so you survived Karachi? You look well.' He grinned, returning her embrace. 'I see you two have met; I'm so sorry I'm late back, Carmel, I was talking to a patient.'

'That's no problem,' she replied, glad to get to the kitchen to make sure her meticulously prepared dinner wasn't burned, and to be out from under the spotlight of Nadia's attention. Sharif led his mother to the lounge area and, taking the bottle from the ice bucket where Carmel had put it, poured three glasses of champagne.

'Carmel, come here when you're ready, I want to propose a toast,' he called as she just covered the meat in tin foil and laid it on the worktop to allow it to rest before carving. Everything else was being kept warm.

She wondered as she crossed the room if she should stand beside him or not, and decided against it, too presumptuous. He took the decision out of her hands when he casually slung his arm around her shoulder and kissed her on the lips.

'Oh, my goodness, am I imagining things? Are you two an item, as they say?' Nadia's eyes were wide with surprise.

'Yes, Ammi, I love her and she seems to love me too, though why I can't imagine,' he chuckled, giving her a squeeze.

'But you never said, we talked and you told me you'd found her, but you never mentioned a romance...'

Carmel was worried, perhaps this changed everything. If Nadia wasn't happy about it, then it couldn't work, she knew how close they were. Suddenly, she found herself enveloped in a fragrant hug.

'Oh, Carmel, this is wonderful news; I am so happy for you both. I knew there was something different about him, he seemed to be glowing, but I could never have guessed... oh, this is just splendid, you've been alone for too long... and you, Carmel, if anyone deserves a bit of happiness, it is you, my dear. Oh, if only Khalid and Dolly could see this, it would be...' she couldn't go on.

'It's okay, Ammi.' Sharif rubbed her hair gently, his arms around both women. 'It's okay, this is how it was meant to be.'

CHAPTER 13

*W*ith relief, Carmel pushed the new SIM card into the slot on her phone. A new life, a new number, now nobody from Ireland could contact her. She punched in numbers to her contacts list. A list longer, she could never have imagined possible before. Various teachers and group activity leaders, some patients' family numbers, Sharif's, of course, and Nadia's, and all the staff members, many of whom she now called friends. Her old phone had had four contacts, Bill, Niamh, Sinead, and Julia. She'd had no life in Birr; the longer she was away, the more obvious it became. Here, she was someone people sought out, texted to see if she wanted to have coffee, someone who got texts from their partner just to say hi. Nobody seemed to see her as poor Carmel. She was a colleague, a girl-friend, a friend, and she absolutely loved it.

She was invited to the cinema to see *Bridget Jones' Baby* with all the female staff, Ivanka, Ivy, Marlena, Nadia, and a few others as well on Friday night and for a pizza afterwards. For them, it was just a regular Girl's Night, as they called it, but for her, it was the first time she'd ever socialized with a group of friends. She was so excited but tried to be as nonchalant as they were.

The first Sunday she was in London, she got up and prepared for

Mass as she had done every Sunday for forty years. Sharif barely stirred because he'd been up most of the night with a patient who was in distress. As she was about to go out the door, she caught a glimpse of herself in the mirror and a sudden realization hit her. She didn't have to go. If she chose not to go to Mass, then she could just not go. She tried to remember if Mass gave her any spiritual support, if it helped her in any way, and came to the conclusion that it didn't. She was a spiritual person, of that she was never in doubt, but the Catholic weekly service meant nothing to her. So, she decided, there and then, that she wouldn't go anymore. She instantly started to panic, thinking something awful could happen, but she resisted the urge to run down to the church. Instead, she went for a walk around the grounds, down past the manicured beds and lawns, around the polytunnels where the residents grew vegetables for the restaurant, and by the little lake, stocked with huge gold koi. On the other side of the little lake was the chapel of rest. It was away from the main area of the clinic and was landscaped with trees and shrubs. It wasn't dedicated to any faith group and so, all the patients, when they died, were laid out there and their families could spend some time with their remains.

She pushed the large oak door and stepped inside. The interior felt cool and calm with gold carpeting and midnight blue upholstered seats. It felt like a spiritual place but without the crucifixes or statues. There were fresh flowers and some soothing looking pieces of art on the walls.

She knelt, even though there were no kneelers, and the pews were individual seats. She blessed herself as she'd done every day of her life. She began to rattle out the prayers drilled into her as a child, when she stopped. Like Mass, they were meaningless. She sat down and breathed deeply.

'Hi, Mam,' she spoke so quietly, though she was alone. 'I've never called you that. I suppose nobody else ever did either. I wish I could have met you. I wish we could have been together. But you wanted me, I know that now, and Sharif and Nadia have been so kind. They talk about you all the time, and I feel like you can see us, I hope you can anyway. I'm so sorry they never let you come for me; I would have loved it if you could have. I had a lonely life, I only know how lonely it was since I've come here. I hope you're happy now, and I hope...well, I hope you're proud of how I turned out.'

She sat in silence for a long time, just thinking. She took the photo album out of her bag and opened it once more. Nadia had given her lots more, taken at various points in Dolly's life, and presented them to her in a beautiful album covered in cream lace and Dolly's name embroidered on the front. Sharif revealed that Nadia had made the album herself. Carmel treasured it.

The only ones of her life before coming to England were the one of Carmel as a baby and the one taken on Dollymount Strand, that just said 'Me and Joe, Dollymount 1973.' It had been taken by a professional photographer and bore the name of a photographic studio long gone from the Clontarf Road, opposite the beach. She'd googled it to see if any trace of it might exist still, but those days when photographers took pictures of couples and they paid a few shillings and collected the snap later, were long gone. Everyone had smart-phones now.

Why would she have included that one, she wondered? Was Joe her father? And if so, Joe who? She tried to see any resemblance between herself and the man in the picture but failed. Everyone who knew Dolly was astounded at the resemblance between her and Carmel, so she wondered if she had any of her father in her at all.

Joe could have been a brother, or a friend, or an old boyfriend. She was born in 1976 and this photo was taken in '73. If he was her father, then he and Dolly would have been together at least three years, and surely then that relationship would have survived an unplanned preg-nancy? Dolly wasn't a wimp. She and this Joe, if he was the father, could surely have taken the boat to England together and had her here and lived happily ever after. They both looked very young in the photo, but surely, three years later they'd have been able to fend for themselves even in holy Catholic Ireland?

Neither Nadia nor Sharif could shed any light on either who Joe was, or who her father might have been. Apparently, Dolly never mentioned it.

'I asked her once, years ago,' Nadia revealed when they discussed it last, 'but she wouldn't say. He was married was all she said.'

'Did he know she was pregnant, do you think?' Carmel didn't know what answer she was hoping for. No, probably, because then he wouldn't have knowingly abandoned her.

'I don't know, I'm so sorry Carmel, I wish I knew more, but for someone so open, she was very, very, private about certain things. We were as close as sisters, but we all have some secrets that never leave our own hearts. Dolly's relationship with your father, whatever that was, fell into that category, I'm afraid.'

She let herself back into the apartment to discover Sharif was gone to the clinic. They were going out to lunch with a doctor friend and his wife and she was dreading it. It was something arranged before he even came over to Ireland and he said he didn't particularly want to go, but the guy was chairing a conference or something that Sharif was involved with, so he kind of had to go.

He thought she might enjoy meeting the doctor's wife. Sometimes, she thought Sharif was totally oblivious to the clear differences between them, but the rest of the world was not. One or two of the less pleasant patients had made catty remarks about her having herself well and truly ensconced in a very lucrative setup, and when she accidentally overheard them, her face burned with shame. They were right, of course, but what they didn't know is that she would love Sharif Khan if he was unemployed and penniless. She cared nothing for money and, funnily enough, despite the fact that he was very wealthy, neither did Sharif.

He believed completely in the idea that prosperity comes easily to those who try to do good with the money they accrue. His primary focus was providing a home for those at the last phase of their lives and making that as positive and as peaceful an experience as it could be. He'd explained, yes, it was an expensive option, and not everyone could afford it. Though several patients seemed to be from very humble backgrounds and still came to Aashna, the vast majority of people had money by the time their lives were ending. They owned houses and so on to sell so they could enjoy some comfort after their years of hard work. Most families would rather see their loved one well taken care of and happy in their final days, weeks or months, than have an extra few thousand in their inheritance. Carmel suspected several of the residents of Aashna were either there on a heavily subsidized basis or free of charge altogether, but Sharif never admitted that.

She had spent what she considered an astronomical amount of money on a dress in Marks and Spencer at the insistence of Ivanka and Zane, who spotted it as they walked through the store on their way to a pub they sometimes went to for lunch. She had tried to take a much bigger size into the changing room until Zane and Ivanka hooted with laughter. She couldn't believe it when the size ten dress fitted her perfectly, all the lumps and bumps caused by years of comfort eating seemed to have melted away. She knew Sharif liked her when they met in Dublin, but she must have seemed so frumpy to him then, at least now she looked much better, even if her insecurities were still there.

The dress was royal blue and very figure hugging, not her usual sort of thing at all, with sheer sleeves and a skirt that stopped just above the knee. Its round neck was encrusted with tiny silver sequins and it looked very glamorous in the shop, but on Carmel, it felt ridiculous. She bought a pair of impossibly high silver strappy sandals that she was sure would result in a trip to A&E but Zane assured her looked fabulous. Ivanka knocked on the door and arrived with a large vanity case. She had promised to come round to do her hair and makeup before the lunch and when she finally looked in the full-length mirror in their bedroom, she had to admit the transformation was remarkable. Her hair was twisted into an elegant upstyle, and pinned with little sparkly clips that caught the light when she turned her head. She'd gone for a trim to the hairdressers the week before and the very camp man who ran the place screamed in horror at the brown dye in her hair, insisting he strip it all out and restore her to her natural colour. He was so determined, she let him, and anyway she hated the brown, it reminded her of that old crow Julia, and so four hours and one hundred and sixty pounds later, she emerged, a blonde once more. Sharif got a fright when he saw her, but he assured her that he loved it and that now her face made more sense. They'd giggled at his description, but she knew what he meant. Her creamy skin and blue eyes worked so much better than with the mousey brown colour. She'd spent more money on herself in the last month than she'd ever done in her entire life before, nudged along by Ivanka and Zane, who had really taken her under their wing. She looked nothing like her former self, and she'd even upgraded her work uniform from a selection of pastel blouses and black trousers to skirts, tops, and even jackets. She still loved her jeans and T-shirts when lounging around, but Sharif always looked so elegant, she felt less dowdy now.

'So,' Ivanka stood back admiring her handiwork, 'you now look beautiful.'

'I don't know about beautiful, but certainly better anyway. I used to look like someone covered me in glue and threw me into a charity shop.' Carmel smiled at her friend. 'Thanks, Ivanka.'

Sharif asked her to meet him there, as he'd had to go accompany a patient to Bedford Hospital for emergency surgery and wouldn't get back to accompany her to the lunch. She ordered the cab to pick her up at reception and got several appreciative comments and even a wolf whistle from Kate and Sheila as she passed, which made her blush.

The restaurant was so posh it could hurt itself, as Kit used to say. It was an old country mansion, all banisters and glittering candelabras and chandeliers. A doorman, in full regalia, held the door open for her, 'Good afternoon, madam, welcome to Grosslyn Court.'

What on earth was she doing here? The urge to bolt threatened to overwhelm her as she stood in the vast entrance hall. Waiting staff flurried about, carrying impossibly heavy silver platters and serving dishes as there appeared to be dining rooms on either side of the grand staircase. She had no idea what to do next, should she try one of the rooms to see if Sharif was there? Or call him maybe? Perhaps people didn't just whip out mobile phones in places like this. Though she thought she looked okay, inside she felt like little Carmel Murphy, nobody's child and completely out of place in such opulent surroundings. She debated going back outside, maybe to wait for Sharif there, but as she deliberated, trying not to get in anyone's way, she spotted him emerging from a taxi outside. Relief flooded through her; it was going to be fine. She smiled and went to meet him, but he didn't see her. He turned to enter the dining room on the left. When she put her hand on his arm, he spun around and gazed in amazement.

'Carmel...I didn't recognize you! You look...Oh, my God, you look absolutely beautiful. That dress, and your hair...I had no idea it was you.'

She beamed with delight. 'Ivanka did it, really, she and Zane made me buy the dress, even though it cost ninety-five pounds!' she whispered in his ear.

He grinned, 'You crack me up. Honestly, you do, the women in here would spend that on a lipstick and not one of them could hold a candle to you. I'm the luckiest man alive. Now, let's take you in so I can show you off to Tristan and Angelica.'

She picked her way behind him to a table where a couple sat

waiting in silence. As they rose to greet Sharif and Carmel, she sensed a coldness in the embrace, especially from Angelica. They were both very rich looking, expensive clothes and shoes, but she was good looking and he definitely was not. He had that high bred look about him, all ruddy cheeks and sticking out ears. His reddish hair was receding, but he had it strategically styled in a not very convincing comb-over, and his voice was nasal and reed thin. She was totally different. All shiny black hair and lots of makeup. The dress was a little too tight and Carmel suspected it was cutting her in half. A life-time spent in the shadows meant Carmel was good at spotting the things more extroverted people missed, and the tension between this pair was palpable.

Tristan was an oncologist as well, and he and Sharif immediately began discussing another colleague's upcoming article in *The Lancet*, leaving her in the full beam of Angelica's inquisitive stare.

'So, Carmel, you're Irish, I understand?' she raised an impeccably plucked black eyebrow. She might as well have said, 'I hear you're a leper,' for all the warmth in her voice.

'Yes, Dublin and later County Offaly.' She tried to sound confident but feared she failed miserably.

'I've never been, Tristan went once, hunting or fishing or some-thing mind-numbing like that but I've never felt the urge. It's terribly green, I believe.' Her accent could cut glass.

'Eh, yes, very green alright. In fact, Johnny Cash wrote a song about Ireland called *Forty Shades of Green*,' she blurted, feeling instantly imbecilic.

'Johnny who? Do we know him? Sharif used to know a chap, years ago, second trombone or some such, with the Berlin Philharmonic? ...' she looked perplexed.

Oh, God, did she have to take this conversation to its mortifying conclusion?

'No, he's an American country singer, well, was, he's dead now.' Carmel could feel the colour creeping up her neck, she took a big gulp of water.

'An American?' Angelica wrinkled her nose. 'Oh, no, I don't know many of those. My father knew some, they were stationed at our country house during the war or something when he was a child, but I tend to avoid Americans where possible. Though it is becoming increasingly more difficult.' She uttered this broad, racist generalization, and dabbed her lips with the starched napkin, leaving a blood red stain that someone was going to have to scrub to remove. Sharif and Tristan were still deep in conversation, so escape looked unlikely.

'I'd love to visit there someday,' she ventured, trying to defend all the Americans she loved to listen to on podcasts and on Ted Talks.

'Well, why on earth would you not go if that is your wish?' She fixed Carmel with an icy gaze as if she were a particularly slow five-year-old.

'Well, it would cost a lot, flights and all of that, I'd have to save up.' Carmel wasn't going to try to keep up with her, it would be impossible anyway.

'Quite.' Carmel could tell she wasn't sure if it was a joke.

The huge leatherbound menus arrived, and to Carmel's dismay, it was written almost entirely in what she thought might be French. She didn't do French at school, it was only needed if you were going to college and she definitely was not, so she did Geography instead. Kids in care were never considered as university material; it was never said outright, but the inference was that she had cost the state quite enough already without expecting a third level qualification as well. She tried to make out what the words on the menu might mean. Sometimes, French words looked a bit like English words she'd heard. But even the bits that were in English were a mystery. The whole thing was confits of this and veloutés of that, she imagined sweetbreads to be a dessert of some kind, but they were being served with samphire, whatever that was, and potato rosti. The only thing she recognized was potato and that couldn't be a dessert, could it? Sharif must have noticed her discomfort and asked should he order for her.

'Yes, please, that would be lovely, I'm just going to the Ladies, you know what I like.' She dared to rest her hand on his shoulder as she passed, and he reached up and covered it with his, holding her gaze for a second. She walked away, happy that he loved her even if she didn't fit in with these surroundings or those people.

When she returned, Angelica was halfway through a bottle of white wine and Sharif had barely touched his glass of red. Tristan was driving, so was only on mineral water. The other woman smiled, but Carmel thought she looked like a particularly hungry fox.

'So, you found it alright? This place is a bit of a maze. I used to come here as a teenager, when the Wesley-Cramptons had it, Old Charlie W.C. as everyone called him, was a frightful goat, one had to keep one's wits about them if he was on the prowl, but the parties were marvelous. One occasion, I recall Grahame Billingsley, do you know him? Top man at London Bridge Hospital, Sharif knows him, anyway, he was caught *in flagrante* as it were with Georgia Samsworth's au pair. Georgia went totally berserk and we all thought she was outraged that he should take advantage of such a girl, but no, it turns out that she herself was involved with Grahame for years and nobody knew. The same night, Grahame's wife was there as was Georgia's current husband, Danny Porchion-Wall. They divorced, but her father was a QC, now sits on the appellate bench, so she got everything.'

Carmel looked at Angelica in bewilderment, but she ploughed on regardless. Carmel had absolutely no idea what she was on about. At least she required no input from Carmel. She droned on for several minutes, name dropping double barrels here and there, and everyone she knew was the top of something. Carmel looked around and took in the splendour of the room until Sharif's voice broke through her reverie.

'Tristan, we have been derelict in our duties to these beautiful ladies, going on about work. Forgive us, we are boring when we get on the subject of molecular mutations in genome sequencing.'

'One of you is boring no matter what he talks about.' Angelica's derisive remark went unheard by the men but not by Carmel.

The afternoon dragged on and Sharif soon saw that Carmel wasn't enjoying it. Angelica was getting drunker by the second, she'd ordered another bottle of wine, having polished off the first one almost single-handedly, and her sneering remarks about her husband were more audible.

Tristan was alright, but he had nothing to say to women, it would seem. He listened politely whenever Sharif drew her into the conversation, but once she'd finished, he'd raise some totally unrelated topic again with Sharif, inevitably one she couldn't participate in. After the main course, where Angelica made a huge deal of how she wanted everything served and then ate none of it, the waiter came offering desserts, but Sharif checked his beeper.

'Oh, I'm sorry folks, we have to go, needed at Aashna.' He smiled apologetically, but Carmel saw the conspiratorial gleam in his eye.

'Oh, for God's sake, can't the registrar do it?' Angelica whined, her red-taloned hand on Sharif's sleeve. 'We've hardly seen you for months and now you're dashing off. Anybody would think you were trying to get away, but then perhaps you are, after all, there's only so much scientific drivel a person can listen to without wanting to stab the talking head with a steak knife.'

Sharif looked at her intently, embarrassed for his friend. 'Perhaps you should cut back on the booze, Angelica, it clearly doesn't agree with you.' Sharif's words were mild but packed a punch all the same.

Angelica reddened with embarrassment. 'Oh, Sharif, don't be such a bore, come on, stay and have some fun.' She tried to recover but it only made everyone else at the table cringe.

Tristan shut his eyes in resignation; he was tired of her constant sniping.

'Well, you must get on, old boy, thanks for coming. I'll be in touch about the call for papers, the conference isn't until the spring, but I'd like to have a strong representation from our end if possible.' He turned his attention to Carmel, 'It was lovely to meet you, Caroline,' he held out his hand to shake hers.

'Carmel, Tristan, her name is Carmel,' Sharif said gently.

'Of course, of course, what did I call you? Something else? I'm so sorry, my dear, I'm a bit...well, you know.' Tristan at least had the good grace to look embarrassed, but she knew he had no more interest in her than the man in the moon. Sharif was clearly his focus and the ladies were mere decorations. His relationship with his own wife left a lot to be desired, and while Carmel felt sorry for him in the way she sniped constantly, if she had to play second fiddle to his career and listen to him droning on about molecules or whatever all day, maybe she had some reason to be so catty.

In the cab on the way back to Aashna House, Sharif held her hand.

'I'm sorry, that was a terrible lunch for you and you looked so stunning... I'm really sorry.'

'Sharif, they're your friends and they seem nice, I suppose, I just don't know the set of people she was on about, the Tingly-Melons or the Farthlewaites or whatever.'

He laughed and seemed relieved she wasn't angry.

'Honestly, please don't feel upset, it was a lovely lunch. I'd never been anywhere so fancy in all my life and the food was out of this world. Did you know Angelica used to visit there before it was a hotel? When it was just a private house, can you imagine?'

Sharif chuckled, 'Don't be fooled by the cut-glass accent. Angelica comes from a long line of social climbers. Her mother was originally a hairdresser and her father a butcher, but they did well, both retiring with huge chains of shops all over London. The ailing and skint aristocracy are desperate for cash and will marry anyone who has it. Poor old Tristan's father gambled everything they had, so when Angelica showed up and set her cap at him, it seemed the answer to both their prayers. Angelica gets status and crumbling old piles to call home and the right honourables get the central heating fixed and patch up the roof with their working-class fortunes. Everyone's a winner, you would think, except that the toffs secretly despise those they need so badly for money and the hairdressers' daughters resent the uselessness of the lords and ladies. It hardly ever works out in practice.'

'And which bracket do you fit into?' she asked with a grin.

'Oh, neither, I'm just a Paki who done good.' He chuckled, putting on a cockney accent. 'Neither group would lower themselves for the likes of me. No, I had to go to The Emerald Isle to find a woman who thankfully wouldn't know the social ladder from one in her stocking and I love her for it.'

He drew her towards him in the back seat of the cab and kissed her.

'Careful, Dr Khan, I might start getting notions of upperosity myself now. A doctor is a serious catch for a girl with nothing and no one to her name. Maybe I'll go for elocution lessons and learn to say 'simply marvellous' or 'what-ho chaps.' Carmel put on a silly posh accent and Sharif chuckled.

'Please don't. I don't ever want you to change, not one single thing. When I was at university, I worked very hard. My mother and father did the same, my father almost worked himself to death when he came here, but he wanted better for me, for my mother. He had corner shops, cliché, I know, but it was a business a young Pakistani immigrant could get a start in, and if you worked hard enough, you could expand it. People see me now, with Aashna House and all of it, but I'm from very humble people, hard-working people, who knew the value of a pound. Their blood is in my veins and yes, now I live in luxury, so does my mother, but it wasn't always like this and I care very little for the trappings of wealth. I'm not a member of their clubs nor do I own a boat or a horse. I'm a simple man, with simple needs and desires. When Jamilla died, I never imagined I'd ever feel like that about anyone ever again. I knew her all my life, our parents were friends and she got it, you know? Her father and mine emigrated together, we grew up together. Weird as it might sound, she would have loved you. She had no time for that whole social climbing business either. She got that I didn't want to be a doctor so I could make lots of money; I did it because I really wanted to make a difference to people's lives.

'I don't fit in with those people, Tristan and Angelica and all of them, they just see the clinic and they calculate the money I must be making and decide to befriend me based on that. I normally refuse all those invitations, but I do want to be involved with the conference, there's some cutting-edge stuff up for discussion there, particularly on the use of cannabis for medicinal purposes. Also, I forgot what a pain Angelica can be and I thought it might be nice for you to make some friends, but they're not your type of people either. I'm sorry, I just want you to be happy here, I don't want you to think you made a mistake.'

'Sharif, I have never been so bloody happy in my life. How can you be worried? I love it here, I love Aashna House, England, the patients, the staff, and I especially love the fact that I can feel closer to my mother here. You've saved my life.'

CHAPTER 14

Carmel's pager buzzed; Marlena had paged her to come to reception. The head teacher from the local primary school wanted to see the events coordinator. For the first time since she got to Aashna, she felt tired. She wasn't sleeping. Her mother was on her mind all the time, so many questions just swirling around her head.

Sharif had taken her to Brighton, to where he and his mother had scattered Dolly's ashes, and showed her the tree they had planted in her memory. 'Dolly Mullane, mother and friend "Que sera sera", was on the inscription. She asked Sharif to put 'mother' on it in case Carmel ever found her, which touched her, but left her with more questions to which nobody had answers.

Who was her father? Was he still alive? Would he want to know her? Why did she feel she had to leave? Last night, she barely slept a wink, eventually getting up quietly so as not to disturb Sharif, she watched the dawn creep across the sky as she sipped a cup of tea in the courtyard. Sharif placing his hand on her shoulder startled her.

'What's up, you haven't slept at all?' He took off his robe, wrapped it around her, and sat down.

She was grateful for the warmth; despite the early summer, it was chilly in the mornings.

'Not really. just…It's like all the questions I had as a kid have come back to the surface again, but I'm sorry, I shouldn't be keeping you up with all of this, you need to rest. I'm sorry…' He turned to her.

'Why are you sorry? What for? You have done nothing…Oh, Carmel, my love, I wish I could take some of this burden for you, I really do. And poor Dolly, if only I could have kept her going for another little while, you'd have met her and she would have told you the answers to your questions.'

She smiled and reached for his hand.

'I don't know what I did to deserve you, but I'm so grateful for you being in my life, for you giving me a life, actually.'

'You're saving me too. We're saving each other. Before you, it was just work, work, work. I never socialized or went on holiday, I didn't see the point. Now, with you, everything is different, I'm living and working, not just working.'

Carmel felt proud as she walked down to meet the primary school head teacher and took her to the day room for coffee. The teacher, a large black lady called Daf, with a growling infectious laugh, said they had been rehearsing for a musical, *The Wizard of Oz*. It was going to be performed for the parents, but she wondered if the patients would like to see it. The school was just across the road from the clinic and was a very inclusive place by all accounts. There was a posher, fancier place at the other end of town, but this school was a real rainbow of nationalities, religions, and ability levels. Sharif always said that if he'd have had children, he'd have sent them there.

Just seeing the kids walk by in the mornings and being collected in the afternoons put a smile on lots of the faces of their patients, a reminder that life goes on.

Of course, Carmel thought it was a lovely idea and made her first executive decision to go with it. Many patients had visitors but some didn't, and to see the little ones singing and dancing could only bring joy. Daf's dark eyes burned with passion when she spoke about the kids in her care. She chatted with Carmel over a coffee and delicious home-baked scones, and it emerged that the drama team at the school was having some trouble sourcing costumes.

Carmel had an idea.

'Maybe we could help you out there? I can sew and I'm running a sewing circle here in the afternoons, well actually, my late mother set it up so I'm just following in her footsteps.' She smiled inwardly at how she dropped the words 'my mother' into the conversation like a normal person. 'Well, anyway, some of the ladies really love it and they're very good. Maybe if what you needed wasn't that complicated, we could help to run up the costumes? Come to think of it, we also have a Men's Shed thing here, some of the men enjoy doing wood-working projects, there are patients involved, but local residents, mostly retired, come too every Friday morning. I'm sure if you needed something made for a set, they'd organize that?'

Suddenly, Carmel found herself lost in a sea of dark curly hair as Daf embraced her warmly.

'That would be amazing! Thanks so much, if you're sure it wouldn't be too much? We just need yellow tunic things for the Munchkins, and they can wear black leggings, and if you could make a lot of red belts as well, just a strip of fabric for around the waist. Something like this, maybe...' she opened a page on her phone.

'That's easy. I'm sure we can do that. How many do you need?'

Daf winced and said apologetically, 'Would fifty be out of the question? We can buy the material or whatever you need...'

Sharif appeared at her shoulder.

'What's all this? Relaxing over cups of coffee when you're supposed to be working? I don't know, Daf, trying to get good staff these days...' He grinned and kissed Carmel on the cheek, perching on the arm of her chair.

'Hi, Sharif, Carmel here is just offering to help with the costumes for the school musical, we're doing *The Wizard of Oz*, and we're going to put on a show here for the patients as well if that's okay?'

'Of course, thanks for thinking of us… We'll be looking forward to it, I'm sure. Carmel is a dab hand with a needle and thread, she gets it from her Mum, and she's got all sorts going on in the sewing class, so I'm sure it will be a great project for them.'

'And I thought the Men's Shed guys could help with the set?'

'Great idea, I think we've quite enough bird feeders, it'll be good to change focus. The bird feeders are attracting so many birds, my car is covered in droppings every day now!'

Carmel loved his chuckle.

'Well, I was just saying that we'd supply the fabric or whatever they need, our fundraising team has been flat out getting sponsorships, if you can just let me know what lengths or whatever, Carmel…'

'No, not at all, we'll pay for all of that,' Sharif was insistent. 'Let it be our contribution. You just let us know what you want and we'll take care of it. It's the least we can do if we're getting the West End Theatrical experience brought to our very own Aashna House. Hey, maybe we could throw a little party afterwards, you know for the kids, some sweets, balloons, music, that sort of thing?'

Carmel caught Daf's glance and smiled, Sharif was like a kid himself, and his enthusiasm was infectious.

'The Kaivalya would be perfect, after the performance, we could take out the seats, have a little party, what do you say, ladies?'

Carmel fought the urge to jump up and hug him there and then. He was so emotional, so full of excitement and fun, the very opposite of Bill. 'I think it would be lovely. Daf?'

'Well, I know the kids would love it but, the Kaivalya here is so beautifully decorated and all that glass and plants and everything, I'm thinking sticky fingers and spilled fruit juice…and as well, wouldn't it be too noisy for the patients? They're a bit hyper at the best of times, but after a performance, they might be very boisterous.'

'No, absolutely not, that's what the Kaivalya was built for; we can clean it up afterwards, no problem. You know what we are like here, Daf, it's not a hushed tones kind of place. These people are sick, yes, but they're not dead yet, and a bit of fun and *craic*, as my charming Irish lady might say, would be good for them. Of course, those that don't want to participate don't have to, but nothing lifts the spirits like the smile of a child; it would honestly do everyone here some good. We'd love to host them here, and lay on some treats and music or whatever, I'll leave the details to Carmel here. Now, I must go, I'm meeting a new patient.'

Sharif kissed her on the head. 'See you later.'

Daf grinned. 'I've known him a long time, and I've never seen him so happy. You two are good together.'

'We are. He's one in a million.'

Daf left, promising to text the details, and Carmel made a note on her phone to speak to the sewing circle and the Men's Shed, then made her way back to the main house to check in with the pottery class.

Walking through the grounds, she observed the patients, trying to imagine what age her father might be. If Dolly was only in her early twenties when Carmel was born, then he was probably around the same age, if it was this Joe, which would make him early sixties now. The fact that her mother included the photo of herself and Joe she took to mean that this Joe was her father, but maybe not. When Sharif found her that time in Dublin, he told her what Dolly had told him, that she was young, and that Ireland wasn't a kind place for young unmarried girls who found themselves pregnant. So, she just assumed the Joe in the photo was her father, but since the trail went cold there, there wasn't any point in further speculation. Dolly had never even told Nadia who Carmel's father was and they were, by all accounts, as close as two friends can be. If it was truly just a young couple in trouble, why the big secret all these years later? In all the letters to Carmel, she never mentioned Joe or any other man, not even once, but then why include the picture? For the millionth time since she'd got here, she wished she'd had even one day with her mother, one hour even, just to talk to her, to ask her things. Maybe she would have told her only child who her father was or maybe not; maybe it was a closed chapter for her. All was well with the pottery class and Carmel decided to knock off for the evening. She was so tired and decided to get an early night. Back in their apartment, she made herself a cup of tea and tried to still her racing thoughts.

'A penny for them?' Nadia asked as she gazed out of the window. Carmel spun around, she thought she was alone.

'Oh, Nadia, I'm sorry…I wasn't expecting…' she was flustered.

'It's quite alright, my dear, Sharif let me in, I hope you don't mind? He's outside talking to somebody, I was passing and I thought I hadn't seen you for a few days and Sharif said you seemed a little distracted; he wasn't telling tales, my dear, he just was worried about you…'

'Oh, I was just thinking about my mother, my father, you know.' She smiled and turned to Nadia.

'Do you feel like a walk?' Something in her tone suggested it wasn't just a stroll in the evening air that was on offer; she gazed intently at Carmel.

'Sure, okay.'

It was a mild enough evening that she didn't need a coat and she and Nadia waved a cheery goodbye to Sharif, who was still deep in conversation with one of the physiotherapists.

'We're just going for a walk,' his mother called and led Carmel away from the clinic, towards the exit of the campus.

'You don't have to tell me anything, Carmel, there were things your mother never revealed to me and you know how close we were. I understand you may want to keep it to yourself, and every woman has her secrets, but it might help.' Nadia didn't look at her but kept clipping along at a pace that belied her short legs. Carmel didn't say anything, she never had anyone to confide in before, so it didn't come naturally to her.

Nadia chatted on, 'Your mother and I shared everything, even Sharif, really. She so longed to have you back and that void hurt her every day of her life. She and Sharif,' Nadia sighed, 'I will be honest, sometimes I was jealous of their bond. When he was a teenager, if he had a problem, it was Dolly he would go to, and it hurt me, but she always directed him to me. Always, she would say that he should talk to me. And Khalid as well, he loved her too.'

Carmel stopped and looked at the other woman in dismay.

'No, not like that, not in a devious way; he was never unfaithful to me in any way, but he loved Dolly and she loved him. She was like a sister, as I said, but there were things she kept from me. In the last year or two before she died, she would go to visit someone and stay overnight, maybe once or twice a week, and she never said who or why.'

'And you never asked?' Carmel was fascinated.

'No, she knew that I knew and she never volunteered the information, so I never asked. It might sound odd, but we respected each other's privacy. Khalid was gone, Sharif was busy with Aashna, and Dolly had this other life that I knew nothing about. It was hard.'

Carmel squeezed her arm as they walked. Nadia was so honest, so warm and open, Carmel thought it might be easy to talk to her. Sharif was wonderful and so understanding, but Carmel needed her mother. She never needed her as much when she was a child, or a new bride or anything like that, but now that she could picture her as a real person, she desperately wanted her guidance. It was all so confusing, she just didn't know how to process it.

'Anyway, enough about me, what has you awake at night?'

'Oh, Nadia, I don't know where to even start...' Carmel heard the despair in her own voice.

'The beginning is usually a good place.'

'I know I should be so happy, and I am, I really am. It's like a dream come true but I just miss her. Like, it's stupid, how can you miss someone you never met? And then I think about my father, and I need to know; I keep thinking I'm seeing him, in the street or on the bus, it's ridiculous I know, even if he's alive, he's probably in Ireland. And this Joe in the picture, like, why did Dolly give me that if he's not my father? I just want to know, when I was little I used to make up stories in my head about my mammy and daddy, but once I got old enough to realize they weren't going to come for me, I forced it out of my mind. I didn't just forget about them, it was different, I wouldn't allow those thoughts in, but now that I'm here and she's real, she lived here, I can't stop thinking, wondering. I never had anyone of my own, except Kit, and I should be down on my knees in gratitude for Sharif and you and all of this, but it's like something has woken in me and I can't let it go. I'm going out of my mind, Nadia.'

On they walked.

'So, what are you going to do now?'

'I don't know, I wouldn't even know where to start to look for this Joe, I don't even know his surname, and anyway he may not even be my father... And if he is, he doesn't deserve to have me land up and wreck his life, a reminder of a girl he knew forty years ago. He's probably living happily and the last thing he'd need is me showing up, destroying everything he's built. He probably doesn't know I exist, or if he knew about Dolly's pregnancy, might not even have told his wife or kids, if he has them.'

Carmel fought back the tears and Nadia squeezed her arm.

'I know what you are saying, and I understand, but have you thought about what might happen if he is happy to see you? He might be your father, and you might have a relationship with him, and all I've heard from you is how he doesn't deserve this or that. The damage you could cause to him. What about what you deserve, hmm? Don't you think you deserve something? None of this is your fault, you're the innocent victim in all of this and I think you deserve a chance to at least find this man. Ask him if he'll take a DNA test. If it proves he's not your father, then so be it, at least he can fill in some more gaps for you about Dolly and if he is, well then, that's a whole new chapter in your life, Carmel. Everything has been on hold for you for too long, you are entitled to a life, you are entitled to know who your parents are. How can you be a whole person, complete, if you don't know where you've come from?' They stopped walking. 'Ahh, Betty's Café, my favourite tea room. Let's rest our legs, shall we?'

Carmel allowed herself to be led into a bright, sunny tea room and gratefully sank into a booth while Nadia ordered tea and cake.

Maybe Nadia was right, maybe she had the right to know. For so much of her life, she was in the way, someone to be taken care of out of duty or necessity. Her needs were met in the most perfunctory of ways, food, clothes, a bed, but nobody ever consulted her on anything or asked her how she felt, what she thought. She was inconsequential. But Nadia and Sharif didn't see her that way, and maybe this Joe wouldn't either, if she could find him.

Nadia sat down as the waitress placed cups and tea pots and two slices of lemon drizzle cake from a tray to the table.

'What does Sharif think you should do?' Nadia asked.

'He says he'll help me in whatever way he can, but I've taken enough from him already. The last thing he needs is me bringing even more trouble to his door, or causing even more expense and hassle. I should probably just leave well enough alone.'

'Carmel, you say he is so far above you or whatever nonsense you said, but he is nothing of the kind. He loves you and I have not seen my beloved boy in love for so very, very many years. You make him laugh so loudly and so often, it does my heart good to see it. He used to be full of fun, but in recent years, he has just been so busy with Aashna and he never took time for himself, and you love him too, I can see that. Dolly sent him to you; I don't know if you believe in that or not, but I do, and I am sure that Dolly sent Sharif to you. You see it as he rescued you, and yes, he did, but Carmel, you rescued him as well.'

'That's what he says too, but Nadia, he could have anyone, I mean all the nurses, every woman we meet looks at him and then looks at me and...'

'And says what a beautiful couple they make, and see how they only have eyes for each other? That's what people see, Carmel, nothing else. But one thing I do know. You have to love yourself before you can truly give or receive love from anyone else. You were never taught to love yourself and that man you married, well honestly, I don't know what to say about him, he did nothing to help, but this is the new you, a second chance. Trust Sharif, and let him help you.'

CHAPTER 15

*J*ust as they were about to go to bed, Sharif's beeper went
off. Immediately, he rang reception.

'Marlena?'

Carmel started clearing up the cups, they'd drunk so much
chai tea.

'Okay, I'm on my way.'

He hung up.

'Some people are in reception, quite distressed, Marlena thinks
they're Irish, will you come? There's nobody else on tonight and if
people are upset…they might need a soothing voice while I examine
the patient.' He was putting on his shoes, the beautiful tan leather slip
on ones she'd admired that first day in Dublin.

'Of course.' She followed him out into the dark night, walking
through the grounds and then in through the back entrance of the
main building.

Unlike hospitals, Aashna House was kept dark at night. Sharif
wanted people to feel as at home as possible, so they walked in silence
along the corridor.

In reception, two men waited, both in their seventies she guessed.

One was sitting on a chair, clearly in great pain and the other rested his hand on his shoulder, clearly worried sick by the look on his face.

Immediately, when he saw Sharif and Carmel he came forward.

'I'm sorry for the late call, and I know you don't have an A&E here, but my friend is in terrible pain...he has cancer...'

'No problem, Carmel, can you get a wheelchair please?' Sharif bent down in front of the man in the chair.

'I'm Dr Sharif Khan, I'd like to examine you if I may, so I'm going to take you to an examination room and we can take it from there.'

The man looked up and nodded, the pain etched deep lines on his face.

'I know who you are; Dolly told me to come here when it got too bad,' he croaked.

Carmel froze. Sharif caught her eye but said nothing, his focus was on the man in front of him. Dolly? There could only be one Dolly. Did this man know her mother too?

Sharif's voice cut through her shock. 'Carmel, if you can just help me to get, Mr...?'

'Brian, Brian McDaid.' Every word was agony for the poor man, so Carmel's questions would have to wait. Together, they lifted him into the wheelchair and Sharif pushed him into an examination room. Once there, they had to help him onto the bed, and then Carmel left.

Back in reception, the other man was waiting anxiously. He was tall and distinguished looking, in a long navy wool coat and a trilby hat, which he rotated nervously in his hands.

'Would you like a cup of tea? Dr Khan could be a while, and he'll page me when he's ready. I'm Carmel, I work here.' Carmel offered her hand and the man shook it.

'Tim O'Flaherty, yes, a cup of tea would be nice, I suppose I can't just stand here...'

The poor man looked distraught with worry and Carmel wondered what the connection was between him and Brian McDaid. She led him to the small coffee dock in the main building and put on the kettle. Tim sat, but she could tell he was beside himself.

'So, is Brian family?' she asked gently.

'er, yes, sort of…we…ah, we live together.'

Carmel took that to mean they were in a relationship, something about the man's appearance, the elegant way he dressed, the clear distress he was in at Brian's condition, convinced her.

'Is that a trace of an Irish accent I can hear?' she asked again, trying to keep his mind off his partner.

'Yes,' he half smiled, 'from Co Mayo originally, but I've been here over fifty years, and you?'

'Dublin, and Offaly after that.'

She knew she shouldn't pry, but she couldn't help herself.

'So, what made you come here rather than A&E?'

'A friend of ours, well of Brian's, really, used to have a connection here, she sort of worked here and later, when she got sick, she was a patient. I've been looking after him at home for the last five years, but Dolly, that was our friend, said that when it got too much, we should come here. Tonight, well, he was in such pain, and the meds just weren't touching it; I hated taking him out of our house, but I was scared…'

'You did the right thing. We don't have an emergency department as such, but Dr Khan is an oncologist and he'll be able to make him comfortable, try not to worry.' Despite Carmel's longing to know if the Dolly he spoke about was her mother, she knew that it wasn't fair to cross examine the man at this point.

'Will he be able to come back home, do you think?' Tim asked, and immediately he apologized, 'I'm sorry, how would you know? I just… he hates hospitals and all of that.'

Carmel handed him a cup of tea and a KitKat.

'This place, Aashna, it's not really like a hospital; it doesn't smell like one or even really look like one. If Brian does end up coming here, it will be okay, I promise you.'

'It's the beginning of the end. I've known for a few months now. Dolly used to visit us a few times a week, and she'd give me a break, let me get out to the bank or shopping or whatever and she'd stay with him; they knew each other since they were children, grew up in

Dublin together. He took her death really badly, he's been going downhill since she died, to be honest.'

Carmel's heart thumped wildly in her chest, it had to be her Dolly. It just had to be.

Just as she was about to ask him something else, Sharif beeped her. 'We can go back now; he's ready to see you.'

Tim rose immediately and followed Carmel back the way they came. The little room she showed him into was cosy and dimly lit and Brian was in the bed, eyes closed and sleeping peacefully, looking considerably less distressed than twenty minutes earlier.

'I've administered some analgesic, a strong painkiller, so he'll be comfortable for the night. I suggest that you leave him here for now; we'll take good care of him and perhaps you could come back tomorrow and I'll do some tests and we can take it from there?' Sharif's voice had a soothing effect on patients and families alike.

Tim seemed relieved to see Brian so peaceful and so allowed himself to be escorted to the reception area once more.

'Thank you, Dr Khan, yes, I'll go home now, and I'll see you tomorrow, thank you for taking care of him, he was in terrible pain...'

'He'll be fine now, from a preliminary exam and from what Brian was able to tell me, I can see he is in the later stages, so I must prepare you, I think all we can do at this stage is palliative, but as I said, we'll talk about it properly tomorrow. If you can bring a list of medications he's currently taking and the details of your GP, I'll liaise with them and we'll make sure he is given the best possible care.'

Once Tim had gone and Sharif had briefed the night staff on the patient's condition, with instructions to call him if anything changed, he and Carmel walked back to their apartment.

'I think he knew my mother.' Carmel blurted once they were outside, 'Tim, Brian's partner, told me that Brian and Dolly grew up together in Dublin and they were friends and that she died here recently.'

'I know. He did know her. She used to visit them regularly, Brian managed to tell me that, despite his pain. We always wondered where she went, and now that I know, it seems even stranger. Why didn't she tell us about them? The fact that they are gay wouldn't have bothered me or my parents, so it can't be that.' Sharif was as puzzled as she was. He stopped and turned to her, 'Carmel, I know you want to know everything, but he is a very sick man, so if he wants to talk, it has to be in his own time okay?'

She nodded. Sharif knew how much finding out about her parents meant to her, but he was this man's doctor first and foremost.

'Okay, I know. I won't go in there first thing in the morning with a list of questions, I promise.'

He smiled and kissed the top of her head.

She slept fitfully in the days after Brian's admission, so many questions going round her head. A week after he arrived, she decided to ask Sharif if she could see him. He was in the high dependency wing and was still very sick, but she was going out of her mind. What if he died? Maybe anything he could tell her about her mother, maybe even her father would die with him. She felt awful for being so selfish, but she was so scared her one chance was slipping away.

She went about her business as normal, but she longed to speak to him. Tim came and went, but he was so upset and worried it wasn't right to bother him with her questions and anyway she wanted to speak to Brian directly.

Sharif knew how she felt, but Brian was just too weak.

'I don't know, Carmel, look, I'll ask him if he'll see you. To be honest, he's rarely awake, the medication needed to control the pain means he is sedated most of the time, but mid-morning is the time he is at his most alert. I know how much this means to you. And in any other circumstances, I'd absolutely refuse to have anyone visit him that wasn't immediate family, but I'll see what I can do. I'm not promising anything, though, alright? It has to be up to him.'

'I understand. And thanks, Sharif.'

Brian was too ill and she tried to put it out of her mind. Sharif promised that if he was in imminent danger of death, he would allow her to see him, but he was hopeful that he could give him a few more weeks at least if he responded to the treatment. She had to be happy with that, and be patient.

She and Sharif had bought two chairs and a table for their little courtyard and she'd planted some flowers in pots, and they loved to have coffee there on the mornings when they were off work, to read the papers or just chat quietly. Even though Sharif had his own place, he had moved in with her after they'd spent every night together for ten days after her arrival, and she was thrilled when he suggested it.

The night he arrived with a box of things, she tried not to flinch when he removed a gilt framed photo of a beautiful young Asian woman and placed it on the table along with some books and clothes.

He caught her looking at it.

'That's Jamilla. I told you about her.'

She could hear the sadness in his voice and once more she was transported back to the kitchen in Birr, her dusting carefully around the picture of Bill and Gretta. She knew it wasn't the same, but she couldn't help the feeling of resentment. Was she to start again, with another dead woman gazing at her every day?

'I can put it away if it makes you feel uncomfortable.'

Instantly, Carmel felt mean and cruel. Why should he be forced to forget his past?

'Of course not, don't be silly,' she picked up the photo and looked deeply into Jamilla's brown eyes. 'She was beautiful.'

'She was. And funny and kind, just like you, actually. You would have liked her. When she died, I never thought I'd recover. The pain, every day, and the fact that I was a doctor but I couldn't save her, it ate away at me. Maybe that's why I threw myself so completely into this place. That's what my mother thinks, I know, that I was using work to numb the loss, maybe she was right. I would work so hard that when I fell into bed at night, I had no energy for thinking, for feeling, and so that was my life for so long. But, time eases everything, even if you don't want it to and one day it hurt a little less and so on until I was in a position to live again. And then I met you.'

'Let's put her here, on the shelf, that way you can see her every day.' She tried to inject enthusiasm into her voice.

'I have a better idea,' he said, gently taking the photo from her. 'How about we put it on the shelf in the spare bedroom? I don't need to see her every day, but sometimes, it's nice to see her smile. I'd hate to put it in a drawer or something, but we cannot live in the past, we must live in the here and now.'

'Are you sure?' it was like he could read her mind.

'Totally sure. I loved Jamilla once, so very much. But she's gone and we are here, she wouldn't want me to be dwelling on her. A little part of me will always be hers, but I told you that before, but the most of me, the part that's alive and loving life is all yours. Jamilla is no threat to you, Carmel, I promise you.'

Sharif had smiled when he saw her one morning in her dressing gown when he came home for a cup of tea after his early morning rounds. She was curled up with a cup of tea and Oprah's book *What I Know for Sure.*

'You look so happy here,' he kissed the top of her head and joined her, the morning sun trapped in the little space.

'I'm sorry, I should get dressed,' she was embarrassed and began to gather her things to go inside.

'Why? I thought you were not in until eleven today? It's only nine thirty.'

She relaxed, he was right. This was her apartment and there were no bells or nuns or anyone else telling her what to do or when to do it, but old habits die hard.

'When I was a kid, all the time I was in Trinity House actually, you

115

got up on the first bell at seven a.m., got washed and dressed before the second bell at seven twenty, had your bed made and were sitting at the table for breakfast by the third bell at twenty to eight. When I married Bill, it was the same, more or less. He had his breakfast after milking but he had tea and a bowl of porridge at 5.30 so I'm used to being up and ready. This lounging around business is new to me.' She grinned to dispel the sadness that had crept across his handsome face. She reminded herself not to tell him any more stories of her childhood; it only made him sad.

'Even on the weekends? Were you not allowed to lie in, or play?'

Carmel put her hand on his. 'It wasn't Oliver, you know, we didn't have to work on a big wheel or up chimneys, it was fine. We did play sometimes, after dinner when the clear up was done, the nuns would let us play cards or there were some board games and the boys went outside to kick a football. They taught me to sew and to knit. It honestly wasn't that bad.'

'Please tell me Bill didn't expect you to get up and feed him at 5.30 every day?' Sharif rarely said anything about Bill, and never criticized him, so Carmel was a little taken aback.

'Well, he kind of told me the schedule the first day, and I just did it and…well, kept doing it, I suppose. He didn't demand it or anything; it was just how things were done. Anyway, when he went milking, then I'd do the housework, and sometimes listen to a podcast or a meditation. I could only do that when I was sure he wouldn't be back, though; he'd have had a stroke if he found me meditating, probably take me down to Fr Lenihan to have me exorcised or something.' She giggled but Sharif didn't smile.

He locked eyes with her as if looking behind them into her mind, her soul. Once, she told him he reminded her of Deepak Chopra, an Indian-born alternative medicine practitioner. Not in the way he looked as such, apart from them coming from similar countries, but there was something deeply spiritual about Sharif. He could be still for long periods and was very connected to himself. He had studied philosophy for many years and continued to do so and was a deep thinker, while also being full of fun and mischief. It was one of the many reasons she loved him so much.

'Will you divorce him?' '

The question caught her off guard.

'Em...I don't know. We were married in the Catholic Church, but divorce is legal now...' She had never really considered it. If she thought about it at all, then maybe she thought he would get his marriage to her annulled.

'Carmel, I'm not trying to pressure you, if you're not ready then that's fine, but you could easily see a solicitor here and start divorce proceedings. You don't need a reason, though the fact that the marriage was never consummated would probably be grounds for a legal annulment.'

'But what would he say? He'd be horrified, to get a letter from England, from a solicitor. I mean I did the wrong thing here; I left him without so much as a note, I don't think I should be the one to...'

'You did not do anything wrong!' Sharif was unusually impatient. 'Listen to yourself, Carmel, you blame yourself for everything. You got dealt a terrible hand in life, it was wrong and you deserved better. You weren't adopted, and that was wrong. Bill married you when he wasn't emotionally available. That was wrong. He treated you like a servant, and that was wrong. He didn't nurture a relationship between his daughters and you, and that was wrong; he allowed his witchy sister to bully you and undermine you, and that was wrong. You are not the perpetrator in any of this, you're the victim and you have got a chance now to leave all those wrongs in the past. You are entitled to free yourself, legally and mentally from him, and you should do it. Who cares what he thinks, or what people in the village think? He is the one with something to hide, he's the one that should be hanging his head in shame.' Sharif, normally so soothing, logical, and calm was unusually worked up. She stood up and went to sit on his lap and he put his arms around her.

Smoothing his silver hair from his temples, she spoke directly to him, 'I'm convinced my mother sent you to me, though I wish she'd sent you a few years earlier; it would have been even better, but maybe I wasn't in the place where I could accept you into my life then, who knows? It must seem ridiculous, a grown woman so unsure of herself and I understand the logic of everything you say, I really do. If someone else told me the story of my life, I'd be like, 'Oh, for goodness sake, she needs a kick in the arse, as we say in Ireland, but it's not that simple. For so long, all my life really, I wasn't important to anyone. That sounds a bit whiney maybe, but it's true. I'm not feeling sorry for myself, I just wasn't loved. And because nobody loved me, or at least nobody I was aware of, I know now that my mother never stopped loving me and that makes such a difference, but I'm not used to it. I didn't expect anything from Bill. I mean, sure, at the start, I foolishly thought we could live happily ever after but the reality was that was never going to happen. He shouldn't have married me, but he saved me. I know it must sound awful to you, the life I had with him, and it was awful in so many ways, it was. But then, I'd see documentaries about homeless people, or drug addicts and so often they grew up in state care and when they reached adulthood they were just thrown out into the world with no skills and I'd think well, at least Bill saved me from that. I had a roof over my head and enough to eat and people thought of me as a normal person, with a home and a family, and when you don't have that, ever, then it's something precious.

'You can't really understand it; you had parents who adored you and a huge extended family, so you knew where you belonged from the start. It's different when you spend your life trying to find a place to be, when everyone else has their spot and you don't. I remember at school one time we were learning about the cuckoo, and how he never had a nest of his own but he used to steal other bird's nests. The teacher was making out like he was a bad bird, compared to all the others who worked so hard on their nests and then he came along and just jumped into it, but I remember thinking, what else was he to do? If you don't have a nest of your own, then you have to try to muscle in on someone else's. The cuckoo never learned nest building because his parents never built nests either, so it wasn't really his fault. All my life, I've been a cuckoo, and that's why I try not to make too many waves or upset people, it's because I'm always the encroacher. So, I know I'm hard to understand, and I will divorce Bill, I'd love to have him out of my life. Don't think for a second that I feel in any way connected to him because I'm not, but when you say you love me, or even when I look around our lovely home, sometimes I don't believe it. I'm afraid that you are going to stop loving me when the novelty wears off or something…though I'm hardly a novelty, but you know what I mean. I'm sorry, it must be such a head wreck as Zane calls it, to be dealing with me.'

Sharif sighed and patted her shoulder, indicating he wanted her to get up. Again, the panic, had she said something wrong? Should she have kept her mouth shut? Maybe he was getting sick of her stupid insecurities. He went into their bedroom and emerged moments later. She was rooted to the spot as he came out through the French doors back into the little courtyard.

Carmel stood in amazement in her dressing gown and slippers as the man she loved got down on one knee in front of her.

'Carmel, I don't want you to be a cuckoo anymore, I want us to have a nest together. I hate the idea that you're afraid that I'll change my mind or go off you or something. I love you so much and I want to be your home and for you to be mine. I know you're not free yet, but when you are, will you marry me?'

He held up a little box containing an exquisite ring, a gold spiral encrusted with diamonds and rubies. It was breathtaking.

'Sharif, I…I don't know what to say…' she could hardly get the words out. She looked down at this gorgeous man, and her heart felt too big for her chest. 'I would absolutely love to marry you.'

CHAPTER 16

*T*wo weeks after Brian McDaid was admitted, Sharif beeped her. He was well enough for a short visit. She rushed across the campus from the Kaivalya, where she was welcoming the local Toastmasters group for their monthly debate, to the high dependency wing.

Sharif met her in the corridor.

'Don't tire him out now, keep it short, maybe you can see him again tomorrow or the next day, talking will exhaust him.' He bent his head and kissed her quickly, 'Good luck.'

Carmel nodded, she was too nervous to speak. Gathering all her resolve, she knocked gently on his door.

'Come in.' The voice was strong, and the accent, unmistakably Dublin.

She was relieved to see how well he looked, sitting up in a chair, in his own clothes. He was bald from the chemotherapy. He had no eyebrows or eyelashes either, but his complexion had much more colour than it had the night he was admitted. His shirt was too big, he was fading away in front of her eyes.

'Hello, Mr McDaid, and thank you so much for seeing me; I know it's tiring to have visitors so I won't keep you long, and if you get too tired, please just tell me to go.' Carmel tried to keep the nervousness from her voice.

'Not at all, I've been waiting to meet you; when Dr Khan told me who you were, well, I couldn't believe my ears.' He smiled and Carmel warmed to him instantly.

'Sit down there on the bed so I can see you. You're the head cut off your mother, that's the truth. I'll tell you what I know, Carmel, but I must warn you, it's not a happy story.'

He waited for her to respond.

'Please, whatever it is, I want to know.'

'Okay, well, your Ma and me were great mates, and we got along so well; I knew her since we were kids, even though there was a long gap in the middle when we didn't see each other for years, anyway, I'll get to that. Are you sure you want to hear this? Once you hear it, you can't ever not know it, y'know?' His Dublin accent was strong and reminded her of the delivery men who used to come to Trinity House.

She nodded, 'Please, go on.'

Brian inhaled almost to gather his strength. Sharif was managing his pain but you could see he was bone weary of it all. He began, staring straight ahead of him as he spoke. 'Dolly, your ma, was going out with my brother Joe since she was sixteen, childhood sweethearts, as they used to say long ago. We all grew up together, on the same road in Kilmainham, Dolly, me, Joe, Kevin and Colm, my sisters Maggie and Orla, and a few other families. When Dolly's mother died, she was only a kid, and Tom, her father, went to pieces, it was to our house she came. My Ma would feed her, wash her clothes, and all of that. My father never liked her, even as a child, said she was flighty, but we took no notice of him. He could only talk with his fists or his belt, and we all, including my mother, got the wrong end of it often. He was a bad man, evil. He wasn't a drinker; if he was, you could blame that, but he just was a cruel man. He gave us all a hard time but poor old Joe got the worst of it. I didn't know why at the time, but later Joe told me he walked in on him attacking our mother. Joe was only twelve, but he was a big strong lad and he hit him a clatter so hard he put the auld fella in hospital for a month. He broke his jaw, and me Da hit his head off the range as he fell. Joe could have killed him, so ferocious the blow was. Guards, social workers the whole lot got involved then and it all came out. You know what Ireland's like, and on a street like ours, where everyone was stuck in everyone else's business anyway, well the place was buzzing. To be honest, I think some of the neighbours suspected; we, and Ma, would regularly appear with bruises and sometimes broken bones, but nobody said anything. It was weird, they'd talk about the neighbours all day long, but then when he was clearly battering all of us, people did nothing. Domestic violence was seen as something to be kept within the four walls, I don't know, it's a kind of screwed up way of thinking over there sometimes. But my father never turned a hair. He'd walk into Mass, Ma with him, and her with a black eye or her arm in a sling, but he'd look like butter wouldn't melt. He was the pillar of the community, you see, collecting the money at Mass, singing in the choir and all that. After that though, people knew him for what he really was, a bully and a coward. People didn't look up to him anymore. He never forgave Joe for that.

Anyway. Dolly and Joe had a special bond or something; when she smiled, his face lit up like Clerys window at Christmas. Since they were kids, you'd never see one without the other. It was almost as if they had a secret language or something, it's hard to explain, but for Joe, there was never another and I think the same was true for Dolly. Anyway, once she got to sixteen, she was allowed to go out with Joe. Tom wasn't happy about it; he was very strict even by the standards of those times, but Dolly convinced him, and anyway, he liked Joe. Dolly's Da had no time for my father either and probably was secretly proud of how Joe handled him.'

Brian stopped and took a sip of water, composing himself once more.

'Joe was apprenticed to a butcher on Capel Street and Dolly was working in Arnott's Drapery department; that's where she learned to sew.

They were stone mad about each other, he walked her to work and collected her every day. They'd walk all over Dublin in the evenings, just talking. Other girls liked Joe too, he was a good-looking lad, but he was oblivious. They were going out for years and they never bored of each other, he would rather be with her than anyone. They had great plans to travel the world once they'd saved up enough money. I remember there was a ferocious fuss made one night when Tom came home early from whatever thing he was at and found Joe and Dolly in bed. He nearly went mental and banned Joe from the house. That sort of thing was unthinkable in those days, even though, by now, they were in their twenties.

Joe begged and pleaded with Tom, trying to convince him that he wasn't just using his daughter, but that he loved her. Dolly loved her Da and was sorry she disappointed him. But eventually, Tom thawed and, after a few weeks, they were back together again, Tom probably knew that Dolly'd defy him if she had to anyway. Nothing would keep them apart.

We were sure that the ring would be produced for Christmas that year. In fact, I knew Joe had planned to propose because the girl our brother Colm was doing a line with was roped in to check the sizes of the rings in McDowell's on O'Connell Street.

Christmas Eve came, and both Dolly and Joe were working late. Ma was in the kitchen getting everything ready for Christmas dinner and the girls were up to ninety about Santa coming and all of that. Us older ones chipped in to get their stuff because my father'd have nothing to do with it. Joe was going to bring Dolly home with him after work and was going to propose on the way.

Instead of the big announcement though, Joe appeared at the back door, ashen faced. He said that Dolly was gone; he waited for her at work and they said she'd not turned up. He went to her house and her father was sitting at the table with a note from her saying she was gone. No note for Joe, no explanation, just a two-line thing to her father saying she was sorry but that she was leaving.

Joe nearly went out of his mind, he just couldn't believe it, that she'd just up and leave him without a word. We shared a room and at night I used to hear him crying over her, she broke his heart so she did. He couldn't understand it, none of us could. Poor old Tom Mullane lost the will to go on after that. Losing his wife, and then Dolly, was too much for him to bear. He used to walk all over Dublin looking for her, he wrote to the police in England, he even contacted some agency in America to see if she could be found, but it was as if she'd vanished into thin air.

She never contacted Joe or her father ever again, never even a letter, nothing. Tom died about four years after she left, a heart attack. Then one day, about six years ago, I saw her. I couldn't believe my eyes, but it was definitely Dolly; it had been decades but I knew it was her, in a draper's shop.

I went in and confronted her, she nearly collapsed. I was so angry at what she'd done to poor Joe, I let her have it; I told her about all the misery she caused him. And her poor father, and what she put him through. She closed the shop and told me to sit down, that was when she told me about you.'

He leaned back against the pillow, the effort of so much talking was weakening him, Carmel could see.

'We can leave it if you want to...' she offered, though she desperately wanted him to continue. She remembered her promise to Sharif. He sipped some more water and took a deep breath.

'No, I'm grand, and I haven't much time left. I want to tell you this if you want to hear it.'

'I really do.'

'Okay, so, even then I was mad, I shouted at her, that she could have told Joe and they'd have brought the wedding forward, they wouldn't have been the first couple to do that, but then she broke down. Just started crying and, well, I was never one for crying females, so I just sat there. Eventually, she told me that the reason she left without a word was that the child, you, might not have been Joe's.

They were always together, and she never had eyes for anyone else, so I was totally confused until she told me who your father was. Are you sure you want me to go on with this? There are some things people are better off not knowing.'

Carmel just nodded, she couldn't speak with the lump in her throat. She blinked back the tears; she didn't want to do anything that would make him stop.

He took a moment to compose his thoughts, whatever he was going to tell her wasn't coming easily to him.

'Apparently, my father got wind that Joe was going to propose to Dolly, and decided he'd hurt Joe in the most terrible way. Get his revenge on him for what my father saw as Joe's ruining of his life. He never took responsibility for anything he did, not to his dying day. As he saw it, Joe had destroyed his reputation and so he would hurt him by taking the thing he loved the most. He waited for Dolly on her way home from work, a few weeks before Christmas. Joe said he was working late that night, so Dolly was to go home without him. It was dark, and my father waited and dragged her into the trees of St Canice's Park. Well, you can guess what came next.'

Carmel felt sick. A wave of cold washed over her, sure she was going to vomit. She didn't, and the nausea subsided, but the blood was thundering in her ears. The idea of continuing the conversation terrified and revolted her, but she knew she had to hear it all. Taking a few gulps of air to steady herself, she managed to croak, 'Go on.'

'I'm not telling you this to be cruel, but you wanted to know… Dolly told me she wasn't sure which one of them was your father but she couldn't take a chance. In a panic, she told my father she was pregnant. To the day she died, she regretted that. If only she'd told Joe or even her own father, but telling Da was the worst mistake she could have made. His plan had been that Dolly would never tell Joe that she'd been raped, she'd be scared what Joe would do. He reminded Dolly that since Joe had attacked his father before, and the guards were involved, if he assaulted him again, he could face charges. My father was happy to know that he'd taken the one person Joe loved more than anyone, and he didn't care if Joe knew; he knew, and that was what mattered to him. He was a twisted man.

'A pregnancy was a whole other matter, though. He saw how panicked Dolly was; Ireland was a harsh place for girls who got themselves 'in trouble' as they said, even if through no fault of her own. My father threatened her that if she said anything to Joe, then Joe would kill him and go to prison for the murder. He then went on to terrify her about what a public trial like that would do to Dolly's father, Tom. She told me that day that she just couldn't do it, be responsible for Joe going to jail, for destroying her father. My father was apparently pleased she was pregnant, delighted he'd caused maximum pain to Joe, and it was he who delivered Dolly to the nuns. She didn't see Joe's father again until two days before he died, five years ago. He lived to be ninety-seven. She read a piece about him written in the local paper on line. Apparently, for years, she used to subscribe to the actual paper and had it delivered to her in England, and then it went on line, so she'd read it every week. It's mostly pictures of kids and football teams, but she said it felt like a small connection with her home. Anyway, because my father used to be still very involved with the church, someone wrote a tribute piece about him, pillar of the community and all the usual rubbish. Anyway, Dolly read it, and whoever wrote it said that the parish sends their best wishes to him in the Mater Hospital and all of that, so she knew where he was.

'So, Dolly went to see him, in secret, of course, convinced as she was at that stage that he had something to do with her inability to find you. She described going over to Dublin and waiting until late at night when she was sure none of the other family would be there, and she went into the room to him. She saw him lying there, ravaged by time and sickness and demanded to know what had happened to you. He laughed at her misery, can you imagine that? She told him about all the years spent looking for you and he cackled, and then he told her the truth. That after he dropped her at the unmarried mother's home, he went in to have tea with the reverend mother. Of course, he said nothing to the nun about raping his son's girlfriend, but just that he'd been indiscreet, that she'd flirted with him and he foolishly succumbed to her wanton ways. The nun readily believed him and almost had sympathy for him when he explained that he was a married man, who didn't want his wife and children upset by this little mistake. He asked them to take care of things short term, and that he'd be grateful. He paid them, you see. Nuns would turn a blind eye to almost anything for money in those days. He told the nun that he might, in time, convince his wife to take pity on the child and allow it to live with them, so in the meantime, no permission for adoption was to be given under any circumstances.' Brian stopped and reached out for Carmel's hand. 'Is this too hard? I can stop…'

'No, please go on.' The words barely audible. 'My birth certificate. I asked for one when I was applying for my passport and the one they gave me had unknown written under the word Father. My birth mother's name was written as D Murphy. How could they have done that?'

'I've no idea, but as we now know, babies born in those places were adopted all over the world without proper paperwork, so they were a bit of a law unto themselves, I think.'

Carmel tried to absorb all this information. Brian was exhausted; she should let him rest.

She was about to say as much when he went on, 'Well, that's all there is to know really. Except that I tried to convince her to make contact with Joe, that he'd love to hear from her, even after all these years, but no way, that's why I was angry with her. I couldn't under-stand why she wouldn't want to see him, to explain, but she was adamant that he was better off not knowing. She said she never wanted to talk about my father ever again, and so many years had passed that it wouldn't do anyone any good. Nothing I could say would change her mind; Joe was married and happy and had a couple of kids and she said she didn't want to drop a bomb like that into his happy life. I said I thought he'd see it differently, but she made me swear to never tell him.'

'And Joe, he's still alive?' Carmel wiped her eye with the back of her hand.

'Oh, yes, in Dublin. His wife died of pancreatic cancer about four years ago, June, she was a lovely lady, but he has a son and a daughter, Jennifer and Luke. They'd be in their thirties now I'd say. I promised I'd never tell Joe, but I never said anything about you because she believed you were lost to her forever. When they told her you'd been adopted, she knew that it was the end of the line; you'd have to try to find her, not the other way round.'

He rested his head back again and she could see the toll talking so long was taking.

'Thanks, Brian, for telling me. I...I don't really know what I'm going to do, if anything, but things are making a bit more sense now. Thank you.' She squeezed his hand and he nodded in return.

CHAPTER 17

Carmel woke the next morning late, her throat sore and her eyes swollen from the emotion of it all. Sharif was at the clinic, but he'd left a bunch of freesias, her favourite flowers, by the bed. Beside them was a note saying, 'I'm sorry I wasn't here to talk to you about B - text me when you wake, I love you. S. xxx' He'd been run off his feet the previous days, and she wanted time to tell him her story, not a quick ten minutes between patients.

She lay there, thinking once again how lucky she was to have him. Just as she was psyching herself up to get in the shower, her phone buzzed. It was Marlena on reception. 'Mr McDaid wants to see you, Carmel, he's very insistent, says he must see you asap.'

Immediately, she jumped from the bed. 'I'm on the way,' she texted and dressed quickly. She looked like a fright, she knew, but she didn't care. Running through the grounds, she wondered what more Brian could have to tell her. She tapped in using her card to the high dependency unit and knocked gently on Brian's door.

'Come in.' His voice sounded even weaker than yesterday. She felt a pang of guilt. She shouldn't have allowed him to exert himself so much.

'Hi, Brian…' she spoke quietly and sat beside the bed.

'How are you? I've been thinking about you and wondering how you were. I've been thinking I shouldn't have said anything...I was wrong to...' a fit of coughing overtook him and Carmel could see a physical deterioration in him even since yesterday.

'I'm glad you did. Thank you, it wasn't easy, but at least now I know.'

'But you don't know, you see, and neither did your mother, the pain it all caused Joe. I love all my brothers and sisters, but Joe and I were very close, we still are, and there are things I've kept from him, not just this... It wasn't that I couldn't tell him...but...' the effort was racking his body, but he was determined to go on. 'Thought I could convince her to talk to Joe at least, but when she said no...it just...' he was out of breath.

'I know. It's been going round and round in my head all night. That Joe might be my father? There's a chance that he is and he's still alive... I feel like I want to tell him, have a test, maybe he is my father, but he doesn't even know I exist.'

Brian gestured that she open the drawer beside his bed, afraid to talk in case it precipitated another bout of coughing. She opened it and, lying there among a few other personal effects, was a small notebook. He nodded and she handed it to him. She watched as his hands, bruised from all the needles, bony fingers covered in almost translucent skin, flicked through the pages until he came to an address. He handed it to her.

JOE MCDAID.
14 FIRGROVE LAWN, KILTIPPER ROAD, DUBLIN 24, AND A PHONE
NUMBER.

She looked at him. 'But I can't just show up, or ring him or whatever. He mightn't want to hear from me at all...he doesn't even know I exist, let alone that he might have some connection to me.'

'Your choice.' His breathing was laboured. 'That's where to find him if you want to. He'll be here anyway soon enough when I die, so you can see him then.' He lay back on the pillows, his complexion ashen and waxy; he looked so much worse than yesterday.

He was going downhill fast, but Sharif said that often happened. As a specialist in palliative care, he saw enough to be sure that once someone decided they had had enough of living, they could shut themselves down. Medicine from that point on could only keep someone alive artificially, once the spirit rests, then so too does the body. She had learned so much about life and death from Sharif, and he had very definite ideas about dignity and honesty around death and dying. Brian knew exactly the situation regarding his cancer and how aggressive it was. Sharif thought it condescending to lie or soften the truth of a person's illness to them. It was their life, their body, not their child's or spouse's or whoever, and they had the right to decide for themselves. It often led to disagreements between him and families, but he was a committed advocate for his patient, nobody else. He also believed that people often needed to face their own death before they felt the need to resolve issues, and sometimes people never did and died at loggerheads with family, or having not put something right. But those that managed to right the wrongs, or say what they needed to say, seemed to then give themselves the leave to fade away. Sharif said it was almost tangible, that moment when the body says to the spirit, 'You're free to go.'

Brian's eyes were closed and Carmel wondered if she should stay or go. This man was either her uncle or her brother. The reality of it hit her. She sat beside him and held his hand, gently giving him a squeeze, just so he'd know she was there. She might have imagined it, but she thought he squeezed hers back. Eventually, his laboured breathing became rhythmic and slow and she was sure he was sleeping, so she stood. The address book still lay on the bed. Before she had time to change her mind, she pulled out her phone and took a picture of the page, then she slipped out.

She worked all day and when she met Sharif in the corridor, he was rushing. He stopped and apologized again.

'It's okay, honestly. You're flat out, I know you are. I'll see you when you finish at home, okay?' she squeezed his hand.

'I've a locum in for me tonight, so I'll be back by seven, I promise. Are you okay?'

She smiled at him, 'I'm fine. See you later.'

The day passed quickly and she had little time to dwell on what Brian had said, until that evening as she watched the sun go down on the evening sky. She sipped a cup of tea in their courtyard and thought about her mother. The lavender and lilacs scented the summer's evening. The day had been sunny, but the evening had a chilly breeze.

Sharif's key in the lock at five past seven broke through her thoughts.

'You feel cold.' He took off his suit jacket and wrapped it around her, and led her back inside. He sat beside her on the couch, drawing a blanket over both of them, her head on his shoulder.

She was grateful for the warmth, and she cuddled up to him, tucking her legs underneath her.

She told him the story Brian had shared with her and he didn't interrupt, but let her speak.

Once she'd finished, he remained quiet, absorbing what he'd heard. Panic set into Carmel. Maybe she was wrong, and he was horrified by the circumstances of her conception on top of everything else and this was the last straw. Or maybe he was angry that she exerted Brian so much by asking him to tell her the story.

'Sharif, I'm sorry...' she had no idea how to reverse the last fifteen minutes and she could feel her entire life crumbling away. He turned to her, his dark eyes shining with unshed tears.

'Why are you sorry? What for? You have done nothing...Oh, Carmel, my love, I wish I could take some of this burden for you, I really do.' She'd never seen him so visibly upset. 'And poor Dolly, carrying that pain all these years when that...man got away with it, and he wasn't content with destroying her youth, her innocence, but he ensured his poison remained potent by making sure you never got a happy home. I'm frustrated to hear he's dead; I would have liked to have confronted him. I'm not a violent man, Carmel, but I swear, I would like to hurt him. I would like for him to feel just a fraction of the pain he caused Dolly, and then you, my poor darling girl.' He held her tightly, soothingly kissing her hair and rubbing her back. Relief flooded her senses, he was still there, he didn't reject her.

Well into the night, they talked, weighing up the various options. He thought maybe she should write a letter to Joe, outlining the fact that he might be her father, she need say nothing about the rape, and see if he would agree to a DNA test. She could then take it from there. If Joe was her father, then she could tell him the whole truth, but if he wasn't, then there was no point in destroying him with the knowledge of what his father did.

'Apart from Brian, she never told a soul. But now, it's out. She's dead and so is Brian's father, so that changes it. She didn't want to tell Joe and maybe I should respect her wishes, but then there's a chance that he's my father. Or even my half-brother. I don't know, Sharif, it's all so confusing.'

'Let it sit for a while, you'll know what to do, you just need to be patient with yourself. Take your time.'

CHAPTER 18

$\mathscr{L}$ife went back to normal, and even though Joe was never far from her mind, she threw herself into her job. Sharif was right, the best thing to do was just to allow herself time to get used to the idea that her father might still be out there. Every time she sat down to write, she gave up. Her life was better than it ever was, she should leave well enough alone. Brian was fading all the time, but she popped in to see him most days. They didn't talk about Joe or Dolly, he was too weak for anything more than hello really, but she liked just to sit with him. Tim visited every single day and she was careful to leave them alone together when he did. Every moment was precious now.

Twenty days after Brian was admitted to Aashna House, Sharif got paged just as they were going to bed. Brian was weakening, the night team was instructed that if he deteriorated, Dr Khan was to be called and Carmel went with him.

Knocking gently and then entering, they saw him lying propped up on pillows, no drips or lines in or out. He seemed peaceful. A nurse was checking his chart.

'Thanks, I'll take over now,' Sharif whispered.

'His systolic b/p is at 66 and his diastolic b/p 44. Recurring apnea and cyanosis of lower extremities.' She handed Sharif the chart and he looked at it.

'No liquids since early morning?'

'Nothing.'

'Okay, thanks.' The nurse left and Carmel sat beside Brian and held his hand.

'Should we call Tim?'

'No. Brian told me three days ago he didn't want him to see it; they've said their goodbyes...'

'Hi, Brian,' Carmel leaned in to whisper in his ear. 'Carmel and Sharif are here now, and we're going to stay with you, okay? You just relax and we'll take care of you. You're not on your own.'

There was no way of knowing for sure, but there was a chance that he could hear them, so they sat either side of the bed and spoke gently and soothingly to him, now and again. There was no need to administer any drugs. That time had passed. He'd had a morphine pump to manage the pain when he was drifting in and out of consciousness, but Sharif said he was one of the lucky ones, he seemed peaceful.

His eyes fluttered open for a moment.

'Dolly...' he whispered, his voice barely audible.

Suddenly, his face seemed to relax, he opened his eyes properly this time and they seemed to be fixed on the top corner of the room. His eyes widened and brightened and his face melted into a radiant smile as if he'd spotted someone he longed to see. The whole thing lasted mere seconds, and then he sighed deeply and was gone. Sharif stood and, after a few moments, checked Brian's pulse and then shut his eyes.

Carmel went to the window and opened it and covered the mirror with a towel.

'Why do you do that?' Sharif asked quietly. 'I've seen it in the Jewish culture but not in Christian families.'

'I don't know, it's just what we do in Ireland. To let the spirit free I suppose, and we cover the mirrors so the soul of the departed doesn't get trapped inside. Superstition, I know, but he was Irish and so am I, so...' Carmel's voice cracked with emotion. Though she only knew

Brian a very short time, he had come to mean a lot to her. Sharif gave her a hug and wiped her tears with his thumbs. 'I'm glad you met him, and he was able to tell you his story.'

'Me too.' She nodded and bent down to kiss Brian's forehead.

Sharif took Brian's medical notes and recorded the time of death, and went out to the office to make arrangements with the morgue.

Carmel looked down at the old man's face, all cares and pain gone. He looked peaceful.

'Thank you, Brian, Godspeed, and say hello to Dolly for me,' she whispered, patting the blankets around him.

The arrangements clicked into motion effortlessly, as they did on an almost daily basis in Aashna House. Each tradition was represented and respected, and every effort was made to give everyone a fitting send-off. That was a duty often falling to Nadia, to talk with the patient and determine what arrangements they would like. She was wonderful at it and it ensured there was rarely a conflict among family members as to how someone's passing should be marked.

'Will I call Tim?' she asked as she entered the little office where Sharif was working.

'Sure, he's expecting it, but it's still a shock.'

Carmel scrolled through her phone for the number. Then she stopped.

'You know, Sharif, I think I might just take a taxi over there, tell him in person. I know we don't normally do that, but I'd like to, is that okay?'

He looked up. 'I'm sure he'd appreciate that; you can bring him back here with you and we can make whatever arrangements he wants. Brian asked me to inform his family back in Ireland, but it's very early. Given the circumstances, I don't know how much they know about his and Tim's relationship. I think we can give Tim some time before involving the extended family. It's four thirty a.m. now, so I'll call them around eight. A few hours either way won't make any difference.'

Carmel rang Tim's mobile once the taxi dropped her outside the door.

'Hello?' Tim was instantly alert.

'Tim, it's Carmel, I'm outside your house.'

'Oh…Oh, right…I see…' He seemed flustered. 'I'll be right down.'

She waited and, after a few moments, she saw his shadow approach the door. He opened it and she stepped inside. He was dressed in pajamas and a brown checked robe and slippers. No words were necessary.

He just looked at her and she nodded slightly. Tim's hand went to his face as he tried to process the news that the man he had loved for nearly fifty years was gone. Carmel put her arms around him and he allowed her to comfort him. Silent tears flowed and they just stood there in the hall.

'He was so peaceful, no pain at all. And at the end, he smiled so happily, Tim, he called Dolly, I think he saw her…'

He released himself gently from her embrace. 'I'm glad. They were as thick as thieves that pair, always laughing or conspiring about something. He told me that he filled you in on the story, it was their only point of argument; he wanted to tell his brother so badly.'

'He did.' They walked through to the lovely bright kitchen and Tim asked, 'Will we have a cup of tea?'

'We're Irish, it's what we do, isn't it?' she smiled.

Tim busied himself with the kettle and getting cups while she chatted. She had seen enough in the time she'd been at Aashna to know grief had many forms. No two people reacted to the death of a loved one in the same way. Sharif always allowed people the time and space to respond in their own way, so she tried to do the same.

Tim sighed. 'I can't believe he's gone, I know that sounds stupid, he was in a hospice, and sick for so long but I just…' His shoulders shook and Carmel went to him. She took the tea pot from him and put her arms around him. Her kindness seemed to open the floodgates. She just stood there, letting him cry.

Brian was laid out in the little chapel of rest in Aashna. Tim seemed reluctant to be there and, while she thought it a bit odd, she understood enough to let him do things his own way.

Standing beside his open coffin, she hoped the sense that she got in the room when he died, that he'd seen the faces of people he loved, was what really happened. She believed in that, and Dr Dyer, Oprah, and others often talked about it, and when she saw the pain and the deep lines on his face caused by the cancer almost smooth out in front of her face, she felt such a strong sensation that he was happy to go and that he wasn't alone.

'Carmel.' She started, snapping out of her reverie to find Sharif at her shoulder.

'Can you come home for a while…?' She smiled, she loved the way he called their little apartment home. He'd moved in all his things and had given his apartment to a new Occupational Therapist he'd hired, so they were really living together now.

'Sure, is everything okay?' she walked beside him across the butter and gold coloured pebbles surrounding the chapel.

'Yes, I just wanted to see you, have some time. It's been so busy and with Brian, I just miss you.' He held her hand as they approached the front door.

She stood on her tiptoes to kiss him as he put the key in the lock. 'I love you, Sharif Khan, really, really love you.'

'Of course you do, I'm fabulous.' He grinned as she swatted him on the bum.

Putting the kettle on while she opened some post that was on the mat, he said, 'There was one thing I wanted to talk to you about.'

'Go on…' She was worried.

'Well, in Brian's living will, you know the thing people can write before they die outlining their preferences, he just asked that there be a simple Mass, no big fuss and that his brothers and sisters be informed. He has two sisters and two brothers living, I believe, so we have contacted them, made them aware of his death, and they are going to come over for the funeral, all four of them, I believe.' She could see he was wary of telling her.

'But shouldn't Tim be doing that?' She was surprised that job had fallen to Sharif.

'Well, the thing is, I don't think Brian's family knew he was gay.'

Carmel nodded, it was making sense now. The way they were together, so united, but so private. It also explained why Tim was so reticent about coming to Aashna now; he was probably afraid of running into one of Brian's family.

'I see. Poor Tim, he can't even be seen to grieve properly, it's a hard situation.'

'Well, yes, it is, but it's their choice, so we just have to do what Brian wanted. I'm sure he and Tim talked about it, so...' he shrugged.

'You didn't say anything to them about me or Dolly or...'

'Of course not,' he led her to the sofa. 'That's your story to tell, whether you decide to tell it or not is up to you. I just wanted you to know they are coming here on Tuesday; I didn't want it to come as a shock.'

'Okay...' she didn't know what to say. Joe was coming here, Dolly's boyfriend and possibly her father.

'Do I have to see them?'

Sharif smiled. 'Carmel, you're forty years old, you don't *have* to do anything. If you want to go to Brian's funeral as a member of Aashna House staff and not ever indicate to his family that your connection is anything more than that, then, of course, that's what you must do. Or if you want to tell them who you are, and who your mother was, then that's fine too. Whatever you wish is fine. I'll be by your side all the time, you'll be safe.'

His voice was so gentle. He understood her insecurities. Growing up in an institution, however benign, didn't, she'd learned, equip you very well for the real world. She was so used to being told what to do and when to do it, first at Trinity House and then all those years with Bill and Julia, that she doubted the power of her own judgment. Sharif recognized that and was gently coaxing her into a life where she was the captain of her own ship.

'Okay...thanks. I don't know what is for the best, I mean, they're grieving their brother, they won't need me barging in on top of them.'

'Well, if you're unsure, then why not just see how it all goes? Maybe it will come out naturally or maybe it won't, either way, you've got me and everyone here as back up. You are not alone.'

'Maybe I should make myself scarce, I mean, it's not really my place anyway to be there; we are related, but not in any way that his family would want to know about...'

'Carmel, you work here. Of course, you can take some holidays if you like, I'm not saying it as the boss, but you have every right to be there as a member of Aashna House staff. If it helps, I spoke to his sister and she seemed very nice. She explained that Brian didn't tell them he was ill. When I asked him about family visits a few weeks ago, he told me he didn't want them fussing. His sister, Maggie, seemed to want me to understand that they hadn't just abandoned him. Apparently, every time they would suggest visiting, he'd say he was away or busy and they couldn't understand why he had rejected them. Joe, especially, was very hurt because they were always close. He texted and emailed and all of that, and he went back to Dublin before the cancer got too bad, but he wouldn't allow them to visit him here. We had a really long chat and I never mentioned what he said, obviously, but I think the burden of knowing what he knew about Dolly and not being able to reveal it to his brother was hard for him to bear, but he made a promise to your mother and he was determined to keep it.'

CHAPTER 19

*C*armel lit a candle in the living room and sat down, back straight and eyes open, taking a deep breath. She exhaled and tried to still her thoughts. It was the day of the funeral and she was still undecided whether to go. Maggie, Brian's sister, and her husband Dominic had arrived from Ireland with the rest of the family the previous afternoon and checked into a local hotel. They came and spoke to Sharif and the undertaker in the evening about the arrangements, but Carmel stayed in their apartment.

She tried to focus on her breath. If ever she needed direction, it was now.

Part of her wanted to go out, to meet Joe, to tell him who she was and to ask him if he would consider a DNA test to see if he was her father. But, the bigger part of her was governed by fear. She tried to analyse it, fear of what? The answer was clear, fear of rejection. What if he told her to get lost, or worse still, resented her intrusion in his grief for his brother, and all of that, leaving aside the whole business of what his father did to Dolly. Every time she thought she had the guts to face them all, she was crushed by an icy wave of dread crashing over her head once again.

Eventually, she decided to take Sharif's advice. Just to go as a member of the staff and see what happened.

She was dressed, in black trousers and a cream shirt, and her hair was brushed till it shone. Before she could start to analyse it again and dredge up all the associated fears, she grabbed her bag and went out the door.

Approaching the chapel, she almost fled but forced herself to walk on. Sharif had offered to accompany her, but she needed to do this on her own. She wore no makeup and hoped her appearance was just neutral. The beautiful engagement ring he had given her was back in the apartment; she felt it was too flashy for a funeral.

She debated stopping and introducing herself to the group standing chatting quietly outside the chapel, but she lost courage, so she just continued inside and took a seat at the back. Only the undertaker and the priest were inside, the coffin was outside in the hearse.

The music began to play, and Brian's family slowly walked in procession behind the coffin as it was pushed on wheels towards the altar. They took their seats at the top of the small chapel and Carmel fixed her gaze on Brian's sisters and brothers, all sitting on the front pew. Behind them were close to twenty other people, wives, husbands, and children, she assumed. She smiled at how Irish they all looked, even the number of people was Irish. She had been saddened at first when she came to England to note how few people went to funerals. She had explained to Zane and Ivy that funerals were as big as weddings in Ireland, bigger often because no invitations were issued. Anyone who had even the most tenuous of connections went, and those who were connected to the family of the deceased too. Colleagues, old school friends of the dear departed's grandchildren, almost everyone in the town or village if it was in the country, everyone went. Back in Birr, she and Bill went to every single removal or funeral in the whole town. It would have been considered the height of disrespect not to. The family was propped up emotionally by their community for a long while afterwards, so the much more understated English system was a mystery to Carmel.

Carmel's heart went out to the McDaid family, they were like fish out of water over here. Back at home, because there was a protocol, a way of doing death, everyone knew what to do. In Ireland, it was as if when someone died, a switch got flicked and the age-old process just cranked into action. Each person knows his or her part, and people are comforted by that. Over here, in this strange country, the McDaids were lost.

Fr. Watson, the local Catholic priest, said the funeral Mass, and the familiar words soothed Carmel's frantic spirit. She felt such a barrage of emotions as she sat there, fear, guilt at not focusing properly on Brian, comfort from the words of the liturgy, all underpinned by a longing for her mother. Brian's nephew Daniel gave a short but heart-felt eulogy. The hymns were traditional, Brian's own choice, and played on the elaborate sound system in the church. The priest blessed the coffin, sprinkling it with holy water as he intoned the prayers of death.

'Into your hands, we commend our brother Brian. Eternal rest grant unto him, O Lord, and may perpetual light shine on him forever, may he rest in peace.'

It wasn't until Carmel stood and the undertaker was arranging with the McDaid brothers and nephews to carry the coffin on their shoulders, that she noticed she was not alone at the back of the church. Tim was behind her.

The Mass ended, and the men in the family carried Brian out to the hearse once more. As they passed, the women were silently weeping, the men stony faced. Of the two older men, one was by far the taller of the two, so she assumed him to be Joe. The only photo she had, taken all those years ago on Dollymount Strand, showed him as towering over Dolly.

Outside in the sunshine, Carmel felt awkward and stood with Tim, slipping her arm through his. She knew he was stoic, but this was killing him. The nephew who gave the eulogy approached them.

'Em...I don't know who ye are, but obviously my uncle meant something to you both, so we'd be happy to have you come with us to the crematorium, and afterwards to the hotel for a bit of lunch?'

Tim recovered first, 'Thank you, that's very kind. We'd love to.'

143

Carmel squeezed his arm in a gesture of solidarity. This was his life partner and yet the last act of Brian's life had Tim playing a bit part, it was so hard.

The cremation was short. Fr Watson said a few more prayers, and the family looked awkward. Cremation was very rare in Ireland, and Carmel guessed it was their first time attending one. The whole ceremony went by as a blur. Thoughts of introducing herself to Brian's family, Joe, in particular, were petrifying. Should she just say she was working there, and since she was Irish, she felt she should go? Or should she admit that she and Brian had been friends, or could she just let Tim introduce himself and let them assume she was something to do with him? To her shame, she wasn't thinking about Brian at all as his coffin slid behind the screen; she was panicking about how to get out of the situation. All the calming, mindful thoughts of this morning were gone and, in their place, terror.

'Have you ever met any of them?' Carmel whispered to Tim as the family huddled together around the door of the crematorium.

'Never. Brian didn't want them to know about us; he wanted to protect me and my life, so he lived a lie all these years for me. By the time it was okay for us to say what we meant to each other, it was too late, too much time had passed, too much had been left unsaid, too many lies told. So, when he went home, he went alone. Anytime he had a visitor from Ireland, which was rare, I made myself scarce. It must seem odd to someone of your generation, everyone is so open nowadays, but it just wasn't like that in our day, and well, we're bad with change, at least we were, it's just me now, I suppose.'

Carmel gave a wry grin, 'I didn't have the liberal upbringing you imagine I had, Tim, nothing like it, so I totally understand.'

Daniel approached them and it took Carmel everything she could do to stay on the spot, the urge to flee was so strong.

'So, ye'll come down to the hotel, will ye? The Davenport it's called. We can do proper introductions there. We've a few taxis coming, so ye can jump in with us or if ye have yer own car?' He was a handsome young man, and his open, honest face drew a smile from Carmel.

'Yes, we have a car, we'll see you there.' Tim squeezed Carmel's arm to his body, murmuring into her ear as they made their way to the car park. 'We're going to need to stick together on this one, my dear.'

'Carmel!' She turned to see Sharif striding towards her. 'Hello, Tim.' He shook the other man's hand, they hadn't met since Brian died. 'I'm so sorry for your loss.'

Tim nodded. 'I didn't know it would be that night, I left earlier than usual and I had a hospital appointment myself early the next morning, and I...' Carmel held his arm as the emotion choked him, 'I...I wanted to be with him, but he said he didn't want me to remember him like that, so we agreed...'

'He wasn't alone. Carmel was with him, and so was I. He had a very peaceful death.' Sharif was soothing.

'He wrote me a letter and put it in a box, to be opened when he died, along with some things that were of sentimental value to us, little souvenirs and things, but the letter...he never was a very publicly effusive man, neither am I, we weren't brought up that way. Maybe people nowadays would say we were a bit stuffy, or formal or whatever, but it worked for us. But this letter, it was everything we felt but never said, he wrote it all. I would have liked the chance to tell him I felt the same.' Tim was struggling to maintain his composure.

'He knew.' Carmel was sure of it.

'So, where are you going now?' Sharif was trying to lighten the mood, he knew that breaking down would only embarrass Tim.

'To the hotel, the Davenport, the family have invited us for lunch.' The dread that Carmel felt was clearly visible on her face.

'Do they know? The family, I mean...who you...or Tim for that matter, do they know who you are?' Concern furrowed his smooth forehead.

'No, no they don't have a clue who either of us is.' Carmel chewed her lip, a habit she'd had since childhood.

Tim recovered and gave a lopsided grin, 'We're debating which of us should explain first.'

'Do you want me to come with you?' he was talking directly to Carmel now, 'Would it help?'

'But your patients, they need you this afternoon surely...' Carmel desperately wanted him there but felt guilty taking him away.

'Well, I didn't know how today was going to go, so I got a locum in anyway. Dr Alexander, the patients are used to her, she often covers for me, so I'm free to go with you if it would help, but if you'd rather do this alone, then I understand, of course.'

She looked up at him, shielding her eyes from the bright sun. 'I'd love you to come.'

CHAPTER 20

Sharif drove them all, Tim was too shaken to drive. They found a parking space, and Carmel and Tim got out, leaving Sharif to make a quick phone call.

'What are you going to say?' he sounded as scared she was.

'I don't know, I can't decide. How about you?'

'Not the truth anyway, that's for sure. Just that we were friends, he was my lodger, something like that I suppose.' The sadness at not just the grief of losing the love of his life, but the fact that he had to deny the importance of their relationship was really hurting him, it was plain for anyone to see.

'Okay, are we ready?' Sharif bipped the alarm on the car and gently put his hand on the small of Carmel's back.

'Yes, well no, actually, not at all ready, but if we are going to do this…'

Before they had a chance to compose themselves, Brian's sisters Maggie and Orla approached them.

'Hello, Dr Khan, it's very good of you to come. I'm Maggie and this is my sister Orla, Brian's brothers Colm and Joe are inside, along with some of our kids. Daniel said you two were friends of Brian's?' Her open face radiated friendliness and welcome even in the midst of her obvious grief at the loss of her brother.

'Yes, Tim O'Flaherty, Brian used to live in my house.' Tim extended a hand and Maggie took it warmly. She was short with iron grey hair and was, what Julia would have called, 'a victim of middle age spread.' A fate that was never likely to befall the angular Julia. Maggie was dressed all in black, but Carmel got the impression she was uncomfortable in the dress, jacket, and tights. Orla was the opposite, very glamorous, with expensively cut and highlighted hair and a well-cut trouser suit. She seemed more wary than her sister, despite the smile.

Both women looked expectantly at Carmel.

'I'm Carmel,' she didn't want to use her mother's surname in case they recognized it, but she couldn't bring herself to call herself Carmel Sheehan one more time. 'I work at Aashna House and I got to know Brian there, what with us both being Irish,' Carmel finished in a rush, desperate to get the words out.

'You look very familiar, I can't place from where, but I feel as though I know you from somewhere.' Orla's brow furrowed, 'I've thought it since I saw you in the chapel. And you're Irish, where did you go to school? Maybe we were in the same one?'

'I...ah...I went to school in Dublin, city centre, but Brian said you were from Kilmainham, didn't you go there?' Carmel was anxious to deflect this line of questioning.

'Yes, we went to Inchicore National School and then to St Jarlath's in Ballyfermot.' Orla was clearly racking her brain.

'Well, I didn't go to either of those; I think I just have one of those faces, people are always saying I remind them of people.' Carmel's laugh sounded fake even to her own ears.

Sensing her discomfort, Sharif interrupted, 'Shall we go in?' Both Maggie and Orla responded instantly to his charm and turned towards him like sunflowers.

'Of course, Dr Khan, it's so good of you to come along.' Maggie recovered enough to lead the little group in.

'Sharif, please,' he smiled as he held the door open for the three ladies. Carmel caught his eye and gave him a look of thanks.

The introductions were made, and nobody seemed to bat an eyelid at the three extra for lunch. The chat was lively and the family even burst into spontaneous laughter on occasion. Despite their pain and genuine loneliness for their brother and uncle, the lunch really was a celebration of a life well lived.

After the main course, waitresses were taking tea and coffee orders, Joe stood up and dinged his spoon off his wine glass, and the family settled down. Carmel's mouth went dry and she was transfixed. Was this man her father? He was tall with grey hair cut short, and an athletic build. She thought he looked in good shape for a man of sixty plus years. His blue eyes were exactly the same colour as hers, and Dolly's eyes were brown.

He waited until everyone was silent and then he spoke. His voice was gentle, and he had a real Dublin accent, just like Brian had.

'Family and friends of my late brother Brian, I just wanted to say a few words. As most of you know, burying Kevin two years ago was a very low time for all of us, and we are really happy that Kevin Junior and Ciara can be here with us, it means a lot. Brian was the eldest of the McDaids and in lots of ways, more ways than he should have been actually, he was the father figure. He was kind and always had time for any one of us, no matter what we ever needed. There was a time when I was a young man that I thought my heart would break, but it was Brian who held me together. When Mammy died, when Kevin was taken from us so early, when the engagements happened, or babies were born, the first thing we did was tell Brian. When he left Ireland, it left a huge hole in all our hearts, but we were glad to see he had a happy life over here. He came home often, laden down with presents every time, and he was always welcome. He texted and emailed us all the time, so he never felt too far away.

I want, on behalf of the McDaid family, to extend a warm welcome to Dr Khan, who is with us here today, and to whom we all owe a great debt. He looked after Brian in the closing weeks of his life, he respected his wishes and maintained his dignity, while at the same time giving him the benefit of expert care. He emailed me a week ago and told me all about you Doctor, how he never suffered, physically or mentally and for that, Dr Khan, we are so grateful.'

Sharif nodded and smiled, and Carmel squeezed his hand under the table. She knew he wasn't comfortable with accolades, he was a true doctor, just wanting to help people.

'Welcome as well to his fiancée, Carmel, who is a Paddy the same as ourselves,' a ripple of laughter, 'I understand that you had some nice chats with Brian in his last days, and we are glad that he had someone from home to talk to.'

'Finally, we want to say thank you and welcome to Tim O'Flaherty, who was a great friend to Brian during all his years over here. Tim, there's a bed for you in Dublin anytime you like. Brian never told us how ill he was, and he didn't encourage visitors, but we never doubted what we meant to him, and I pray that he knew how much he meant to us too. Thanks.'

He sat down to thunderous applause. Then Daniel stood up, 'Raise your glasses to Uncle Brian. Hip hip...' the gathered group answered 'hurrah' and once again, the lunch became a jovial affair.

Carmel chatted with one of his nieces, Colm's daughter Aisling, and she was so funny and refreshing, telling stories of the shenanigans of her uncles and aunts when they all got together. They sounded like such a happy family, and the cousins were clearly all good friends. Carmel wondered what it would be like to grow up like that, so happy and loved and surrounded by your people, to know that you were part of something.

Tim, sitting on her right, was just observing the whole family, the pain of loss and grief hidden behind his eyes and his smile.

'How are you bearing up?' Aisling had popped to the bathroom so Carmel had a chance to speak to him quietly.

'Okay. You know...they loved him, of course they did, but in an old uncle over in England kind of way, not...'

'Not the way you did.' She placed her hand on his. 'I know. It must be so hard behaving like an outsider when you're, in fact, the chief mourner.'

Tim nodded, his mouth set in a hard line, trying to hold it

together. 'I think I'll go, actually. Thanks for today.' He pushed his chair back and without a word to anyone, he was gone.

Sharif caught her eye. He read her glance correctly, that she too, had had enough and she wanted to go. He made his farewells and helped Carmel into her coat.

'Thanks for having us, it was so lovely to meet you all. And I'm sure wherever Brian is now, he's looking down and smiling,' Carmel managed to say and with waves and warm handshakes, she took her leave of the McDaids. She hadn't spoken to Joe at all, deliberately placing herself at the other end of the table.

As they made their way across the car park, they spotted Tim waiting on a cab. They'd forgotten he had come to the hotel with them, his car was back at the crematorium.

'Tim,' Carmel called, 'come with us, we'll take you back to your car.'

He didn't answer, just raised his hand, suggesting he was fine. Carmel and Sharif walked over to him. He looked as if he was just about holding it together, but when Carmel linked his arm, suddenly, tears were pouring down his lined and age-spotted face. Without a word, they led him to the car and Carmel got in the back with him. She held his hand as he wept, 'He was my world.' She sat beside him as Sharif drove home. 'What am I supposed to do now? Everyone else will be a bit sad, but they'll go back to their lives but...Brian was my life. Without him, I just don't know how to be, what to do.' Carmel held his hand and said nothing. He just needed to talk, to articulate the pain. She wished she could ease it for him, but there was no way around grief, just through it. The familiar streets passed by in a blur.

'Would you like to go for a cup of tea? Or something stronger?' Once they were back at the crematorium, it didn't feel right just to let him go off, back to the home he'd shared with Brian for so many years on his own.

'Thanks, and you've both been so kind, I really appreciate it, but no, I think I'll just go home. It's been a long day and I just want to get into bed and be alone with my thoughts. I hope you understand?'

'Of course, we do. It has been a really hard day for you, made harder by the fact that you couldn't grieve properly. But, Tim, cele-brating a life, remembering, having those precious memories, they don't mean much today, but they will in time become important, and all of this today, irrelevant.'

Sharif had a way of speaking to the bereaved that constantly impressed Carmel. It was if he knew what to say. He wasn't at all morose or dreary, quite the opposite actually, he was full of fun, but he had a deep compassion and understanding of the human condition.

They saw Tim to his car, waved him off, and headed home to Aashna. Carmel longed for a soak in the bath, a gin and tonic, and an early night. It had been a grueling day, and even though the McDaid family had no idea who she really was, she still felt the burden of the knowledge she had, thanks to Brian, weighing heavily on her. Maybe she should have said something, but it wasn't the right time. She sat heavily on the couch, kicking off her shoes and examining a blister on the sole of her foot, caused by the new shoes she'd bought for the occasion. Maybe there would never be a right time; she was too tired and wrung out to even think about it anymore. Sharif had some calls to make and needed to do his evening rounds, but before he left, he ran her a bath, lit a candle for her in the bathroom, and made her a drink.

'Now, you relax there, listen to some music, and try to let the strain of the day melt away. I'll be about an hour. Will I bring you something from the kitchen? Are you hungry?' He was in front of her, gin and tonic in hand.

'How on earth did I get you?' she took the drink and put her hand on the side of his face. He turned his face and kissed her palm. 'Seri-ously, Sharif, I don't know how I'd have got through today without you. Thank you.'

'We're a team now, Carmel. Together, there is nothing we can't do. Now, relax, have a soak, and I'll be back soon.'

She watched his departing back as he left the apartment, his mind now on those people who needed him and she laid her head back against the sofa. She tried to imagine Bill ever doing anything thoughtful for anyone.

So many times, she'd started a letter to him, but it always sounded crazy. She and Bill never talked, they had no relationship, and to try to talk to him as her husband, as someone she should be close to felt so uncomfortable she ended up throwing all her efforts in the bin.

In the end, their break up had many of the characteristics of their marriage. A cold empty nothingness, with no explanation or attempt to soothe from either side.

She went into the bedroom to undress when there was a knock on the door. Her heart sank. It was probably Nadia, calling to see how she'd got on, or Zane with some Grinder crisis that could only be solved by Chardonnay and lots of analysis. Normally, she would have been thrilled to see either of them, but she was so drained she couldn't face company. She just stood in the bedroom and hoped the person would go away. They might assume she was in bed already if she drew the curtains.

The knocking was insistent, however, and she knew she'd have to go out and answer the door. She threw her pajamas and dressing gown on and stuck her feet in her furry mule slippers and went out, determined to make her excuses.

The bubble glass meant she couldn't make out who was there, but it certainly wasn't ebony skinned Zane nor the tiny Nadia. She opened the door.

'Joe.' His name almost caught in her throat.

'I'm sorry for calling unannounced, but…can I come in?' he looked shaken and drawn.

'Er…yes…of course…come in. Sharif isn't here if it's him you want to see, he's doing his rounds over at the main building…' she knew she was babbling, but this was just too close for comfort.

'It was you I wanted to see, Carmel.' His strong Dublin accent took her back to her days in Trinity House.

'Oh…oh right, em…sure…em…what can I do for you?'

'You can tell me how someone the living spit of Dolly Mullane ended up at my brother's funeral for a start.'

Carmel felt the colour drain from her face, her insides turned to ice water, and a cold sweat prickled her skin.

153

'There's no point in denying it. The minute I saw you, I knew. Don't ask me how it happened, but you're something to Dolly Mullane, I'd put my life on it. Am I right? Brian had something to do with it...I know that much. Something he said a few months ago, about Dolly, I don't know...he never let on, but I had a feeling always that he knew something about what became of her. And then you show up...'

'Would you like a drink?' Her voice sounded stronger than she felt. She needed to play for time, to think how she was going to handle this.

'By the look on your face, I think I'm going to need one.' He tried to crack a small smile.

She made herself another gin and tonic and made one for Joe as well.

'So, am I right? Are you related to Dolly?' he asked as she handed him the drink.

There was no point in lying, but Carmel had no idea where to begin. She took a deep breath and tried to steady herself. Eventually, she spoke.

'Yes, Dolly was my birth mother.'

'What do you mean birth mother?'

'Well, I never met her, she died before Sharif found me.'

Seeing his confusion, she knew she had to tell him the story from the beginning, leaving nothing out. There had been enough secrets and lies, now was the time for truth. Filling in the blanks in the story between Brian's, Nadia's, and Sharif's recollections of Dolly's life, she told Joe everything she knew. His face when she told him about his father's attack, and Dolly's subsequent pregnancy almost broke her heart. The raw agony, it was as if it had happened yesterday.

He allowed her to tell her story, everything about his father and the ban on her adoption, and when she was finished, they sat in silence.

'So, my father is your father?' He could barely get the words out.

This was it, the moment when she told him that he might be her father. Suddenly, it all felt like too much. What if he rejected it? Told her she was lying? Could she cope with him refusing to accept responsibility for her? She wished Sharif was there. Taking a deep breath, she blurted it out.

'Possibly, or it might be you. Dolly didn't know, it could have been either of you, but your father threatened her, and so she left. She couldn't tell you because if she did, your father said that you'd try to kill him and that you'd end up in prison, and her father would have the scandal of that to add to his pregnant daughter...she did the only thing she could. Your father put her in the home for unmarried mothers run by the nuns.'

'And you?' He could barely bring himself to ask. 'Did they hurt you?'

'No. Not like abuse or anything, it was okay.' Then she told him all about Bill and his proposal and his jaw tightened.

They sat in silence for a long minute, Joe trying to absorb what he'd heard, Carmel trying to see his reaction. Rage, upset, sorrow, pity, it was all there on his face.

'I can't believe that he wouldn't let you be adopted. He was an evil man, I always knew that, he was horrible to us as kids and to our Ma, and he couldn't bear us challenging him. He drove Brian away because he tried to defend me. For a year after, he'd goad me about Dolly, saying she must have left me for a real man all that sort of stuff, and my heart was broken, it hurt so much. Brian told him to shut up one night, to leave me alone, and he made his life hell after that. If only she'd told me, or written even...even if she did it after he died...'

'But you were married then, had children of your own; she didn't want to upset your life, I suppose, thought she'd done enough damage.'

'But, June, that was my late wife,' he added. 'She knew all about Dolly, sure we all grew up together. I remember one night, after our son Luke was born, thirty-two years ago now, and Jennifer was a toddler, she says to me, 'I know you'll never love me the way you loved Dolly, but is this enough? Is what we have enough for you?'

His voice betrayed the emotions going on inside.

'I told her that it was, that I loved her and the kids so much, and I was telling the truth, I really did and we had a great marriage, but she knew...'

They sat and talked for over an hour, Carmel filling in what she knew about her mother's life in England, most of which she'd learned from Nadia and Sharif, and Joe told Carmel all about growing up in Kilmainham, and what Dolly was like as a child.

'So, now what do we do?' Joe looked uncertain.

'About what?' Carmel knew exactly what he meant, but she needed to hear him say it.

'About you and me, and us figuring out if we are father and daughter, or brother and sister.' The words fell between them like lead weights.

'What do you want to do?' Carmel heard herself swallow.

Joe turned on the couch to face her and took her hand in his. He sighed deeply, the weight of all he'd discovered bearing down on him.

'What I want, can't happen. I want to turn the clock back to the day before he attacked her. I want Dolly to have come to me forty years ago, telling me that she's expecting and that we have to get married. I'd have married her in a heartbeat. I want to have raised you as my daughter with Dolly as your mother and my wife, and maybe a few more along with you to keep you company. I want none of this to have happened. For that pathetic excuse for a man to have never laid a hand on my lovely Dolly, for you not to have had a lonely childhood with nobody to love you, for you to have never married that culchie who couldn't be a proper husband to you, I wish lots of things, but wishing won't change the past. All we have is now.'

So many thoughts and questions were rushing through Carmel's head. Did this man want her to be his daughter? Did he want to find out? Did he wish he'd never uncovered this awful secret? Was he still in love with Dolly? Did his children know that he loved Dolly before their mother?

It was too overwhelming; she needed a minute to process her thoughts.

'I want to show you something.' She got up and went to the bedroom where she kept the letters and the photos Dolly had left for her. She still looked at them every day. As she rooted in the box, she caught sight of her reflection in the mirror, she looked haggard and drawn. Then she stopped and really looked into her own eyes. Others saw her mother there, perhaps she could too.

She spoke silently to her. 'Mam, Dolly, please help us all here, I don't know what to do, what to say. You seem to be guiding me, and so far, it's been for the best, bringing me here, to Sharif, and Nadia, I finally have a life of my own, but this, with Joe, I'm lost. Please, help me.'

She found the photo she was looking for and brought it to Joe. She handed it to him and instantly she saw the flood of recognition in his eyes.

'Where did this come from? God, we look so young, we must only have been twenty or twenty-one then. I remember the day it was taken, out on Dollymount. We'd both been paid, so we went to the seaside on the bus and had chips and ice-creams and swam in the freezing cold sea. That night, we came home and Dolly's father, Tom, was out. We made love for the first time then, a first for both of us. If we were caught, he'd have strung me up, but Dolly was sure he was out for the night. He did catch us another night, and threw me out and was raging with Dolly, but he softened in the end. He knew I was stone mad about her, and she wasn't the kind of girl that went off with this fella and that fella, she wasn't like that at all. But, she and me, we had a bond, since we were kids. We loved each other.' Tears welled up in his eyes, and he wiped them impatiently with the back of his hand.

'It was in a box, with some letters and photos she gave to Sharif to give to me if he ever found me. Apart from one of me as a baby, it's the only picture from her life before she came over here.'

Suddenly, she needed Joe to know how hard Brian had fought for him to know the truth.

'Brian and Dolly fell out, you know, though she looked after him and visited him and all of that, but he was so angry with her. He wanted to tell you as soon as he stumbled across her that she was alive and about me and everything, but she wouldn't let him. She made him swear to keep it all to himself.'

'But I don't understand why. I mean, she knew I loved her and that even after all these years, I'd want to know.' Joe was so sad, it hurt Carmel to hear the pain in his voice.

'She just felt that she'd hurt you enough, I think, that you were happy with a family of your own and that anything she said at that stage would just upset that. She just didn't ever want you to know what your father did to her, and to me, it wouldn't have helped.I'm only basing this on what Brian told me; I never met her and I so wish that I had, even for one day.'

'I wouldn't mind a word with her myself, now that I know what I know. It's so strange for me, to be here, looking at you. I can't tell you how much you look like her. I never knew Dolly when she was your age, she was gone from me a long time by then, but I can see her in you, clear as day. Your eyes are different though, hers were dark, and yours are blue, like mine.'

'I know.'

She wanted to ask what colour his father's eyes were, but she couldn't.

'Everyone says that I look like her. I never looked like anyone, so it's strange for me too, I can assure you. She and I are different in personality, though, she was much more outgoing than I am, much braver too probably.'

'You're remarkable. You don't seem to be angry, I'm bloody furious, and yet it was to you all of this happened and you seem okay with it.'

Carmel didn't know how to take that, perhaps it was a criticism but she couldn't be sure.

'There's no point in harbouring anger, it would only hurt me, and those people who didn't behave as they should have, well my being a mess wouldn't impact on them in any way, would it?'

Joe smiled, 'You're right, of course you are, but still. You say you're not like your mother in personality, but I think you are in some ways. She was kind of pragmatic as well. When her mother died, and her father was hard to deal with, she just accepted it and tried to make the best of it. Even her life over here, she was obviously torn apart after losing you, but she tried to make the best life for herself that she could.'

They chatted away easily, there was no awkwardness or wondering what to say next, and Carmel stopped fretting about his reaction to the news. As usual, Sharif was gone much longer than he'd anticipated, but Carmel was used to it and she knew he'd be back when he'd got everyone settled for the night.

Sharif's key was in the door and his face registered surprise to see Joe sitting there.

'Don't worry, Sharif, I'm not in here trying to charm your fiancée.' He smiled and stood up to shake Sharif's hand.

'I should hope not.' Sharif chuckled and kissed Carmel on the cheek. 'I take it you two have been chatting?' The enquiring look he gave Carmel meant he was checking who knew what before he continued with any conversation.

'Yes, Joe knew who I was right away; apparently, I couldn't be anyone else, only Dolly Mullane's daughter. I've told him the whole story, or as much as I know anyway, everything Brian told me and also about her life here, from your Mum and you.'

'It's quite a tale, is it not?' Sharif poured himself a glass of red wine and joined them in the lounge area.

'It certainly is,' Joe agreed. 'What we have to decide now is what to do next.' The words hung in the air, all the time they'd been talking they had both studiously avoided the question of a DNA test. From Carmel's perspective, she wanted to know, but then she wondered if she might be better off not knowing? The idea that Joe was her father, now that she'd met him properly, was such a lovely one, and the alternative was horrible. Maybe if they never found out, they could just carry on and...she stopped herself from that crazy train of thought. Of course, he would want to know.

'What do you want to do, Carmel?' Joe asked gently.

'I don't know.'

He leaned over and held her hand. 'Well, will I tell you what I think?' She nodded, not trusting herself to speak.

'I think you're my daughter. Maybe I only think that because I want it to be the case, but I don't know, I just think you are. You have my eyes. I'd love it if you were, and I know once I explain to Jennifer and Luke, they'll welcome you with open arms. They're great, and you'd love them. And if you want to do a test, I think they can do that now fairly easily, then that's what we'll do, but if you don't, well that's fine with me too.'

Carmel felt the reassuring weight of Sharif's hand on her shoulder, and it calmed her.

Joe went on, and his words were a like soothing balm on a raw wound. 'I want to be your Dad, it's late in the day now, but even so. I can't just walk out of here and say, well, best of luck with your life and leave it at that. It would drive me crazy. So, Carmel, the ball is in your court, as they say. I'm here, and I would love to call you my daughter and try to make up even in a small way for all the pain, but if you don't want that, well then, I'll be very sad, but I'll accept it.'

He stood up to leave. 'I don't want an answer now, there's no time limit on the offer. I know this must be so overwhelming. It is for me too. So, I'll leave ye both to talk it over, and maybe we could meet up before I go home tomorrow night? Or if that's too soon, here's my number,' he handed her a card, 'ring anytime, or visit, whatever suits you, Carmel. No pressure.'

She stood and took a step towards him as if it was the most natural thing in the world. He wrapped his arms around her and she laid her head against his chest. The overwhelming feeling was one of safety and peace. He kissed the top of her head and was gone.

That night, she and Sharif talked about it in bed. A part of her wanted, needed, to know the truth and another part of her just wanted Joe to be her father and for her to be in his life. The idea that

THE CARMEL SHEEHAN STORY

he would accept her as his, even without knowing the truth, was a testament to the kind of man he was. He was obviously worthy of the love Dolly had for him all those years ago.

After going around in conversational circles for hours, Sharif leaned up on his elbow and looked down into her face.

'Carmel, I have an idea. Say if it's a terrible one, but you've had such a harrowing few months. It must feel sometimes like you're being dragged under a sea of emotions. I was thinking, why don't we take a holiday? Take a little time out together? Just the two of us? It's been so busy since you came over here, I'd love just to spend some time with you away from all the distractions. Just for a week maybe, somewhere sunny and calm, where we can just relax and get away from all of this. What do you think?'

She'd never had a holiday, even when she and Bill had gotten married, they drove home to Birr that evening and he was out milking within half an hour of arriving at the farm. The idea of a honeymoon was never suggested.

'That would be absolutely amazing, even though our life here is a kind of endless holiday for me, you never take a rest. Your mother was only saying last week that it was ridiculous that you never take any time off. And I must say, the idea of having you all to myself for a whole week...well, it is just bliss.'

'Hmmm...' he kissed her neck, sending shivers of desire through her body. She had no idea that her body could react that way until he'd kissed her that very first time outside the pub in Dublin, the very first day they met. 'Of course, I *am* all yours now...'

CHAPTER 21

*C*armel was on a coffee break in the bright, sunny restaurant, sitting opposite Zane and Ivanka.

'Ah, no, I mean thank you, it's a lovely thought but I don't think we...' she fought back panic.

'Ah, come on, the last big bash we had here was for your mum and it lifted everyone's spirits. We are all so happy for you and Sharif, it's like a fairytale, him finding you, and you falling in love...' Zane was coming over all weepy.

The more practical Ivanka chimed in, 'Why not? It's just a party to celebrate your engagement, a few drinks, some nice food, a band maybe? What's so terrifying about it? All your friends around you, the patients who are able, and Nadia, it will be fun, not scary at all.'

Carmel was desperately trying to find a way out, 'I don't think it would be Sharif's thing, honestly...' she protested but Zane interrupted her.

'He's fine with it, we asked him already because we knew you'd say that. He said he's happy to have it but it's up to you. So, if you don't say yes, you'll be letting him down too.' Zane winked cheekily.

'Ignore him, he's just looking for an occasion to strut about like a pigeon.'

Zane hooted at Ivanka's word confusion.

'It's a peacock struts not a pigeon, don't you have peacocks in Siberia?' he nudged her playfully, the banter between them was relentless.

'How many more times? I am from Ukraine, not Siberia, and, yes, we do have every kind of bird there, but sometimes I get confused with this English, okay? At least I am bilingual not like you only speaking peacock English...' she winked at Carmel.

'It's pigeon...Ahh...I see what you did there, very clever...for a Ruskie, I suppose,' he grumbled good naturedly. 'Anyway, back to the party, it's going to be great, pleeeeeeeease, Carmel, pleeeeeeease?' He was on his knees in the middle of the Aashna restaurant making a total show of himself, and them. The patients dotted around smiled; they were used to Zane and his antics, he was like a ray of sunshine around the hospice.

'I hate being the centre of attention, guys, really I do, and all those posh doctor friends sniggering at how Sharif fell for an Irish nobody with only one name...' Carmel was failing miserably to quell their enthusiasm.

'What do you mean? Only one name?' Ivanka was curious.

'Oh, you know, they all seem to be Belinda Parker-Willington and Montgomery Clifton-Barrett. I've been to two doctor social things and the only one I could talk to was the waitress. We'd have to have all of them and it would be dreadful...' she begged them to understand.

'No, we don't! It's your party; you invite who you like. Sharif isn't really like that at all anyway, you know that he has to go to those events sometimes but he wouldn't choose the Humpty Bumpingsworth-Bladderfuls of this world and you know it.'

They both giggled at Zane; he really was hilarious.

'Okay, so, are you saying we can do it if we only have Aashna House staff and patients, and Nadia?' Ivanka moved in for the kill.

Carmel knew when she was beaten, 'Okay, I suppose so. But low-key, and not too expensive, I don't want flash, okay?' Zane smirked at Ivanka.

'Zane, I mean it, nothing flamboyant or over the top, just a few friends for a get-together, okay? Promise?'

'Promise, promise, it will be just a stale, curled up fish paste sandwich and a cup of lukewarm tap water.'

'I mean it, Zane.' She swatted him on the arm with a grin. 'Please, low-key, right?'

The other two clapped and high fived each other. The Good-cop/Bad-cop routine had obviously worked.

As she walked across the lawn on her way to the recreation room after lunch, she was going over all the things she needed to do. The costumes for the *Wizard of Oz* were coming on wonderfully and the kids were coming for a preliminary fitting this afternoon. The Men's Shed group was getting stuck in with set building as well, and Carmel and Sharif were thrilled how getting involved in the production was really giving a powerfully positive energy to the place. There were more supplies to buy, but she'd wait until she spoke to Daf. They'd ended up taking over the entire costuming and she was giving lessons on needlework to anyone who was interested. She had organized some snacks for the kids the last time they came to rehearse, and they loved visiting. They stayed for ages, talking to the patients and showing them things on the internet while munching crisps and buns.

She took advantage of the calm before the storm and sat on a bench in the garden, kicking off her sandals and resting her eyes. She was trying to practice her mindfulness and being present in order to extract the maximum from her day. Sharif was always trying to get the staff to take time for themselves during the working day, he really believed it led to a more productive, positive atmosphere for everyone if stress could be avoided.

Before she came here, she spent most of the day on Facebook, chatting in groups who were interested in all aspects of spirituality. She would have loved to meet those online friends in person and even once considered asking Bill for the money to do a meditation weekend at a gorgeous Buddhist Retreat Centre in West Cork but she baulked at the last minute. He'd have refused anyway, she reasoned

THE CARMEL SHEEHAN STORY

with herself; he probably thought anything to do with mind, body, spirit was a load of old codswallop.

As the sun streamed down on her face, she was transported back to Birr, another lifetime ago. She used to try to dismiss Bill and her old life from her thoughts but one of Deepak Chopra's guided meditations said that it caused stress to try to constantly police your thoughts; instead, he advised just to let them flow into your mind and out again.

She smiled at the thought of explaining meditation to Bill. He knew she was interested in it because he must have seen her books and CDs of Deepak Chopra, Sharon Salzburg, The Dalai Lama, and, of course, her favourite, Dr Dyer, around the house, but he never said a word about them. For him, spirituality was strictly Catholic. They went to Mass at 10.30 every Sunday without fail, Bill, Julia, and herself, rain hail or shine and Carmel tried to find meaning in the words the priest would say, but she failed. She had been brought up in that tradition, daily Mass, weekly confession, the sacraments, but for most of her adult life, it was entirely without meaning for her. Probably because there was never a discussion, never a chance to question or explore the faith, it was just presented as a fait accompli; there it was, ready to go, just take it on and off you go. Do what you're told and it will all be fine but if you dare to stray, by word, deed, or thought, then it's 'straight down to the hot fella' as Sister Catherine, her junior infant teacher would say, describing the eternal fires of hell to five-year-olds with what she now realised was inappropriate enthusiasm.

Carmel could recite the prayers of the Mass by heart and say the rosary in her sleep, but it didn't touch the core of her. She would look around at people, some truly connected to the experience but most were like her, she imagined, going because it was what you did in an Irish town. Since the scandals of child abuse in recent years, the numbers attending were dwindling but the Mass was still well attended. The new Irish, those who had moved to Ireland in the last decade from Poland, Lithuania, Latvia, and Nigeria, were making their mark on the liturgy as well, so churches were being revitalized by the waves of immigration. She would have loved not to go, to stay at home and meditate or go for a walk and connect with God that way, but Julia would have had a stroke and Bill would probably have an even more advanced version of the 'I'm really disappointed how my life turned out' face he always wore.

At least Julia didn't sit with them at Mass, she was in the choir. Her screechy, reed thin voice was unmistakable, deliberately trying to drown everyone else out, Carmel was convinced. She would hold the note at the end slightly too long, so for a few seconds, she was doing a solo. Her sister-in-law thought she was a great singer but honestly, and Carmel tried to steer away from negative thoughts, she was like a crow. Even Bill squirmed a little when the whole congregation was treated to her squawky version of 'Nearer my God to Thee' with the rest of the choir doing their best to negate it. For most of the choir, and indeed the congregation, she was Miss Sheehan, principal of the primary school, who terrorized their childhoods, so they were power-less against her.

Outside Mass one Sunday, a new curate suggested to Julia having a children's choir as well as the adult one at Sunday Mass, but she vetoed that immediately, 'Father Creedon, with respect, I know the children of this parish and the houses they come out of in a manner that you simply cannot. I can tell you with one hundred percent certainty that there are no children in this parish who possess the musicality or temperament to be successful in a church choir. I have dedicated my life to the education of the children of Birr, many of whom are no better than they should be considering where, and more importantly who, they came from, and one of my God given talents, my singing voice, has been sorely tested, I can assure you, trying to teach them even the most basic melody.'

Carmel remembered the red spots of indignation on her sister-in-law's gaunt face as she seemed almost to grow taller in her righteous indignation. Her terrifying stare, the severe bun which dragged her sparse hair back over her skull, and the light blue eyes that bore down on him did not put the young priest off, however.

'Ah, now, Miss Sheehan, you can't surely be telling me that out of two hundred or so youngsters in the school, not one of them can carry a tune? That seems unbelievable to me.' His smile was gentle but there was steely determination behind the words. The parish priest, Fr Hourihan had made himself scarce, deciding, quite sensibly, to leave the formidable Miss Sheehan to the young curate.

She really was something else, Carmel mused, so glad to be in Aashna and not back there. The months since she left Ireland had given her some perspective, and each time she told Sharif a story about her ex-sister-in-law, he was incredulous that she could be so manipulative and bossy, and even more disbelieving that the Carmel he had come to know just accepted it.

She tried to explain to him how when you're brought up in care, being told what to do and being expected to obey without question was so deeply ingrained she never really thought about it. She didn't like Julia, certainly, but the idea of standing up to her was alien. At least it used to be. She had recently been to see a solicitor who had begun the divorce proceedings but she had yet to hear anything back, either from him or from Bill. Thoughts of confrontation caused her to worry but she tried to face the anxiety and tell herself that she would deal with it when she had to, and on top of that, it would be with Sharif and now Joe on her side.

Her reverie was interrupted by her phone beeping. A text from Joe. 'Hi, C, how's things today? Had a dream about you last night, where you were singing on stage in a pub in Wicklow?! Mad, eh? Going to Jennifer's for dinner tonight, so am going to tell her about you. Is that okay? x'

She had met him for lunch the day after the big chat and it had been easy and fun. She told him that her head was in a spin and asked if he'd mind just getting to know her and she him before making any big decisions. He was happy to do it and they ended up drinking a bottle of wine and having a really good laugh. He was charming and funny and she liked him a lot. Since he went back, he'd been texting and she texted back, chatty newsy texts.

'Sure, if you like. I'd like to meet her sometime, she sounds lovely.'

She paused and thought for a second, before adding an x and a ☐. Sharif was gently teasing her about it being like a romance, texting and getting to know each other, but in some ways, he was right. She was nervous of what she said in texts even though she talked so easily to him when they were together. She had never put a kiss on a text to Joe before, though, much to Sharif's amusement, her texts to him were littered with emoticons.

The more time went on, the more she felt like Joe was her real dad. He certainly behaved as if he were, telling her to be careful walking at night, or telling her to ask Sharif to examine her when she had a cough. She was fine, but it felt so strange, in a nice way, to have someone care so much. One night, he rang and she noticed he sounded breathless.

'Are you okay? You sound a bit wheezy?'

'Ah, yeah, I've a touch of asthma, I've had it all my life. I'll take a puff of the inhaler now in a second and I'll be grand again.'

She didn't tell him that she had asthma as well. Sharif said Dolly didn't, so she wondered if she got it from him.

She put her phone back in her pocket and realized she should be getting going. She and Sharif were leaving for the South of France tomorrow for a whole week and she couldn't wait for the holiday. They'd chosen accommodations together off the internet, and Carmel nearly had a fit when she realized the price of the villa with private pool, but Sharif insisted.

'Carmel, okay, I see this is a conversation we need to have.' He looked so serious. 'We are going to get married, yes?'

'Yes, I really hope so, unless you come to your senses,' she tried to joke.

'Firstly, stop that talk, I don't want to hear it anymore, about how you are getting such a catch in me and I'm somehow slumming it, that is ridiculous and not true. We love each other and that's all there is to it. And, on that note, we are an equal team, from now on, we share everything, emotionally, practically, and financially.'

She was about to interrupt when he held up his hand, pleading for her silence.

'So, you should know this. I have worked very hard for almost twenty years to build this place up. I didn't take holidays and every spare penny was ploughed back in here, but now, and for the past few years, that hasn't been necessary. Therefore, I have a lot of money; I can show you the bank statements if you want to know specifics, so please, let's just spend it. That is what it's for. I didn't over the years, not because I was saving or anything, but because I was so busy I never had time. But now, I have you and I can't tell you how happy that makes me. We are equal. We share everything because I can't be in a relationship with someone who thinks they are inferior to me in any way. Is that okay?' He put his head to one side and looked deeply into her eyes. His silver hair was swept back from his forehead and his liquid, almost black eyes searched hers, and she knew he was being totally honest.

'But I can't just swan in here and take your money, you worked for that, not me.' She was trying to be reasonable.

'Oh, my God, woman! Sometimes, you're just infuriating! Why can't you just accept it? I've spent years avoiding gold digging women who pretended to like me just because I am wealthy, and when I do find someone special, she won't even take my money.'

His frustration caused her to get a fit of giggles and they ended up kissing passionately.

He had given her a credit card and a debit card for his account but she preferred to use her own money. It drove him crazy but she would never again be beholden to anyone, even Sharif if she could help it.

She got up and stretched. She would have been far too self-conscious to rest with her eyes closed in public or to stretch herself like a cat before she came here, but here in Aashna, it was the sort of thing people did. As she slipped her feet back into her sandals, she spotted Zane in animated chat on his phone on the other side of the garden. She'd have to have someone keep a very close eye on him if he was organizing an engagement party while they were away. She just knew he would use their absence to recreate an unholy alliance of Strictly Come Dancing meets Cirque du Soleil.

'Hi, Carmel,' she was interrupted from her thoughts by Oscar, the yoga teacher, walking barefoot across the grass, Birkenstocks in hand.

'I hear congratulations are in order? Delighted for you both.' His smile was warm and genuine and not for the first time Carmel felt overwhelming gratitude for the life she now lived.

'Yes, I'm still in shock, to be honest, but yes it seems like we are doing it.' She chuckled, fizzing inside at the thought of marrying Sharif.

'Well, good on you both, you deserve to be happy. I'd better move on, I've a class in the Kaivalya in ten minutes.' He gave her a wave and wandered off. She longed for his inner peace, he always seemed so serene and chilled out. He was a fascinating man and she always enjoyed talking to him, and sometimes if she had time, he taught her a few stretches so she was building up her sun salutes and downward dog pose. The first time she tried it out at home, Sharif came home unexpectedly and she jumped up, flustered and embarrassed, but when he joined in for a few minutes, all her worries disappeared. Her reactions to things were still pre-Sharif as she called it, but she was learning. He wasn't Bill, and she was a grown adult who could make her own decisions. She repeated the mantra often in her head and gradually, in infinitesimally slow steps, she was starting to believe it.

For once, Sharif was home before her and had made a salad and mixed an omelette, which he put in the pan when she arrived. She loved that he could cook and that he seemed to enjoy it. Coming from a life with such clearly defined gender roles, it was a revelation to meet a man who cooked and ironed his own shirts.

They ate and chatted about their upcoming trip. Just as they were clearing up, his phone beeped. She handed it to him and saw a shadow cross his face as he read the text. It wasn't any of the patients; the staff always used his beeper to contact him if he was needed.

'Everything okay?' she asked, trying not to sound nosey.

'Oh...er...yeah, fine.' His smile recovered instantly, but something had bothered him.

'Are you sure?' Carmel looked concerned; she thought he'd been a little preoccupied in recent days.

'Yes, it's probably nothing, but you know Mrs Johnson? She's in the early phases of dementia, as well as having stage three Adeno-carcinoma.'

Noting her look of confusion, he added, 'Lung cancer. Well, her son pulled me aside a few days ago, saying he wasn't happy with the care she was getting, and that I wasn't giving her the appropriate medical treatment and all of this. I told him that the care plan had been coordinated not just by me, though I led it, but had input from a variety of health professionals and that his mother was getting the best possible treatment for her condition. He left it go then but I don't know, there's something about him I just don't trust. Mrs Johnson, when she's lucid, doesn't seem happy with him either, and the staff in the restaurant were saying he was complaining, claiming he'd found a hair in his food… I don't know, he just seems to be a bit of a trouble-maker. I've known her for years, but he's new to me. I don't think I ever even heard her talk about her son but he's turned up out of the blue and seems to be determined to cause trouble. Marlena just texted me to say he'd been up to reception to say his mother's room was freezing cold and that she was shivering in the bed. That just couldn't be, but she sent someone from maintenance to check it out. The whole building is on a thermostat and everywhere is fine. I don't know why he's so determined to find fault…'

Carmel felt a surge of protectiveness for Sharif but also for Aashna House. 'God, he sounds awful. I think I know him, kind of rough looking? And his mum is lovely, a really gentle person. Maybe he resents her money being used to pay for her treatment; he sounds like the kind of person who'd be happy to dump her in a state nursing home and let the taxpayer pick up the bill.'

'Well, she was a cleaner here in the hospice when I first started up. She was such a help to me, in the early days when I didn't have too many staff, she'd not just clean but she'd feed patients, or push them around the garden in their wheelchairs. She was invaluable and she always used to say how lovely it would be to end your days someplace like here. When she got the diagnosis, she was a chain smoker so it wasn't a surprise really, she came to me and asked if she could come here. Of course, I said she could and so she moved in. Not a mention of this Derek. I know her husband died when she was a young woman, long before I met her. So, this guy just shows up, he lives in Hammersmith someplace but suddenly he's the caring son? She's been here over a year at this stage, and he's only turned up in the last few weeks. I'm not convinced.'

'Well, you know what they say, where there's a will, there's relatives.'

'That's true, I've seen plenty of greed here over the years but this guy, I don't know, there's something dangerous about him. Also, she doesn't have a bean, so I just can't figure out what he's after. I like his mother a lot, though, and she said she wanted to be treated here and so treat her we will. I just wish he wasn't part of the equation.'

Sharif was normally so unflappable, it was unusual to see him so perturbed.

'I know, but we don't get to pick who comes through the doors, nor do we get to choose their relatives, unfortunately. I know you're worried, but the others are well able to handle anyone with a problem, Dr Alexander will be here as well as the junior team, and Nadia is going to move in here for the week, just to be extra safe, so let's just enjoy our holiday and try not to think about this place. Johnson has no grounds for complaint; it's not like we're doing anything wrong. His mother, like everyone else here, gets the very best of care, and the staff are aware of him now, so try to put him out of your mind, okay? Your mum told me the last holiday you took was actually to go to a medical conference in Madrid eleven years ago! And, well, I've never had a holiday in my life, so let's just go and relax and have some fun together.'

'Fun? What sort of fun did you have in mind?' he grinned, drawing her close to him.

'Oh, you know, Monopoly, Scrabble, that sort of thing...' she winked and he lowered his head to kiss her.

The holiday was wonderful. They wandered hand in hand around the old city of Saint Emilion, popping in and out of little caves selling local wines, cheeses, and foie gras. Carmel loved it all, though she drew the line at the foie gras once she learned how it was made. They marveled at the vast cathedral carved out of rock rather than built from the ground up, they bought baguettes and had picnics on the secluded lawn of their villa. Sharif taught Carmel how to swim in the pool, her first time ever being in water other than a bath. He stopped asking her how it was that she had never been to a beach or a swimming pool or even a cinema because he hated to see the look of shame in her eyes. She tried not to be too wide-eyed and astounded at everything but it was so hard. She never imagined the world was actually like this, so beautiful and warm and welcoming. She realized, living as she had through all the years of her marriage through Facebook, that her world view was kind of distorted. She imagined all conversations to be political in nature, and people to be much more aggressive than they actually were.

She and Sharif sat outside cafés, the sun brightening everything it touched, delighting at the simple beauty of it all. Each day for lunch they'd investigate the mystery of the plat du jour. She deliberately never asked what it was and was determined to try as many things as she could. She ended up trying escargot, deliciously swimming in their parsley butter, moules served in a large silver bucket and cooked in shallots and white wine, all mopped up with crusty baguettes; confit de canard that just fell off the bone and melted in the mouth with the most delicious chips she'd ever tasted. She was sure she must have gained ten pounds and marvelled at the slim French women. How did they live here and stay so slender, she wondered, as she and Sharif tucked into the buttery croissants and pain au raisin for breakfast each morning. The little kids blathering away in French fascinated her; she expected the adults to speak the magically romantic sounding language, but the children just blew her away.

She and Sharif never tired of each other's company as they told stories of their respective childhoods and lives up to the time they met. They talked about Dolly, Nadia, Joe, and the whole situation and she never felt as if she was boring him or droning on. To her utter amazement, he found her a constant source of delight and would often laugh out loud at something she said or stop her mid-sentence to kiss her. She never imagined happiness like this existed.

'So, the wedding? What do you want to do?' He was pouring her a glass of Sancerre on the terrace of the villa after they'd strolled home, having had yet another delicious dinner.

'What do you mean, what do I want? To get married as soon as I can…though I'll have to go on a diet at this rate or I won't get a dress to fit me after all this food.' She patted her still flat belly.

'You have a delicious figure, and anyway, I don't care about that. Those emaciated models never did anything for me, give me a real woman any day with curves. I've never understood those androgynous females, skin and bone, and I've never met a man who finds them attractive. No, I meant, do you want to get married in the UK or Ireland or abroad or where?'

She thought fleetingly of the sad little ceremony seventeen years earlier in the church down the road from Trinity House where she married Bill.

'Not Ireland anyway, that's for sure. I don't know, what would you like?'

Sharif thought for a moment, 'Well, weddings are generally a bride's domain, especially in my culture, so I haven't thought much about it, but I think I'd like something small, maybe at Aashna? And if it was nice weather, maybe the reception in the grounds. We could have a marquee for the food or something, and set up a bar and a dance floor and all of that… is that like something you'd like? Or would you prefer something else?'

'That sounds gorgeous. But there is the business of the divorce first. I know in Ireland it takes years, like you have to be separated for four of the previous five years, I checked it out online.'

'But in the UK, it's nothing like that. You just apply and the court grants it, simple as that. In terms of the marriage being an Irish one, well, that doesn't matter as far as I understand it. You can divorce Bill from here, and get married here because under British law you are divorced.'

'It's so strange I haven't heard from them. I mean, he must have gotten the letter the solicitor sent by now, he posted it six weeks ago, and because of that, he'll know where I am, he had to put the address on the letter, and I've not heard anything. I know he didn't care for me, but he'd surely want to speak to me or even Julia would, don't get me wrong, I'd dread to get a letter from either of them, but even so, it's weird, don't you think?'

Sharif sighed and sat down opposite her, giving her the glass of wine and holding her other hand.

'To be honest, I find the entire relationship weird. The idea that a red-blooded man would have you beside him in bed every night for seventeen years and he never laid a finger on you. I just don't get it, we're simple creatures, carnal, and either his restraint is remarkable or there is something deeply wrong with that man. I suspect the latter. And as for that witchy sister of his, I mean, what on earth is that all about? She was horrible to you because she wanted to be some kind of pseudo wife to her own brother...as I said, the entire thing is a mystery to me.'

Carmel smiled. Sharif had a few glasses of wine with dinner, so he was a little more candid than normal. Generally, he just remained silent on the subject of Bill and her years with him.

'I just hope he agrees and just lets the divorce go through. Every time there was a referendum in Ireland on the subject, and there were three, it was the church that came out most strongly against it. It was only finally allowed in 1995 but the rules are still fairly draconian. Bill and Julia are pillars of the community and of the church, and even though people in Ireland have been getting divorced for over a decade now, in certain sections of society, there is still a stigma. Bill and Julia would be part of those sections.'

'So better to stay miserable than be free to find happiness elsewhere? Seems mad to me.'

'More or less, yes. What God has joined together and all of that.'

She took a sip of her wine, it was delicious. The scent of the lavender that ringed the garden was being released by the evening sun and Sharif was captured in a beautiful buttery light.

'You look like an angel.' She held up her hand to shield her eyes from the setting sun. 'Maybe you are, a gorgeous, sexy angel sent to me by my mother. Sometimes, I really think that, like, I know I never met her, but in Aashna and when I'm with you and Nadia and even Joe, I feel her, and I sense that she's with me. Do you believe in all of that?'

'I do, I suppose. I was reared a cultural Muslim, though not a very devout one, but like you with Catholicism, I have more or less walked away from it. The faith itself is not the problem, in fact, it has some good advice about how to live, just as the Bible does, but I want no part of what it means in the modern world. Religion only divides people in my view, and something I have observed in all my years in oncology and palliative care, no matter who we are, men or women, black or white, old, young, rich, poor, Christian, Hindu, Muslim, atheist, whatever, we all are born the same way and we all die the same way. We all want to be happy, to be loved, for our families and friends to be safe and well. Our bodies may look different on the outside but we all have the same internal organs, we are all the same.

'As for the idea of angels and spirits and all of that, absolutely. If you have seen as many people die as I have, you couldn't think otherwise. Something often happens in the last moments, a peacefulness, a joy, the pain just seems to go, and the person is at peace. They are moving on, to where or what I don't know, but this is not the end. You saw it with Brian, but I've seen that same thing, many, many times, with people from all sorts of backgrounds.'

'Do you think Dolly sent you to me?'

'I don't honestly know. What I do know is she wanted so desperately to find you. And I know that she loved me. It does seem strange that in all the times she went over there and searched, she got nowhere and then that I would find you in a Facebook group. I'm not even on Facebook; there's an Aashna page but someone else manages it, but when Wayne Dyer came to speak here, it generated huge interest and he was such a large presence on social media, it was interesting to see people's reactions. I do believe the dead are not gone, their energy, the essence of a person continues on in some form, but whether or not they can influence things in this world is the great unknown.

So, to answer your question, I couldn't be sure, and I am first and foremost a clinician, so I'd probably be drummed out of the Medical Council for saying so, but possibly, she did, yes.'

'Now, on that note, Joe and the DNA test. I don't mind, obviously, it's your decision but have you come to any conclusions about what you want to do?'

Carmel sighed. She had thought so much about it but she was no closer to a resolution.

'I don't know, Sharif, honest to God, I have no idea what's for the best. He is wonderful, and I feel a real connection to him, you know he told me the other day on the phone that he has asthma? Immediately, I was happy, not that he has it, but that I might have got it from him, you said Dolly didn't have it. But then, maybe his father had it and that's where it comes from. I don't know, Sharif, it's all such a muddle. I want him to be my dad, but if he's not, then all of that is fake, isn't it? I don't mean he's a fake but I mean, what's the point? I'm forty years old, I don't need a dad now, so it's not like he can be a surrogate dad, like it would be different if I was a kid, am I making sense?'

'Yes and no. I understand that you want him to be your father, and you feel like if he was then you could build up a loving relationship with him, so you are afraid to do the test in case the alternative is the case and it is his father who is your biological father. But have you thought of this? I'm not advocating any position, just a thought, but Joe feels like he is your father, he's told you so, and you feel that he is,

177

or maybe you wish it to be the case, so why not leave it at that? What good would finding out do?

'I know people always say truth is the best way forward, people should know the truth, and so on, but I'm not too sure about that. I'll tell you something that nobody knows. When my parents were young, and I was just a child, my father had an affair. He told me when he was dying, he needed to confess to someone, I think. And when I asked him if my mother ever knew, he said he didn't tell her because it would only have hurt her. He loved her deeply, always did, but he was foolishly flattered by another woman's attentions and so he was unfaithful. It was over in a matter of weeks and it meant nothing to him. He explained to me that his punishment for himself was to bear the burden of the guilt on his own, to spare my mother the pain of his betrayal. Of course, I was furious at first and accused him of not telling the truth to protect himself, not me or my mother, and I stormed out. But then, I spoke to Dolly. She was like the grave if you confided in her; you could guarantee her silence.

She said to me, "Sharif, the truth is overrated. It usually hurts, and more often than not does no bloody good at all, sometimes the best way to love someone is to protect them from the truth. Your father is very sorry for the mistake he made, he regrets it and he never did it again. Your mother loves him and you and the life you've all had together all these years. Breaking that up over something so inconsequential as a brief affair with someone he didn't love would be to make you and Nadia pay for a crime you didn't commit. He chose to bear the guilt himself and spare both of you, you should be thanking him, not angry at him."

And after a while, I calmed down and realized she was right. It would have broken our family; my mother is a proud woman, she could never have taken him back, and then what would her life, and my life have been like? My father worked so hard for me to go to university, and every penny he earned was for us. He never bought things for himself, he had the same car for fifteen years, but he would spare no expense when it came to my mother or me. He was a good man.' Carmel heard the catch in Sharif's voice and knew how private he was, so the fact that he confided something like that in her, made her feel so loved and trusted.

'He did the right thing. Your mum talks so fondly of him, and it's clear she adored him.'

'She did, we all did. Dolly too. He was so good to us all, and he carried that his whole life. That whole experience has made me rethink the value of the truth.' Carmel got up and went to sit on his lap, her arms around him as he rested his head on her breast. Together, they sat in the silence of a fragrant French evening.

CHAPTER 22

*T*he holiday really refreshed them both and brought them even closer. Sharif talked about Jamilla, and how losing her was the worst thing that had ever happened to him. Carmel just listened and, even though she knew Sharif had once loved Jamilla so much, she didn't feel the confusion and hurt she felt about Bill and Gretta. Probably because Sharif was so anxious to point out that she was dead and they were living. They owed it to her, and to Dolly, to live the best life they could.

Two days after they returned, they were having breakfast before work.

'I was thinking of inviting Joe and maybe his kids over for the engagement party, what do you think?'

'Sure, good idea. He's told them about you, so I'm sure they're curious; I know I would be.' Sharif was talking to her but reading something on his phone at the same time.

'Yes, well, he said they were okay about it but...' she stopped. 'Sharif, what's the matter? You seem worried.'

'Oh, I just asked Marlena to keep a log of all the complaints coming in from this Derek Johnson, and she's just emailed it to me. Claims that his mother wasn't given her medicine at the right time, the room is too cold, the food is making her sicker, staff are rude, the physio is too rough, and he said he didn't want Ivanka working with her anymore, something about her swearing at his mother! He mentioned something to her about malpractice, he actually used that word. This is outrageous; I can't have this any longer, I'm going to speak to him today. If he is not happy with the service we provide, then maybe he…oh, I don't know…Mrs Johnson wants to be here, and she expressly asked me, and he's her next of kin, and now her dementia is advancing and there doesn't appear to be any other family. This is such a mess. I just have a feeling he's building up to something.'

'Like what? I mean, he can't do anything to hurt you, can he?'

'Well, a malpractice suit is every physician's worst nightmare. It's damaging beyond repair, even if it's totally groundless; it can drag on and on in court and the patients' advocacy groups are very resourceful if they take up someone's cause. Even a complete lie could close us down.'

She'd never seen him so solemn. Surely, that can't be true? Sharif was a wonderful doctor and Aashna House was such a special place, surely one malicious person couldn't tear down all he'd built just out of spite.

'But why would he want to, even if it was possible?' Carmel couldn't understand such viciousness.

'Well the deal is that if people want to come here, the state funds it partially, but in return, their pension and whatever income they might have is taken into consideration. The state means tests people, and then based on what they can contribute themselves, they make up only the difference. If he had his way, he'd probably take her home, say he'd care for her, which he wouldn't be able to do even if he wanted to, but he would then inherit the house and whatever bit of money she has. You'd be amazed at how many children of elderly sick parents are against them coming here, not because the offspring themselves have to pay, but because they see it as eating into their inheritance.'

'Oh, what a nasty piece of work. How could he do that to his own mother?'

'Easily. He sees her death as a windfall day for him, and he wants to make sure he gets the maximum amount possible. By complaining that everything is wrong here, that I'm being negligent or unprofessional or whatever, he has grounds to remove her from our care. Poor Mrs Johnson is not lucid most of the time now, so she's easily manipulated. That's a very sad element of this, but worse, there's the threat of him reporting me as an incompetent physician, and that would be a disaster.'

'Don't you have insurance against that? And, as you say, Mrs Johnson's needs are complex and there's no way he'd be able to take care of her properly.'

'Yes, but the problem is the process takes so long, people believe in the no smoke without fire theory, even if the accusation is totally false, the damage done to reputation is irreparable. Even one malpractice case has been known to close down so many healthcare professionals. As for him taking care of her, well, I dread to think. She would be in terrible pain if it's not managed, and she's not lucid most of the time, so she wouldn't even be able to complain or get help.'

Carmel was trying to think. It was an area about which she knew nothing but she desperately wanted to help Sharif.

'Perhaps you talking to him isn't the best idea. You know, it might end up being used against you, especially if you get cross or whatever. Why don't I have a go, you know, casually, I could be popping into Mrs Johnson and I'll try to strike up a conversation, see if I can't get some information out of him? I promise I won't make the situation worse, if I can't get him to open up, then fine, we try another way, but it might be worth a shot? It could be that he's just an old loudmouth, looking for something to moan about, but he won't go any further.'

Sharif thought for a moment. 'Maybe you're right, I hope you are, but just be careful. He's very aggressive and if this does go to court afterwards, and it emerges, as it's bound to, that you and I are in a relationship, then it could be misconstrued. In the meantime, I'm going to call my solicitor to get his take on it. See if there isn't something to be done before this Derek Johnson does anything worse.'

Carmel hated to see Sharif threatened in this way. He was such a good man, and such a conscientious doctor, the idea that someone could just come along and tell a bunch of lies and threaten everything he worked so hard to create seemed so very unfair. She made it her business to pop into Mrs Johnson several times during the day, but of her son, there was no sign.

The day flew by, just like all the others.

Eventually, she spotted Derek Johnson leaving the hospice and getting into a very old car. Carmel approached him as he was throwing an Aashna House plastic bag, which probably contained Mrs Johnson's clothes for washing, into the back. Carmel noticed several other bags like it littering the back seat. There was a laundry service, but in general, patients' families were encouraged to do the patient's laundry at home, and most people did. Clearly, this Johnson was taking the dirty clothes, but not doing much else with them. The entire floor of the car was covered in junk food wrappers and beer cans.

'Hi, Mr Johnson, I'm Carmel, I work here. I was wondering how your mum was today?'

He looked warily at her.

'What's it to you? You're not a nurse or a doctor.' Carmel tried to ignore the rudeness in his tone and the dismissive attitude. Not only was he an odious personality, but he was a physically repulsive specimen as well. His grubby Guns N' Roses T-shirt didn't quite cover his voluminous beer belly and his trousers were shiny with wear and, she suspected, dirt. He badly needed a haircut, greasy curls almost reaching his shoulders, and he was unshaven. He smelled fairly pungent as well, but Carmel was determined to be pleasant and to keep the conversation light.

'No, no, I'm not, but I organize the events here.' She nailed a smile on her face.

'Look, my mother ain't goin' to be goin' to any events. She's nearly dead, thanks to this excuse for a hospital.' He opened the car door and got in.

'Well, perhaps if you and I had a chat, maybe we could address some of the issues you appear to be having?' Carmel knew she was grasping at straws, but she was trying to get something she could take back to Sharif.

'You're having a laugh, right? I ain't got nuffin to say to you or to that Paki what owns this place. Why don't you lot all bugger off back where you came from, eh?' He slammed the door and drove away, the car backfiring and emitting bilious black smoke.

Carmel stood in the car park, stunned.

'Carmel! You okay?' Zane ran across the car park. 'I saw him talking to you, was he having a go?'

Carmel relayed the conversation to him, incredulous that someone could be that horrible.

'Oh, welcome to my world, darlin'. It happens. Most people are nice, glad to live in a multi-cultural society, but there's always a few, and he's one. Don't give him the time of day, he's horrible to everyone, it's not personal.' He grinned and gave her a peck on the cheek. 'He called me the N word the other day.'

'He didn't!' Carmel was shocked.

'Water off a duck's back. Have you seen the state of him? And the smell off of him? He's mingin'. I don't rent out space in my head to people like him. Now, it's knocking off time. A post work drink to settle our nerves after all of this?' He winked at her and flashed her one of his irresistible grins.

She had been going to tell Sharif of the exchange but she decided to leave it. She hadn't found anything out apart from the fact that Johnson was a racist ignorant pig. Anyway, he was at a multidisciplinary conference with the team to discuss some patients with very multifaceted needs, so he wouldn't be home for another two hours at least. She might as well go and try to forget about Johnson.

'Sure, will we text Ivanka?'

'She and Ivy are already there; it's been one of those days.' He threw his eyes heavenward dramatically and linked her arm as they walked to the pub.

The school production was almost ready and excitement was at an all-time high. The set looked fantastic and was being painted and sanded by several of the patients, and even those who were too ill to participate were enjoying the buzz created by the kids around the clinic. Daf was thrilled and she had the children make a huge card, full of drawings and messages for everyone at Aashna, where it proudly took up most of one wall of the Kaivalya.

Carmel had a few things to organize for next week's cookery course, so she needed the calm of her office. Sai, the chef, was Indian and his cuisine was legendary, so he was giving five half-hour cookery demonstrations and the patients were looking forward to it. Though it was unlikely any of them would be using their new skills again, Sai was a character and he made everyone laugh. The Derek Johnson situation was never far from her mind, but there was nothing she could do about that, so she was just doing everything she could to remove any other responsibilities from Sharif's shoulders.

Oscar waved as she passed the sun-filled yoga studio. It was one of her favourite rooms, with bleached pine floorboards, polished and varnished to a shine, and one full wall of glass that overlooked the gardens. There were comfortable chairs around the walls, and a beautiful grand piano in one corner, but the main floor area was clear. There were all sorts of activities in there from meditation to tai chi, ballroom dancing to yoga.

'Hi, Oscar, how's it going?' she popped her head round the door.

'Hi, Carmel, all good, thanks. How about you?' Oscar had a way of asking how you were that made you feel like he really wanted to know.

'Fine,' Sharif had spoken to a few of the staff about the situation with Johnson but she wasn't sure who. She suspected he'd probably told Oscar but she didn't want to say anything just in case.

'I hope you're going to make the engagement party on Friday? Zane, Ivanka, and now Ivy have taken over the organization, so I'm in the horrors about what they've planned. They are so enthusiastic, I need someone calm by my side.'

'I certainly am, wouldn't miss it. I'll have to go home after the strippers, though...' He laughed out loud at the look of dismay on Carmel's face. 'Oh, I fear I've said too much.'

'Tell me you're joking, honestly, with Zane anything is possible.' The closer the party was getting the more stressed she became. Joe was coming with his two kids and that terrified her. He said that they were fine about everything, but she didn't know what he'd told them. She had tried to pluck up the courage to ring him but she baulked each time she was halfway through punching in the number. She knew she was being stupid, but texting, she could handle, conversations, either on the phone or in person, about everything, stuff she hadn't even processed herself yet, were just too much. Then there was the thought of being the centre of attention; Zane even said she'd have to make a speech, which actually made her feel nauseous. Sharif knew how she felt and offered to call it all off, but she said she'd feel even more ridiculous and anyway, everyone was looking forward to it. Everyone except her. Oscar, realizing she was upset, led her to a sofa at one end of the studio and sat her down.

'Hey, are you okay? You look a bit stressed. Don't worry, Carmel, it's just a party. A bunch of people who like you and Sharif very much, and are happy to see how much you mean to each other. It's going to be fun. Ignore Zane, he's just winding you up, you know what he's like. There are no strippers or speeches or anything, I promise you; Sharif has spoken to them and said it's to be kept low-key and not too many people. Ivy and Ivanka will curb the heights of Zane's enthusiasm, and even if they don't, the rest of us will. Okay?'

Carmel shut her eyes and took a deep breath. She needed to centre herself, to find her inner calm.

'Okay.' She gave Oscar a watery smile. 'I know he means well, and he's been such a great friend to me since I got here, you all have. I never had a bunch of friends before, that sounds mad, I know, but where I grew up it wasn't encouraged and then afterwards, well, it was a kind of empty life, so I'm just not used to this, and I'm a bit socially pathetic, to be honest.'

Oscar walked over to the grand piano, took a mirror off of it, and walked back to her, handing it to her.

'Look.' His voice was gentle.

'At what?' Carmel was confused.

'Look and tell me what you see.'

'Myself, I see my face.'

'Who are you, Carmel?'

She looked up into his kind face as the silence hung between them.

'I have no idea,' she whispered softly.

'Well, isn't it about time that you found out? What the world sees is a kind, funny, beautiful woman, who has come here, to this place, the place that the mother you never knew loved, to be with a very special man. We all like you, Carmel, and nobody thinks of you the way you seem to think of yourself. My wish for you is to see that, to see when you look in the mirror what the rest of us see, what Sharif sees. Anyone who cares for him knows how he has dedicated his entire life to this place, it's not just a hospice, you've seen it with your own eyes, it's something much more enriching and fulfilling than just some place people go to die. People find their life's purpose here, often at the very closing of their lives, and they die with dignity and peace. Sharif created that. He doesn't care a jot for wealth or flashiness, you know that about him, he could be a millionaire but he allows so many people in here free of charge, but never mentions it. Sharif sees goodness, kindness, fun, humility, humanity in you, Carmel, and so do we. Nobody here judges you because of your background, the only one doing that is yourself.'

Such kindness and friendship should have made her feel better but she didn't. What on earth was wrong with her? She had a life now, one she could never have dreamed of, and here she was being a big baby over everything. She was so angry with herself, berating herself and wishing she could be the woman Sharif deserved.

'I'm sorry, Oscar,' she scrubbed her eyes roughly. 'I'm just being stupid. Ignore me.'

'You're not being stupid. You are feeling a bit worried about a big event coming up and you're talking it out with a friend. We all need that, Carmel, me, Sharif, Zane, everyone. Nobody is as composed as what we present to the world, and what happens in childhood matters. Sometimes, in order to make sense of things we can't comprehend, we pack away beliefs about ourselves, maybe not the healthiest beliefs either, when we're kids. Then we just live our lives accepting these beliefs as truth, when, in fact, they're not. We sometimes need, as adults, to take these deep-rooted beliefs out and examine them, check if they are actually true.'

'Maybe you're right. It's just there's a lot going on at the moment.'

'Isn't there always? Anyway, if you ever want to talk, you know where I am.'

'Thanks, I really mean it, thank you.' She looked at his kind face and wondered, 'Have you got kids, Oscar?'

He grinned, 'Yes, three. Twin girls from my first marriage, Ellie and Daniella, and while I was a total nightmare, my ex was a trooper. Not only that, she never turned them against me, which she could so easily have done. I would have deserved it, but I have a great relationship with them. They stay with me at weekends and we try to co-parent as much as possible. They're thirteen now, so they can be challenging, but they are great and I adore them. And I also have a two-year-old son with my partner, Caroline, he's called Teddy and he's fabulous. How about you?'

'Me? No. My ex had two daughters, twins as well, actually, but they really missed their mother so they never took to me I'm afraid. They have an aunt they're close to, so I wasn't needed. Your kids are so lucky, having you as a dad; I bet they'll grow up really happy confident people.'

'I hope so. We are all doing our best to lay the foundations of that anyway. It's so important to build kids up in childhood; otherwise, life can be very hard. My mum was accused once of giving me and my brothers a superiority complex, and she explained that there was a very hard world out there only too willing to knock the confidence out of anyone, and so if the sense of self-worth wasn't built up at home, then what did you have to fight with? Of course, I was a total plonker, obsessing about money and deals and thinking I was so important, so maybe it backfired a bit, but I'm reconciled to that now. It took time though, Carmel, and a lot of self-examination to get to here. I don't know your background, apart from the bit you've told me about growing up in care and an unhappy marriage, but it sounds to me like you need some investment in yourself. See someone, talk to them, work this stuff out for yourself; we all deserve to be happy, Carmel, but it's something generated inside, the outside world can't provide it. Money, success, power, even other people can't make us truly happy, we need to find that in here.' He pointed at his chest and Carmel knew he was right.

'Thanks, Oscar.' She stood up and he drew her into a hug. Normally, physical contact like this with anyone except Sharif made her squirm; she never knew what she should do in return, but this time, she just relaxed. She'd been hugged more in the six months she'd been at Aashna, than in the forty years before that.

'I never got a hug, as a kid. Or as an adult, now that I think of it.' The words were out before she even realized it.

Oscar sighed but didn't let her go. 'The wonderful thing about this life we've been given, Carmel, is we can change it. We can reinvent ourselves as often as we want to. It's not easy, we need to let go of a lot of nonsense that hurt us in the past, but it can be done. If I can go from an arrogant city broker, obsessed with power and status and things, to the man I am today, then you can be a happy fulfilled woman who believes she is worthy of someone's love. Regret and guilt are two of the most pointless emotions. The past is over, it happened and nothing we can do will change it, but we can decide to not let it be our future. It's a long road ahead, but you can do it.'

189

The moment was interrupted by her phone ringing. It was Marlena on reception.

'Hi, Marlena.'

'Carmel, I'm so sorry about this but someone is here demanding to see you; I told her you'd call her if she left a number but she's most insistent. Can you come up?' Marlena, usually unflappable, sounded harassed.

'Sure. I'm on the way.'

'Thanks for the advice, Oscar, I'll do it. I better go, someone is looking for me. Marlena sounded a bit stressed, some of these sales people can be very pushy.'

'See you, Carmel, nice to chat.'

She hurried across the grounds towards the large glass reception area. It was beautiful inside, with tropical plants thriving in all the heat and sunshine captured by the glass-domed roof. She'd become accustomed to sales reps coming and trying to sell various products to Aashna House and she surprised herself at how forceful she could be in return when people were too pushy.

She went in the back and stopped dead in her tracks.

'Carmel. So, this is where you've been hiding.' Julia's words dripped icy disdain as she stood squarely in front of her.

'Julia…How…I wasn't expecting…' Carmel could hear the tremor in her voice.

Her sister-in-law looked at her as if she were a very slow five-year-old. 'You sent a letter, or at least some solicitor did? Or do you not recall the tiny matter of your husband and family in Ireland? Did you just expect us to pay up and walk away?'

Visitors and various staff members were milling around and Carmel really didn't want to have this conversation here, in public.

'Em right…can we go to my apartment…it's not far…to talk…' she was sweating and could feel the rivulets of perspiration running down her back.

'Yes. Let's go to *your apartment*, Carmel.' Julia's tone suggested the idea of Carmel having an apartment was highly suspect. Carmel didn't dare catch Marlena's eye as she quickly exited reception. Not a word passed between them as she walked towards the residences. Panic was rising up inside her.

'Don't be stupid,' she told herself as she almost sprinted back. 'She can't make you do anything, she can't force you to go back. You're a grown woman with her own right to live wherever you want...' However often she told herself that thought, she wished she could believe it.

It took three goes to get the key in the lock, but eventually, she managed it. She opened the door and Julia walked past her into the lounge. Carmel caught the look of surprise in Julia's eyes at the beauty of her home. The oatmeal sofas, the flat screen TV, the lovely rose-wood dining table, and the high-gloss fitted kitchen with French doors out to the courtyard were a far cry from the 1970s time-warp that was Bill's dreary farmhouse.

'Can...Can I get you a drink, tea?' Carmel knew she was coming across as pathetic but she couldn't help herself. She should throw her out, not be offering her tea.

'No. I don't want anything.' Julia spoke slowly, taking everything in.

Thank goodness, she'd put the framed photo taken in France of herself and Sharif in the bedroom. A couple they'd struck up a conversation with offered to take it, and it was a really nice one. Nadia had got it framed for them as an engagement gift. Carmel felt a knot of anxiety rise up like bile within her as Julia's eyes rested on the 'Congratulations! You're Engaged' cards on the shelves beside the TV.

'So, whose hospitality are you encroaching on now? This is clearly not your apartment, whatever you may want me to believe, and I doubt that any couple, recently engaged, wants you hanging around.'

Carmel knew she should say something, something to defend herself from Julia's scathing remarks, but she just couldn't. She busied herself with cups, despite the rude rebuff of her offer of a drink. Hands shaking, she dropped a mug from the countertop, where it smashed on the floor.

Julia's look said it all. Typical Carmel, can't do anything right.

'So, are you going to explain yourself, what you are trying to do over here in this Godforsaken place?'

If anywhere was Godforsaken, she wanted to yell, it was the miserable farmhouse on a lonely bit of a farm in Birr County Offaly. Aashna was beautiful, and even Julia could see that. For some reason, the insults about Aashna were more cutting than those directed at her.

Carmel brushed up the shards of mug in silence, her head down, and opened the bin.

'You seem to have your feet firmly under the table here anyway, however you've managed it. It's very sterile, though, no personality.' The suggestion was clear that Carmel was behaving deceitfully, hoodwinking some innocent with her imagined tale of woe.

After years of living with Gretta's knick-knacks and ornaments, Carmel loved the bare surfaced simplicity of the apartment. Sharif, too, was not a collector of things, his clothes, his washing things, and a few books were all he owned really. He loved his clothes, she found that so funny at the beginning, he had a style all his own, but whenever he bought something new, which he did often, he donated something else to the charity shop on the high street.

Julia's inquisitive and judgmental gaze stopped to rest on an Islamic painting hanging beside the French doors. Nadia brought it back from Karachi, from her parent's house when they died. When she gave it to Carmel, she explained that where she had placed it was the Qibla, the place where Muslims would pray in the house. She knew that Sharif wasn't religious, but they were delighted to accept the gift. When Nadia asked if she'd object to it being up in their living room, she had explained that people often had religious paintings or statues in their houses in Ireland as well, even if they weren't religious at all. Sometimes, they were family heirlooms or just a tradition. Sacred Heart pictures, crucifixes, images of the Virgin Mary were common in Irish homes and so she was happy to have this symbol of Sharif's culture in theirs. Besides, she loved the blue and white geometric designs, it was soothing to look at.

'It's from Pakistan,' she managed to say, as Julia's eyes rested on the picture.

'Really? It looks like something the children would do in school. Pakistan, you say, and what might one ask, would you know about Pakistan?'

This was it. She had to summon up the courage to tell her the truth.

'Sharif Khan, the doctor who runs this place, is from there.' She was disgusted at herself. Why couldn't she have said, Sharif, my fiancée, owns it, his mother gave it to us as a gift? Because she was pathetic, that's why.

'And does this man allow you to live here, in return for working in this hospital, or whatever it is?'

'Yes, I am the Events Manager here.'

'Pah!' Julia barked. 'You are in your eye, the manager of anything. Listen to me, Carmel Murphy, I know what you are, I've always known what you are, and you might have fooled these eejits over here, thinking you're all sweetness and light, but I know your game.'

'I don't know what you're talking about, I don't have a game...I don't want...' Carmel began.

'Oh, don't you now? Is that why you sent a solicitor's letter to my brother, demanding half of our family farm? Because you have no plans, is that it? You must think I'm a total simpleton.'

'I did not demand anything, I saw the letter myself, the solicitor was simply asking to start divorce proceedings, and so he wanted a valuation of the land and so on, it's standard practice...' Carmel wished she felt as confident as she sounded. She was nervous when the solicitor sent it, despite him explaining that this was perfectly routine.

'Standard practice! Listen to yourself, standard practice indeed. That is our family's land; it has been in the Sheehan family for four generations and you think a nobody like you, born out of dirty carnal sin, is going to take it away from us? Do you?' she spat.

'But, Julia, it's Bill's farm anyway, not yours. We've had this

conversation already. Bill and I will come to an arrangement...'
Carmel was trying to be reasonable.

'Bill will do no such thing! Not while I have breath in my body.
You tried to kill me once, I won't forget that; you're lucky I didn't go
to the guards but you caused enough drama I didn't want to add to
poor Bill's problems. That land was my mother's, my father only
married in, it is as much mine as it is Bill's and I won't stand by and
have our land carved up to pay off a gold-digging tramp.' She grabbed
Carmel's arm and squeezed.

'Julia, let me go...' Carmel's arm was really hurting; the woman
was surprisingly strong.

'Get your hands off her immediately!' Sharif ran into the apartment and Carmel shook her off and ran to his arms, knocking Julia
off her feet in the process. The situation would have been funny if
she wasn't so shaken. Julia fell backwards over the arm of the
couch and was looking most undignified, legs in the air, as she
tried unsuccessfully to right herself. She fumed as her skirt rode
up and her thick brown tights and beige corselette were on
display.

Sharif made no effort to help her up.

'I have no idea who on earth you are, but get off my property this
moment or I will call the police and have you arrested for assault.'
Carmel had never seen Sharif so angry. Fury glittered in his dark eyes
and his voice was cold as steel.

He kept his arms around Carmel, protecting her.

'And who do you think you are? You will do nothing of the kind.'
Julia was struggling to right herself. Eventually, she was upright, but
two red spots of fury glowed in her cheeks. She had been humiliated
and Carmel knew this wasn't going to be taken lightly.

'I was speaking to my brother's wife, and if you knew what she had done, then you'd not be so quick to defend her.'

'Oh, you must be the dreaded Julia. I am Dr Sharif Khan.' Carmel noted the look of shock on Julia's face that Sharif knew who she was.

'Oh, I'm sure she's made up plenty of lies about me and poor Bill to make you feel sorry for her and give her a job and a flat. She's good at that, taking advantage of people's generosity. But it is all just that, total lies, and if she thinks we're going to take this lying down, her sending solicitor's letters and threatening Bill, well then, she has another think coming. I'd say you should check who you have as a lodger, or as a cleaner, or whatever she is because little Carmel is not the sweet innocent she's pretending to be, I can tell you that.'

Sharif stared at Julia.

'Carmel, *my fiancée*,' he emphasized the word deliberately and watched the news penetrate Julia's self-righteous indignation, 'told me about you, and how you treated her. How you constantly criticised her, how you tried to dictate her every move. How you're so greedy you're determined to get that scrap of land and all this concern for Bill is a joke, you just have your eye on what you'd like to get when he dies. And she told me about Bill, treating her more as a slave than a wife. She has told me everything and I know she is telling the truth...'

'Oh, she has a right eejit made of you...' Julia was dismissive.

'Get out of our home.' Sharif was cut-glass icy.

'Your home, ha! That's a good one...shacked up with this...' She looked Sharif up and down, trying to think of a racist word to describe him.

Sharif moved so he was almost toe-to-toe with Julia. His six-foot frame towering over her tiny one.

'Go on, say it. I dare you to show your true colours. You are a twisted, bigoted, old harridan, but you can't hurt her anymore because she is free, free of both of you.'

Julia pointed her finger at Carmel, each word dripping hatred and vitriol. 'You'll come crawling back, madam, you mark my words, and you'll get the door slammed in your stupid, sponging face. He'll get sick of you when the novelty of a white woman in his bed wears off.

He'll get sick of you scrounging off him, and he'll see through you, just as everyone who ever knew you did…you better call off that solicitor and don't even consider seeking a divorce. That land is Sheehan land and it's staying Sheehan land, do you hear me?'

'That's enough!' Sharif shoved Julia towards the door. 'Get out, you venomous woman, and as for that brother of yours, tell him he is pathetic and that he will never hear from Carmel again. All dealings from now on are to be through our legal teams and, believe me, ours will be seeking just recompense for the years of unpaid slavery Carmel has done for your family. You can wave goodbye to that little farm and if you, or he, ever appear here again, I will have you arrested for trespassing, threatening behavior, and assault.'

Giving Julia a nudge in the back, he shut the door behind her.

Carmel tried to stay strong, but she dissolved into tears. 'I'm sorry, Sharif, I had no idea she was coming. I was hopeless…'

'Hush, my love, it's all okay. She's gone.' He wrapped his arms around her once more. 'They can't hurt you anymore, not really. I know they are awful but they have no power over you. You're a free agent, free to live where you choose, with whomever you choose. Now, did I go too far, threatening to take the farm? It's your business what you do; we don't need their money but what they did to you was wrong.'

'No, you were right. I'm not going to be bullied anymore. Let her stew. I don't want anything to do with the stupid farm but it's worth it to rattle that old crow. Sharif, I should have told her about us, but I just couldn't. I feel terrible, like I was denying you or something, but I wasn't, I just…'

'It's okay. She knows now anyway. Look, we've sent them packing and hopefully, that's the end of it. You weren't exaggerating when you described her. She even looks like the wicked witch in the fairy stories, all thin and pointy features and long greasy hair. She must have left her broomstick outside.' He grinned and was happy when she returned it. 'I know she freaked you out by just showing up, and if she ever does that again, just beep me and I'll come, but let's just put her behind us, okay? Marlena buzzed me, saying she looked a bit mad and you seemed shaken, I'm so glad she did. Bill and Julia are from another life, and they've no place in this one.'

'Okay.' She smiled weakly. 'I'm just going for a shower. I feel like I need to...I don't know... wash her off me or something.'

'Sure. I'm not going out again, so I'll cook something, shall I? And try not to picture Julia upended on our couch.' He gave her a grin and she smiled back. Maybe it really was going to be okay.

Over dinner, they discussed the party. She didn't tell him about the encounter with Johnson; there had been enough upset for one day.

As they tucked into Dhal Bhat, spicy lentils and chapattis, Carmel marveled at how her taste buds had changed. The first time Sharif made this dish, she thought she'd pass out it was so spicy, but over time, the flavours had grown on her and now she loved it. Irish food, while very tasty and flavoursome, didn't go big on spices.

'Well, this party is looking more like a gala event every time I over-hear something. I know you want it low-key, and believe me, it's considerably lower in key than what Zane had in mind first day. I don't care, I'm dying to show you off to as many people as possible. It's close to impossible to curb the enthusiasm of Zane I think, even Ivanka and Ivy are powerless in the face of his extreme party planning.'

Carmel sighed, 'I know. It's a waste of time talking to him; I'm imagining Moulin Rouge with me appearing half naked on a swing if he got his way! I was talking to Oscar about it today. Before Julia turned up. He calmed me down about it anyway. It's just a party, and they're just people we know who want to wish us well. Joe is coming and he's bringing Luke, Jennifer, and Jennifer's husband and their baby. I'm half looking forward to it and half dreading it, to be honest; he texted that he'd told them, but what he told them I've no idea. And what if they think, "Who the hell is she, bursting into our lives" or whatever?'

'Carmel, we've been over this. They're coming, that must mean they want to meet you, doesn't it?'

'Or kill me. Julia came too, and look how that went.' The ridiculousness of the entire situation made her laugh. Sharif joined in and within moments they were both laughing at the hilarity of her monosyllabic ex and his dreadful sister.

CHAPTER 23

'There. You look absolutely stunning.' Ivanka was delighted with her work and smiled as she was packing away her brushes, potions, and lotions. 'I'll leave you to get dressed, so we'll see you at the party.'

She'd insisted on doing Carmel's makeup. She really was talented, and when she finished, Carmel looked like a more polished and elegant version of herself. The creamy foundation made her skin look flawless. Her blue eyes were accentuated with smoky liner and gold and warm brown eye shadow, and much to Carmel's initial horror, she had plucked and shaped her eyebrows, darkening them slightly. The effect was amazing. Carmel had drawn the line at cherry red lipstick, opting instead for a coral shade, and the whole effect was, she had to admit, much better than she could ever have imagined. She'd spent the afternoon at the hairdresser's, having her blonde wavy hair done in an intricate up style, which swept the hair back from her face and twisted it loosely behind her head.

She looked warily at her dress once more. It seemed perfect in the shop, but now she wasn't so sure. It looked expensive, and it was. She'd never worn a silver dress in her life, and this one was clinging in all the right places, according to the sales lady, but Carmel feared it was too much. It was knee length but the skirt was split on one side, revealing some recently tanned leg. She pulled it on carefully, trying not to damage her hairstyle. She didn't look in the mirror until the whole look was complete. The sandals were silver as well, strappy and high, and would probably be excruciating after an hour or two, but she loved them.

When she was ready, she turned to face the slide robe floor-to-ceiling mirror. Even she had to admit she looked good. Not bad for a girl nobody wanted, she thought to herself. Sharif was going to be home any minute, his clothes were pressed and ready in the walk-in wardrobe. He was wearing a cream suit and an amethyst silk shirt. She'd bought him a lovely mauve handkerchief to complete the outfit. On anyone else, it might look a bit effeminate, but not on Sharif; he was tall and broad, muscular, and with no extra fat, and he looked exotic and beautiful when he dressed up. His silver hair contrasted so mesmerizingly with his dark skin, he sometimes took her breath away. Comparing him to Bill, sweaty and bulging out of his best suit, bought three decades ago, was impossible. Bill was like an old pig and Sharif like a sleek jaguar.

'Oh, wow! You look amazing. Oh, Carmel, I always thought you were beautiful but you take my breath away.'

She spun around to see him standing at the bedroom door; she had the radio on and didn't hear him come in.

'Is it okay? Not too...'

'Not too sexy, or too glamorous, or too drop dead gorgeous? Yes, you're all of those, and I'm going to be the proudest man on earth with you on my arm this evening. I'd kiss you but I'm afraid I'd smudge you...' He just stood and gazed for a moment before he walked past her and called from the *en suite*, as he stripped off to shower before dressing. 'By the way, the Kaivalya looks great. I stuck my head around the door as I came up; Zane has been there all day making sure it's all perfect. Fresh flowers, sparkly lights, everything. We've brought in extra care assistants to help the patients who want to come get ready, and the band is tuning up nicely. It's going to be a lovely party, really, don't worry about a thing.'

He stepped into the shower and began singing. She grinned. He really couldn't carry a tune in a bucket but she loved to hear him belting out Bruce Springsteen numbers, even if the words were the only way to recognize them by Sharif's off-key rendition.

Despite her jangling nerves, she was kind of looking forward to the evening. She'd never even had a birthday party in her life, so this being her first-ever party in her honour, it was going to be something to remember. She wondered if Joe was here already, and what his children, her possible brother and sister, would be like.

Twenty minutes later, they were walking hand in hand across the grounds. They could hear the music, and thankfully, it wasn't deafeningly loud or techno as Zane had suggested, but a great 1940s swing band. The catering was all in place and neither of them had had anything to do with the planning. Even if they wanted to, they wouldn't have been allowed to involve themselves in the logistics.

They entered and were immediately greeted by everyone in the room. Wheelchairs were pushed, so some of the older residents could shake Sharif's hand or give Carmel a kiss on the cheek. It took twenty minutes for the crowd to disperse and for them to get a drink. A smiling waitress offered them some champagne and they accepted gratefully just as the band leader announced,

'Well, ladies and gentlemen, it appears the guests of honour have arrived, and I know you'll all forgive me for deviating from the 1940's vibe for a moment to venture into this number, sing along everyone!'

The opening bars of Cliff Richard's 'Congratulations' gave everyone the courage to sing along, and soon every guest was singing as Carmel and Sharif danced together in the centre of the room. As she looked into his eyes, he mouthed, 'I love you,' and she kissed him, causing whoops and cheers from the gathered crowd. Sheila and Kate looked fabulous in matching outfits, and they had made a special bird table for their courtyard, with love birds carved on it for them as a wedding present. Tim was there, and Carmel was delighted to see him. Zane was in his element, accepting compliments on the fabulous party and flirting outrageously with a member of the band. The atmosphere was magical.

As the dance drew to a close, the crowd was calling, 'Speech, speech,' and Sharif took Carmel's hand as he approached the stage. The lead singer handed him the microphone but Sharif looked questioningly at Carmel. 'Ladies first?' he whispered. Carmel paled at the thought of addressing all those people, but her need to thank them all and to publicly proclaim her love for Sharif outweighed her terror.

'Okay,' she said, trying to control the fluttering in her stomach and the dryness in her mouth. She took the microphone and squeezed it tightly, hardly daring to look up at the sea of expectant faces.

'Em…I've never given a speech, so…em…forgive me if I make a mess of it but I…I just wanted to say thank you. To all of you here to celebrate with me and Sharif tonight. As most of you know, my birth mother, Dolly Mullane, lived here at Aashna House, and was great friends with Nadia, Sharif's mum, and indeed Sharif and his Dad as well, and somehow, through some strange twist of fate, I find myself here. Not alone that, but I have a life here, friends, a job, a home, and someone to love. I never had anything like that before. I want to say thank you from the bottom of my heart to Nadia for welcoming me like a daughter, to all of you, the patients and staff here at this very special place. To my great friends, Oscar, Ivy, Ivanka, and of course this party wouldn't even be happening, let alone be the amazing extravaganza it is, without Zane, someone both Sharif and I agree is such a vital cog in this machine. I also have to thank one more person. He promised my mother that he wouldn't stop looking for me, even after she died, and he didn't. Despite being so busy here, and all his other commitments, he made the time to find me, and he showed me that there was a way to be happy, and more importantly that I was deserving of that, that I should be happy. He brought me here, he mended my broken heart and puts up with all my crazy insecurities. He's made sure I'm not going to be a cuckoo anymore,' she looked up into his eyes. 'I love you, Sharif, and thank you for rescuing me.'

He hugged her and held her tight as the crowd clapped and cheered.

Then the band leader gave him the microphone.

'I don't really know how to follow that but I'll keep it short.

Dolly brought us together, she loved me and she loved Carmel, and as those of you who knew her know, she bore the pain of her daughter's loss every day of her life. But she was great 'craic' as she, and now my soon to be wife, say. I'm the luckiest man in the world to be marrying this funny, kind, clever, beautiful woman. I adore her, as you all know, and I can't wait to marry her. Thank you all for everything you have done for me over the years. Zane and the others have done a spectacular job, so eat up and drink up and enjoy yourselves.'

As they moved away from the stage, Carmel spotted Joe sitting at a table with two others. He smiled and waved at her as she approached them. Sharif got waylaid by some friends but she didn't mind, she wanted to meet them on her own anyway.

'Carmel, you look absolutely lovely, really smashing. I can't believe how much like Dolly you are, not that she was ever in such finery when I knew her.' Joe hugged her warmly, 'Now, this is Luke and that's Jennifer. Lads, this is Carmel.'

Carmel judged Luke to be in his early thirties, tall, thin, and kind of artsy looking. He was in frayed jeans and a grandfather shirt, over the collar of which curled his brown hair. He had an earring in one ear, a small silver hoop, and he stood up. He smelled of sandalwood as he gave her a huge bear hug.

'Carmel, it's great to meet you; Da is after telling us a bit about you and your background and that, but we're looking forward to getting to know you better.'

'Me too,' Carmel smiled, instantly relaxed with him. Was this guy her little brother? It was mind blowing if he was. She then turned to Jennifer, tall like her brother, with short dark hair in a pixie cut, and blue eyes. She too was dressed very casually, in a tunic and leggings, and her face was perfectly heart shaped and very pretty. She looked nothing like Joe or Luke; she must take after her mother, Carmel guessed.

'Hi, Carmel,' her voice, though unmistakably Dublin, was gentle. 'Thanks for asking us, it's a lovely party.'

'Thanks for coming, I...well...it means the world to me. Joe said

203

your husband and baby were coming as well?' She wondered where they were.

'Oh, yeah, Damien is staying at the hotel with Ruari; he's asleep by now. If we brought him here, you'd know all about it, I can tell you. He's just crawling now, so nothing is safe.' She grinned and Carmel relaxed. They seemed so nice, not out to kill her. As usual, Sharif was right.

'Did you get a drink? Some food?' she was anxious that they be looked after, especially after coming all that way.

'We're grand, fine altogether. Now, don't feel you have to be minding us all night, right? Go off and enjoy your party. We might slip away soon just to get Jennifer back to Ruari, but maybe we could have lunch tomorrow?' Joe was so understanding, he meant what he said, no strings, no pressure.

'I would love that. Why don't you all come round to us? I'll make lunch and we can have a long chat and get to know each other properly.' Carmel had the invitation issued before she had time to analyse it. Normally, she'd weigh up how likely they were to refuse and probably resist offering for fear of rejection. She smiled hopefully, glad she at least had the guts to ask.

'Sounds great,' Jennifer smiled, putting her head to one side. 'Y'know, I know everyone says you look like your mother, and I'm sure you do, but I can see a bit of McDaid in you as well, can't you, Luke?'

'Yerra you know me, Jen, I can't see resemblances in anyone. Sure, people tell me I'm the spit of the Da but I hope not, cause he's a banjaxed auld fella and well, I'm in my prime!' he laughed and nudged his father.

'Go 'way outa that, ya pup, I was in me prime once too y'know and I'd have left you in the starting blocks, I can tell ya that.' He winked at Carmel as he took a long draught of his pint of Guinness, the barrel of which Zane had shipped from Ireland because British Guinness wasn't the same stuff at all.

'That's great, I'll ask Nadia as well, that's Sharif's mum, she's lovely. I'm really looking forward to it.'

'Me too.' Joe sounded so sincere and she warmed under his gaze. 'Now, go off and be chatting to all these people who've come to see you and we'll see you tomorrow, okay? Have a great night, pet.' He put his arm around her protectively for a moment and Carmel felt five-years-old again. She trusted this man, and she just knew, on some deep level, that he was a good person.

Carmel kissed Joe on the cheek and went off to mingle. As she moved around the party, people complimenting her on how lovely she looked stopped her several times, and she was enveloped in a group hug by Zane, Ivanka, Ivy, and Oscar. They dragged her out on to the dance floor and she was soon bopping away to Don't Sit Under the Apple Tree with her friends. The patients were all having a great time as well and the canapés being circulated by the waiting staff were delicious. She spoke to patients and their families, met Oscar's partner who was just like him, so chilled out and happy, and Zane insisted on being introduced to Luke, despite Carmel saying she didn't think he was gay.

'With all due what's it, Carmel darlin', I think I'm the better judge of that sort of thing,' he winked and dragged her back to Joe and his children.

Carmel introduced them and went to look for Sharif; she hadn't seen him since the speeches over forty minutes earlier. Everyone seemed to be having a great time and the music complemented nicely the lively buzz of chat in the room. Being so tall and with his distinctive hair, she could nearly always spot him in a crowd, but as she scanned the room, he wasn't to be seen. Hoping nobody would notice, she stepped out into the corridor joining the Kaivalya to the main building, the silence was instant. All the doors in Aashna House were soundproof so the party noise didn't spill out. Perhaps he'd got a call about a patient, she thought. She would just go to reception and check if he'd been called. Marlena was at the party, as were most of the regular staff, so there were several temporary and agency staff on duty. Sharif probably just wanted to check everything was okay.

Reception was empty, most of the patients would be in bed by now, and a young man, presumably from the temp agency, was on the desk.

'May I help, Madam?' he asked politely.

'Yes, I'm em…I'm Carmel, I work here. I was just looking for Dr Khan, has he been called to a patient?'

The young man seemed uncomfortable. 'Well, em, Dr Khan is with somebody at the moment, perhaps I can give him a message for you?'

'A patient?' Carmel sensed some reticence in the man's answer.

'No, Ma'am, not a patient, a family member, but I'm sure if you leave a message, I'll make sure he gets it…'

They both turned on hearing raised voices coming from the office behind the reception desk. Suddenly, the door burst open and Derek Johnson emerged, 'Well, let's see what my solicitor has to say about you partying while my poor mother lay in her own filth, half starved. I've got photos, so don't even try to deny it! You're a crook and a criminal and I'll see you pay for this, mark my words, you will pay…' he barged past Carmel and out into the night.

Carmel could see Sharif standing behind the desk in the office through the open door. Quickly, she went to him.

'Madam, if you could just wait…' the receptionist began, he'd clearly been given instructions not to disturb the doctor.

'It's okay, thanks, but it's fine.' She went into the office and closed the door.

'What on earth was all that about?' Carmel had never seen Sharif so shaken.

He gazed at Carmel, then shook his head.

'He's claiming that when he came in to see his mother this evening, she was lying in sheets covered in excrement and blood, that she hadn't been fed, that she was in mental and physical distress, and somehow, he has photos to back up his claim.' He sat down heavily in the seat.

'But that's simply not true; I mean, it just couldn't be. Mrs Johnson was fine when I popped in this afternoon. She'd just had her lunch. They were clearing it away when I arrived. I even remarked to her about the cottage pie, how I'd had it for lunch as well and how delicious it was. She smiled, the way she does you know, and seemed to understand. There's no way that what he is claiming has a grain of truth.'

Sharif sighed deeply. 'I know that, and you know that but it's our word against his, and he's got photographs on his phone. I've seen them. She's sitting in a wet, dirty bed, and she's crying. It doesn't matter what the truth is, what matters is how it looks. He's threatening to take it legal, or go to the papers with his so-called evidence. He could destroy us, destroy me.' He ran his hand over his jaw.

'But all the staff here, we'd all testify...'

He interrupted her. 'And what would they say? Of course, the staff of the private clinic would back it up, they don't want to be found to be professionally negligent either...no, Carmel, I don't know what to do, but fighting him is probably not the answer. I mentioned him to David Harrison, you know the solicitor you're dealing with as well, the last time he was shooting his mouth off? His advice at the time was to ship Mrs Johnson out. He said that, in his experience, it never ended well when someone was making claims against doctors. And fighting it in court can take years, is cripplingly expensive and ultimately fruitless because the reputational damage is already done.'

'But you didn't move her because you promised her you'd take care of her. Oh, Sharif...' She went to hug him, and together they stood in the quiet office, clinging to each other.

After several moments had passed, he broke the silence, 'We'd better get back to the party.'

'I suppose so,' she sighed, 'but it's honestly the last thing on earth I feel like doing now. But you're right, they've gone to so much trouble and we've all those people yet to speak to.'

'Yes, I'm just going to check on Mrs Johnson, see what on earth is going on, and I'll join you then. Can you just say I've been called to a patient?'

'Of course, do you want me to come with you?'

'No, better one of us is at the party at least. I'll see her and talk to the night staff. He picked tonight on purpose because of all the agency staff. It's not a coincidence. Everyone here watches out for him, hovers around when he's in, but these people wouldn't have known.'

They smiled good night at the young man on reception and Sharif instructed him to beep him if there was anything unusual happening and they walked hand in hand down the corridor.

'It's going to be okay, Sharif, we can survive this. I don't know how, but you can't be punished for being kind, the universe doesn't work that way.'

He squeezed her hand, 'I'd love to think you're right, my love, but I'm not that confident. I've seen so many malpractice cases, especially in recent years. A college friend of mine was being sued for sexually harassing a patient's wife when the truth was she had a crush on him. He rejected her and she took it very personally and the result was the loss of his practice, the near collapse of his marriage, and the alienation of his kids. She was very convincing. It was proved later to be totally fabricated, but, the damage was done. More often than not, doctors settle. Even if there's no truth in it whatsoever, and I think that's what Johnson is after, money.'

'We'll talk later.' She stood on her tiptoes and kissed him once they reached Mrs Johnson's room and he gave her a watery smile.

CHAPTER 24

'What a lovely party last night.' Nadia was her usual effusive self as she arrived at the apartment for lunch the next day, giving Carmel and Sharif each a warm embrace. 'I've made Carrot Halwa for dessert, Sharif, I know how much you love it!'

Joe and the family had yet to arrive. Jennifer was bringing Damien and Ruari as well, so they'd have to squeeze up. Sharif had called maintenance for another table and more chairs and Nadia was busy decorating the long table beautifully with candles, flowers, and ornaments.

Sharif had been up since the dawn; they'd talked long into the night once all the guests had gone and they decided they would have to address all the staff on Monday morning, explain what was happening, and ask them if they knew anything. Carmel was devastated for Sharif, his whole life's work threatened by some horrible greedy man, but she was glad he could share his worries with her. The way he spoke, we will do this, we will say that, made her feel like an intrinsic part of Aashna House, and her desire to defend it and Sharif was intense. That man could not win. It was almost four in the morning when they eventually fell asleep.

Sharif must not have slept at all because he had the entire meal ready when she woke.

'I couldn't sleep anyway, so I thought I might as well keep busy. I made Aloo Gosht with naan, I hope they'll like it. It has potatoes in it.' He smiled. It was a running joke of theirs that potatoes would have to be cooked every day, just as Bill demanded.

'I'm sure they will; it's not too spicy, is it?' she looked a little worried. While she was getting used to the sensation, and quite enjoyed it now, she was nowhere near being able to eat what Sharif and Nadia could in terms of hot spicy food. She suspected Joe might be the same.

'I don't think so, I tried it and to me, it tastes bland, so it's probably about right for the Irish palate. Here, try,' he offered her a spoon from the pot.

The glistening sauce dripped from the piece of lamb he offered her. She tasted it and while it was certainly on the spicy side, she could eat it without feeling the need to run her head under a tap. She hoped Joe could handle it. She was less concerned about Luke, Jennifer, and Damien. Dublin had become so multicultural in the past decade, everyone was used to food from all around the world. The baby, Ruari was seven months, so Sharif had bought some little yoghurts and fruit purees in case Jennifer needed something to feed him.

The shock from last night and her worry about Sharif had totally replaced her nerves at meeting the family properly. They seemed so nice last night, she was sure it was going to go well. She heard a cab pull up outside and went out to greet them. Joe was in the front and Luke, Damien, Jennifer, and the baby tumbled out of the back, complete with buggies and bags of all descriptions.

'I'm sorry, Carmel, we look like we're moving in, I know; I honestly don't know how one small baby needs so much stuff, but he does.' Jennifer laughed as she gave Carmel a one-armed hug, Ruari lodged on her other hip.

Luke and Damien carried the rest of the things and Sharif directed them to the spare bedroom.

The sudden cacophony of chat and laughter seemed to diffuse the sense of impending doom they were both feeling.

'Now so, Ruari this is Carmel, Carmel, meet Ruari.' Jennifer waved the baby's fat little hand in her direction and his face cracked into a wide gummy grin. He was adorable and Carmel felt a pang, how lucky Jennifer was to have this little baby in her life.

'Hello, Ruari, how lovely to meet you, and what a handsome little man you are, yes, you are. Oh, Jennifer, he's just gorgeous.'

'Ah, thanks, I have my moments.' Damien piped up from behind Jennifer.

Carmel instantly liked him.

'I meant the baby,' she chuckled. She stuck out her hand, 'I'm Carmel, lovely to meet you, Damien, thanks for coming, oh, and thanks for doing the honours last night so Jennifer could come to the party.'

He grinned and Carmel could see how his smile was reflected exactly in Ruari's.

'Not a bother, Jen says it's not babysitting when it's your own kid, parenting or something she calls it!'

Jennifer gave him a good-natured thump on the arm. 'Now that he's off the boob there'll be much more of that, I can tell you, so you better get used to it. He got away with murder the last few months. Do you know I overheard him telling his mam how Ruari never wakes at night? I couldn't believe my ears! Because I can tell you, there's only one person in our house that doesn't wake at night, and it sure as hell isn't Ruari.'

Nadia was deep in chat with Joe, and Luke and Sharif were joking about football. Sharif was a Luton Town fan, despite their lowly status, and he'd been going to games since he was a child. Luke was a Liverpool supporter, so the inevitable joking around began. Carmel had no idea what they were on about, but she was happy to see Sharif relax and relieved that the McDaids blended seamlessly into the gathering.

The food went down a treat, it turns out that Joe lived in England for a period during the sixties when there was no work at home and had developed quite a taste for Asian cuisine.

'I used to share a flat with a lad from Bangalore; we were working together in a big abattoir out near Finsbury. The flat was absolutely tiny, but we didn't mind. I remember him telling me how tightly squeezed in they were back where he came from, and I explained to him about being one of six in a two-bed terraced house in Kilmainham, so we got on grand. He'd cook, at the start it used to blow the head off me, so it would, but after a while, I got into it. Cardamom and garam masala and all sorts, and then being in the abattoir, we had access to the end cuts if we wanted them. We lived like kings and never spent a shilling.'

The table erupted in questions at the image of Joe and his Bangalore friend eating together every night in cramped quarters. Sharif was engaged with everything, though, undoubtedly, the situation with Derek Johnson couldn't be too far from his mind.

Carmel just sat back and observed everyone, chatting and joking with each other. Joe and Nadia were getting on famously, each telling stories of Dolly. Luke was playing on the floor with Ruari, and Sharif, Jennifer, and Damien were discussing the situation in the North of Ireland. It struck her that, even though these people were from very different cultures, they had so much in common. She'd never had more than a passing acquaintance with anyone other than native born Irish before coming to England and was still amazed that the worries, joys, and preoccupations of people she knew back in Ireland were replicated here, no matter what colour or religion people were.

Ivanka was worried about her elderly parents back in Ukraine, her dad had Parkinson's and, though she sent money back, she felt guilty about not being there. Zane was openly gay but his dad was a macho West Indian and couldn't accept his son's sexuality. Ivy's daughter was in the middle of a bitter divorce and she was worried about her and her grandkids, and Nadia was dreading a visit from her very pernickety sister, who was insisting on coming from Karachi, to criticise, according to Nadia.

These two families blended so effortlessly. Maybe that's what having a family meant, that you weren't a lone entity in the world, that there was strength in numbers, so you could explore the world and other people with a bit more confidence. Then something occurred to her, these people didn't just belong to each other, they kind of belonged to her as well. In fact, she was the common denominator. She had never before had a family to call her own and yet, looking around at Nadia and Joe, Jennifer, Luke, Damien, and Ruari and, of course, her darling Sharif, she realized that for the first time ever, she was part of a family. Tears came unbidden and she decided to start clearing plates rather than make a total show of herself in front of everyone.

Immediately, everyone tried to help, but Jennifer stopped them. 'I'll help Carmel, and you all sit here, ye'll only be in the way if we all try to do it. Why don't we clear up and then the men can take over coffee and desserts, right?'

There was general agreement.

'Well, I was slaving over a hot...'

'Visa card.' Jennifer finished for her brother. 'Don't try to make out you baked that, Luke.' She nodded in the direction of the pie they'd brought, along with wine and chocolate and a lovely bunch of flowers. 'Don't you know the trick? If you want it to look homemade, you need to take it out of the box, pop it on a plate of your own, and bash the sides up a bit. Those perfect rounds are a dead giveaway.'

'Ah, Jen, do tell me that lovely apple tart you feed me is made by your own fair hands?' Joe's mock anguish caused them all to chuckle.

'Sorry, Dad, Tesco's all the way!' She smiled sweetly and kissed him on the cheek.

'What a disappointment you've turned out to be. Carmel, how about you? You wouldn't pawn off some mass produced auld muck on me, now would you? I bet if you made an apple tart, it would be better than Jennifer's, from this day forward to be called Tesco's.'

Carmel smiled weakly and went to the kitchen. She stood at the sink, fingers gripping the cold stainless steel. She didn't dare catch Jennifer's eye. She must be devastated to hear her father suggest that Carmel could be a better daughter than her. She knew he was only joking but still, Jennifer had had her father's undiluted adoration all her life. She was probably either hurt or mad that Joe would say such a thing.

Jennifer landed a pile of dirty plates on the worktop and started scraping the scraps into the bin. Carmel couldn't make eye contact. Perhaps she should say something, something to show Jennifer that she wasn't trying to muscle in.

'Your tableware is beautiful. Where did you get it? It reminds me of the stuff my granny had when I was small, so delicate.' Nothing in her tone suggested the outrage she must be feeling. Carmel dared raise her eyes but she was greeted by Jennifer's open, happy face.

'Em...Nadia gave them to us; they were actually my mother's, apparently, but she gave the set to Nadia when she was dying. She saved up to buy all the different pieces.' Carmel gently placed each one into the dishwasher.

'It must be so hard for you, to be here in the place where she was, and still to have missed seeing her by just a few months. My mam died but I have loads of memories, and even though I really miss her and some days it's harder than others, I can picture her clearly, hear her voice, and I don't know, it doesn't feel so lonely I suppose.'

The two women worked easily together, clearing the many plates and serving bowls. Carmel was glad of the distraction. Amazingly, Jennifer didn't seem at all put out by the apple tart remark.

'Well it is, but I never knew her, and to be honest, growing up, I tried not to think too much about who my mother was. I believed she had me, chose for whatever reason not to keep me, and that was all there was to it really. It wasn't until I met Sharif that she became a real person to me, but yeah, hearing Nadia and Sharif talking about her, and now your Dad, it does make me wish I could have met her.'

'He was so happy you turned up. When he came home from Brian's funeral, he texted from the airport to say he needed to talk to us. We didn't come over because Ruari was too small to fly with at that stage and Luke couldn't go because he was on a case.' She noted Carmel's look of surprise. 'Oh, he didn't tell you? He's a guard, well, more special branch, like a detective; don't be fooled by the homeless hippie look, he's a smart cookie, my brother. Not much gets past him.'

'Anyway, Dad came back and one night he took me and Luke out to dinner and told us about you. Hearing him talk about your mam, we'd never seen him like that before. Like, he loved my mam, no doubt about it, but even she told me that she wasn't his first love. Everyone round them knew how gutted he was when Dolly left. My mam told me that the night before their wedding, she went round to Dad's house and asked him straight out if he was still in love with Dolly, and if he was, then he shouldn't marry her. He told her the truth, that a bit of him would always love Dolly, but that he wanted to marry Mam and that he'd be faithful and loving towards her till the day one of them died, so she accepted that and they really did have a great marriage.'

'I'm glad. He's such a nice man, he deserves to be happy.' Carmel didn't really know what to say. Had Joe told her that he was Carmel's father? Or had he told them about the ambiguity, and, if so, did they know the details? She wished she'd had a chance to speak to Joe on his own but it was too late for that now.

'What are you thinking about the whole thing? It must be incredibly weird for you...suddenly finding a family you never knew you had?'

'It is. Really strange, but in a nice way. I don't know, I'm still just processing it all, I suppose.'

'Are you going to have the test?'

The tone was gentle but the question was definitely direct. Carmel had lived a life where nobody said anything of any consequence, or at least not to her, and so when people were forthright or inquisitive, she found herself at a bit of a loss.

'Do you think I should?' Carmel was surprised at herself for meeting such a blunt question with one of her own.

Jennifer smiled and sighed. 'I don't know, honestly, I don't. I've gone over this and over it. Dad wants you to be his daughter, and he believes you are. I'm just thinking, are ye better off just assuming that you are, if it's what you both want, rather than risk finding out that you're not his biological child and ruining everything? Like, I think you are, I can see a resemblance even, not so much to Dad but to my aunties and cousins, but if your dad is just some random bloke Dolly was with some time, then won't it hurt both of you?'

So, Carmel was relieved to note, Joe hadn't told them about the grandfather. He must just have said that maybe Dolly had a relationship or something with someone else. Though Carmel knew logically Dolly hadn't done anything wrong, as Sharif was constantly pointing out, she was delighted that Jennifer and Luke didn't know the truth.

'And what about you? How would you feel about it?' Carmel tried to keep her voice light but she was sure Jennifer could hear her heart thumping in her chest from across the small kitchen.

'I'd love it.' She shrugged, 'I've always wanted a sister. I mean, I'm probably past the robbing your clothes and makeup phase, but it would be lovely just to have a sister, y'know? And for Ruari to have an auntie?' Her voice cracked with emotion and Jennifer reddened, clearly embarrassed.

Carmel crossed the kitchen and embraced her. 'Do I know? Oh, yes, I know. I'd love a sister too.'

Releasing her, Jennifer asked, 'So where does that leave us? We want you in our family, we think you are our sister, and we can find out for sure or leave well enough alone, what do you think?'

They were interrupted by Sharif arriving in the kitchen to make coffee. Nadia was busy unwrapping her Halwa to appreciative sounds and Luke was making a great show of battering the outsides of the chocolate cream pie he'd bought. Jennifer accepted the little yoghurts that Carmel had bought for Ruari, exclaiming that they were his favourite, and Sharif gave her a squeeze. Carmel wondered if she knew before this that it was possible to be this happy.

After desserts, there was coffee and delicious Bailey's Irish Cream chocolates, which everyone said they couldn't possibly touch, but still managed to polish off almost the entire box. Sharif tapped his glass. The room became instantly quiet, even little Ruari was resting peacefully in Jennifer's arms.

'I'm not much of a man for speeches normally, but there is something I want to tell you all. Seeing everyone here today, so relaxed and happy in each other's company, it feels like we are family already. Carmel and I can't make any plans for our wedding until she can get a divorce, but as soon as she does, we will be getting married, and I know I speak for her too when I say we would love it if you'd join us on that day.'

Joe was sitting beside Carmel and he put his arm around her shoulders. She turned to him and smiled. He winked at her and her heart melted. She realized now for sure, she wanted this man in her life. But maybe Jennifer was right, what would a DNA test prove? If it was positive, and he was her father, then they were exactly where they were now, and if not, well if not, who knew what anyone would feel?

'The second thing is something to do with the clinic. I know I've only just met you and normally I am a very private person on such issues, but Carmel and I are going to need your support in the coming months. In a nutshell, I am being sued for malpractice.' Even saying the words out loud was causing him pain, Carmel could see it.

Nadia was outraged, 'By whom? That's ridiculous, you are the most diligent, conscientious...' Sharif smiled as he saw the mother lioness emerge, protecting her cub.

'Ammi, I know you think that, and I will, of course, fight this if I can, but basically, a patient who is suffering from dementia was photographed by her son in soiled, wet sheets and he is claiming that, on a regular basis, we neglect her.'

'But, Sharif, my darling...how can he say such a thing? It's that Derek Johnson, isn't it? I knew he couldn't be trusted. You are letting his mother stay here, with top facilities for nothing, just because she asked you to and now this is how he repays you?'

Sharif had never told Carmel that Mrs Johnson wasn't a paying patient, but she suspected. That made the whole thing so much worse.

'That's irrelevant, the thing is, it's not true, he must have brought those sheets in and put them on the bed and then photographed her. In the pictures he showed me, her nightgown was all stains and her hair very disheveled, as well as the dirty sheets and rubbish all over the room. There was even a full ashtray. He clearly staged the whole thing, but as I was explaining to Carmel, malpractice suits are notoriously difficult and costly to fight, and often the damage is actually done by the suspicion anyway. Most of the time, doctors settle. I've spoken to my solicitor and he's put me on to a legal team that specializes in this sort of thing, but their advice is going to be to settle, I would imagine.'

Carmel placed her hand over his as he sat down.

Joe was the first to speak, 'Sharif, I don't know anything about you, really, but from what my brother said about this place, I know that man is lying. Surely, he can't just come up with a load of rubbish like that and expect to get away with it?'

'Well, it seems he can. It's not fair, but then…life isn't fair sometimes. Anyway, there you have it. We'll need your support as I said and I just thought it was better to tell you what was going on; I know I don't need to say this, but I'd appreciate it if you kept this to yourselves.'

'Of course, that's awful.' Jennifer and Luke both reached out for Carmel's hand at the same time and for an instant, she felt a sibling connection.

'Now, I don't want this to spoil our lovely day, so let's not talk about it anymore, but I wanted you all to know. It will all work itself out, I'm sure.' Sharif smiled with a confidence Carmel knew he didn't feel but he was right, there was no point in dwelling on it.

'So, how long are you all staying around?' Carmel hoped she'd have some time with them on her own before they went back to Ireland.

'Well, myself, Damien, Luke, and the little prince here are going back tomorrow, but I think Dad is staying around for a few days, aren't you?' Jennifer must have known her father was a little nervous, afraid of outstaying his welcome, so she was encouraging.

Carmel jumped in right away, 'Oh, that's wonderful. I'm really sorry you guys are going back so soon, but I know how it is with work and everything, and I'm so grateful that you came over, really, travelling with Ruari and everything, it's meant the world to us. And, maybe we can spend some time together, Joe, over the next few days?

That's if the boss will give me the time off, he's a bit of a tyrant.' She winked at Sharif.

'Somehow, Carmel, I think you have him wrapped around your little finger.' Joe looked relieved that she was pleased.

'She certainly does, Joe, I'm a slave to her whims.' Sharif was mock mournful.

'Hey, say if this is a bad idea now,' Damien spoke up, but how about if myself and Joe mind the small lad and let Jennifer, Luke, and Carmel go out for a drink or something? We're all going back tomorrow and maybe...' he got embarrassed then, unsure of how to finish because nobody had yet said anything about the situation of Carmel's parentage.

'I'd love that. If it suits you two?' Carmel knew Jennifer was anxious to welcome her but she'd love to talk properly to Luke as well. The family lunch was wonderful but it didn't allow for any real conversation on the future.

'Perfect. Now, I need to get over to the clinic, check on everyone, so I'll take my leave of you all. We had a lovely time, thank you so much for coming and please come over again soon.' Sharif was picking up his keys and making for the door.

'Or, you could come to visit us?' Luke grinned.

'Maybe. Dublin was where we met, so maybe we could go back for a visit sometime?' Sharif knew that Carmel had no desire to ever return to Ireland but maybe a family of her own over there would be enough of a lure.

'Maybe.'

'Don't worry about clearing up. I'll do it when I get back.' And Sharif was gone.

Nadia and Joe began removing the dessert plates and the glasses as Damien took Ruari off to change him into his pyjamas.

'Right, Carmel, show us the highlights of this bit of the urban sprawl,' Luke joked as he shrugged on his jacket.

'Well, we are just a teeny bit too far out to be considered urban anything, but we could go in, up the West End or something if you'd like, or we could just stay around here? Whatever you two would like.'

'Well, maybe this single lad is looking for a bit more action than a night with his sisters, but I'm happy to stay local.' Jen smiled and Carmel coloured at the casual way she dropped in the word sisters.

'What more could a fella want? I already had one nagging sister, now it seems I've got two. Brilliant.' He threw his eyes heavenward, and with a martyred sigh, offered them an arm each. 'Right you, where are you taking us?'

Carmel thought quickly, 'I'm not much of a pub goer but my friends Zane and Ivanka hang out at The Dog and Duck and they say it's fun. We go there for lunch some days, so will we try there? We can walk, it's about twenty minutes or we can call a cab?'

'Oh, let's walk. I'm stuffed after that lunch, I could do with some exercise.' Jen patted her belly.

Luke looked doubtfully at his sister's high boots. 'Are you going to be able to walk in those, and not be whining after three minutes? You know what you're like and I'm not carrying you!'

'Hmm, good point.' Jenifer looked down ruefully.

'What size are you? I can lend you a pair of pumps?'

Jennifer looked at Carmel and grinned, 'Maybe it's not too late after all to be borrowing your stuff! I'm a six?'

'Me too, come into the bedroom and see what you'd like.'

'Here we go,' Luke moaned dramatically, 'One pair of shoes, Jen, and only to borrow, a thirty-second decision, not a half an hour, okay?'

'Yeah yeah, whatever...' she punched him playfully on the shoulder.

Five minutes later, Jennifer emerged wearing a pair of flat ballet pumps and a cream and gold jacket of Carmel's.

'I love this jacket, it's so unusual.'

'Ivy gave it to me, actually, someone bought it for her as a present but she's in her sixties and she felt ridiculous in it. Keep it if you like.'

'I couldn't do that, it's yours.'

'And now it's yours. I like the idea of you having it, you can think of me when you wear it.'

'Okay, now that the fashion show is over, can we please get going?

One sister was bad enough...' he grinned and kissed Nadia on the cheek and gave his Dad a hug.

Jennifer did the same and Carmel followed their lead. She was never quite sure what to do in these situations. Certainly, as a child, there was no physical contact at all, and during her years with Bill, it was kept to an absolute minimum. The twins would give her a peck on the cheek when they arrived and left, and she shook hands with people when it was time to show the sign of peace at Mass, but apart from that, she wasn't really touched by anyone. Over here, she was constantly being hugged and kissed by Sharif, friends, Nadia, and while it was lovely, she was always a little unsure about what she should do.

'Be careful and mind each other,' Joe called as they closed the door behind them.

'So, tell us more about this Johnson fella.' Carmel was surprised at Luke's interest, but she told him all she knew.

'So, he just rocks up out of the blue and says he's her son and starts all this trouble?'

Carmel remembered that he was a detective and assumed that's where his interest lay.

'Well, we've no reason to believe he's not her son, but yeah, that's more or less it. Poor Sharif, it's killing him inside, I just wish there was something I could do.'

'Well, just be there for him, I suppose, y'know, what you're doing. Imagine if he didn't have you?' Jennifer linked Carmel's arm.

'Well, I hope I'm being some use, but to be honest, I doubt it. I approached him the other day in the car park and he was horrible. Apparently, he hates Paddies and Pakis, so we are both equally bad. You should see him and his car, filthy, smelly, and I just can't believe that he's suddenly the caring son. None of it fits. I haven't told Sharif that I spoke to him. Maybe I should? I just wanted to help him, but what if I've made things worse?'

'I doubt that. He sounds like a piece of work. If you want me to, I could ask someone I know at Scotland Yard to run a check on him? If we knew a bit more about him, then it could help find a way to deal with him?'

Carmel felt so touched at Luke's offer to help, and the way he seemed to see it as a collective problem, not just Sharif's.

'I'll speak to Sharif, see what he says, thanks so much, Luke, you don't really need this crap in your life, but we really appreciate it.'

'I deal with criminals all day every day, in general, they are cowards under all the bravado and nearly always have something to hide. Find that, and you have leverage. Simple really, when you know how!' He winked.

'Do you think he's a criminal?'

'Well, so far, he's falsified evidence, made unfounded accusations, and made racist remarks. Let's just say, I wouldn't be stunned if it turns out he has a record. Normal, law-abiding people just don't do things like that.'

'And you could find that out for us?'

'I would imagine so. Yeah.'

Carmel looked at him and wondered if the whole student look wasn't a sort of disguise. He came across as jokey and very much the baby brother when he was goofing around with the family, but now that he was in business mode, he was focused and professional.

'If we can help in any way, Carmel, we will, you've been through enough in your life, you deserve a break. And it's just so unfair that now that you and Sharif have found each other and your story with your parents is just starting to emerge, that you have to deal with this awful man and his horrible threats.' Jennifer was sincere, Carmel just knew it.

'You have no idea what it means to me to hear you say that, both of you. Seriously, I was terrified before the party that you were coming over to tell me to back off, to leave your Dad alone. You're both so easy to talk to. I don't know because families were a bit of a mystery to me, I learned everything about relationships from TV soaps. To be honest, I thought it was always fraught. But seeing Sharif and Nadia together, and Joe and you lot, it all seems so easy. I can't believe I'm actually in one, a real proper family. I just sat and watched you all over lunch, talking, eating, laughing, and I felt such awe, and then I realized I was actually part of it, not outside looking in, the way I have been all my life. I know that sounds pathetic, but honestly, I was breathing in and out and going through the motions but I wasn't living, not really.'

'What was Trinity House like?' Luke asked as they walked along. In some ways, Carmel realized, it was easier to talk properly when walking, eyes straight ahead.

'Okay. Like, I wasn't abused or anything, that's the first thing everyone thinks these days when they hear I was reared in care. So, there wasn't anything like that, thankfully, but I was just there, nobody cared really. We were fed and educated and all of that, but we were just numbers, I suppose. We went to the local school, and I remember I used to dread when there would be a note to go home to have signed for different things. Each one of the normal kids would be given a note and then when it came to us, the kids from Trinity, they'd say, "Ye don't need to take one, it's been sent." I used to cringe with shame. My First Communion, Confirmation, all of that, it was the same. We went with the others to the church, they even found dresses or whatever for us, but no photos, no family lunch, no cash from your aunties and uncles. The usual stuff kids think about, I suppose. So, it was lonely and embarrassing, and empty, but they weren't cruel.'

'But no love?'

'No. Nothing like that.'

'And you must have been wondering why you weren't adopted?'

Carmel knew now that Jennifer and Luke didn't have the full story, so she couldn't explain about the order Joe's father had made.

'I just supposed that nobody wanted me. Like, once you go past four or five, it's almost impossible anyway. People really only want babies, so I remember on my seventh birthday deciding I wasn't going to think about that anymore. It wasn't going to happen and that was that.'

Luke said nothing but put his arm around her and gave her a squeeze.

'Is that why you married that fella from down the country?'

223

She shrugged. 'I was well over eighteen, time to be out of care and well, I'd nowhere else to go. I didn't have any qualifications, I got my Leaving Cert, but without a proper address or some experience, I couldn't even get a job in a shop. I could sew, and I used to make clothes for the kids in Trinity or adjust the stuff out of the charity bags that were dropped in, but there wasn't any need for that anymore. I thought that because he had kids, and their mother had died, that they'd need me. I used to look after the little ones at Trinity House, and I like kids, so I just thought... Well, anyway, they didn't need me or want me, as it turned out. I think Bill only got married to keep his awful sister out of his house and a bit for the girls I suppose, but then when they didn't want me, it was all a bit pointless.'

'How old were they?' Jennifer was clearly upset at such cruelty.

'Oh, they were only six when Bill and I got married, but Julia kind of dominated them.'

'Oh, she's the one that showed up the other day? She sounds like a right wagon.'

'Oh, she's a piece of work alright. Sharif says she looks like a witch in a storybook, all pointy.'

'And did you not want to have a child with your man?' Luke was so direct, it must be the policeman in him, but Carmel found that she didn't mind.

'This is going to sound mad, but we never actually...well, you know. He was still married in his head to his dead wife, and so he never touched me.' Carmel couldn't believe she was admitting this to them, but somehow it felt safe.

'Are you serious?' Luke was incredulous, and Jennifer had tears in her eyes.

'And you're so gorgeous, and he never wanted... Oh, Carmel, you poor thing, that must have been so hard...' Jennifer was trying her best to hold it together, Carmel could see, but it was impossible. Once again, she was surprised at the impact of her story.

Luke stopped walking and drew both of them into his embrace.

'Come on now, we're supposed to be celebrating, so let's try to focus on that, eh? They're out of your life now, well almost, just the divorce to get sorted, and then you've got all sorts of options.'

The pub was half full and there was a nice buzz of conversation. Carmel went to the bar, despite Luke's efforts to buy the first round.

'What can I get you, love?' the barman asked as Luke and Jennifer went to sit down.

'I'll have a gin and tonic please and a glass of red for my sister and a pint of bitter for my brother.'

The barman looked a little askance, generally, people didn't specify who the drinks were for but Carmel wanted to say the words.

'Have you decided what you're going to do?' Luke asked as he lifted his pint to his mouth.

Carmel fought back the panic. She realized now that she was emotionally underdeveloped. She'd been reading a lot about children reared in care and how the normal human responses that happen between parents and kids and between kids and their siblings are often absent, and so it leads to emotional delay. Sometimes, she felt like she was in a foreign world where everyone else spoke the language except her. Sharif understood and wasn't put off by her odd reactions sometimes, but she hoped she could explain it properly to the McDaids.

'I don't know. Jennifer and I spoke about it briefly earlier. I'm a bit weird, that's the truth, Luke. I've had such a peculiar life compared to virtually everyone else I've met, that I'm afraid to move forward in case I mess it up. I don't really understand about families, as I said, and what it's okay to do and say. And I don't even know if I am part of your family, so...' she sighed heavily, knowing she was making a hash of explaining it to him.

He waited to see if she would go on and when she didn't, he spoke, 'Will I tell you what I think?'

She nodded at him.

'My dad thinks you are his child and so, if he's sure, then that makes you my sister. And, if you want to be part of our family, then we'd love to have you. When Dad first told me, I must admit I was a bit like, I don't know, not shocked or anything, but just a bit slow to change things, y'know? Like, we're grand just the three of us. And, there was Mam as well, like, was it disloyal to her or something? And, let's face it, none of us like to think of our parents as sexual beings, right? And you being here meant that he did it with someone other than our mam, so that was a bit, I don't know, weird to process as well. But now that I've met you properly, and Sharif, as far as I'm concerned anyway, you're my sister and I think you should have the test.'

Carmel stopped and looked up into the intelligent hazel eyes of this man who might be her brother.

'And if I'm not?'

'Well, it won't matter to me. Or to Jennifer or to Dad, I'd say. I think the test will just confirm what we already know. You look like him, that's the main reason I think so. It's inconceivable that you don't have McDaid blood in your veins, looking like you do. But even in the very unlikely event of it being negative, it will matter, of course, on one level, but it's not like we'd all just walk away and say, okay, then, Carmel, nice knowing you.'

'But then I'm not your sister, I'm just some random woman who is the child of a woman your father used to go out with. Our only point of connection with your family is someone I've never even met. The bond is so...well, it's not there, is it? I think I don't want to do it because I'm afraid of what I'll find out. Wanting something to be true and it actually being true are so different.' She sipped her drink.

'I love reading books about the law of attraction, like, that our thoughts are things and that we can alter our lives by shaping our thoughts to what we want, *The Secret* and all of that, but then, when I was a little girl, all I wanted was a family. Like, I prayed and wished and daydreamed all the time, but it never happened. And if the pure thoughts of a little child can't do it...'

Luke covered her hand with his and gave her a squeeze. He was just like his father, strong and protective, even though he was at least a decade younger than her.

CHAPTER 25

'Relax.' Sharif put down his newspaper. 'It's going to be fine. You'll have a great day. It's going to be warm in Central London, though, so don't forget your sun cream.'

'I know. And I don't know why I'm so nervous, it's like a date or something... that sounds stupid I know but I just...oh, I don't know, Sharif...' Carmel leaned against the countertop with a cup of coffee in her hands.

'It's just a day out with someone you like and trust, what's to stress about? See the sights, I got Marlena to book front row seats for Jersey Boys at the Odeon, and you have a reservation for pre-theatre dinner at The Five Fields in Chelsea; have a few glasses of bubbly. Now, have you got your card? No scrimping now, okay? I know what you're like.'

He stood and gathered his keys and wallet.

'Well, I'm seeing this new legal chap this morning so I'd better get my skates on. I love you. Hopefully, if Luke can find out if this guy has a criminal record, then we can get a bit further with it.' He kissed her and was gone.

Joe was picking her up in twenty minutes, having seen Jennifer and the others to the airport, and then he and Carmel were taking the train together into London.

She'd had a lovely evening in the pub with them the night before, all stories and laughing, and she couldn't tell if she was so relaxed and happy around them because they really were her siblings or because she desperately wanted them to be. They didn't raise the subject of the DNA test again and just enjoyed each other's company. She observed Jennifer and Luke's interaction with a mixture of affection and envy. They were constantly teasing each other and had so many stories of the things they'd done together, not just as kids, but as teenagers and young adults as well. They'd gone to Australia working for a year together as part of a bigger group of friends and cousins, they'd backpacked around Thailand and Malaysia, they'd done so much and clearly were devoted to each other. They were exactly what she imagined brothers and sisters to be like. Her only other experience was Bill and Julia which, the more time and distance she put between them, the more bizarre that set-up seemed to be.

She checked her wallet for cash. It never ceased to amaze her that she had money of her own. Bill gave the girls wads of cash when they visited and Carmel used to look in amazement at his largesse when she had virtually no money. The local shop was on an account, which he settled each month, and everything else was paid for by the month, so it never occurred to him that she might like to have some money. Once, she saw an ad up in the local shop for a housekeeper job in the town and she mentioned it to him. He looked at her as if she was stark staring mad.

'Skivvying for the neighbours, would you have sense?' was all he said, and wearily went back to his farm, leaving Carmel with the familiar sensation of having let him down once again.

It wasn't that she wanted to buy anything in particular, but it just would be nice to have her own money, to be able to pop into The Cosy Corner Café for tea and a scone or to buy herself a book or a new top or whatever. Bill had an account in Cotters, the local draper's shop, where he bought three shirts every year as well as six new vests, six new pairs of underpants, and pyjamas. Every five years, he bought a suit. The girls usually got him a pullover and socks for Christmas, and Julia bought him slippers. The suits had three phases, The Good

Suit, the newest, used for Mass, weddings, and funerals; the five-year-old suit, used for going to the mart, for a pint, or the occasional football match or hare coursing event; and the ten-year-old suit was then used for farming. Once, she saw overalls on special offer in the drapers, so she bought them for him, thinking it would be better than the suit, but he told her to take them back, they were a waste of money. The drapers had some women's clothes as well and she did get a few things there, but the owner, Mrs Cotter, was a lady in her seventies and her taste in stock reflected that. Pastel cardigans, pleated skirts, and lilac or pink blouses seemed to be the only things she had for sale. Carmel had taken to secreting a little of the 'housekeeping' money. Bill put twenty Euros a week in a jar for sundries in case they ran out, and she siphoned off a few Euros each week. Over months, she managed to save up enough to buy an occasional pair of jeans or a top, suitable for someone under the age of seventy, in the large department store at the edge of town. Every Christmas, the girls bought her a scarf, usually some shade of blue, she had seventeen of them now, and Julia bought her slippers too. Bill just gave her money, it was an excruciatingly formal and embarrassing exchange each year, but she managed to make it stretch to pay her phone bill and a few small personal items. Her life now was the opposite, a wardrobe full of lovely clothes and a drawer containing silk lingerie, and on the fitted shoe rack, there were sixteen pairs of shoes. It seemed almost criminal decadence.

The knock on the door startled her out of her reverie. She took one quick glance in the mirror and decided she looked okay. She was wearing trainers because there was going to be a lot of walking, light blue jeans, and a cream hoodie. Her blonde hair was tied up in a ponytail and she was wondering if she was a bit old for such a girly look; she was going to take it down when Joe knocked again. Dismissing her hair concerns, she opened the door.

Joe smiled and enveloped her in a hug.

'Coffee?' she asked, hoping her voice didn't betray her nerves. This was ridiculous, it wasn't as if she had never met him, but this day, this time alone together, was a first and she felt so unsure.

'Please, if you're making some anyway.'

'I've it made already.'

'God, Carmel, I...I might as well tell you, I was so nervous coming over here. I was trying to give myself a good talking to. Like, I know you and everything now, but I don't know...'

'Me too. I feel exactly the same.'

'It's like a first date, isn't it?' he chuckled.

'Well, since I've never had that experience, I don't know; I never went on a date with Bill, and Sharif just sort of showed up and we were together and that was that. No dating as such...though I'm not complaining, mind you, I don't know what I'd say or do on a proper date with a stranger.' Carmel felt she was babbling but it seemed to relax them both.

'Well, whatever way ye got together, it sounds to me like a great day's work. He's a lovely man and he's mad about you, anyone can see that. I'm so glad he rescued you from that desperate situation. You deserve to be happy after all you've been through. I just wish you didn't have to...'

Joe seemed visibly upset, thinking about Carmel's life up to the time Sharif appeared.

'It wasn't that bad, honestly,' she tried to reassure him.

'You say that, but I hate the thought of you in that home, and then with that thick farmer, when all the time you could have been in a happy family, adopted by people who'd love you properly, all because of my father...' Joe wiped his eye, brushing away a tear. 'I'm sorry, Carmel, I'm a big eejit, dragging all that back up again when you probably want to forget it, but it just sickens me when I think about it.'

Carmel handed Joe his coffee.

'Look, Joe, it wasn't great, okay? Nobody's saying it was, but it wasn't that bad either. I keep telling people that, but they don't want to believe it. I was fed and clothed and educated and, honestly, it was fine, and the years with Bill, well it wasn't like he was cruel or hurt me or anything. It was just, well more of the same really, I suppose.'

'But we all need love, Carmel.'

'Maybe, and a life where you're loved is, well, I can't explain just how wonderful it is, but I never knew what that felt like anyway, so I never knew what I was missing. I thought families were always fighting and people cheated on each other all the time, either that or they lived in totally unrealistic situations, all my education about real life came from TV and watching the soaps, you see.'

Joe leaned against the kitchen counter, cupping his coffee with both hands.

'Just because you knew no better doesn't make what he did acceptable. I hated my father long before I knew about you, really hated him, and the day he died was a great day, God knows, we waited long enough. He was a bully and a liar and he made our lives and my mother's life hell. What saved us was each other. Myself, Colm, Brian, Kevin, and the girls, we looked out for each other and for Mam too. Brian told you about the time I battered him, put him in the hospital because I came in to find him hitting my ma and I just saw red. What he didn't tell you was it was Brian that pulled me off him. I'd have killed him, Carmel, I find that hard to say, I'm not a violent man, never raised my fists in anger at anyone before or since, but something about him, the smug, holier than thou way he went on. He'd make you sick so he would, up there on the altar at Mass, doing the readings and giving out communion, looking like butter wouldn't melt, when all the time, he was anything but. I pressured my ma to press charges but she wouldn't. It was peculiar back then, like, the woman was somehow shamed as well if her husband was beating her, or maybe she was just afraid of him; anyway, she wouldn't make a statement to the guards. I made sure that people knew though, me and Dolly. I was over at her house after the fight happened, I couldn't go home, and I remember my hands were all swollen up and I had all of these cuts on my knuckles and she was patching me up. I was giving out that my ma wouldn't go to the guards and says she, "Listen, Joe, if the reason you want her to go and report him is so that his reputation as a pillar of the community is shattered by having to turn up to face charges in court, well, that's easily done. Just tell Bina O'Leary. She's got the biggest gob in the parish, and just watch the story take on legs and arms and all sorts. People love something to gossip about, they half know anyway, so we'll leave it to Bina to fill in the juicy details, she'd love nothing more. Don't you worry, they'll be giving each other knowing glances and secret sneers by next Sunday if he's out of hospital in time for Mass.'"

He chuckled, 'Of course, she was right, Bina ran the small shop at the end of our road and prided herself on knowing everyone's business. Dolly went up to buy some disinfectant, even though we had loads and told Bina the whole story, all upset like, and sure enough, the whole place had it by the next day. Not just that he was battering my ma, but the girls as well, and that he'd been cautioned by the guards, and that he was facing prison if he did it again, oh, the whole nine yards. My mam was upset at the start, but she didn't know how it got out. She never did, and you know, people were kind. Not as judgmental as she thought they might be, and in a way, it protected her. Now that it was out what kind of a man he was, she couldn't be going around saying she walked into the door or whatever, so he had to lay off a bit. When he got out of hospital, he went into the church, to make sure nobody had usurped him in his position of chief arse licker. Fr O'Mahony, a big gruff fella from Connemara, gave him the road apparently, saying he'd want to mend his ways and repent of his sins before darkening the door of his church again. The priest knew because my ma had gone to him once or twice when we were kids, looking for help. He used to give her a few bob or get a box of grub sent around. He was a grand man really and I'd say my father's carry on, being all holy for show and a tyrant at home, appalled him. My father was finished then, but bitter. What he did to Dolly...my lovely Dolly...she was brave as a lion, Carmel, she really was, nothing scared her, and she was so loyal. That's why, when she left without a word, I was devastated for years. It was so unlike her, I could never accept that she just walked away from everyone, from me. She wasn't that kind of person. My wife June knew all about it, everyone did, I looked such a misery for so long after, we didn't talk about it, but when she was dying, we talked a lot. She said she thought I never really got over Dolly leaving, and she was right. But knowing why she had to go, well, it's so hard to come to terms with.' He sighed heavily. 'Would you listen to me, dragging all this up on a sunny morning when we are supposed to be going for a nice day out. I'm sorry, Carmel.'

'Don't be. It's our shared history, and it's good that we can talk about it. Dolly carried that secret, and then Brian did, and now it's ours to carry, but at least we have each other.'

Joe looked deeply into her eyes, neither of them speaking.

'I'm a simple man, Carmel, I'm going over this and over it since Brian's funeral, and I just keep coming to the same conclusion. As far as I'm concerned, you're my daughter and though I don't know you well yet, I love you, and I want the best for you just as I do for my other two kids. I'm happy to go to my grave with things just as they are. So, it's up to you, if you want to do the test, or if you never do, then that's okay. Forget all about tests, and DNA, and all of that. But I have to ask you this,' he took a steadying breath, 'do you want me to be your dad?'

It was as if a dam was released within her. Carmel couldn't stop it, all the years, all the rejection, just seemed to take on a molten quality and fell as scalding hot tears. She tried to speak, but no words would come. She was five again, seven, twelve, twenty-one, a bride, lonely.

Joe just stood, right in front of her, not touching not speaking. The tears racked her body and she found it hard to breathe. She had no idea where all of this was coming from, and it frightened her. She gulped air, she tried to steady her breath but she couldn't, she was so overwhelmed by her reaction that she couldn't even feel embarrassed at her lack of control.

Pain seared his face, seeing her in such anguish, and eventually, he stretched out his arms. He made no move towards her but his arms were welcoming her. If she moved into his embrace now, then that would be it. She wanted to, but she was afraid, she desperately wanted him to be her father, to love and protect her. Even though she was forty years old, she felt like she was a child. Suddenly, something propelled her forward, she didn't know what it was, but she had the same feeling she'd had that night outside the pub in Dublin when Sharif asked her to come back to London with him. They were singing her mother's song, 'Que Sera Sera' at a party in the pub and Carmel felt her, urging her to trust Sharif. She felt it again now.

She took the two steps towards him and felt his arms around her, she sobbed into his shirt, and he rubbed her back and kissed the top of her head, soothing her gently.

'I do,' she managed to croak.

'Well, then, I am. It's okay, darling, you're home now. It's alright, I've got you, nothing will ever hurt you, I've got you, my lovely baby girl, you're safe.' He murmured those words over and over again and she eventually felt herself relax and her breathing return to normal. The front of his shirt was soaking and she could hear his heart beating through his chest. He smelled of washing powder and aftershave and she felt so safe. They stood together for a long time, the sun streaming in the window, locked in their own little space in the world together. Eventually, he released her and they smiled at each other.

'Thanks.' She wiped her face with a tissue he offered her. 'I'm sorry about that, I don't know what happened there, just years of...I don't know.'

'Anytime, pet, I've a lot of making up to do.'

CHAPTER 26

They had a fantastic day walking all over London. Joe took her to see where he lived with his Bangladeshi friend off the Tottenham Court Road years ago, and she showed him some of the things Sharif had shared with her. They held hands on the London Eye and shared their meals at the fantastic restaurant Sharif had booked for them, realizing they both were mushroom lovers but were very dubious about cheese. Sharif sent her a few texts during the day, just checking in with her, and she assured him that she was having a wonderful time. They sang along to all the songs in Jersey Boys and after the show went for a drink in a cosy old pub.

They were so engrossed in each other's company, it was as if the rest of the world didn't exist. He told her all about his years working for the Irish Steel Company, having decided that a life of chopping up animals was not for him. How he'd been able to take early retirement because he'd bought a few houses in Dublin when they were cheap and had done them up himself. He loved DIY, so now he could live on the rental income on top of his pension. He told her about the apartment he bought in Spain and how it was for anyone in the family who wanted to use it. She told him that she'd never been to anywhere but England before the week in France with Sharif and that she'd love to go to Spain with him sometime. They were lost in conversations about tapas and sangria when they were distracted.

'Excuse me, do you mind if we sit here?' an elderly couple interrupted them, indicating the other end of their table.

'Of course, no problem.' Joe smiled and moved up a little. While the man went to the bar, the woman sat down and began to chat.

'We've just been to see Jersey Boys; our son bought us tickets for our anniversary. We don't normally come into the West End, we're from Croydon, but it's nice, isn't it?'

Carmel really just wanted Joe all to herself, but she seemed like a nice old lady, she did hope, though, that once her husband came back they'd be left alone again.

'Yes, we've just seen it too, we really enjoyed it.'

'Really? Isn't that funny? Well, I suppose it is just across the road so maybe not that much of a coincidence. My Ernie is always saying I'm seeing signs where there's nothing, maybe he's right. Very superstitious I am, can't help it, always have been since I was a little 'un. One night, during the Blitz, we were worn out from going down the tube station night after night. My dad said he was sleeping in his own bed and if Hitler wanted to come, then let him. So, we all stayed, but I woke up and went into my parents' room. I was only five or six and I told them to get up, the Germans were coming. Of course, they told me to go back to bed, there hadn't even been a siren but I insisted, and eventually, my mum said there was something about me, so she bundled us all up and back down the tube again, dragging my dad grumbling behind her. Next morning, our house was gone, flattened in a direct hit. Anyway, listen to me, blathering on. So, is it a special occasion for you too, anniversary or something?'

Joe grinned at the idea that he and Carmel were a couple.

'No, well yes, actually. Joe here is my dad and we've only just been reunited. I never knew him growing up, but he's back in my life now and it's just wonderful.'

'Well, isn't that just smashing! I love that show, Long Lost Families, you know the one with Davina McCall and that other chap where they find people all over the world? It's amazing, and then people are so happy to see each other again; blood is thicker than water, isn't that the truth? Sometimes it doesn't work out, of course, but looking at you two, you're going to be fine I'd say. Don't force it would be my advice, Que sera sera as the old song goes, do you know it? Doris Day. What will be will be…The future's not ours to see…' At that moment, Ernie came back, nodded politely at them, and led his wife to a table that had just become vacant at the other end of the bar.

Joe and Carmel smiled incredulously. She'd shown him the video of Dolly singing that song at her birthday party, and he told her that it was her party piece, even as a kid. Then she told him about how they were singing it in the pub that first night she met Sharif and now this.

They sat together in the back of the cab all the way home, Carmel nestled against him, his arm around her shoulder. He told her stories of his childhood, his mother and his siblings, they talked a lot about Dolly, and Carmel felt the picture was coming clear.

Sharif and Nadia had told her so much about her mother's life in London, and now Joe was able to fill in all about her life in Ireland. Carmel's maternal grandfather had been dead many years and, according to Joe, he was heartbroken when Dolly left without a word. Joe had plagued him for months, convinced he knew where she was, but eventually, he'd had to give up when Tom Mullane broke down, something nobody had ever seen, and roared at Joe to leave him alone. 'Wasn't it bad enough that he'd lost his wife and then his only child without the neighbours mithering him day and night about the whereabouts of his daughter?'

'He was a nice man, Carmel, your granddad, easy going, quiet. He was of his generation, not great with the feelings and all of that, but Dolly was his whole world. Sometimes, I'd see him watching her and she trick-acting around him, and his face glowed with love and pride. He'd never say it, even to her, but she meant the world to him.'

'Maybe we could go to see his grave sometime if I come back to Dublin?' Carmel wanted to connect, even if it was to lay some flowers on his grave.

'Of course we will, pet, and I'll take you to Nana Mac's as well, that's what all the grandkids called my ma, she was lovely. It will be some party when we tell the extended McDaids about you! Well, you met some of them at Brian's funeral, so you know what they're like, so imagine that multiplied by about fifty. Actually, my niece, Aisling, she's Colm's daughter, is getting married in a few months, I'm sure she'd love you to come, Jen and Damien and Luke, of course, will be there too. Would you and Sharif come?'

'If she wouldn't mind, then we'd love to.'

'Nah, she'll be delighted. Aisling's gas, did you meet her at the funeral?'

'I did, she seemed lovely.'

'Speaking of the funeral, I was wondering if I should make contact with Brian's friend, the landlord man who came to the funeral? Do you know him? What do you think?'

Carmel had discussed this with Sharif and they had concluded that if Joe brought it up, then the best thing would be to tell him the truth.

'Tim, yes. I've gotten to know him since Brian was admitted. Dolly told Tim to bring him when it got too much. I see him now from time to time, he's heartbroken, really he is.'

'Well, if he and Brian were such friends, I'd like to meet him again, I don't know, English people are different to us. Do you think he'd see it as an intrusion?'

Carmel sat up and turned to face him, 'No, I don't. The first thing is, he's not English, he's from County Mayo, though he's lived here for years...' Joe sensed her hesitation.

'And the second thing?'

'Well, the second thing is,' she hoped her revelation wasn't going to shock Joe or make him think less of his brother. 'He and Brian weren't just friends. Brian was gay and he and Tim were together for over fifty years.'

'You're joking.' Joe was astounded. 'Seriously? I can't believe that. Like, we had no idea...'

'Are you shocked?'

'No, not like shocked horrified or anything. I'm a bit sad, I suppose, that he felt he couldn't tell us, tell me even; I thought we were closer than that…I thought he felt he could trust me.' Carmel hated to hear the dejection in Joe's voice.

'He absolutely did trust you, and when we spoke about everything, he told me how close you two were, how much he felt for you when Dolly left, and how hard he went on her to allow him to tell you the truth. He cared about you so much, genuinely, but I think he just wanted to keep his private life private. To be honest, it was for Tim's sake, he was married for years and years and had kids and everything, so their relationship had to be kept secret. Apart from the fact that for many years it was illegal. The reason he never told you was because Tim was afraid his kids would get wind of it. Tim still sees them and they have no idea; they think Brian was a lodger. Apparently, he had his own room, anyone walking into the house would never think anything other than that two bachelors were sharing a house. It's not as strange over here as it might be at home, property is so expensive here, loads of people share.'

Joe digested this information and made a decision.

'Right, okay, well, in that case, I definitely want to go and see him. Will you come with me? It would be easier, I think, if you were there.'

'Of course, I will, you're stuck with me now…Dad.' It was the first time she'd ever called him that and, though she couldn't see his face as she nestled back into him in the cab, she knew he was smiling.

She crawled quietly into bed beside Sharif who was fast asleep. He instantly woke with the movement.

'I'm sorry; I was trying not to wake you,' Carmel whispered.

Sharif turned and gathered her into his arms. 'I was only dozing, I knew you were on the way; thanks for the text. You know I didn't mind if you wanted to stay out, but it's nice to know you're okay. Did you have fun?'

'Oh, Sharif, we had the best time, but I'll tell you all about it tomorrow. Go back to sleep.'

'No, it's okay, I've been resting all evening, tell me everything, how was the show?'

'Amazing, we were singing along and everything. The strange thing is, on the way there, we were trying to think of Frankie Valli songs we might know and came up with around two, and then we knew every single one. It was such fun, and then we met this lady in the bar who actually said Que Sera Sera, I mean, those words, I know some people might think that's a load of old rubbish, but I don't, I think it was Dolly telling us that she was happy Joe and I were reunited.'

'And did you talk about that, the test and everything?'

She told him everything, all about the breakdown in the apartment before they left, and about the test and Tim and everything they'd discussed.

'I'm glad you told him, I could never have, confidentiality and so on, but Tim told you and therefore you could tell Joe, and I think it will be nice for them to meet properly. It must have been so hard for Tim, being the person Brian was closest to and having to behave like they were something less than that. Joe is such a nice man, I'm sure he'll welcome him to the McDaid family, just as he's welcomed you.'

'He really is special, you know, the more I get to know him, the more I think Joe's just like the fathers I imagined as a kid, strong, kind, funny, that sort of thing. I was sitting in the back of the taxi, and he had his arm around me and I was cuddled up to him, and I just didn't feel forty, I felt about ten, and he made me feel safe. It's scary for me, I'm not used to all this affection, either from you or from him, and yet it all feels natural, right, somehow. I just keep thinking this can't actually be happening to me.'

'So, are you going to see Tim with him?'

'Yes, tomorrow afternoon if possible. Joe is going to call him in the morning and see if he's free. I think he's kind of nervous about it; he was sad that Brian never told him, and he seemed genuinely surprised.'

'I suppose Brian wasn't in the least bit camp or anything, not that all gay men are, but he didn't conform to any of the stereotypes of gay people we see on TV or whatever. He was very straight-laced, I suppose, and even when Tim visited, if anything, they seemed kind of formal with each other.'

'I suppose when you have to live your real life in secret, you build up walls like that.' Carmel sighed. 'Poor Brian, it must have been so hard.'

'Well, he at least had the guts to get up and live the life he wanted to live, unlike many of his compatriots. It's the same in my culture, worse actually, as homosexuality is still technically illegal in Pakistan, and even if the law isn't enforced that much, there's still a terrible stigma. Britain has proved to be such a sanctuary for so many gay people. If Pakistanis didn't have British Passports in the past because of being in the commonwealth, well, I dread to think.'

'You wouldn't want to let a bunch of Irish nuns hear you say that, we were fed a strict diet of the trials and misery brought down on our heads because of the English for eight hundred years. They'd go mental if they heard someone saying being ruled by Britain was actually a good thing.' Carmel grinned, leaning on one elbow and looking down into Sharif's face.

'I don't think any Irish nuns would approve of a good Catholic girl consorting with a Pakistani Muslim either.' He smiled ruefully. 'Especially one facing a malpractice suit.'

'Tell me if you don't want to talk about it but, how was your day? Meeting the other solicitor, how did that go?'

He sighed deeply and she saw the worry cross his face once more.

'Alright, I suppose, it seems that all he has are these photos, which are definitely fake, the sheets are not ones we use, they have patterns on them, and everything we use here is white, so he obviously put the stains on them, brought them in, and put them on his mother's bed and photographed her. The dirty tray, the ashtray, I've never seen any of it before, but he said the same as my own legal people, that it would be best to settle. Luke rang, apparently this Johnson does have a record, but it's all for petty things, so nothing we could really use. The solicitor reckons he's not even going to try to take it into court but that he might just try to blackmail me, say he'll send them to the papers or something, post them online, who knows? He's sent a letter, I got a copy this morning, outlining all his grievances, not just the dirt and all of that, but that people here are cruel to his mother, that she doesn't get her meds on time, that she's just not being taken care of generally. His solicitor is not one my man had ever heard of, but that doesn't mean anything.'

'This is just so wrong!' Carmel was struggling to control her temper, 'How the hell can he just come up with all this stuff? And poor Mrs Johnson can't even speak up for us; we've done nothing but be kind and courteous and look after her, like we do for everyone, and this awful money-grabbing man can just...I've a good mind to find him and ...'

'Shush, getting mad doesn't help. Trust me, I was stomping around the office when I got the letter, I just went for a run, pounding the roads seemed to work the temper out of me. I know the temptation, darling, to find him and force him to withdraw his ridiculous claims, believe me, I have fantasized about this myself, but we must do nothing that would make us in any way culpable. All the legal people agree on that. Do not approach him, and to keep an extra close eye on Mrs Johnson. Her charts, her paperwork, all up to date and verified. I am having another consultant come in tomorrow to assess her and write a report on her care, just to have it. I've asked Tristan to recommend someone, not anybody I know, to have an independent assessment of her for our files. It's going to be a rocky road ahead, Carmel, and I can't tell you how glad I am to have you beside me.'

'Well, I've a confession to make, I actually did approach him the other day in the car park. He basically told me that we should both go back where we came from and stop scrounging off the British state.'

Sharif laughed out loud.

'Says the only one in this whole sorry story on benefits! He really is a piece of work. Was that all; I hope he didn't hurt you?'

'No, just verbally abusive and racist. What you'd expect. He is so smelly and horrible and his car, ugh, gross.'

'I know. Look, it will hopefully be okay, and you know how I know that?' He put his arms around her.

'No, how?'

'Because I have you in my corner. I'd be so much more worried if I was facing this alone, but having you beside me, well, it's just great.'

'Always. I don't know how much help I can be, but I'm here one hundred percent.'

'I know you are, now we had better get some sleep, busy day tomorrow.' His dark eyes fixed hers, 'Unless you're not sleepy?' a slow smile crossed his handsome face.

Feeling quite wanton as the nuns might have put it, she ran her hand over his chest. 'No, I think I could stay awake if I was busy...'

CHAPTER 27

Carmel's beeper buzzed her to reception. She tried not to show her frustration, everyone was so busy with the final dress rehearsal for the *Wizard of Oz*, fixing costumes or putting the finishing touches to the set. Things were somewhat chaotic, sets falling over, zips bursting, and the PA screeching feedback, much to the delight of the children. The entire staff found reasons to stop by at one time or another to enjoy the fun. The Kaivalya, recently the home of their very beautiful engagement party, now looked like a bomb site. The show was due on stage the following evening and all the kid's parents and families were coming. The life the production had brought to the hospice was palpable. Even those not involved were excited to see how it all came together.

Carmel was kneeling, mouth full of pins and the Lion stood before her with an almost entirely detached tail. Apparently, he'd closed the toilet door on it and when he turned to see what the problem was, he ripped his tail off, as well as tearing quite a large hole in the costume. The little boy, Noah, was very upset, so Carmel, along with Jill and Winnie, two patients, were doing their best to soothe him while repairing the damage. Similar catastrophes were being handled throughout the room. Daf assured everyone, big and small, that the dress rehearsal was always a total fiasco but that it would be alright on the night. Carmel hoped she was right, but then realized that once the kids had fun, and the patients saw the fruits of their labours on stage, who cared if it wasn't West End standard? Leaving the Lion in Jill's care, she reluctantly made her way to the front desk.

She really wanted to get the show all sorted before meeting Joe. He had arranged to call to Tim's house at six and was picking her up at five-thirty. She took out her phone again. She'd read the text several times already, but she couldn't stop herself.

'How's my girl this morning? Really had a fantastic day yesterday, pet, one of the best of my life. Meeting Tim at his house at 6, will I pick you up at 5.30? love, Dad xx'

She'd offered to meet him earlier but he said he had a few things to do, and he was flying back to Ireland the following morning, so he'd see her later. She wondered what he could have to do here in London, and while she wanted to spend as much time as she could with him, she was glad to get to pitch in with the musical. She had to keep reminding herself that Joe and his family were in her life now and that there would be many more chances for them to meet.

As she made her way to reception, her phone beeped again. Another text, this time from a number she didn't know.

'Hi, Carmel, I'm Aisling, Uncle Joe said he'd like for you to come to my wedding, so if you and Sharif are free on the 15th of September, I'd love to see you again. We spoke briefly at Uncle Brian's funeral, but I'm looking forward to meeting you properly. Hope you can come, Aisling xx'

Carmel was so touched by the message. That Joe had asked Aisling to invite her in the first place, and then that Aisling had taken the trouble to contact Carmel herself. Every moment since making the decision not to have the test had made her realise what a good choice it was. She felt like Joe's daughter, she wanted to be part of his family, and finding out for sure might jeopardise all of that, so she was glad. To go from having nobody at all, to having not just Sharif and Nadia, but to now be part of this big, noisy family, well, it was a dream come true.

She would wait till later to reply when she could word it properly, something to convey how grateful she was for their acceptance.

Joe was standing in reception.

'Is everything okay?' She rushed over to him, he looked a little shaken. 'I thought we weren't meeting until later?'

'Yes, don't worry, everything is grand. I just needed to see you, I need to talk to you, you and Sharif, urgently. Is he around?' Carmel could tell from his expression that something had definitely happened. All sorts ran through her head. Maybe he had decided against taking on Dolly's daughter, maybe someone in his family had talked sense into him.

'Em… yes, I can have him beeped. Let's go in here.' She led him into an office off the large sunny reception area. Before entering, she turned to Marlena, 'Marlena, can you beep Sharif, please? Tell him it's urgent, thanks.'

She closed the door and they both stood in silence. Whatever had happened, Carmel knew it was not good. Joe looked stern and preoccupied.

'Can I get you a drink? Tea? Coffee?' It sounded so ridiculously formal after the intimacy of the day before.

'No, pet, nothing, I'm fine.' At least he called her pet, that was a sign he still loved her, wasn't it? Or maybe he used that term of endearment to lots of people and it didn't mean anything special with her. He stood with his back to the room, gazing out the window.

'Joe, Sharif is on the way, but please, can you tell me what's wrong? Did I do something wrong?'

He turned, 'You? You do something wrong? Ah, Carmel, my love, you're completely innocent, but somebody's doing something wrong alright…'

Sharif opened the door. 'What is it? Are you okay, Carmel?' Worry was etched on his face; she'd never had him beeped before.

Before she had time to answer, Joe spoke, 'Sit down, both of you. You're going to want to hear this.'

Carmel and Sharif exchanged a glance, neither having a clue what was coming next. They sat and Sharif reached for her hand.

'So, Carmel, this morning I went to see a solicitor, I had to sort out some things regarding Brian's estate, he left all his paperwork in perfect order so I knew where to go. I also thought I could kill two birds, as it were, and make my own will. I know I could have done it at home as well, but I wanted to have something to show you this evening, just so you'd know I was serious when I said I want you in my family. Luke and Jen are always onto me about doing it, and so I decided I was going to split my estate three ways, equally between my three children, you, Jennifer, and Luke.'

Carmel had no idea what to say, such a huge gesture was really overwhelming. Before she had time to process it, however, Joe went on.

'So, I went into Bedford this morning, that's where Brian's solicitor is based, at Old Weir Legal Centre. It's only a mile or two from here, actually. There I was anyway, waiting in the sort of communal area, it's like a chambers for loads of legal people, you know the place?'

Sharif nodded, 'I do.'

'Well anyway, I was a bit early so I was just waiting when two people came in. He was fiftyish, unkempt looking, tattoos and all that, and he was with a woman, similar age. The first thing I noticed was she had an Irish accent, and then I looked again. They walked past me and sat kind of around the corner, and though they were talking quietly, they didn't imagine they could be overheard, but I got most of the conversation. The woman was clearly in charge and was telling the man what to say to the solicitor. Apparently, they were meeting someone new since their old solicitor appeared to have abandoned them and their case.

She was telling him not to play up anything too much, apart from the photos, that that was their downfall the last time because all of that was going to be contested by staff but that the camera didn't lie. Lads, she was talking about here and Mrs Johnson.'

Sharif shook his head, astounded. 'I got a call from my legal people this morning, saying that they didn't know why, but Johnson's old

247

solicitor just rang to say he wasn't dealing with the case anymore, he wouldn't go any further apparently, just that.'

'Exactly, well, according to this pair, the old solicitor was hopeless and didn't want to bend the rules, so their mission was to engage another one; that's what they were doing at the law firm.'

'Describe the woman.' Carmel's voice was monotone, she had a horrible feeling she knew who it was.

'Very thin, darkish hair drawn back from her face, I didn't get a good look at her because as I said, they were around the corner. He never referred to her by name, but she was definitely running the show, he's English, a bit of a half-wit, at least that's how he came across.'

'It's Julia.' Carmel was shocked but certain. 'I'd put my life on it. This whole thing is her doing, she said I would pay for what I did to her, back in Ireland and again the other day, and so she's using this Johnson eejit to get back at us, get back at me really for daring to try to divorce Bill and break up the farm.'

'I think you're right. He kept going on about how much they should settle for, trying to calculate Sharif's worth. I was called in then, and I didn't want to go, but if I didn't it would have looked suspicious and I didn't want them to know they'd been overheard. I made my excuses to the solicitor, I think she thought I was just too upset over Brian, so she was very kind and told me there was no rush and to call back when I'm ready. I came straight here.'

Sharif, Carmel, and Joe sat in silence for a moment.

'Did you actually hear them say it was a fake photo?' Sharif asked.

'No, no I didn't, just that he was to leave the talking to her, and to stick to the photos, that nothing else was provable.' Joe was disappointed that he hadn't more conclusive proof that Julia and Johnson were in cahoots.

'So, what should we do now? Surely, this shows they're telling lies?' Carmel felt sure it must mean something.

'I don't know, I'm totally out of my depth here. Should we go to the police?' Sharif wondered.

'Maybe we should ask Luke. Like, I know it's policing in a different jurisdiction, but he might know what to do?' Joe suggested.

'Can't hurt.' Sharif was thinking, 'But we're going to have to be very clever about this, this might be a breakthrough, but it's still only your word against theirs, and you are Carmel's father, so you'd be bound to defend her. You said there was nobody else there?'

'Not a soul. Unfortunately. So, will I ring Luke now? See what he says?'

'Please do, thanks, Joe.' Sharif just looked frustrated as Joe went over to the other end of the room to contact his son.

Carmel felt such guilt she had to say something, 'Sharif, I'm so, so sorry, this is all my fault, bringing that evil witch into your life...I just...'

'Stop,' he whispered, trying not to disturb Joe as he tried to make contact with Luke. He cupped her face in his hands and spoke directly to her, 'None of this is your fault, nor mine, not anyone else's but Derek Johnson's and possibly your ex-sister-in-law's, if it is her.'

'It is. I know it is. She's capable of it too. Maybe I should try to talk to her, reason with her?'

'No, definitely not, we can't approach her, Carmel. She's clearly a very dangerous person if she's willing to go to such lengths. Let's listen to Luke's advice and take it from there.'

They both watched as Joe finished up his conversation with Luke.

'Okay, well, if you're sure... I'm sure she'd appreciate it, okay... I'll tell her, bye son, thanks.' Joe hung up.

'He's coming over in the morning. He's got some contacts in Scotland Yard and he'll see what's to be done. If it's extortion or blackmail, then that's a crime, obviously, but it's just a matter of proving it. Anyway, he said to tell you to do nothing for now and that he'll see us tomorrow lunchtime.'

'Joe, there was no need for him to drop everything and just come over, I mean, we only rang for a bit of advice.' Carmel was overwhelmed at her brother's generosity.

'He knew you'd say that, and he said to tell you that there have to be some perks to having a cop in the family, so to take advantage of it and he'll see you tomorrow.' Joe's voice was full of pride, despite the circumstances. 'Now, as he said, in the meantime, the best thing to do is do nothing. Just sit tight until we know more. But it's a bit of light at the end of the tunnel, isn't it?'

'It is. Thanks, Joe. Aren't you booked to go back to Ireland in the morning, though?' Sharif was grateful and didn't want to inconvenience him any further.

'I was originally but I'm after changing my flight to next week. If that's okay? I just want to help you two during this time if I can, and I'd like to spend more time with you, Carmel, if you don't mind, that is. If I'm in the way, please just say it and I'll go back in the morning.'

'Of course, you're not in the way,' Carmel began, but Sharif interrupted her.

'We'd love you to stay and we'll need all the support we can get, so, if it's not inconveniencing you, then we are delighted. Now, if you're staying, then you must come and stay with us, we have a spare room. What do you think?'

Joe looked at Carmel, the question hanging between them.

'I'd love you to stay with us, I really would.'

'Well, if ye're sure.' Joe smiled gratefully.

'We are, let's go round later and collect your bags, check you out of the hotel, and move you in with us.' Sharif was glad to be able to do that, at least, for the man who was throwing him a life line.

'Should we go to Tim's?' Carmel didn't really feel like it but there was nothing they could do at this stage anyway until Luke got there, so they might as well.

'Sure, I suppose we should, though it's hard to concentrate on it after this. I just wish I'd had the sense to record them, I could have done it with the phone if only I'd have thought. I could kick myself. I was just so angry, listening to them plotting away, that everything else just...'

'Don't worry, we'll get to the bottom of this, at least we now know who is pulling his strings. I always maintained Johnson wasn't sharp enough to come up with all of this on his own.' Sharif was thinking, 'Maybe there is some way out of this mess, after all, though I've no idea what. Maybe if we can prove there is a connection between Julia and him, or something, I don't know. Imagine being so full of venom that you'd want to destroy someone? She's a piece of work, Carmel, you were right.'

They were a little early for Tim's, so Sharif suggested they go for a coffee. As they walked through the grounds, Joe was trying to make sense of it all.

'I mean, if anyone should feel a grievance, it's this Bill character, not that you owe him anything, but it's his farm that's at stake, but why would his sister go to such lengths, it seems mad.'

'I know it does, but on the other hand, I know what she's capable of; I lived under her thumb for long enough.' Carmel wanted them to be under no illusions about what they were dealing with. 'She's poisonous. There were so many examples of it over the years. Like, I might have had a chance to make a relationship with the twins if she'd have allowed it. And she claims to love them, but I remember Sinead was going with this really nice lad years ago, but his family weren't elevated enough in Birr society, so she told Sinead that he'd cheated on her. Of course, he hadn't, but Sinead trusted her aunt so much she never spoke to the poor fella again. Apparently, years ago, one of the kids in school called her a withered up auld virgin, and she nearly beat the poor lad black and blue. The child's mother was afraid to complain because Julia would take it out on all of her kids if she did. She terrorized the whole town, and because it was the only primary school for miles, people had very few options. She really has a terrible temper. She's said horrible things to children about their families and she always sucks up to the doctor's kids, the well-to-do in the town, but to anyone weak or vulnerable, she shows no mercy. And she had such a streak of righteousness in her.'

Sharif thanked the young girl who delivered their coffees.

'Only that I've met her, I can believe it. She's horrid alright,' he agreed, sipping his drink. 'But it seems extreme, even for her.'

Carmel went on, 'She's well capable, honestly, Sharif, I wouldn't put anything past her. One time, a young woman, Lily her name was, came to join the choir in the church, her husband was the new guard

251

in the town and she knew no one, so she thought it might be a way of getting to know people. She had a beautiful voice and everyone commented after Mass. Anyway, I could see Julia was fuming, and the following week, the choir leader suggested that this Lily do the psalm at Mass, to sing it solo, you know? Well, Julia said nothing at the practice but when she called to Bill's house after choir, I could see the bile rising up, almost choking her as she droned on and on at Bill and me. A few weeks later, Lily left the choir, and her husband was suspended pending investigation. Apparently, someone had made an allegation of misconduct, of a sexual nature with a minor, he was training a local under 10s football team. Julia never said anything directly, but she did buy football boots and a jersey for one of the Donnelly's kids, whose father was an alcoholic, and I'm almost sure she put young Donnelly up to saying the guard did something. Of course, nothing came of it, but he was moved on, and Julia was left cackling and croaking her way through every solo once more. She's vicious. Nothing would surprise me, even this.'

CHAPTER 28

*J*oe leaned forward and pressed the doorbell beside the lovely ornate Victorian door with the stained-glass panels. Flowers grew in profusion all around the beautiful front garden, this was clearly the home of a gardener. Carmel gave him an encouraging smile as a shadow appeared behind the door.

'Tim, great to see you again.' Joe's greeting was effusive to hide the trepidation he obviously felt.

'Hi Joe, and Carmel, so glad you could come, it's lovely to see you both, come in.' Tim opened the door wide and they entered. The house was like others on the street, detached with a double bow front, but modest in size. Carmel thought it absolutely gorgeous. She'd been here very early on the morning Brian died but she took very little in during that visit. Her sole focus was on breaking the news to Tim and being there for him. Now that she had time to take it all in, Carmel thought it was like a picture you'd see in a child's story book or one of those ads off the TV at Christmas. The décor was tasteful and unique. Nothing like what one would expect in the home of two bachelors in their seventies. There was no clutter, no hall-stand filled with jackets and outdoor shoes; instead, the house was calm and unfussy. The hallway was painted a dove grey with what looked like hand painted birds of paradise here and there. Coloured light flooded the space through an ornate stained-glass ceiling and straight in front of them were distressed pine double doors leading to a large open-plan kitchen and dining room that opened onto an amazing looking back garden.

'I hope you haven't eaten? I've made supper.' Tim smiled shyly and Carmel knew at once he was as nervous as Joe. She wondered if she should have called him ahead of arriving, given him some indication that Joe knew the truth about his relationship with Brian, but she decided against it. She trusted Joe to be gentle with him and to let the story emerge in its own time.

'We haven't, not that we were expecting it, we were planning on going to the pub afterwards but this smells divine.' Carmel was touched he'd gone to so much trouble.

'It's just chicken in white wine and some new spuds. I don't bother cooking much these days, it's nice to have the excuse.' The pain at the loss of Brian was as raw as it had been at the funeral, but they could tell he was doing his best.

'It's a gorgeous place you have here, the house and the garden. It's like a little oasis of peace in the hustle and bustle.' Joe was looking around, admiring everything.

'Well, I'm into interior design a bit, more the DIY side than the design really, I suppose, but the garden was all Brian. He would spend hours out there, doing God knows what. I'm clueless, wouldn't know a dahlia from a daisy.'

Joe chuckled, 'I'm the same, everything I plant I manage to kill, even the stuff they assure me I can't destroy, I seem to have the knack. We didn't have a garden growing up, so I wonder how he got so good at it?'

'Apparently, when he came over first, he was trying to make a life here, I suppose, and he was working and all of that, but he took a night class. In fact, he signed up to do landscape painting, but he showed up on the gardening class night by mistake and decided he'd stay at it. It's just as well, really, since he turned out to have very green fingers but he couldn't draw a straight line!' Maybe it was because she knew what they meant to each other, but she felt there was something proprietary in the way Tim spoke about Brian. Something intimate and special, her heart broke for him.

'Now, can I get you a drink? A glass of wine?'

'I'd love a glass of white, please.' Carmel was really blown away by the house. It was so elegant and restful. The huge range cooker built into the island at the centre of the room, the bleached wood table with fabulous carved benches on either side. She could imagine how happy Tim and Brian had been here.

'I'd love a glass of anything, Tim, I'm not fussy.' Joe smiled his thanks.

As they took their drinks out to the patio outside to catch the evening sun, they sat in companionable silence for a moment and then Joe held up his drink.

'This is a beautiful home you two made, and a magnificent garden, I can see exactly why my brother dropped anchor here. To Brian.'

'To Brian.' Carmel and Tim clinked glasses.

'So, you know?' Tim asked quietly, staring at the ground between his feet.

Joe sat back and shielded his eyes from the sun, and sighed.

'I do. Carmel told me last night. I can't say I had any inkling before and, I'll be honest, I was a bit sad that he never felt he could tell me, but I'm very glad he had such a great life...' Joe took a sip of his wine and gazed at Tim, whose head was still down, 'such a great love.'

Long seconds passed before Tim spoke quietly, never lifting his head.

'He didn't tell you because of me. It was something that caused him pain, I know it did, but he knew that my kids could never accept our relationship, so he didn't tell anyone. I'd hate to think you were hurt that he didn't say anything to you, he definitely would have told you if my situation was different. He did that for me. The split from my ex was very bitter, she had every reason to be; I married her knowing I couldn't love her, not the way she should be loved. That destroys a person over the years, when she finally found out, she, well she couldn't bear the shame of anyone knowing, so she made me promise to never reveal to anyone what I really was. Giving in to her request was the only thing I could do to lessen that pain I'd caused, so I promised.'

'And your children, they still don't know you're gay?'

'No, their mother is alive, and well...I gave her my word. I've kept it up this long, it won't be so bad to keep it up for the rest of my life at this stage. To be totally honest with you, I'm not entirely sure what the point of my life is anymore. My children are grown up, and while I love them, they've got their own lives to live. I see them every few weeks but...it's so lonely without Brian.' Joe caught Carmel's eye as they heard the anguish in his voice.

Joe leaned over and placed his hand on Tim's, it was a strange gesture Carmel thought, for two Irish men of their age, but it was the right thing to do.

'I miss him too, he was always there for me as well. Every day, especially these last few weeks, I've instinctively gone to ring him and then it hits me again, he's gone. It makes me feel better now that I know the reason he never said anything. Brian was that kind, if he made you a promise, he stuck to it, no exceptions. I presume you know all about Dolly and all that story?'

'I do, it was hard on him, he tried everything to get her to tell you but she was adamant. Between me and her, we put a lot on his shoulders.' Tim topped up their glasses.

An easy silence descended once more, each lost in their own thoughts. Carmel eventually spoke, 'I can understand why she didn't want to tell, especially after what happened to her, but I think both Dolly and Brian would be glad how things have turned out.'

The two men nodded. Carmel then turned to Tim, 'Joe and I have decided, well I'm not sure what the term is, but anyway, he's my dad and I'm delighted he is.' Carmel looked at him and thought how she could never get enough of his twinkly smile.

'So, you've had the test?' Tim seemed surprised.

'No, and I'm not going to. What we have is perfect, we have found each other and we want to be in each other's lives, and finding out that he wasn't my biological father would be so hurtful and hard, especially given the situation. I think we'll let that information with the dead, where it belongs. Joe's family, Jennifer and Luke, have been amazing, and so welcoming, for me, this is just perfect.'

They chatted easily over a delicious dinner and they even laughed. Tim showed them a photo album, normally kept hidden from view, of holidays he and Brian had taken together, where they could be less formal than they were in England. While there weren't pictures of them kissing or holding hands or anything like that, there was a closeness there, it was undeniable.

As Joe turned the pages slowly, he spoke to Tim, 'Lots of people go their whole lives without a love like that, I know the pain of losing him is tearing you apart now, but it will get better, and soon the memories will keep you company and it won't seem that bad, or at least it becomes bearable.'

Carmel marvelled at how Joe was so intuitive to what people needed, he would make such a good counsellor. He had empathy and kindness and yet he was fundamentally a jovial kind of man.

'Were you like this after your wife died?' Tim asked.

Joe thought about his answer. 'Yes and no. June, she was a great mother and wife and I miss her every day. We had such a great marriage, open, respectful, loving and she was great craic as well. But, I'll be honest, the greatest loss I ever had in my life was Dolly. Even now, all these years later, I think about her. Carmel showed me a video, the one taken at her birthday party at Aashna House, and even though a lifetime had passed, and time had done its work, there she was, my Dolly, still the same, the same glint of mischief in her eye. She was a rogue, that one, she wasn't afraid of anyone or anything. At least she was before...' a darkness crossed his face. 'She was like a tiger, so loyal and fierce. That's why it must have almost killed her that she couldn't get you back, Carmel.'

Carmel sat with these two men, people she never even knew existed a year earlier and felt a profound sense of connection to them.

They chatted all evening about Brian, Tim filling them in on his life in London, Joe telling stories about Brian as his brother. It was a warm and gentle evening and it did both men good to reminisce. Carmel asked about Tim's plans.

'I don't know, really, Brian and I had an idea to rent this place out, maybe go travelling for a few months. He wanted to go to Norway to see the Northern Lights and I wanted to see the migration of the butterflies to Mexico, so we had a bucket list. Unfortunately, Brian decided to kick that before we got to live out our plans. I'll have to go back to Mayo sometime, there's land and a farm there and I honestly don't know what's happening with it. I was an only child and so the farm came to me. A local farmer is using the land but as for the house, I don't know. Though, to be honest, I don't relish it. My father caught myself and a local lad in the barn one night, so many years ago now, anyway he threw me out, and told me never to come back again, so I didn't while he was alive. I went to my mother's funeral but that was over twenty-seven years ago.'

'I know how you feel,' Carmel agreed, 'Ireland isn't exactly calling me either. If I never go there again, it will suit me just fine.'

'Ah, now, ye're being a bit harsh on the old sod, if ye don't mind me saying so.' Joe seemed genuinely indignant.

'Ye are both Irish, and you each had your own, very valid reasons for leaving, but it's not fair to blame the whole flippin' country. Seriously, Tim, you'd see lads and girls walking down Grafton Street on a Saturday afternoon, holding hands and canoodling of all kinds, straight, gay, transgender, gender fluid, whatever the hell that is, I don't know, but the point is, the Ireland you left was a very different place. We were the first country in the world to legalise gay marriage by popular vote, you saw that on the news, and people are kinder, there was nothing good about the good auld days, certainly, but it's a very different place now. And from what I know of Mayo nowadays, it's all café culture and craft beers and fellas wearing shorts and going sailing. I think you'd be very surprised, but in a good way.'

Tim held his hands up in capitulation, 'Okay, okay...I never anticipated a Bord Failte representative! The Tourist Board should recruit you.'

'Well, I just love my country and I think you're letting one bad experience colour your view of the whole place, and as for you, young lady,' he pointed at Carmel, mock stern, 'Ireland is your home, it's in your blood, and no matter what, you need to reconcile yourself with that. You're coming over for Aisling's wedding with Sharif. Why don't we make a little holiday of it? Travel round a bit, I bet you've never even seen the West Coast, have you? Tell her, Tim, is there anywhere nicer in the entire world than the West Coast of Ireland on a summer's evening?'

Tim nodded, 'He's right, Carmel. It's like paradise, the crashing waves, the green hills rolling to the sea, tumble-down old castles beside white painted cottages, bright till eleven o'clock at night and then watching the orange sun sink below the horizon of the Atlantic, I miss that alright.'

'Hey, why don't you come too, Tim, we could all go together, rent a big people carrier and drive out west, stay in little B and Bs, and explore our country. You could sort out whatever you need to do with your homeplace, but at least it would be in the company of friends, maybe less sad. God knows, enough tourists do it every year and there we are, Irish people, and we not taking advantage of the bit of heaven on earth God chose to land us in. We're lucky people. I know it's hard, and life had been tough for all of us at one time or another. I'm not diminishing it, but there's something soothing to the soul about standing on the soil of your own land, watching the sea birds nest on the big cliffs, drinking a pint of Guinness and eating fresh fish, while a bunch of hairy fellas belt out tunes on pipes and fiddles, come on, are ye with me?'

They both burst out laughing at his impromptu sales pitch.

'Well, are ye coming or what?' His face was like a child's, full of enthusiasm and fun.

'Fine, okay, yes, I'll come,' Tim agreed.

'Carmel? There's no backing out now if you say yes. Sharif will love it and he needs a holiday.' Joe was determined, and she knew he wouldn't accept procrastination.

'Yes, I'd love to drink a pint of Guinness, the first of my life, with you two somewhere in Ireland.'

'Great! I'll book it all when I get back and let you know the dates, August sometime, okay? Would Nadia come, do you think?'

Carmel laughed at the thought of them all, bouncing around the west of Ireland. 'Well, I don't know, but you can ask her. I'm getting the feeling you're a hard man to refuse.'

Tim smiled and, for a moment, the pain of his loss dulled a little.

Luke landed at Luton the following afternoon and Joe went to pick him up. They all met, along with Nadia, in Carmel and Sharif's flat. As usual, Nadia brought some amazing smelling pastries.

'If we are having a council of war, then an army marches on its stomach, and we'll be no exception.' She smiled, but there was steely determination behind it all. Nobody threatened her son and got away with it.

Carmel was surprised how Luke's demeanor had changed. Gone was the jokey, semi-student to be replaced by a serious law enforcement professional.

'Okay, so what we're looking at is blackmail, and that's an offence under section 21 of the Theft Act 1968. Basically, it means someone being convicted of the act of making an unwarranted demand with menaces with a view to making a gain or causing a loss.'

'Which is exactly what Johnson is doing,' Nadia was adamant. 'And this Julia woman. I wonder if he had this idea and she spurred him on or if it was all her doing? She is definitely the brains of the operation. Johnson has been moaning for ages but going to a solicitor, the photos, he's not smart enough to do all of that on his own. And how did they meet? It seems so odd that she from Ireland would know this Derek Johnson.'

Sharif spoke up. 'I wondered that too, but I got a few key members of staff together this morning to fill them in on what's happening. I don't want it broadcast, obviously, but we have a great team here, so I spoke with them. Johnson was complaining long before Julia arrived, but we do know they had a conversation on the day Julia appeared in Aashna House. Oscar, the yoga teacher, mentioned that Johnson was in the car park, complaining about everything again, he stormed off on Carmel earlier that day but he must have come back later. Julia went over to him and started a conversation. She was on her way out after I more or less threw her out of here. Oscar thought nothing of it until I told him what was going on.'

'Well, yes, that makes sense.' Luke was thinking aloud. 'She's got a grudge against you, Carmel, and now Sharif as well, if she thinks you're behind Carmel wanting a divorce, and Johnson was the willing stick she could use to beat you with. That's almost certainly the truth, but proving it is the tricky bit. I spoke to my opposite number in Scotland Yard off the record this morning, and he was of the same opinion as me. To just wait and see what happens. Do nothing.' He noted their faces.

'Look, I know it's so frustrating just to watch and wait, but he's claiming that his mother was badly treated and he has some evidence, however fraudulently achieved, to that effect. As Sharif has been advised, malpractice suits are notoriously hard to fight and very costly. You could pursue them through the law, and you should, I suppose, they are engaging in criminality, but this is the brother, not the cop speaking, it's a long drawn-out process and all the reputational effect of all that negative publicity could never be quantified.'

'Well, what about we play her at her own game? I mean she's a school principal over in Ireland, for God's sake; surely, she won't want her employers to know what sort of thing she's involved with over here. We could threaten to expose her,' Nadia's eyes flashed with fury.

'I know why you feel like that, Nadia, but honestly, Sharif has the high moral ground here; he's done nothing wrong, so if we threaten her, or make any suggestion of blackmailing her, then it becomes a tit for tat thing and that's much murkier from a legal perspective.' Luke was the voice of reason.

'But, Luke, I heard them plotting; surely, they can't just get away with this, it's not right.' Joe was getting aggravated.

'I understand that, Dad, and if this wasn't family, I'd probably be saying get straight down to the local cop shop, but I know how these things work. They are taking, or threatening to take, a civil case. In essence, by involving the police, you are turning this into a criminal case. So, you'd effectively be upping the ante on something that you really just want to disappear. Do you see what I mean? They haven't escalated it yet, and maybe they'll never have the guts to do it; the evidence is very flimsy, I think Johnson's hoping you'll just pay up and then he'll scurry off into the corner. As for Julia, well she just wants to break you both. You can call their bluff, certainly, say sure, let's see how this plays out in court, but then you're back into negative publicity, no smoke without fire and all of that. And, with hospitals and doctors, there are always more moaners willing to jump on the bandwagon. Some other person's family who sees a chance to strike gold. And to add to it, if the legal end of things doesn't work out for him, he could just send the photos to an unscrupulous daily rag, and they'll print them. It's rotten, I know, but it's how it is.'

'So, is your advice just to pay them off?' Sharif spoke for the first time.

'My advice, and that of my colleague over here is just to sit tight and see what they do next. They've sent the letter to your solicitor, along with the photographs. They never made a demand. Now, we know from what Dad overheard that the first solicitor is after dumping them; clearly, he or she realizes this is fraud, so had the good sense to put the run on them. Most solicitors won't even take this kind of thing on. Of course, there are some sleaze balls who will, but it might be tougher than they think. So, my advice is to wait. See what happens next. I know it's hard and it's a worry hanging over you, but if it was me, that's what I'd do.'

Neither Nadia nor Joe was happy. They were both indignant and with good reason, that someone as unscrupulous as Johnson and now Julia, could just throw a grenade into Sharif and Carmel's lives out of spite.

'I appreciate what you're saying, Luke, and I know on one level it makes sense, but even if they can't get another solicitor to take a legal case on their behalf, what if they just email the photos off to the local paper? We are ruined then, either way. I just hate that they hold all the cards.' Nadia was so angry, her black eyes glittered. Sharif looked shaken and Carmel knew he was ruminating on what Luke told them. He was the best authority they had, him and the solicitor, both of whom were now suggesting that they sit tight and hope that this died down. She knew that such a passive approach wasn't in Sharif's nature; he didn't get this place up and running by taking adversity lying down. There were many hurdles to cross in those days and he went at each one head on. This was killing him.

As the conversation went on around her, she took it all in. These people had given her a happy, love-filled life, something she never imagined she could ever have. She knew what she had to do.

CHAPTER 29

'*A* dhaoine uaisle, ta failte roimh go leir to Baile Atha Cliath. Ladies and gentlemen, you are all very welcome to Dublin. We hope you enjoyed your flight and look forward to welcoming you on board another Aer Lingus flight very soon. In the meantime, Slan agus beannacht.'

Carmel hadn't heard Irish spoken in months, and even though she wasn't brilliant at it when she was at school, it still was nice to hear. Maybe Joe was right, Ireland wasn't to blame for her life, she shouldn't write off the whole country. She stood up to retrieve her carry-on bag from the overhead bin. She'd never flown before, but she was figuring it out.

She showed her passport and was waved through security, and within moments, she was in the terminal building. She made her way to the Bus Ticket kiosk and purchased an expressway ticket into the city centre. She'd have to start from there.

The streets seemed so familiar and yet so alien to her now. The reflection of her face in the bus window blended with the buildings *en route* to the main bus station. She marveled at how cosmopolitan Dublin had become. Though she had grown up here, she rarely had reason to venture into the city as a child, and since marrying Bill, she'd come to the capital only three or four times. The last time she was here was the first time she met Sharif and then, well, after that, everything changed.

He'd be up by now, would have seen her note, begging him not to worry, assuring him she'd call later tonight. She'd turned her phone off because she knew once he realized what she was going to do, or where she was going, he'd try to talk her out of it, but she was sure, surer than she'd ever been about anything that this was the only way out of the mess Sharif and Aashna House were in.

The familiar accents and sounds and smells of Ireland assaulted her senses as she waited in line for another ticket. The central bus station was a hive of activity and all human life was there. Students engrossed in smartphones, earphones jammed in their ears, mothers trying to control unruly toddlers, elderly ladies on day trips, availing of the free travel for all pensioners the Irish government supplied, and of course a good smattering of tourists, drunks, and homeless people.

'Next,' the bored looking woman called from behind the glass.

Carmel stepped forward.

'Birr, please.'

'Single or return?'

'Single...I mean return, I thought you meant was I single...return. I'd like a return, please...' Carmel mumbled, feeling her face redden in embarrassment

'One-day, three-day or twenty-one-day?' the bored voice again.

'Pardon? Sorry, I don't unders...'

'Do you want to come back today? In three days? Or in three weeks?' the woman spoke slowly and loudly, clearly used to dealing with all sorts of people.

'Er...I don't know...it depends...em...'

The woman eyeballed her, exuding disdain and frustration from every pore.

'I'll just take a single, I think,' Carmel eventually said weakly.

'Eight seventy.' The woman tapped some things into a computer and a credit card sized ticket was generated.

Carmel paid and took her ticket. 'Do you know where the bus

leaves from?'

The woman pointed at a gigantic screen indicating which bus left from which lane.

'Oh, right, thanks...'

She was putting everything back into her purse when the woman yelled, 'Next,' and Carmel shuffled away, trying to close her purse as she went.

She examined the board for quite a while, finally finding the bay and bus number she needed. Grabbing a bottle of water and a chocolate bar in the little shop, she made her way to the bus, secretly begging her mother to make sure there was nobody there she recognized. She'd been doing that a lot lately, not that she'd admit it to anyone, but it gave her comfort. She saw feathers and felt her presence quite often and was convinced her mother's spirit was with her. It gave her strength.

Thankfully, she was one of the first to take her place in the queue and found a seat at the very back, minimizing the chances of being seen. She had to change buses at Athlone and take another bus to Birr. Once she arrived in Birr, she didn't exactly have a plan. The farm was three miles outside the town, and there wasn't a bus. On her once-weekly trips for grocery shopping, she took the weekly community bus that took all the elderly people into town, to the clinic, the library, or for a few messages. But that bus only went on Wednesdays and this was Friday.

She wished she knew where Julia was. The school was off for the summer, so she probably wasn't there. She may well be still in England. Part of Carmel hoped she was.

The journey was uneventful and she tried not to look too guilty or conspicuous as she got off the bus at Emmet Square. She prayed again to meet no acquaintance. It was hard enough being back. Everything looked so familiar, the shops, the streets, but she wasn't that person anymore, she was someone else.

Gripping her overnight bag, she made her way west of the town, passing the entrance to Birr Castle and Demesne. She remembered how she used to watch the families gather for picnics there often, the riverside walk was lovely, grounds nestled in the lee of the imposing castle walls. There was a playground and she'd sometimes sit near it and wonder what it was like to have children. Couples walking hand in hand, fathers carrying little kids on their shoulders, friends power walking and gossiping, all of it was right in front of her, but might as well have been on Mars for all she knew about it. She'd been on the outside looking in her whole life, until now. How she longed to be back in London with Sharif, safe and loved, but she needed to be here. He'd done so much for her; he had given her a chance at happiness and she owed him this.

The sun was high in the sky as she walked, and her bag felt much heavier than it had when she crept out of the apartment at five this morning. Sharif was sleeping at the clinic in the on-call room. He did that sometimes if someone was dying and wanted him near.

She climbed the hill and saw their house, or Bill's house, as she always thought of it, in front of her. His car was parked outside as usual; he didn't like to drive it into the yard in case it got dirty. Bill was very particular about his car.

'Okay, Dolly,' she spoke to herself, 'If I ever needed you, I need you now. Firstly, keep that witch Julia away. Whatever hope I have of managing this without her there, I'll have none at all if she turns up.'

It was as if ice was churning around in the pit of her stomach. The chocolate she ate on the bus was the only food she'd taken and she was feeling light-headed. This was insane, what was she doing here?

'Calm, Carmel. Use your breath to steady yourself, you can do this.' She repeated the mantra to herself as she approached the house. What should she do? Knock on the door? Go around the back? The back door was usually never locked, or should she just take the spare key from under the milk churn with flowers in it and open the front door?

Eventually, she decided to knock on the back door. She didn't even know if he'd be there, but there was a chance.

With trembling hands, she made a fist and knocked on the back door. Nothing. She was about to knock again when she saw the shape of someone through the bubble glass, and the door opened.

'Hello, Bill,' was all she managed.

He stood there for a long moment just looking at her, then turned back into the house, leaving the door open. Assuming she could go in, she stepped inside to the back kitchen and followed him into the main room of the farmhouse. Everything was exactly the same, the décor, the ornaments, the Waterford crystal-framed wedding photo of Bill and Gretta. The only thing different was a kind of sour smell like the place needed a good clean.

He stood with his back to the range, his hands in his pockets. She thought he looked old and tired. He needed a haircut and had cut himself shaving, there was blood on the collar of his shirt.

'Are you coming back?' he asked, eyeing her small bag.

'I...I...Well, no but I just wanted to talk to you, in person...face to face, you know?'

'About what?' his voice was leaden.

Carmel took a breath; clearly, he wasn't going to engage in small talk.

'I'm sorry I left you the way I did. I should have said something, it was wrong of me.'

He rested his eyes on her, taking in her new clothes and hair, she was sure. She looked like a different person. Not just looks either, she was a different person.

'It was.'

'And so, I want to say I'm sorry.'

'So, your fancy man, that darkie, he kicked you out, did he?'

Carmel tried not to flinch at the racist description of Sharif. She couldn't let this turn into a fight.

'No, no, he didn't.'

'So, what are you doing here?'

'I wanted to talk.'

'About what?'

'About us, about the future,' she took a deep breath, 'about Julia.'

Again, the silence, his eyes raking her face for a clue.

'There's nothing you can say to me that I'd care to hear. Your solicitor and mine will be hammering out the details, but don't be expecting much. This is my land and I won't be giving it up, for you or for anyone else for that matter.'

Carmel thought it might have been one of the longest sentences he'd ever addressed at her.

'Well…If you'd just hear me out anyway.' Carmel was doing her very best to stay neutral and reasonable; Bill would baulk immediately if she started crying or got upset. This was her only chance, she had to take it and make the best effort she could.

'Sharif knew my birth mother. That's why he came to see me, to give me some letters she wrote to me. She never wanted to give me up, but she was raped, you see, and she had no choice. The man who raped her insisted that I never be adopted, and so I never was. When I met you, I really hoped I could be part of your life, your family, but I wasn't, I couldn't. I did try, I swear to you, I did. I wanted to be a mother to Sinead and Niamh, but there just wasn't room for me.'

She tried to see if there was any hint of understanding or anything at all on his face, but he was just standing there, hands still in his pockets, his face giving nothing away.

'I…I was so lonely, Bill. I…wanted you to love me, but to be honest, I wasn't sure you even liked me. You married me; well, for years I wondered why. Until that day you told me it was to stop Julia moving in.'

The silence between them was thick and heavy. If he refused to speak now, then she might have blown it.

Just as she was beginning to think he was never going to reply, that she'd have to take her bag and leave, he spoke, 'Do you want money? Is that it? Because I'll give you money if you don't go after the farm.' She thought she heard some emotion in his voice, but she couldn't be sure.

'Bill, listen to me. I don't want your money or your farm. I don't want one single penny from you.'

'Your solicitor does.'

'I don't and he works for me. He was just doing what is standard practice. I'm with Sharif now and we have enough money. I just want us both to move on with our lives and try to be happy.'

Carmel looked at Bill and he looked so much older than his sixty-eight years. She felt a sudden surge of almost affection for this man who she'd called her husband for all those years, but, in fact, was a total stranger to her.

'Bill, can we sit down?' she kept her voice gentle, not wanting to break the spell where he actually spoke. She moved to the kitchen table and pulled out two chairs.

He sat down, and she sat opposite him. Her voice was steady and confident, infused with kindness.

'Gretta was the love of your life, sometimes you only get one of those.'

He looked up at her and sighed, nodding slowly, as if not trusting himself to speak.

'And this fella, is he that for you?' Bill's blue eyes were locked with hers. If she was to have any hope of getting him to understand, then this was it.

'I think so, yes. I love him, Bill, and he loves me.'

More silence.

'Right so. That's it.' He went to stand.

'But, Bill, there's something else.'

'What?' He was wary again, any shred of intimacy dissipated.

'I don't want anything from you, I swear. I know I've hurt you or embarrassed you or something, and I'm truly sorry for that, but I just want us to divorce and get on with our lives.'

'Fine. Send whatever papers you need me to sign.' He got up to go.

'Julia is blackmailing us.' She blurted it out, fearful he was going to leave and the chance would be lost.

'What?' he turned, his brow furrowed.

'It's a long story, but there is a man trying to claim that Sharif isn't taking proper care of his mother, an elderly patient. It's lies, of course, but Julia is involved. She is going to solicitors and she got him to take photos of his mother in dirty sheets and with ashtrays all around and all of that, totally fabricated, but she wants to hurt me and Sharif. She came over a while ago, threatening me to leave the farm alone, and things got a bit heated, she was so angry, so she wants to hurt us. I know you probably don't believe me, but I have witnesses who have overheard her plotting with this man…' Carmel knew she was getting over excited in her efforts to have him believe her, but she was frightened he'd just dismiss her and walk out the door.

Bill sat back down, clearly thinking. Carmel stopped talking. She knew that he'd only say something when there was space to say it.

Bill sighed deeply, obviously tired of it all.

'We had words, after that day. She told me all about your set-up when she came back. I didn't know she was going over there; I wouldn't have allowed it had I known. She's had too much to do with me and the girls since Gretta died. Gretta couldn't stick her, actually.'

Carmel couldn't believe her ears.

'Can you get her to stop?' Carmel didn't want to interrupt his flow, but she was so unsure as to how to handle this new verbose Bill that she decided to strike while the iron was hot.

'As I said, we haven't spoken since that day.'

'Could you try? I know I've no right to ask you for anything, after what I did, but Sharif has worked his whole life to build that place up from nothing. You get that, don't you? If someone threatened the farm, you'd have to fight back? And it really is such a special place, and it seems that malpractice suits are so hard to fight…'

'That's wrong. She's a spiteful woman, always was.' He went to the phone, which was attached to the wall.

He lifted the receiver and consulted the little brown address book he kept hanging beside it on a piece of twine. As he punched in a number, Carmel wondered, hardly daring to breathe, about what was going to come next.

'Julia? It's Bill.'

'Yes, I am, of course, at home, where else would I be?'

'Listen to me now, and stop your blathering. I know what you're up to with that fella you met over in England, trying to tell a load of lies about that hospital or whatever it is. Now, listen carefully, if you ever want to speak to me or the girls ever again, you stop this right this minute. And find some way of stopping that other fool you're after getting yourself tangled up with. Do you hear me?'

Long silence while he listened.

271

'That's your own business; you got yourself into this and you may get yourself out of it. I am warning you that this is to stop unless you want the whole place here to know what you're at, and that includes Father Hourihan, who is the chairman of the board of management of the school above and Father Creedon as well.'

Another silence.

'Won't I? Well, you'll just have to wait and see about that now.'

And he hung up.

Carmel was astounded. On so many levels.

'Right. She'll call it off. Now, I've got to go.' He went to take his coat from the back of the door.

'Bill.'

He turned.

'Thanks, it means the world to me that you helped me out. And, I'm sorry, I really, really am.'

He stopped and, for a moment, she thought he was just going to leave without another word, but he turned and crossed the room and stood in front of her. She could almost see him formulating the words in his head. Eventually, he spoke.

'Tis I should be sorry, dragging a young girl in here, and being... well...not right. And that day when you asked me why I married you, well I was a bit harsh. I'm not one for much chat, but I could have made things nicer for you. Gretta would be very vexed with me for the way I treated you, so I'm sorry too. I hope you'll be happy.' He held his hand out to shake hers, the only voluntary touch in nearly two decades of marriage.

She ignored it and leaned in and kissed him on the cheek.

'I wish you happiness too, Bill. I really do.'

He nodded.

'Will I run you down to the bus?'

'That would be great, thanks.'

They pulled away from the house for what Carmel knew would be the very last time. She didn't look back, there was nothing to see.

CHAPTER 30

'Good afternoon, ladies and gentlemen, and you are all very welcome aboard this flight EI 348 to London Luton. Please ensure your tray tops are secure, seats upright, and seat belts fastened. Our flight time today is fifty-five minutes...'

She switched her phone back on for a moment and wrote a text to Sharif and Joe. As she expected, there were several missed calls from both of them.

'Hi, am okay. See you later, will explain then. C x'

She switched it off again. This wasn't a conversation she could have over the phone and anyway, she just needed some time with her thoughts.

Luckily, there was a flight back to London that evening and she'd bought a ticket, smiling to herself at how competent a traveler she had become in just a few short months. She dozed on the flight and only woke to the bump as the plane touched down.

The taxi dropped her at reception of Aashna House, and even though it had only been a day, it felt different. She hoped Sharif was there; she needed to see him.

'Oh, Carmel, hi, we were starting to worry! Sharif has been in and out all day asking if you were back yet.' Marlena smiled as she was getting ready to leave for the night. 'Well, he was until this evening. Mrs Johnson has gone down rapidly, he's with her now. Will I beep him for you?'

'No, no that's okay, Marlena, I'll find him. I don't want to disturb him if he's with a patient. Er...is Mrs Johnson's son there?' Carmel lowered her voice, even though the entire area was empty.

'No. He was here this afternoon, seems he took a lot of her things, jewellery and so on, and left. The staff told him that the end was close, she's been in and out of consciousness all day really, but he didn't seem to care, he didn't even say goodbye to her, and now he's not picking up his phone. He told them something like he won't be back...' Marlena's normally perfect English became more accented if she was upset. 'He is so awful, this man. Really not a nice man.'

'Yep, you're not wrong there.'

Carmel made her way to Mrs Johnson's room, deciding she would just peek in. If Sharif was attending to her, then she would leave and wait for him at home, but he could just be sitting with her. He was insistent that nobody should leave this earth alone, so when patients had nobody, it was often Sharif who held their hand as they took their last breath.

It was late by now, most of the night staff were on, but they were quiet and the lights were dimmed. The door to Mrs Johnson's room was slightly ajar and, as she suspected, there he was, sitting beside her bed, her small hand in his.

He looked up as she entered and sighed.

'You're back,' he whispered, 'I was worried.'

She kissed the top of his head and sat beside him.

'I'm sorry. I went to Ireland to see Bill. I asked him to speak to Julia, to call this whole thing off.'

Sharif turned and gazed intently at her.

'And?'

'And he did what I asked. He told her to stop everything, or she'd never see him or the girls again, and he threatened to report her to the

Board of Management of the school. He also told her to find a way to get Derek Johnson to withdraw his case as well.'

'Really?' Sharif's brow was knitted in confusion, 'Why would he do that for you, for us?'

'You know, it was strange. We had a good chat, actually, probably the first one ever. I told him I didn't want the farm. He said he was sorry, that he hadn't really been in a position to marry again, and he shouldn't have. He was kind and wished me all the best, as I did him. It was amazing, really.'

He gestured to her to move outside as Mrs Johnson stirred but resumed her peaceful sleep once more. Her breathing was shallow but she seemed not to be in any distress. Once out in the quiet corridor, he whispered, 'That all makes sense. Johnson stormed in here today, very agitated, furious I'd have said, and he took whatever Mrs Johnson had, money, jewellery, and when Julianna, the staff nurse told him that his mother's condition had deteriorated, he basically told her to eff off and stormed out. We've tried calling him several times this evening, she won't last too much longer I would think, but his phone is switched off. Julia must have taken Bill's threat seriously.'

'Well, the way he spoke to her, I was there, he wasn't messing around. Bill isn't a man for idle threats. Either way, it's over. Oh, and he said he's not going to be difficult about the divorce, just have our solicitor send whatever he needs to sign and he'll do it.'

Sharif drew her into his arms, something he never did within the clinic.

'You're amazing, do you know that? Simply amazing. I can't wait to be married to you.'

'I know.' She grinned, winking at him. 'Now, would you like me to sit with Mrs Johnson for a while? You take a break?'

'No, I'm okay. She and I go back a long time. It won't be long now. You can come in with us if you like, or are you exhausted?'

'No, I'm fine. I'll just go and call Joe, he and Luke are out visiting some more McDaids in Reading or somewhere before heading back to Ireland tomorrow. I texted him from the taxi, he was worried too.'

'I know. I'm so happy and grateful that you managed to solve this. You really should have told me your plan, though…'

'You'd have tried to talk me out of it.' Carmel was matter of fact.

'Well, maybe I would, but please, no more solo runs, okay? We're a team and we make decisions together.'

'Are we having our first fight?' she grinned.

'I hope not because if today is anything to go by, I'll be on the losing side every time.'

'You might do well to remember that.' She smiled at him and squeezed his hand.

She walked away down the corridor to an alcove with easy chairs and a sofa.

She scrolled and pressed call.

'Carmel, so you turned up?'

She could hear the grin in his voice. Briefly, she outlined the events of the day, and both he and Luke were delighted. It sounded like they were having a great time and so she left them to it and returned to Sharif.

Mrs Johnson's breath was very ragged now, and noisy. Sharif had explained to her before that the loosening of mucus in the airways causes what is commonly called the death rattle. Her skin appeared paler too, and her hands were cold, Carmel sat on the other side of the bed from Sharif.

She seemed a little more agitated than earlier, and Sharif spoke soothingly to her.

'It's alright now, Dorothy, you can go. Everything is all right with the world, everything is fine. Slip away, you're free to go.'

She never opened her eyes, but seemed to take a deeper breath and exhaled slowly. Instantly, her face became more peaceful, she seemed to release all her pain in that last breath.

Sharif sat holding one hand and Carmel the other. A few moments passed, and he stood and took her pulse and noted the time of death on her chart. Carmel watched him brush her hair back from her face and lean down to kiss her gently on the forehead.

'Thanks for all you did for me, and for this place. Godspeed,' he whispered.

He notified the morgue team and the all too familiar process began.

Quietly, Sharif took Carmel's hand and together they walked home.

EPILOGUE

The day dawned bright and clear and Carmel allowed herself to luxuriate in their large bed for a few moments before getting up. It felt strange to sleep alone, but Nadia insisted that she should spend the night before her wedding away from Sharif. He, Joe, Nadia, and the rest of the McDaid's were staying at a hotel a few miles away.

She switched the alarm off and threw back the covers. The wedding was going to be at noon and Ivanka was coming to do her hair and makeup. Her dress was so simple it would be on in a moment. Nadia had helped her choose and she was delighted with the raw silk strapless gown. It was fitted to her waist and then fell to her ankles so gracefully she felt like a princess.

'I think I'm a bit long in the tooth for princess dresses,' she said ruefully when the saleswoman suggested it originally, but at Nadia's insistence, she tried it on. It was perfect on her and there and then she decided she would wear it. So what if she was forty? She'd never dressed up like this before and she was only doing this once.

Nadia had been so understanding last night when she said she wanted to be alone before the wedding, just to go over to the little chapel and have a talk with her mother. Perhaps it was her Catholic upbringing and all the time spent in churches, or maybe not, but she felt close to her there. Nadia said Dolly often went there to be alone as well and today she wanted to feel that connection before all the excitement started. She'd sat there, for an hour, and just chatted to her mother, and for Carmel, her mother was there with her. When she came back to the apartment, she found Nadia in the spare room, looking at the photo of Jamilla.

The older woman was embarrassed to have been caught, 'I'm sorry, Carmel dear, this must look awful, like I'm wishing things were different, but I assure you...'

'Nadia, I understand. Jamilla was a huge part of Sharif's life, and of yours and Khalid's as well, of course she is going to be on your minds today. Please, don't be sorry.' Carmel wanted to reassure this woman who had been so welcoming and kind to her.

They stayed up later than they intended, drinking chai and talking about Jamilla, Khalid, and, of course, Dolly, and it was lovely.

Nadia had left for the hotel earlier that morning.

As she made her way into the shower, there was a knock on the door.

She sighed, much as she loved everyone at Aashna, she hoped it wasn't anyone calling to wish her luck or anything, and immediately regretted the thought. What she would have done this time last year for some friends, someone to love, a home of her own. She opened the door to a UPS delivery man asking her to sign for a smallish box he proffered.

The box was addressed to Carmel Murphy, a name she hadn't used for years, and she didn't recognize the writing. She opened the box with a knife and was intrigued to shake out an 'On your Wedding

Day' card and another box, this one containing a Waterford crystal large empty photo frame. She opened the card,

'TO CARMEL AND SHARIF, *I wish you all the best on your wedding day. I hope you have a very happy life, you deserve it. The frame is for your wedding photograph.*
Best wishes,
Bill.

SHE SAT DOWN and stared at the present, incredulous that Bill would have gone to such trouble. The frame was almost identical to the one she dusted every day on his mantelpiece of him and Gretta, and for a moment, she was transported back to those empty lonely days.

Bill had kept to his word, Julia and Derek Johnson disappeared, he never even turned up at his mother's funeral, and once the divorce was granted, she wrote to Bill telling him of her wedding plans and thanking him for his cooperation. She heard nothing in reply until now.

She thanked him quietly and went to get ready. Life really was so strange.

At her kitchen table, she sat alone, savouring the peaceful solitude. She'd come so far, from a child of the state to the wife of a man incapable of loving her in any sense, to here. Nobody could have predicted her life path. For the millionth time, she wished Dolly could have lived to see this day, but it was not to be. She said a prayer for her, and for Brian, and asked them to watch over her and Sharif, today and always.

And then it was time. Ivanka had outdone herself, and as Carmel looked in the mirror, she thought, you look lovely. Not, not-too-bad for a kid from an orphanage, or passable if you don't notice the flaws, but really, really, lovely, and she felt proud. She was so happy to marry Sharif, she loved him with all her heart and he loved her. He had given her everything, this beautiful life, but she owed him so much more than that. He gave her the confidence that most kids get from their parents, that sense that she is worthy and precious, and under his love, she grew up.

When Joe arrived, he simply stared at her, beaming.

'Well, my darling girl, you look radiant, absolutely glowing with happiness.'

They walked arm in arm across the lawn to the marquee erected for the wedding. Oscar was a humanist celebrant, so they asked him to perform the ceremony, and everyone she loved was gathered inside waiting for her.

'Ready?' Joe smiled down at her and squeezed her arm close to him. She nodded.

All eyes turned to her as she entered the beautifully decorated marquee, and her mother's voice, singing *Que Sera Sera, whatever will be will be, the future's not ours to see, Que Sera Sera* recorded at her last ever party, accompanied her forward to her future.

THE END

CHAPTER 31

BOOK 3 - WHAT WILL BE

*C*armel sat on the side of the bath trying to breathe normally. Sharif was in the living room watching a documentary about whales, and Nadia was happily surfing the internet on her new tablet. Nadia had decorators in her place, so she was spending a bit more time with Carmel and Sharif to allow the workmen to finish the job quickly. Jen had called Carmel to tell her the exciting news that she was pregnant again. Carmel was thrilled for her sister, of course she was, but why did the news bring stinging tears to her eyes and a pain in the pit of her stomach?

She gazed at her reflection in the mirror over the sink. She looked upset; Sharif would know something was wrong if she came out now. Her naturally blond hair was shiny and sleek, having just been to the hairdresser's today, and she would touch up her makeup, but no matter how she looked, he had a way of seeing past all of it, into her soul.

She'd have to pull herself together. She was forty-one years old, for goodness sake, she'd had her life transformed in ways she could never have imagined, and she a had a home of her own, a loving family, friends, and the love of Sharif, so why on earth was she feeling so despondent? She knew the answer, though she didn't even want to admit it to herself. She wanted a baby.

'Carmel, do you want some tea?' Sharif tapped gently on the bathroom door. The programme must be over.

'Eh, yeah, thanks, I'll be out in a minute,' she called.

'Is everything OK? You've been in there a long time...' She heard the concern in his voice.

'Yes, fine. I'm...reading something on my phone,' she lied, reddening, even though there was nobody to see it. She just wanted him to go away, for a moment or two, to give her a chance to recover.

She tried to keep it together, to not cry.

It was so peculiar, so strong, this longing for a child, and the feeling had taken her totally by surprise. She had never imagined herself as a mother. She'd thought her only chance at motherhood had been her failed attempt with her ex-husband Bill's girls nearly twenty years ago. But even though they were only little when they'd lost their mother to cancer and Carmel and Bill married, the girls had been monopolised by their aunt. There'd been no room for Carmel.

Now that she'd found such happiness with Sharif, she felt frustrated with herself. Why couldn't she just enjoy it? But she couldn't. All she wanted was a child of her own, just one—a boy, a girl, she didn't care.

Being raised in state care in Ireland meant she'd never had a family, never felt part of anything, and now that she was married for love, at long last, things should've been perfect. Sharif was her soul mate, no doubt about it, and his mother Nadia had become almost a surrogate mother to Carmel, as well. Nadia had been best friends with Carmel's birth mother, Dolly, for so long, she was able to bring Dolly alive through her stories. Nadia still felt Dolly's loss keenly, and she sometimes expressed frustration at knowing how close they came to reuniting Dolly with Carmel. But it wasn't to be. Dolly died months before Sharif finally found Carmel on Facebook. He had promised Dolly he wouldn't give up the search, and he was true to his word. After she died, Nadia and Sharif had helped Carmel in every way imaginable, giving her a life, a home, helping her connect with Joe, her dad, and Jen and Luke, his children. She had so much more than she'd ever imagined she could. They would have done it anyway, even if she and Sharif had not fallen in love, but the fact that they had was a happy coincidence.

The hospice they all ran together, Aashna House, was so busy but such a rewarding place to work, she should have been content. More than content. She should've been doing cartwheels. But here she was crying in the bathroom because her sister, who she'd only known for a year, was pregnant.

Carmel was forty-one and Sharif was forty-six, so they were no spring chickens. He didn't have any children—his first wife had died, and afterwards, once he came out of the cloud of grief, he threw himself into creating Aashna. When he and Carmel had talked about children, ages ago, he seemed to be under the impression that that ship had sailed, and he was mildly regretful but not sad. He was just so grateful and happy to have found love a second time, that was enough. At the time, Carmel said she'd never envisaged herself as a mother, because she was afraid to say what she really wanted. The thoughts swirling around her head at night, as Sharif slept beside her, told her she would probably be hopeless at parenting anyway—she had no experience. What would someone raised in an institution know about being a proper mother? The care workers in Trinity were fine, and even the nuns were all right, but you wouldn't describe any of them as maternal. She wouldn't know where to start to be a mother, she knew that, but nothing would make the yearning disappear.

She was on the pill, and apart from that one conversation with Sharif, the subject was never raised again.

Something had come over his face that day they talked about kids, something she couldn't read, and she was afraid to pry. After all, he'd plucked her from her miserable marriage and delivered letters from Dolly, who had spent her life looking for her only child, to no avail. Apparently, the loss of her daughter was the heartache of her life and the years spent searching and getting nowhere meant she'd died unfulfilled. The thought of it all made Carmel happy and sad in equal measure. She would have loved to meet her and regretted deeply the fact that her mother was unable to find her, but the knowledge that she hadn't been abandoned as a child, discarded like something unwanted, served to heal some of the broken bits inside her.

She took a deep breath and tried to bring herself back to the present. She needed to pull herself together. She was afraid Sharif would think she wasn't happy, or that she was ungrateful. She knew deep down he would think none of those things, but the insecurities she carried, deeply ingrained by twenty years of state care, followed by seventeen years of an empty, cold marriage, were not easily erased.

Before she went back out, she took one more look at herself in the mirror over the sink. The strong spot lighting, ideal for putting on makeup or shaving, hid nothing, and the pain was there in her eyes. Both Sharif and Nadia were very perceptive; she'd have to do a better job of acting like everything was fine.

'Chai or Barry's?' Sharif asked as she emerged.

She smiled. 'Chai, please.' He handed her a cup of chai, which she'd initially found revolting. At first, she'd been afraid to say she hated it, because Sharif never drank normal black tea, even though he wouldn't have cared if she did. But after almost a year of living with him, she'd actually come to like chai.

'Are you sure you're OK?' He put his head to one side, his brown eyes looking intently at her.

'Honestly, I'm fine.' She smiled and kissed his cheek. 'Thanks for the tea.' She sipped it.

'Does it still taste like boiled weeds?' He grinned, teasing her about a remark he'd overheard her make to her sister Jennifer on the phone months previously. The very next day, he'd gone out and bought her a big box of Barry's tea bags from Ireland.

'Well, aromatic weeds, I'll go that far.'

'So how's Jen?' he asked.

'Good, she's fine. Joe is doing a job for them in the house, and Luke has a new girlfriend, it seems.' She didn't tell him about the pregnancy; she just couldn't get the words out. She was spared further elaboration when Sharif's beeper went. He was needed in the hospice.

He glanced at it and kissed her cheek. 'I've to go. I don't know how long I'll be, but text if you need me, OK?'

'Sure.' She hugged him. He was so muscular and smelled of sandalwood and soap. She felt a familiar stirring of attraction.

Something in her embrace caused him to pause and give her a slow smile. 'Mmm, you're so gorgeous. I'll try to be back before you go to bed.' He murmured it all so his mother didn't hear.

'I'll wait up,' she whispered back.

Nadia was so deep in a very animated FaceTime chat in her native Urdu with one of her relatives in Karachi that she wouldn't have heard them even if they spoke normally. Likewise, Carmel hadn't the faintest idea what Nadia was saying. Sharif could speak Urdu too, as it was the language of their home as he grew up. Carmel sometimes felt bad that they had to speak English around her all the time, so as not to exclude her, but they assured her they were equally comfortable in both languages.

She slipped into their bedroom, leaving Nadia to chat, relieved to be alone. Something made her pick up the phone and call her dad. The discovery that Joe even existed was still new, but in many ways, she felt as if she'd known him all her life. They spoke every day, sometimes several times a day, on the phone. Sometimes just for a minute or two. She knew he wasn't a phone chatter, but he seemed to understand that she needed to have that connection, and to make her feel less needy, he called her as much as she called him.

'Hi, darling, how are you?' he answered on the first ring, his strong Dublin accent immediately soothing her troubled soul.

'I'm OK. You?' She tried to inject some enthusiasm into her voice. She wished he was here in London; she could've really used one of his bear hugs.

'Grand out, pet, flying it. Your cousin Aisling's wedding is taking up everyone's time here. I'm telling you, there was fellas put on the moon with less organisation. I'm staying out of it all as much as I can, but she just rang and asked me to make a sweet cart or something. I thought she was losing her marbles, like sweets like a child would have, at the wedding reception, only there's no kids going. And I sez to her, Aisling, pet, when people are drinking pints and glasses of wine or whatever, the last thing on their minds are fizzy jellies or smarties or whatever, but she wasn't having a bar of it. Tis all the go now, apparently. Sweets, did you ever hear the like? So off with mad old uncle Joe to the hardware place tomorrow to get the stuff for it. I don't know, more money than sense...'

Carmel chuckled. She loved to hear the stories of the extended McDaid tribe.

'Now, yourself and Sharif and Nadia are still on for the trip, aren't ye? I've a great itinerary set up. Come here to me now, you're the very woman for this job. I was talking to Tim earlier, and he was saying he didn't think he'd be able to make it, and I didn't like to pry. I know he has some things to sort out over in Mayo with his parents' land and everything, but he was all up for the trip the last time we spoke, and now he's backing out. Could you talk to him? See what's going on? He and Brian were very private about their relationship and everything—well, they had to be, on account of Tim's family—and I know Brian was my brother and we were close and everything, but I just don't feel comfortable pressing Tim.

'There's something up though, I know it, so maybe you could get it out of him? He trusts you. I think it would do him good to come over; it's been decades since he set foot in his native country, and I think it would be to his benefit to lay a few ghosts to rest. Anyway, it's his choice, but ye can fly into Dublin, and we can all rent the minibus and take off for the West of Ireland, have a proper holiday, not just a weekend for the wedding. Jen, Damien, and the baby, and Luke are coming as well, so we'll have great craic.'

'Yes, we've the flights booked and everything. Though I can't say I'm looking forward to being back.' Carmel loved that she could be so honest with Joe. Their relationship had started out that way and had continued, no pretence, no saying what she thought he wanted to hear. It was such a departure for her after a lifetime of watching what she said, trying to please, to fit in. 'I'm excited to go to Aisling's wedding, of course, but I just feel happier out of Ireland, you know?

287

Like I escaped. And I'm scared to go back in case I get sucked back in or something. Stupid, I know...'

'Ah, 'tisn't one bit stupid, my love, not a bit of it. But as I'm always telling you, the reason your experience here was so bad, so empty, was because of the behaviours of a few people, not the whole country. You're Irish, Carmel, your mam was Irish, and so am I, and no matter what, this place is in your bones. It wouldn't do you any good to build up a big wall between you and it. Like, Sharif is Pakistani, he doesn't live there or anything, but he knows who he is and where he comes from. That's important to the human spirit. I think it is, anyway.'

'Maybe you're right. I'm trying just to see it as a holiday, but do me a favour? Keep me away from Birr, County Offaly, OK?' She smiled.

'Well, I have no notion of going near any town that is home to your ex and his mad witch of a sister, so yes, we're staying out of that part of the country entirely, just in case. But wait till you see where I am taking ye, you're going to love it. We need to spend a few days in Westport, to let Tim get things sorted legally with his family farm and all of that, provided of course that you can convince him to come. I'm going to show you all the places I wish I'd been able to show you when you were small, when I could have been a proper dad to you.'

Though his words were tinged with sadness at all the time that was lost, his enthusiasm was infectious, and she felt her mood lighten. 'You're a proper dad now,' she said quietly. 'And I'm so glad to have you.'

'We've a lot of making up to do, Carmel, a lot. Please God we'll have lots of years together. I used to think my job was done, and after June died, I was very low. Jen and Luke were reared and doing grand, so I felt like I was only filling in time, but now that you're in my life, I feel like I want to live for years and years to try to make up for all the time lost.'

Carmel felt a rush of love for this man, her dad. She used to dream about her parents, when she was small, but she couldn't have dreamed up a better man than Joe McDaid.

'You will. Sure you're fit as a trout, as Sister Kevin used to say. Actually, Sharif was saying the other day he was at a conference and there's a new drug for the treatment of asthma in trial that is having great effects, so we might both be even healthier in the future.'

'Imagine that.' Joe chuckled.

'Oh, and I'll ring Tim tomorrow, invite him for lunch,' Carmel promised. 'He's finding the days long without Brian, and Christmas was so lonely for him. He doesn't go to his daughter or his son, but I've never raised the question with him. As you said, he's very private, but I'll do my best. I can't think why they are estranged; they could be such a comfort to him now that Brian is gone. It seems such a waste.'

'I know, the poor man. He gave his whole life to my brother, they had a long and happy marriage, even though the state would never recognise it as such, but that's what it was, and his heart is broken, I can hear it in his voice. No wonder himself and his children aren't close. If I had to keep something as big as that—the pain at losing the only person I ever loved—from Luke and Jen and you, I wouldn't be close to ye either. The only reason people are close is because they trust each other. If there's no trust, then there can't be anything else either.'

Carmel loved it when he said things like that. As if she was as valid as the son and daughter he'd reared from infancy.

'I know. Maybe he just can't go there now, after all this time. Who knows? I mean, his children must be in their fifties by now; he was only married for a short time when he was very young. I'll try to bring it up with him anyway, or at least figure out why he's backing out.'

'Sure that's all you can do.'

'Well, we're going to be a right motley crew on this bus trip you've planned, but we'll have a laugh, I'm sure.'

'We sure will. Now, pet, I'm going to have to love you and leave you, there's a meeting in the parish hall about trying to do something about the homelessness situation. It's awful, you know, families living in hotels and the whole city full of empty properties. I'm volunteering to get them into habitable shape.'

'Sure, you are a marvel, you do know that? Give me a call tomorrow if you get a chance.'

'Will do, pet, night night.'

Carmel ended the call and realised that talking to her dad had made her feel better. She wondered if she ever might confide in him about her baby dreams. She doubted it. Despite all the love and family and everything she'd been gifted with, she still felt separate and alone sometimes.

CHAPTER 32

'*I*t is quite impossible. I mean, honestly, what am I going to do?' Nadia was fuming as she paced around Carmel and Sharif's kitchen the next day. 'I didn't even invite her, and she just announced she was coming. Booked flights and everything without a word! Who does that? I can't have her! She will drive me insane...'

'Maybe it won't be so bad. After all, her husband isn't long dead; maybe she just needs to spend some time with her sister...' Carmel was trying to be supportive; she knew how much Nadia's sister Zeinab irritated her.

'And what about our trip to Ireland? Her so-called visit is right in the middle of it. It is as if she knew the very worst time and picked it on purpose.'

Carmel tried to suppress a smile as Sharif grinned behind his newspaper.

'She could come with us,' Carmel suggested. 'I'm sure Joe won't mind.' Sharif winked at Carmel—he knew how her suggestion would go down with his mother.

'Come? Come to Ireland? Have you lost your mind? All of us stuck in a little bus with Zeinab and her ailments and her complaining and her snobbery? It would be hell, absolute hell. No, I'll just have to cancel, there's no other way.' Nadia was devastated. Carmel knew how much she was looking forward to the trip. She and Joe got along so well, and at one stage, Carmel had even though there might have been a spark of romance there—but no, they just really had fun together.

'She will come over here, and complain, and criticise, and tell me how my house is too small, my bottom is too big, my *gajar ka halwa* is too dry—I can't bear it. There is a reason I live five thousand miles from my older sister.' Nadia's tiny frame was almost quivering with frustration. Her normally serene brown eyes glittered.

Sharif sighed and put down the paper. He stood, resting his hands on his mother's shoulders. His six-foot-two bulk dwarfed her. 'Ammi, you're making this worse by getting yourself into such a state. If you won't contact her and say not to come, which you are perfectly entitled to do, by the way, then you'll have to come up with a way of not letting her get under your skin. You have to come to Ireland; you've been looking forward to it and now it's all set up. Carmel's right. We'll just take her with us. I think Zeinab might actually enjoy Ireland, and she'll have Joe, me, Tim, Luke and Damien, not to mention little Sean to fawn over. You always said she's an old flirt and behaves much better around men, so maybe it's the best idea.'

Carmel smiled as Nadia managed to calm down. Sharif had that effect on people. Somehow, he managed to make people realise that nothing was ever as bad as it seemed. Nadia sighed and relaxed a little.

'Ah, Sharif, why does she do this? Always the same. Remember the time she came over to help when your father was ill? Dolly and she nearly came to blows, and I was so stressed, trying to keep her away from poor Khalid. The man was dying, and still on and on she would talk, jabbering away incessantly about people we don't know, always this one and that one from Karachi society. It was all to show off how well connected she and Tariq were, as if Khalid gave a hoot about that... Even if we did ask her to come to Ireland with us, she would find some reason not to. She would refuse simply because she would know I want to go.'

Carmel was so fond of her mother-in-law, she hated to see her so wound up. Sharif adored his mother, too, but sometimes thought she was inclined to be a bit melodramatic. She was just a really animated person, the kind who talked with her hands and told great stories. Carmel, after years of people being guarded and detached with her, loved Nadia's spontaneity and how she wore her heart on her sleeve. Which gave Carmel an idea. 'Look, why doesn't Sharif call her? He can explain that we're all planning a trip to Ireland, about my cousin's wedding and all of that, and how we can't change it at this stage so if she wants to visit then she'll have to come to Ireland with us. You said yourself she idolises Sharif, and she'd never refuse him anything.'

Carmel tried to quell her own anxiety. Confrontation and outbursts of emotion unsettled her, though she was trying to learn that they were a normal part of human interaction. Since she'd never experienced it in her life before, sometimes normal family interactions confused her. Once, when her friend Zane had described an argument he'd had with his sister one Friday, Carmel had been horrified and really worried about him all weekend. But when he came back to work on Monday, he was full of how he and his sister had had such a laugh at a wine tasting on Sunday. And the first time Carmel had had an argument with Sharif, over something silly, she'd convinced herself the relationship was over. But he'd come home, and they'd talked and solved it.

Carmel had even confided her fears to him, and he'd explained that people who loved each other sometimes fell out—it was no big deal. She was trying to be more relaxed about conflict, along with about a million other life adjustments she had to make every day.

But Nadia seemed genuinely distressed at the prospect of her sister's arrival. Maybe the trip to Ireland wasn't such a good idea after all. Carmel didn't really want to go back, Tim was backing out as well, and now Zeinab was arriving.

The holiday had been mooted as an idea by Joe last summer, before she and Sharif were married, as a way of helping Tim go back to Mayo and sort out his family affairs, as well as giving Carmel some time with family and to see the sights of her country she'd never seen before.

Carmel wondered why Tim was suddenly reluctant. He'd told her his story briefly, how as a young man, he had been found kissing one of the local lads in the barn by his father and was told to get out and never come back. The man never again wanted to see his son. Tim had taken his father at his word and had only returned once since the old man died, for his mother's funeral. Tim moved to England and married in London, as was expected, but of course, the marriage was a disaster. So one day his wife confronted him with her suspicions and left, taking their little son and daughter with her. Tim met Joe's brother, Brian—or perhaps he knew him before the marriage broke up, Carmel never asked—and they'd lived happily and quietly together until Brian's death last year.

The idea of going back to Ireland, even with Sharif and all of her new family, made Carmel nauseous, so maybe Tim felt the same. She was convinced there was nothing there for her anymore. The shy, insecure, lonely woman she was still lurked inside somewhere, but she was stronger now than she could have ever imagined. A big part of her believed that strength would disappear the minute she set foot on Irish soil.

'Carmel is right,' Nadia said with a sigh. 'Perhaps if you speak to her, Sharif… She is not so difficult with you…'

Sharif gave his mother a squeeze with one arm. 'That's the spirit. It will be fine—I'll call her this afternoon and smooth it all over. Now, don't you have to meet with the family of Juliette Binchet?'

Nadia glanced at her watch. 'Yes, and I'm late. She was a difficult woman too, and her daughter and son are now at loggerheads about the funeral, mainly because the daughter wants a very flashy affair to show off to her friends and he doesn't want to spend the money.'

Carmel smiled at Nadia. 'You'll sort everything out beautifully to everyone's satisfaction, like you always do.'

'We'll see. These two would try the patience of a saint, as Dolly used to say. Anyway, see you two later.' She gave them each a quick kiss on the cheek and was gone.

Once they were alone, Sharif put his arms around Carmel, his eyes searching her face. She loved how his eyes crinkled up when he smiled.

'OK, I've tried waiting for you to tell me what's wrong, but you won't, so I see I'm going to have to extract it.'

He led her to the courtyard of their apartment. The plants she had sown last summer, when she arrived, were blooming in profusion, and the fragrance of the lilac and sweet pea was heady.

'If we have to sit here till tonight, I want to know what's up. You've been distracted for the last few days, and sometimes I watch you and you're a million miles away and, judging by the look on your face, it's not somewhere pleasant, so I'm worried.' His voice was soothing and gentle as always. 'Remember, we agreed—no secrets, no keeping things in, we say what we feel.'

Carmel sighed. 'OK... I don't want to go to Ireland.'

'OK.' He paused. 'The first thing is you're a grown adult...'

'I know, I know...' She finished his mantra: 'I'm a grown adult who can make her own decisions.'

For her first forty years, she'd never had any autonomy. Everyone else had decided what would happen, and she was expected to fall in with it. Sharif was gradually trying to give her back that independence.

'But my dad has gone to so much trouble, and he loves Ireland so much, and he hates that I just don't feel the same way about the place. If I back out, I'd feel like I was letting him down—I *would* be letting him down—and they've all done so much, been so welcoming, especially considering a year ago he didn't even know I existed.

'I know it's not too much to ask to go on a little holiday with my family. And, of course, the wedding, it will be the first time I meet all these cousins and aunts and uncles, and I know he's dying for me to meet them. I longed for a family for most of my life, but it just all feels...I don't know, overwhelming? And then there's Tim; he's getting cold feet as well, apparently, for different reasons maybe—I don't know. I told Dad I'd speak to him. And now Nadia needs some way to cope with your auntie, which is a further complication, and to be honest, I'm happier here than I've ever been anywhere, and I just don't want to go back.'

'All right, now tell me exactly why you hate the thought of it so much.' Sharif held her hand, making small circles on her palm with his thumb, which she found strangely relaxing.

Carmel thought for a moment. 'Because I think—and I know this is mad—but I'm afraid I'll be that person, the woman I was when you met me first, if I go back. My independence, the courage I've got, is all to do with moving away from all of that, and going back, well, it feels...terrifying, if I'm honest. Back there, I didn't know about my mother, my father, nothing. I was nobody.' She tried to keep the tremor out of her voice. 'Here, in Aashna, I'm not nobody. I'm Carmel the events manager, Carmel the friend, Carmel the daughter. Here, I'm your wife. Things I never dreamed I could be.

He drew her into his arms and held her tight. 'What would Dolly say?'

Carmel didn't answer.

'I'll tell you, shall I?' He took her phone from her pocket, scrolled to her videos, and selected the one of Dolly's last birthday party, in Aashna, a few months before she died. Carmel watched the video every day.

There her mother was, in a wheelchair, wearing a blue dress and red lipstick, and a birthday girl hat. She sang in her unmistakable Dublin accent:

'When I was just a little girl, I asked my mother, what will I be? Will I be handsome? Will I be rich? Here's what she said to me. Que sera, sera, whatever will be will be. The future's not ours to see, que sera, sera.'

Sharif paused the video before Dolly gave her speech, and looked down into Carmel's eyes.

'When *you* were a little girl, she moved heaven and earth to find you, but your grandfather made sure she never could. If she was here now, she'd say, "What will be, will be, Carmel, my love, but go forward, face the future with bravery." You are one of the bravest people I've ever met, and I know it must be scary, but you're a different person now, you're stronger, and you can do this. You might even enjoy it. But in this, just like everything else, we're a team. If you decide you can't or you really don't want to go, then I've got your back, 100 percent. Always.'

She thought about bringing up the other thing, the pregnancy or lack of it, but didn't. 'Thanks. I know you have, and I really appreciate it. It'll be fine, I suppose, and I'll have everyone with me, and Joe assures me we're not going near Birr, County Offaly.'

'I don't know, maybe Julia would invite us all for tea?' Sharif teased.

'Unless you wanted it laced with arsenic, I wouldn't be drinking anything she made you.' Carmel didn't need to remind him of the lengths her ex-husband's sister was willing to go to hurt them. She'd tried to destroy Aashna last year, colluding with a criminal to bring a malpractice suit against Sharif. In the end, Carmel had had to visit Bill in Birr to get him to call her off. Carmel swore she would never go back to Ireland that day—the day she left Bill and the lonely farm for good—and yet here she was, making plans to return to the country of her birth.

CHAPTER 33

*C*armel strained to hear the actual words of the announcement over the tinny PA system of the airport. The screen said the flight from Karachi was due to land in forty-five minutes, and she and Nadia were sitting in a coffee shop killing time. Nadia stirred her coffee so much it was as if she was trying to wear through the cup. She drummed her fingers and fidgeted constantly.

'Nadia, can you just try to relax? If you meet her like this then it's going to start off on the wrong foot and that's only going to upset you.'

Nadia had been up since the dawn trying to identify and rectify anything with which Zeinab could find fault. Sharif couldn't accompany her to the airport as he was in meetings all morning, so Carmel offered her services as a chauffeur.

'I know, I just wish...'

They both knew what she wished: that Zeinab hadn't decided to soothe her allegedly broken heart in London with her only sister. Nadia had seemed unusually silent every time Zeinab went on about her 'darling Tariq.' Whenever Carmel tried to talk to Nadia about her sister in the weeks leading up to the visit, it had ended with Nadia listing all the reasons why the idea of Zeinab visiting was so terrible.

Eventually, after much gentle probing on Carmel's part, Nadia had told her the story of how she and Zeinab had grown up together in Karachi's Garden East area, called so because it was surrounded by the Karachi Zoological Gardens. Carmel loved to hear stories of life in Pakistan, and Sharif promised her they would visit his home country just as soon as they got some time. It all sounded so exotic and magical. Interestingly, up to then, Nadia's stories about their childhoods had always showed Zeinab in a good light.

This time, though, Nadia explained how Zeinab had married Tariq, a man older than her but with excellent credentials, a business associate of their father's. Nadia confided in Carmel how she and Zeinab used to make fun of Tariq when he came to the house to discuss business. When their parents sat her older sister down and told her that Tariq had asked for her hand in marriage, Nadia had laughed uproariously at such a suggestion, but Zeinab had agreed, much to her sister's horrified bewilderment.

From Nadia's point of view, the match made no sense whatsoever, but their parents were traditional, and arranged marriages were the norm. Though, Nadia was quick to point out they were more enlightened than many of their friends and would never have forced their daughters into a marriage they didn't want. Nadia tried to talk her sister out of it; Tariq was as old as the hills, she claimed, and had hairy ears, and was too short, and his breath smelled bad. Despite her giving Zeinab any amount of other reasons why she should not marry Tariq, Zeinab was determined. Tariq had a fabulous apartment in Clifton, overlooking the beach. He had lots of staff, so his new wife would not need to lift a finger, and all the international designer stores were on their doorstep.

Even the night before the wedding, Nadia begged her sister to reconsider, trying to make her see that money and status were no substitute for love, but Zeinab accused her of being jealous and naive. Things were never the same between the sisters after that.

Two years later, Nadia married Khalid Khan, a man her family didn't really approve of because he wasn't from the right neighbourhood and his family were not wealthy, but they finally agreed to the match because they saw how much the young people meant to each other. Nadia often told Carmel the story of the day she met the man she would marry, when her scarf blew away in a sudden gust of wind and this young man ran to retrieve it. He walked beside her all the way home, telling her stories and making her laugh. It was not the done thing for young ladies from respectable backgrounds to be seen walking with strange men, but Nadia was so taken with him she didn't rush away. He begged to meet her again, and she slipped out to the market the following day, claiming she needed something, just to see Khalid. After weeks of secret meetings, where they would meet for a few moments of conversation, he asked to meet her family. He professed his love and his desire to marry her before they'd even held hands.

It was a topic Nadia loved to talk about, so Carmel thought it might be a good way to pass some time now in the airport.

'Tell me again about the night your parents met Khalid; I love that story.'

Nadia smiled. 'I know what you're doing, and I appreciate it, Carmel, but I'm not yet an old lady in a nursing home telling the same story over and over you know!'

A young couple with a toddler and a baby and a huge amount of luggage squeezed past them into the cafe. Carmel noted the baby sleeping in a sling on the woman's chest, and she felt a longing so intense it almost took her breath away. She tried to get back to Nadia; such thoughts were not helping her at all.

She smiled and placed her hand on Nadia's. 'I know you're not, but I never had any stories like this when I was a kid, so I like hearing them now. It makes me feel more connected or something, so go on.' Carmel made a funny face, and Nadia grinned and retold the story. Carmel wondered at the glow that came over the older woman's face as she recounted her own personal love story.

She began as she always did, with the first night he came to their house, when she was so nervous she threw up. If her parents were not seduced by Khalid Khan's charm, the marriage would be forbidden.

He had no fortune, and his father had only a small shoe shop in Orangi Town, not the most fashionable of areas.

When she asked if he could come, both her parents were horrified. Firstly, that she would suggest a man not of their choosing, and secondly, that this was someone she had clearly lied to them about in order to meet. He was not connected to their circle in any way, so she must have had unchaperoned and unsanctioned meetings with this man. It wasn't the best of starts.

As the crowds milled around, waiting for the flights coming from places Carmel had never even thought about, Nadia reminisced.

'Oh, Carmel, the fear. My father was a gentle, kind man, but he was a proud Pakistani and a Muslim, and this was just not how things were done. It was a testament to how much he loved me that he even considered meeting Khalid. My mother said nothing, but I knew she didn't approve, either. Khalid arrived, bless him, in his best suit and in a pair of shoes I later realised had been handed in to his father's shop for repair. He brought my mother flowers from his mother—in our culture, it isn't appropriate for a male visitor to give a female a gift unless it came from another female. Then he and my father withdrew to the study.'

Carmel smiled at how the other woman's eyes shone with love for this young shoemaker's son, even now, all these years later.

'So, obviously, it worked—he charmed them?' Carmel asked.

'Yes, it worked. My father saw a bright young man, who, though he may not have come from money or status, was a very hard worker, and he knew Khalid would take care of me. It was a great leap of faith for someone like my father, but he took it and agreed to the marriage. Zeinab told our parents they were being foolish to allow it, and that they were always too soft when it came to me. She always said that, that they were harder on her, but I don't think that's true.

'She said there was no way she could associate with me if I insisted on marrying someone so far beneath us in social status. On and on she went about how embarrassing it was for her and Tariq, what would people say and all of that rubbish. Where Tariq was heavyset and short, with a gruff attitude and terrible table manners, Khalid was tall and handsome and funny and everyone who met him fell under his spell. I think she was just envious. Tariq gave her a lovely lifestyle, true enough, but he was constantly unfaithful.'

She noted Carmel's look of surprise. This part of the story was new to her.

'Oh, yes, that's one of the strange things about some people in our culture. Not everyone, of course, but a significant cohort of Pakistani men, back there anyway, enjoy a forgiving society when it comes to extramarital affairs. Sometimes, faithfulness is not expected, and society would not condemn a man for cheating, often not even the wife. Of course, for women, no such understanding is shown. Tariq was discreet, spending time in clubs where women were available and such, but never in public. He would have considered that the height of consideration for Zeinab, almost like she should be grateful he was being so considerate. Some other men in his circle would have made no secret of their mistresses, which is humiliating for the wife. Zeinab knew about his affairs, he didn't try that hard to hide them, but she never confronted him or even admitted she knew.'

'How awful for her,' Carmel murmured.

'That's not the half of it. One evening, soon after Khalid and I were engaged, Tariq came to our house. I was in the kitchen helping our mother, and she was called away to deal with something, and when she left, he came in and made a pass at me. I was horrified and reacted angrily—he really was a horrid old goat—but Zeinab arrived just as I was giving him a good dressing down. I was not the typical demure Pakistani girl, even then.' She chuckled her deep, throaty laugh.

'Oh my God, did Zeinab realise what had happened?'

'Yes, and she was mortified, but instead of taking it out on her awful, lecherous husband, she blamed me. She accused me of flirting with him, as if I would, and we had a terrible fight.'

'Oh, no,' Carmel gasped.

'Over the years, things mellowed a little, and we got on up to a point, though she never stops criticising. The only reason there hasn't been a huge blow-up between us is because I live here and she stayed in Karachi. Whenever we've visited over the years, it has been tense, and we've spent as little time together as possible. So why she is now coming here, after everything, is a total mystery.'

'But she likes Sharif?' Carmel asked.

'Oh, yes, she loves him, and she loved Khalid too, in the end. He was relentlessly charming, long after he needed to be, it was just his way. But she never really forgave me. Our lives were in such sharp contrast. Khalid never would cheat on me, he treated me wonderfully, I was his whole world. Even though, as far as she sees it, I married beneath me in terms of class, I got to marry for love, to a man who adored me, and to add even more insult to injury, I had a son. She never had children, and I think it made her so sad. I heard that Tariq had two children with one of his mistresses, but that might just be gossip. That's why it is so complicated between us. I feel sorry for her, of course I do, who wouldn't? But she makes it so difficult to like her.'

'She must have felt like you got it all,' Carmel said. 'That must be hard.'

'Yes, exactly, and on top of it all, she was jealous of Dolly. Your mother was much more of a sister to me than Zeinab ever was. Any time they met, they knocked sparks off each other. Zeinab accused me of confiding in Dolly more than her, of loving Dolly more than her, and of course she was right. That's the sad thing. She was absolutely right.'

Nadia just stared at the table, lost in her own thoughts.

Carmel thought back to the secret Sharif had shared with her about his father. On Khalid's deathbed, he'd confessed to his son that he had been unfaithful to Nadia years earlier, but that it had meant nothing and that it was just once. Some woman he had known years ago in Karachi, she came to London and they'd had one night and she returned to Pakistan, never to make contact again. Sharif had told Carmel how he had been so appalled and accused his father of keeping quiet not to protect his family but to protect himself. He told her how he'd stormed out of the hospital, horrified that his beloved father would betray his mother in that way. Sharif had spoken to Dolly about it at the time, knowing he could trust her, and he'd told Carmel he would never forget the answer she gave him.

Apparently, Dolly had claimed that the truth was totally overrated. She calmed Sharif and explained that if Khalid had admitted it to Nadia, the marriage would have been over. She would never have taken him back. Nadia, unlike her sister, was not one of those who would turn a blind eye to a philandering husband. And so, by bearing the guilt alone all those years, Khalid had saved his wife the heartache of betrayal and spared his son a broken home. According to Sharif, Dolly had a way of explaining things that made the most incomprehensible things seem simple.

For the millionth time, Carmel wished Sharif had found her just a few months earlier. She would have given anything for just ten minutes with her mother.

Carmel dismissed the futile dream and returned to the matter at hand.

Nadia never knew her darling husband had been unfaithful to her, and she never would.

'Poor Zeinab, of course she resented my mother,' Carmel said gently. 'I mean, I know she can be a pain, but she's had a lot to deal with too. Look, we'll get through this, I promise you. Sharif and I will be there a lot. If it gets too much, you can come round to ours and scream or punch things. And if we can convince her to come to Ireland with us, then the McDaids will charm her for sure.'

Nadia smiled and sat back, thinking for a moment. 'When it became evident that I was only going to have one child, I convinced myself Sharif was all anyone could want. And he is—I adore him, as you know—but it is so nice to have a daughter. Your mother and I talked about you a lot, never knowing where you were, how you were getting along, but we would look at women out shopping with their little girls and we both felt it, a little pang. I feel like we're getting the chance now, not just me, but Dolly, too.'

Carmel swallowed the lump in her throat as a tear threatened to spill. She couldn't speak but squeezed Nadia's hand.

They hadn't much more time for chat as the flight had landed, so they made their way to the arrivals area. And, eventually, behind a stack of suitcases, manoeuvred by an airline staff member came Zeinab, being pushed in a wheelchair.

They watched as the large woman wearing the most beautiful lilac-and-gold *shalwar kameez*, the loose-legged trousers and tunic top synonymous with Pakistan—tipped the young man fifty pounds. He could hardly believe his luck, the usual tip being closer to five.

'Thank you, my dear.' Zeinab waved regally, as he handed her over to Carmel and Nadia.

'Zeinab, what happened? Did you hurt yourself? You never said!' Nadia was shocked to see her sister in a wheelchair.

Zeinab ignored the question, launching straight into criticism. 'Oh my word, Nadia, it is so cold, how can you endure it? And look at you —not enough clothes on.' She turned to Carmel. 'You must be darling Sharif's new wife! I saw the photos of the wedding, even if I wasn't invited. It looked like a big affair.'

Though the words were delivered with a sweet smile, Carmel felt the barbs. Nadia had insisted that Zeinab would ruin the day, and anyway, at the time, Tariq was dying, so if she had been asked she would have said they were being insensitive. According to Nadia, you just couldn't win with Zeinab.

'Hello, Zeinab, how nice to meet you. Nadia's told me all about you. I'm so sorry you missed our wedding, it was quite small actually, but Nadia and Sharif didn't want to add to your pressures, as you were caring for Tariq, God rest his soul.' Carmel began to manoeuvre the heavy wheelchair as Nadia struggled with the trolley and Zeinab's four large suitcases, two duty free bags, and an enormous jewelled handbag. Nadia shot her a grateful glance, and Carmel had a moment of exhilaration at how well she'd handled it. The old Carmel would just have reddened and muttered something apologetic.

Once they were at the car, Zeinab calmly got out of the wheelchair, walked to the passenger door, and sat into the front seat, regally allowing Carmel and Nadia to load up her many bags and return the wheelchair.

Carmel and Nadia exchanged a glance that said more than words could ever say. Nadia was gritting her teeth in frustration already, and Carmel stifled a grin. This Zeinab, clearly perfectly healthy, was certainly a piece of work.

Carmel sat into the driver's seat and tried to look confident. She wasn't driving long, but she had passed her test first time and Sharif bought her a gorgeous Renault KADJAR as a birthday present. She was determined not to look incompetent in front of his aunt.

Nadia said nothing but seethed in the back as Carmel switched on the sat nav.

'Do you not know how to get home?' Zeinab asked incredulously, looking in distaste at the screen.

'Well, I'm not from London, I've only been living here less than two years, and it's a huge city, so I'd get lost without the sat nav.' Carmel tried to keep the frustration out of her voice. Nadia wasn't wrong, though—Zeinab was a bit of a weapon all right. That said, she couldn't be any worse than Bill's sister Julia, and Carmel had managed her for seventeen years, so she was sure she'd cope with Zeinab for a month. 'I imagine Karachi is the same?'

'Oh, I rarely leave the house, and when I do, I have a driver, so I wouldn't know,' she answered imperiously.

'London is very rundown, is it not?' Zeinab gave a running commentary as they drove, criticising everything: the congestion, the buildings, the jaywalkers... And as they came closer to Aashna House, she ramped it up.

'I'm surprised Sharif did not act on my suggestion for gold gates for this place. At the moment, anyone can just drive in. It doesn't give the right impression. And also those cars in the car park, they are so small, surely he has a separate staff car parking area? What will people think? If you come to Aashna House, it is for the exclusive treatment by my nephew and his team. You don't want to have to park your Mercedes beside some old dirty *Japanese* car.'

Carmel smiled. Zeinab had Sharif so wrong. He wanted patients, families, and staff to realise the place was open to all and that money didn't matter. Those who could pay did, but many more did not.

306

As they drove through the grounds, verdant lawns stretched either side of the avenue, and a tinkling fountain sparkled in the sun. Aashna House itself was an old stately home, so the main building was protected, but behind it, Sharif had built so many wonderful spaces for the patients and their families to enjoy. The one thing he was adamant about was that it should neither look nor smell like a hospital.

The Aashna restaurant, which specialised in organic locally sourced food, was used by everyone in the locality and was housed in a huge glass building along with yoga studios, class-rooms for all sorts of things, therapy suites and a pool. On the other side of that building was a beautiful garden full of trees, flowers and shrubs, cared for in the main by the patients and anyone else who wanted to get stuck in. There were gardeners for the heavy lifting, but they really only encouraged and supported anyone interested in getting their hands dirty. Carmel had been delighted to discover she, too, had a love of plants, having never grown anything before. Bill would not have seen the point in wasting grazing land, and in Trinity House where she grew up, there was just a yard.

She felt a surge of pride as they drove slowly past the main house to the apartments at the back of the property, where she and Sharif, Nadia, and other staff members lived. She waved at the children from the local primary school who would come in and help the patients with the garden. There was even a group from a young offenders rehab place coming twice a week, and they were teaching some of the older people who were interested how to use the internet. The patients seemed to love them. Initially, she and Nadia had been reluc-tant when Sharif suggested it, but she had to admit it was working out great. Though, if Zeinab saw any of them with their tattoos and earrings, she would probably run away shrieking.

They pulled up outside Nadia's apartment, on the other side of the staff complex from Carmel and Sharif's place.

Zeinab demanded her handbag from Nadia, who was holding it on the back seat, crushed by suitcases. Nadia shoved the enormous

Michael Kors bag forward with a heave, and Zeinab took it without a word of thanks and extracted her huge Versace sunglasses.

'The sun in England is much too glary,' she announced.

Carmel caught Nadia's eye in the rearview mirror. It was going to be a long month. It was with a sigh of relief she left the sisters to it, inviting them both over later.

CHAPTER 34

hey arrived before Sharif finished work, but when he did arrive, he found himself enveloped in the voluminous embrace of his aunt before he even had time to register her arrival. He was barely in the door, and Carmel marvelled at the transformation in Zeinab.

Though Carmel had invited them for dinner, Nadia said she would bring something, not because she didn't love Carmel's cooking, she did, but because she would hate for her daughter-in-law to get the full inevitable lash of Zeinab's tongue on day one. Nadia had been cooking feverishly all week to prepare for the welcome dinner, and Carmel remarked to Sharif how it was touching, that even though Nadia exclaimed how annoying her sister was, she was going to such lengths to impress her.

'My darling boy, look at you! You are so handsome and so fit looking, I cannot believe some Pakistani beauty did not snap you up, though of course, it is impossible to replace dear Jamilla! Oh, what a lady she was; you must miss her terribly to this very day.' She laid her hand on his cheek.

The photo of Sharif's first wife, who'd died of cancer when she was only twenty-nine, had pride of place on the shelf beside the TV, and both he and Nadia spoke of her often, but never in a way that made Carmel feel inferior or left out, which was exactly Zeinab's intention.

'Hello, Khalla Zeinab,' Sharif answered, extricating himself from her hug. 'It's nice to see you.' He crossed the room and put his arm around Carmel protectively. 'Hi, darling, how did you get on with the traffic?' He knew she'd been nervous about driving to Heathrow.

'She did wonderfully, like a pro.' Nadia smiled while she chopped coriander, and her son kissed her cheek and gave her a quick squeeze.

'How are you, Zeinab? You must be lonely, finding it hard to adapt to life without Tariq?' Sharif had a way of being both direct and gentle. Carmel had seen it many times with the patients who came to Aashna to die. He never used fluffy words, or euphemisms, but he was so empathetic, people seemed to be able to take it. Not only that, but she had seen the trust in his patients' eyes. When everyone else would skirt around the realities and refuse to tell the person in the last phase of life the truth, they knew Dr Khan would.

'Oh, I am finding it very hard. He was my world, my whole world, and life without my dear Tariq is just hopeless.' She sniffed for dramatic effect.

'Well, hopefully, you will find some peace and joy here with us, even if just for a while. Company is good, even if you don't feel like it, especially in the early days.' He smiled kindly. 'Be gentle with yourself; it will get better even if it doesn't feel like it now.'

Zeinab replied in Urdu, which caused Nadia to roll her eyes and Sharif to say, 'I'm sorry, Zeinab, Carmel doesn't speak Urdu so we use English. But if there's something you don't know then of course I'm happy to translate. Now, I haven't eaten yet today, so I'm really looking forward to whatever Ammi is working on in there.' He grinned to lighten the mood after his gentle reprimand of his aunt.

'Your mother has been making something in there, though I don't recognise the smell.' Zeinab dismissed all Nadia's hard work with a wave of her jewelled hand. 'I feared at first we would not be eating properly. Tariq and I always found the food in England dreadful whenever we visited in the past, despite only staying in five-star hotels. All fish and chips and boiled vegetables. But I'm sure Nadia won't poison us.' She had a horrible, tinkly laugh.

'Tell me, Carmel, can you cook?' she went on. 'I hope so. If nothing else, you'll need to be a good cook to keep this handsome nephew of mine at home!' The implication was clear: Carmel did not appear to be in possession of any other traits that might keep her husband at home.

'I love cooking, Zeinab,' Carmel replied smoothly, 'and I've learned a lot about Pakistani cuisine from Nadia and Sharif, so we eat half Pakistani, half Irish I would say.' She smiled, marvelling at her ability to take Zeinab head-on. The Carmel that was raised to be quiet and grateful for any small kindness because she had no entitlement was not gone but was definitely on the back foot.

'Irish? Oh, dear me.' That laugh again. It was really grating on Carmel's nerves.

Zeinab was oblivious to the insult and carried on. 'I suppose they eat the same as the British but insist on calling it something else. The Irish are a total mystery to me, I mean, where is the gratitude? They don't seem to realise, as we in Pakistan did, that without the British Empire's civilising care they would still be savages. Instead, all they do is try to create havoc, for a reason nobody understands, not even the Irish themselves, I daresay.'

Carmel knew it was now or never. She'd bitten her tongue often this afternoon, but she knew if Zeinab was allowed to speak to her like this at the outset, it would never change.

'Well, Zeinab, we Irish understand the whole situation perfectly. And we don't see it like that. The British never cared for us, as you put it, they invaded and subjugated us, stole from us, terrorised us, and over the centuries eroded our most basic human rights, such as the right to speak our language, or practice our religion, or own our own land. We were ruled from Westminster with an iron fist, and woe betide anyone who dared to object. So, no, we are not *grateful*. We got rid of them through force of arms, the only language they understood at the time, after eight hundred years. That is something Irish people, me and my family included, are very proud of. I would have thought

311

you as a Pakistani would appreciate that, given your country's long history as a colony of Britain also.'

Silence descended on the room as Nadia studiously chopped and Sharif grinned, giving Carmel a squeeze and a kiss on the top of her head.

'You'd better be careful what you say to my wife, Zeinab, they are feisty, these Irish ladies.'

Zeinab tried to appear nonchalant, but Carmel knew she had thrown down the gauntlet. Zeinab looked her up and down as if she was not worth her attention.

'I recall that Irish woman—what was her name—who worked for you, she was very outspoken as well,' Zeinab replied haughtily. She was clearly fuming that Carmel would speak to her like that but dared not say anything further.

Carmel watched her reaction carefully. She might've been a snob and a pain in the neck, but she wasn't stupid. She'd taken in the situation and realised that Sharif wouldn't stand for anyone coming in and upsetting either Carmel or his mother, so Zeinab was realising she would have to tread more carefully than when the women were alone together.

'Dolly,' Sharif said. 'She was—'

'Dolly was my mother,' Carmel finished. 'I never met her, though it was my dearest wish, and still is, to have even a few moments with her. But Nadia and Sharif have kept her alive for me.'

Zeinab could not hide her shock. She opened her mouth to speak and closed it again.

'Well, I must say I am'—she noted Sharif's warning gaze—'*surprised*. You never mentioned this before, Nadia.' Zeinab turned on her sister.

'It wasn't relevant. Sharif and Carmel fell in love, and both I and Dolly, if she were here I'm sure, would be thrilled. Dolly loved Sharif, and she spent her whole life looking for Carmel. I think the whole thing has a nice symmetry to it, don't you?' Nadia smiled a genuine smile, willing Zeinab to keep her nasty thoughts about Dolly to herself.

'Oh, yes, I can see a resemblance, now that you mention it.'

There was no doubt in anyone's mind that Zeinab did not see that as a good thing, but Nadia only sighed—it could have been much worse.

Dinner was served and was so deliciously tasty, they washed it down with a lovely bottle of Merlot. Initially, as Sharif went to pour some wine for his mother, she placed her hand over the glass, refusing.

'I'll just have water,' she murmured. Drinking alcohol was frowned upon by polite Pakistani society.

'But you love this one, I got is specially.' Sharif smiled innocently, but he knew perfectly well what he was doing. If she refused a drink now, Nadia would not have one for the entire month her sister was here, and while Nadia wasn't a heavy drinker, she loved to unwind with a glass over dinner. Sharif was not going to have his mother deprived of her pleasure because of Zeinab.

'Can I tempt you, Zeinab?' he offered.

She looked at him like he had ten heads. 'I don't drink alcohol, I never have, so no, thank you, Sharif. I was not brought up that way.' She looked pointedly at her younger sister, who was now sheepishly sipping her wine.

Carmel could empathise perfectly with Nadia. Though she was a very capable and confident person, something about being back with the people of your childhood makes you revert to who you were then. Nadia was intimidated by Zeinab, and who could blame her? Zeinab was twice the size of Nadia and dressed so ostentatiously, complete with an arm full of very expensive bangles, both hands adorned with jewelled rings, and a hand-embroidered dupatta covering her head. Though she looked in no way like Carmel's ex-sister-in-law Julia Sheehan, Carmel realised there were lots of similarities. Both women were only happy when they were undermining someone else or pressing their own advantage.

'Well, maybe you should start.' Sharif was cheerfully topping up Carmel's glass. 'It is a wonderful way to relax, and we have a glass of wine most evenings, so if you change your mind...'

'I don't think I will, Sharif, but thank you,' Zeinab said primly and went on eating, and even had seconds, without ever once complimenting the cook.

'So, have you ladies filled Zeinab in on the surprise we have planned?' Sharif asked. Neither Carmel nor Nadia responded.

'A surprise for me?' Zeinab beamed. Now this was more like it.

'Yes, a really special one, actually,' Sharif said enthusiastically.' As you know, Dolly, our family friend who died last year, was Irish, and when she gave birth to Carmel, she was forced to give her up for what she thought would be adoption. For a variety of reasons that I won't go into, Carmel never was adopted, and therefore was raised in state care. When I eventually found her, as I promised her mother I would, she was married to someone else, but it was not a happy marriage, so she left and came over here.' Carmel kicked him under the table. This was excruciating. Nadia had deliberately kept the details very scant in her communications with her sister.

'So you are a *divorcee*?' Zeinab's eyes bored into Carmel.

'Y…yes,' Carmel admitted, all previous courage seemingly having deserted her.

'Well, you must consider yourself very lucky indeed then, to have snapped up a man such as my nephew. He could have had anyone.' She rested her jewelled hand on Sharif's proprietarily, but he removed his immediately.

'Oh, I'm the lucky one, Zeinab, not Carmel, make no mistake about that.' His voice was quiet but firm. This dinner was excruciating, but they needed to get everything out in the open. He went on, 'Anyway, in that process, and through a connection we have over here, Carmel was reunited with her father, Joe McDaid. He is a lovely man, and he has a daughter and a son besides Carmel, so she not only found her dad but she got two siblings into the bargain. The connection we have with him is through two friends of Dolly's, a gay couple, Brian and Tim. Well, Brian died last year, but he was Joe's brother.'

Sharif carried on despite the look on Zeinab's face, horrified at the mention of illegitimate children, long-lost parents, and now homosexual men. 'Anyway, his surviving partner, Tim O'Flaherty, needs to return to Ireland to attend to some legal affairs there, regarding his family land. Carmel's father has arranged that we all go and take a tour of the West of Ireland. Tim hasn't been back to Ireland for years, and since it is to take place while you're here, we've checked with Joe and we have room for one more. Isn't that exciting?'

Zeinab looked like she would rather have had a root canal than go on this trip with these awful people. She was clearly appalled, but she managed to recover her composure. She clearly longed for Sharif's approval almost as much as she wanted to undermine Carmel and Nadia. Carmel glanced quickly at her husband. He was suppressing a smile; he seemed to enjoy scandalising his aunt.

'Well, it will be lovely to spend some quality time with you. You've always been so busy when Tariq and I visited before. And I have never been to Ireland, I hear it is very...er... green?' This last was addressed to Carmel with the fakest smile she had ever seen.

'Oh, yes, very green indeed, and lovely.' Carmel smiled. 'It's a special place; you're going to love it.' She hoped her parents would've been proud of her defence of her homeland.

CHAPTER 35

'Would you mind horribly if I pulled out?' Tim asked as he percolated the coffee in the bright, sunny kitchen he had lovingly decorated with Brian. Carmel had rung earlier to see if he was free, and he'd been delighted. They'd enjoyed a lovely lunch together, and Carmel felt she'd cheered him up a little. Brian's death had taken so much out of Tim, and he seemed suddenly much older than he had when Brian was alive.

'The right thing to say is of course not'—she grinned and made a silly face to make him smile—'but the truth is yes, I would. Look, Tim, I don't want to pressure you, though I kind of am, I know, but you being there was going to make this trip easier for me. So, selfishly, I do really want you to come. I was dreading it too—well, I still am, I suppose—but, to be honest, of late, I've not had much time to think about it, what with Nadia's sister being here. And now that she's coming to Ireland with us, well, you'll see for yourself, but she's a handful.'

Tim stopped and looked at her.

'I made one last attempt to speak to Rosemary and Charles last week.'

Carmel waited. He never really discussed his son and daughter; Carmel just knew they were estranged.

'I thought now that Brian is gone, they might... Anyway, they made it very clear they still want nothing to do with me, not now, nor at any time in the future.' The pain was written all over his face.

'Why not?'

He poured her coffee.

'I approached them a few years ago. I never said anything about Brian or anything at that stage, but they were not willing to even meet me. Then, soon after Brian died, I don't know, I just wanted to see them, to explain things in my own way, not the version they would have got from Marjorie, so I convinced them to meet me in a hotel bar. I told them everything; I mean, they are middle-aged people now. But they said that as far as they were concerned, I had abandoned them when they were very young, they'd grown up without me, and they didn't need me. They are very bitter at how I deserted their mother, as they see it. The realisation that I was gay seemed to be something they found disgusting, by the way they reacted, but it changed nothing. In fact, it made things even worse. So, I left that day, devastated, but there was nothing I could do. Now that I have this land in Ireland, I was going to offer them each a fifty-percent share, call it bribery if you like, and so I wrote to them both and made the offer. I got this last week.'

He pushed a letter towards her.

Carmel took it out of the envelope and unfolded the thick cream paper. It was a solicitor's letter threatening a barring order if Tim ever tried to make contact with either Rosemary Taylor or her brother or any member of their family in the future.

'Oh, Tim, I'm so sorry.' She wanted to hug him, but she resisted. He stood tall and erect, his white hair brushed back from his high forehead. He wore a shirt and tie every day of his life, and while he wasn't forbidding exactly, he was somewhat private and a little bit aloof. She knew he'd told nobody about his life, his loss of Brian or his children, except her, and she was profoundly touched.

'So that's that. I never had a relationship with them to lose, but any

317

hope of a reconciliation is truly dead in the water now, isn't it?' He shrugged.

Carmel nodded. There was no point in giving false hope.

'We are a lot alike, you and I,' she said. He nodded slowly. 'We're both a bit outside of the world, a bit, I don't know, separate. Others seem to interact more easily with society.'

'They had normal upbringings by people who loved them. I think that's the difference.' Tim sighed. 'But, yes, we have a lot in common.'

'So this is the reason you won't come to Ireland?' Carmel asked, glancing at the envelope with the solicitor's letter.

'There seems no point. There's a young couple renting the place, farming it; their family and mine have been neighbours for generations. I have enough money, my needs are few these days, so I just haven't the heart for it.'

Carmel knew going back to Westport would be hard for him, but she believed it would ultimately do him good, as it would her. Bury the ghosts, as it were.

'Please reconsider, Tim. We are your friends, and Joe and the McDaids are Brian's family, which makes them yours, too. My dad was only saying the other night that you and Brian had a long and happy marriage, and that makes you a McDaid, too. Sure, neither of us exactly fits the bill, but they are offering us their hospitality, their homes and hearts, and maybe we should take it. To hell with your children; they've made their choice. Let's go over to Ireland, to Brian's family, and tell them who you really are. Claim him as yours after all these years. Let them know their uncle was loved and had a full life, a happy life. You can let them know how much their uncle Brian meant to you, be authentic for maybe the first time. I know you probably think I'm begging you for selfish reasons, and I am to a certain extent, but I really do think it would do you good as well.'

She saw the impact her words had on Tim. He wasn't able to speak for a second. Then he said, 'Maybe you're right. It would feel good to be honest, especially with people who loved Brian, too. I hated sneaking around. I always wanted to reassure him that it wasn't because I was ashamed of him, or of what we had, but because I promised Marjorie I wouldn't ever reveal what I was. She felt it was the least I could do for her after treating her so badly...'

You could only barely hear the hint of an Irish accent, after sixty years in the UK.

'And now the thought of going back,' he went on. 'Dublin would be OK, but Mayo... I don't know if I can. I was forcing myself to go as it was, thinking if it would fix things with Charles and Rosemary, but now that it won't...'

'Are you not even a bit curious to go back, to be in the house where you grew up?' Carmel hoped she wasn't being insensitive, but the idea of having a home and having no interest in it was a hard one for her to grasp.

'No,' he said firmly. 'I've no happy memories there. It wasn't a particularly happy house, even before my father threw me out. My mother was fervently religious, to the point of obsession actually, and my father was a bigot. They were well matched. I never fitted in, and back then, nobody spoke about anything. Really, they didn't. Farming, the price of things, the neighbours—that was all they talked about. I knew there was something wrong with me, from a very young age, but I could never tell anyone. I didn't even know what it was to be honest. But when the local lads were chasing after the local farmer's daughters, driven on by lust and greed for land, I just didn't get it. I definitely lacked the lust part, and the idea of farming even more land filled me with horror. I didn't want to farm the land I had, but as an only child, my future seemed set in stone.

'One girl, Kitty Lynch, was my friend. She seemed to just like me for me and didn't make any demands. She was the one that got me into gardening, actually; her parents' garden was the talk of the town. Brian took over the garden here, but he was into all the exotic plants. I love wild flowers. When I lived back in Westport, I planted a wild flower garden in some waste ground at the back of the house. Mam could see it when she was at the kitchen sink, and she said it cheered her up no end to see the different flowers coming at different times. I think it was the only time in my life that I pleased her. My father thought it was ridiculous, of course, that a young fella would be planting flowers when there was farming to be done, but he ignored me most of the time anyway. Just more proof that I wasn't what he wanted in a son, I suppose. All through my late teens, and up to the time they threw me out really, Kitty and I would pal around, getting wild flower roots in the hedgerows all around, so everyone thought we were the makings of a match, though we were never more than friends. If it wasn't for her, I'd have cracked up. I left without a word to her. I've always regretted that.'

'Is she still there?' Carmel asked. 'I've no idea, though I doubt it. She'd be seventy-seven now. She didn't come to my mother's funeral, so I'm assuming she's either dead or has moved away. I wouldn't blame her, getting out of that God-forsaken place.' He sighed heavily.

'Were you never tempted to go back, after your father died? See if you could patch things up with your mother at least?' The idea of having a mother, knowing she was there, and still choosing not to have anything to do with her was strange to Carmel.

'No, never. That night when my father found me in the barn with Noel Togher, well, it wasn't pleasant. Noel was married, the previous summer, but he was gay. He and I sought each other out, almost intuitively, but there was no relationship—we never talked, we just met occasionally and, well, it was the release valve we both needed, I suppose. I hated myself, and in a way, I hated him too. It was complicated; I was so screwed up, as they say nowadays. My father came into the barn, I think he might have seen us go in, and he was armed with a big shovel. He clouted Noel across the back of the head, knocked him out, drew blood and everything, and then he beat me up. I let him, even though I was bigger than him by that stage. I don't know, maybe I felt I deserved it or something, but he really tore into me. Blood, broken ribs, the whole lot. He called me all the names he could think of, and then he told me to get the hell off his farm and to never darken his door again. So I didn't. I left that day. I didn't even stop to say goodbye to Kitty. I felt terrible, but I was in such a state after the beating my father gave me, I would have frightened the life out of her, and anyway, I couldn't face her. I was so ashamed.'

Carmel sat in silence. Tim had given her the outline of the story before, but this was the first time she'd heard the details.

'The only place I could get to was England,' he went on. 'I had no money, no real skills, no friends... I was so lonely at first over here, I wrote to my mother. She replied, care of a priest I knew down in Cricklewood. I don't know if my father told her why he threw me out, but I don't think he did because she didn't mention it. All I got back was a short note, all about saying my prayers and going to mass and all of that, but nothing more. She wrote again, later, to tell me my father had died. He got cancer,' he paused. 'I didn't go back. The next time I had anything to do with her was arranging her funeral. I lived up on the Kilburn High Road at that time. I'll never forget the feeling, turning the key in the lock of my flat when I came home after burying my mother, the emptiness, the loneliness. I'll take that feeling to the grave with me.'

'Is that why you married?' Carmel asked gently. 'Because you were lonely?'

'I suppose so. I thought if I could just ignore the part of me that was attracted to men, then everything would work out. Marjorie was nice. She was a well-brought-up girl who wouldn't dream of having relations before marriage or anything, so I was off the hook on that front, for the entire courtship. She would say how lucky she was to have met someone so respectful, when her friends' boyfriends were forever trying to grope them in the back row of the pictures. She was nice, and she used to bring me home to her parents' house for tea. It felt so comforting to be in a proper home. I was living in that flat in Kilburn, that's where all the Irish were, and I'd got a job in Lloyds Bank. Just a clerk to start with, but I was making progress, so from Marjorie's perspective, I was a good, safe bet. I didn't drink or smoke or go with women. I was steady and likely to be able to provide for her. So she angled for a ring, and eventually, when I could think of no more excuses, I proposed marriage.'

Carmel was confused. 'But you surely didn't think it would work out?'

Tim sighed and sat back in his chair, the home he and Brian had built together all around him, giving him comfort.

'I don't know. I just thought maybe I could deny that part of me. I'd never had any relationships with men after the Noel experience, and that wasn't a relationship at all. Marjorie was going to break it off if I didn't propose, so I asked her. I know, to someone of your generation, it seems mad, but I can't tell you how different things were then, not like now, where homosexuality is fine, no problems. It wasn't like that then. Back in Ireland, you could be arrested, put in prison, made to take chemical castration drugs. It was terrifying, and even in London, society was not accepting. Marjorie and a nice safe life was a much more appealing prospect.'

'So you married, and then what?' Carmel was intrigued.

'Well, we married, and she had the children, Charles first then Rosemary. I managed that much, though I doubt it was much fun for her, and for me, well, it was awful. And then, once the children were born, she announced that she was more or less done with the sex thing. Lots of women of her generation felt that way, I'm told, that it was a nasty but necessary business, and once you had your children you could happily dispense with it all. That suited me perfectly, and you know, Carmel, we kind of rubbed along together fine for a while. The children were lovely, and I was promoted in the bank. We had a nice house, played tennis, went to drinks parties, it was all fine.'

Tim stopped, and Carmel wondered if he was finished with his confidences. Even though she'd known him almost a year, this intimacy was new.

'I'm sorry, this must be boring you to tears, listening to my tale of woe.' He went to gather the cups.

'No, quite the opposite actually. It's so interesting. What happened between you and Marjorie if everything was going along fine?'

'Brian happened.' She could hear the pain of losing Brian McDaid in Tim's voice, as raw as the night she came to tell him Brian was dead. He died in Aashna with her and Sharif beside him, and she'd wanted to be the one to break the news to Tim. They'd said their goodbyes, and Brian hadn't wanted to put Tim through watching him die, so he'd asked Sharif not to tell Tim that the end was as close as it was.

'I met him through a work thing. He was in insurance, I was in banking, not exactly rock and roll, or what you'd imagine two young men in the late sixties to be like. Films and so on always present the sixties in London as all Carnaby Street and flares and outrageous behaviour, but we were so conservative. Suits every day, church goers, neither of us drank in those days... But when we met, I don't know, something just clicked. We played tennis together, a perfectly reasonable activity for two young men; we even took up golf. We were both hopeless, but it allowed us to spend time together without arousing suspicion. I... Well, *we*, I suppose... We fell in love, and for me, it was the first time. For him, too, I discovered, and we just couldn't get enough of each other. He'd heard about places, down in Soho, where men would go, to be together, so one night we arranged to meet, and down we went.'

Carmel tried to visualise Tim and Brian, terrified but excited to go somewhere they could relax together. Life was so hard for gay people then, compared to now. She thought of her friend Zane, the care assistant at Aashna, with his endless swiping left or right on Grindr, the gay dating app.

'How did it go?' She was almost afraid to ask.

'It was...marvellous, really, an eye-opener, no doubt about that. We must have stuck out like sore thumbs, the scene was so very camp, even then. Lots of sequins and colour. We got two beers and sat at the bar, another first for us, and just took it all in. It was the first time in my life I didn't feel like a freak of nature.'

'Did Marjorie find out? Is that what ended it?' Carmel was hanging on every word.

'Yes and no. She didn't like Brian; she was very racist against the Irish. A lot of people were; signs up on digs: no blacks, no dogs, no Irish. It was rampant, and even though I was Irish, she always complimented me on having lost my accent completely. I never spoke about Ireland, never wanted to go back, so as far as she was concerned, that was fine. I suppose I lost my accent on purpose, immediately I landed here, but Brian, as you know, was a pure Dub, and there was no getting rid of his Dublin accent. Marjorie hated that. Maybe on some level she knew, sensed something, who knows? Anyway, she said she didn't like him and she didn't trust him and that she didn't want me seeing him anymore, like I was a child. We fought, and she demanded to know why I was so determined to go against her wishes. So, I just blurted it out. I think I actually wanted something to happen. I wasn't happy sneaking around with Brian while simultaneously playing happy family with Marjorie and the children.'

'So you just told her you were gay?' Carmel was incredulous, trying to picture the scene.

'Well, I told her I loved Brian. The word *gay* wasn't used in those days. *Temperamental, theatrical* were the kinder words, but there were others, and to my horrified amazement, she knew them all. I never saw such venom and hatred. The vitriol just poured out of her; it was truly shocking to me, this mild-mannered girl, in a twinset and pearls, screaming all sorts of profanities at me. And so, I found myself banished from my home, once again, for being who I am. She said that I could never see her or the children again, that it was more bearable to be seen as a deserted wife than the wife of an unnatural beast. She even said she feared I would interfere sexually with the children.' The raw anguish of the reminiscence was etched on his face.

He went on, 'She made me promise to leave and never contact her again, nor was I to flaunt my disgusting habits around London in case any of her family or friends found out what I really was. There was a threat in there, I suppose, that she'd report me, to the bank, to my colleagues. She wanted me to remain a closet homosexual all my life to spare her, and so I agreed. I felt so guilty, I suppose...'

'But wasn't it legalised in the late sixties?'

'Yes, but *legally allowed* and *socially acceptable* are two very different things. I'd have lost my job, so would Brian. We'd have been pariahs. And I wanted to try to make it up to her. It was stupid, I know.'

'I don't think it was stupid at all. I think it was too much to ask, but the fact that you kept your promise all these years, well, it means something. Brian understood, and he loved you for it.' Carmel leaned over and covered his hand with hers.

Tim allowed the tears to fall, and for a long time they just sat in the bright kitchen. Eventually, Tim asked, 'So, we're doing this, are we? The pair of Irish misfits going back home, not knowing what awaits us?' He managed a weak smile.

'It's going to be OK,' Carmel found herself reassuring him, though she was also filled with trepidation. 'We'll all be together, and there's strength in numbers. I'm nervous too, but we'll stick together, and we'll be grand. To be honest, I think we'll have our hands too full with the famous Zeinab to be dwelling on our own issues.'

'OK, I'll come. For you, and for Brian.'

CHAPTER 36

*C*armel waited in line in the local Boots pharmacy for her contraceptive pill prescription. Beside her on the shelf were a whole lot of different pregnancy testing kits. What she wouldn't give to be buying one of those instead.

She'd never had occasion to buy one when she was married to Bill, since they never had sex, but she could just imagine the horror of walking into Quigley's Pharmacy in the square in Birr and asking for a pregnancy test. She doubted they even stocked such a thing, and if they did, all it would take is for one of the locals to walk in behind you and your business would be all over the town within the hour. She was still getting used to the indifference, in a good way, of the British. Nobody really cared what anyone else did, or who they did it with. Sharif thought it was funny when she asked, 'What will people say?' about particular things, and he always responded with 'What people?'

Life here, though only an hour away by plane from Ireland, was light years away in virtually every way. Well, the way Jen and Luke described Dublin it was probably more like London, with everyone going about their business without the crippling fear of what the neighbours would have to say about anything, but her experience was of a town in the midlands, where people had very definite opinions about other people's business.

For example, she was fascinated by Zane's openness about his sexuality. He was gay and proud, and she'd admit to having been a little shocked at his antics at first. Or how Oscar, the yoga teacher at Aashna, dressed in baggy trousers and tie-dyed t-shirts and wore beads around his neck and wrists and probably never thought he looked a little odd. And over here, he didn't, but any man wearing clothes like that or bangles and beads in Birr would definitely have been on the gossip radar. Ivanka, the occupational therapist, had explained nonchalantly one day how she did a pole dancing class for exercise and loved it, not even considering for one second how her choice of exercise looked to anyone else.

When Carmel brought it up with Sharif, he was circumspect.

'I, and I suspect most people here, only care what the people they love think. If you or my mother thought I was being ridiculous, or doing something stupid, then I would take notice. But as for anyone else, people I don't know, or barely know, why would their opinion of me have any impact on my choices? I don't care what they do, it's nothing to do with me, and they presumably feel the same way about me.'

She knew he was right, but it was still hard to shake off the feelings of a lifetime. She paid for the pills and smiled her thanks at the Sikh man with the saffron-coloured turban who served her.

She buried the little purple oblong box of pills, in its paper bag, in the bottom of her handbag. Her period was due tomorrow.

She went into the bakery section of Waitrose and bought herself a Danish pastry and a takeaway coffee. Sitting in the lovely public park, munching her snack and drinking her latte, she smiled. There was no way on earth she'd have been seen eating a pastry in the castle grounds in Birr. Public eating was another taboo. She could picture the mothers, taking their kids on the swings, whispering to each other, 'No wonder she's got a muffin top, eating cakes all day long.' Both the muffin top and the gossipers of Birr were long gone from Carmel's life, but sometimes she had to remind herself of that fact.

Many's the long discussion she and Joe had about her perceptions of Ireland. He was of the opinion that she was ridiculously negative and that people were not as she imagined them to be at all. Maybe he was right, maybe the women in the park in Birr would care nothing about whether she ate a bun or not, or maybe they'd think to themselves, 'That looks delicious, maybe I'll pop in and get some for myself on the way home.' It was hard to know. Her life there had been one of isolation.

Despite living in the town as a respectable married woman, her husband a reasonably wealthy farmer, and the sister-in-law of the formidable Miss Sheehan, local school principal, Carmel had not been part of the community in any meaningful way. Partly it was the fault of the people around her, but she'd been forced to admit that some of it was because she didn't try to connect with people, either. She'd been insecure and worried people wouldn't like her because of her background, but she may have come across as standoffish.

She sat on the bench, watching life go on around her. A man was teaching a little boy how to ride a bike on the path beside the bench where she sat. Two old ladies were walking their chihuahuas around the lily pond, chatting animatedly as their little dogs pranced along on their tartan leads. A young couple lay on the grass to her left, studying and testing each other.

CARMEL MARVELLED at how she now felt part of this world, not like an outsider looking in, unsure of how to enter this world of living people. She knew it was crazy—she'd evolved so much as a person since leaving Bill and Ireland and the person she was—but she was still afraid to go back.

She checked her watch; it was time for her appointment. The first meeting she'd had with the counsellor, Nora, she'd felt so intimidated, but now that she'd been a few times, it was actually something she looked forward to. Seeing someone had been Oscar's suggestion, and initially, she'd been hurt when he suggested it. She was of the belief that only people who were mentally ill went to counsellors. She remembered Donie Kinsella in Birr, who was convinced that Sheila Moriarty who worked in the post office was, in fact, Saint Seraphina, to whom he had great devotion. Nothing would convince him otherwise, even a punch from Mr Moriarty one day when his wife was driven to distraction from Donie saying prayers to her and trying to touch her cardigan every time she came out of the post office for a cigarette. Eventually, Donie was admitted to the county home, where a psychiatrist, and presumably some heavy medication, cured him. He was reintroduced to Birr society after about a year, and he scurried sheepishly past the post office. The poor man was mortified, and nobody ever forgot his obsession. Carmel had resisted Oscar's suggestion of talking to someone more than once, until one day, Oscar cornered her.

He said he understood her concerns, but he went on to explain, 'Carmel, I'm only thinking how hard it has been for you. There's been so much to process, and we all need to take a time out sometimes, to talk to someone who has no emotional investment in us, someplace safe. When I flipped out, lost a ton of my clients' money and was a demon to my ex-wife and kids, spun out of control, I went for counselling, and it really helped.

'Now, you're not like I was, but everyone you confide in—Sharif, Nadia, me, or Zane, or Ivanka, your family in Ireland—we all want what's best for you, but we all have ideas about how you should cope that's all loaded with our own agendas. And how you react, well, that's loaded, too. You don't want Sharif to get sad, so you temper the stories of your childhood; you don't want to seem ungrateful, so you don't tell Nadia the things that bother you; you want your friends to like you, and they do, but you hide bits of yourself that you think are less attractive. We all do it. That's why speaking to someone outside of your life, where you can be totally honest, it is so cathartic. Just go once, and if you hate it, well, fair enough, but I'm confident you won't.'

He had given her the number, and one day, she made the call.

She'd told Sharif that night, and to her surprise, he thought it was a great idea. He'd echoed Oscar's thoughts, and she'd felt better about it.

329

'Hi, Carmel, how are you doing?' Nora took her jacket, and she took her usual seat, opposite the counsellor. The room was lovely, in the attic space of an old house, full of light coming through the two enormous skylights. The walls were covered with bookshelves, and multicoloured rag rugs covered the polished rosewood floor. Nora had told her she often burned sage, an ancient Native American and also Celtic custom for clearing a space of negative energy, and the aroma lingered in the air.

'Fine, thanks.' The first few minutes were always a bit awkward. Carmel never knew whether to launch into chitchat about the weather, stay silent, or get straight to the issues.

Nora was so still, the most serene person Carmel had ever met, yet she also had a wicked sense of humour, and Carmel liked her enormously. 'How was your week? Last week you were telling me you were all waiting on the arrival of your husband's aunt?'

'Oh, yes, Zeinab. Well, it turns out Nadia wasn't exaggerating—she is a handful. She doesn't think much of me, nor anyone from my country, it seems, so our upcoming trip to Ireland will be interesting, I'm sure.' Carmel smiled.

'And does it bother you that she doesn't think much of you?' Something about Nora's gentle voice made Carmel feel safe.

'Well, it shouldn't, I know that, but I suppose it does, and I'm nervous that she'll be rude to Joe or the others. Sharif says he'll have a word with her before we go, and he'll warn my family not to take any notice if she says something racist or offensive, but I'm dreading it.'

'Is Zeinab the only reason you're dreading it?'

Carmel went on to explain just why she hated the thought of returning to Ireland, of slipping back into who she was.

'That won't happen, Carmel. Who you are now is who you are. You've grown so much, you're your own person, and while the emotions you experience are going to be challenging sometimes, you must remember that the person you have become, that's the real Carmel. Do you understand that?'

Carmel nodded, not trusting herself to speak.

'I want a baby,' she blurted.

She had not intended to just say it like that, no warning, no buildup.

'Are you pregnant?' Nora asked.

'No... My period is due tomorrow, but I just can't stop thinking about what if I did...' Tears stung her eyes.

'Have a child?' Nora probed gently.

'Yes... I'd love to have a baby, with Sharif, but I think I'm too old, or maybe I'm infertile or something. We haven't really discussed it...' She reddened. 'Anyway, I'm on the pill.'

She began to cry, unsure why, but Nora just sat in her chair and allowed Carmel to let it out. Eventually, the sobs subsided.

'Why have you not spoken to Sharif about your dreams to be a mother do you think?' Nora asked.

Carmel took a breath to steady herself.

She'd wondered this herself. She could talk to Sharif about anything...but this, for some reason. He and his first wife, Jamilla, hadn't had children, but Carmel assumed it was because Jamilla was ill. A shadow of grief crossed Sharif's face when he spoke about her still, so Carmel didn't bring it up for fear of upsetting him. But Sharif was so gentle, so approachable. Maybe there was another reason Carmel couldn't bring it up.

'I'm not sure,' she said slowly. 'I think he still misses his wife, and the way she died...and so young... They didn't have a family, but I imagine they would have wanted to, and I don't want to make him talk about it, I suppose.' She paused. 'Or maybe I'm just hiding behind that. Maybe I'm afraid of sounding ungrateful? Or perhaps I'm afraid he would think someone like me, with no experience of being a parent—or indeed, being parented—wouldn't be up to the huge task of rearing a child. I try not to air such thoughts, because it hurts Sharif. He never says it, but he gets upset when he hears me think so little of myself.'

She went on, and it felt good to be honest about her feelings without having to consider the effect her words had on the other person. 'He gets it on one level, that no matter how confident and secure I seem now, during the important years, and so many of them,

I was disregarded. A lifetime of that can't be erased in a year, no matter how much a person is loved. Maybe it never can be.' Tears stung her eyes, and she wiped them away, embarrassed. She was so unused to being open and honest about how she felt, it was difficult—but surprisingly cathartic.

Now, at least, she could express all those feelings of inadequacy to Nora and be spared seeing the fleeting hurt in Sharif's or a friend's eyes.

'Carmel, your emotions are not a reason to feel ashamed. You feel what you feel, and you don't need to apologise for it. Own your emotions instead of trying to stifle them. Why do you think the prospect of not becoming a mother upsets you so much?'

Carmel thought for a moment. 'I want someone of my own to love and for them to love me,' she whispered.

'But you have lots of love in your life now. How would a child change that?' Nora sat forward, shortening the space between them.

'I never knew my mother. And my father—and I'm not even sure he is my father—has only been in my life for about a year. Sharif and I, we love each other, but he could leave, he could die, anything could happen. I suppose I want a baby because that boy or girl would be mine, and I'd be theirs, or something. I don't know. It's mad.'

'Why are you not sure your father is your father?'

Carmel sighed. If she was to go forward with this and really heal all the years of pain, she'd have to be upfront and honest with Nora. The story of her conception was one that hurt her deeply, and she'd never spoken about it with Nora, even though this was her third session. She took a deep breath to steady herself.

'My mother used to go out with the man I call my father, Joe McDaid. They grew up together in Dublin. She and Joe were sleeping together and had intended to get married. Joe hated his father—he was a bully and violent and all of that, terrorised his wife and children. So, one night, to stop his father attacking his mother, Joe got into a fight with him. He beat him up and put him in hospital, but more than that, everyone now knew what the old man was like. He was holier-than-thou, you see, reading at mass and being the real

Catholic on the outside but a demon at home. Anyway, he knew how Joe felt about my mother, and so to punish Joe for exposing him, he dragged my mother, Dolly, into a wooded area one night and raped her.' Carmel shuddered at the words.

She took a drink of water to steady herself and went on. 'My mother discovered she was pregnant, and in a panic, she told Joe's father. She didn't know which of them was the father, and he arranged for her to be put into a place run by nuns for girls who got pregnant outside of marriage. What he did then, he never told Dolly. He paid the nuns handsomely, I'm sure, but he lied to the Reverend Mother. He said he'd been foolish and had a relationship with Dolly but he was a married man. He told the nun he was going to try to convince his wife to take the child—me—when she got over the shock of him having an affair. He never said *rape*, of course, called it a little mistake, flattered by the attentions of a lovely young woman, all of that. Dolly was never consulted.

'Anyway, he insisted to that end, that I never be adopted, and so I was never even eligible for adoption. I was born in a mother and baby home and immediately transferred to Trinity House on the other side of the city. I used to hope and pray that someone would come for me. I saw other children adopted over the years, but nobody ever showed the slightest interest in me. I assumed I wasn't pretty enough or something. I didn't know why they didn't want me, I just knew they didn't. I spent my whole life there. In fact, I outstayed my welcome. We were supposed to leave at eighteen, but I had nowhere to go, so the nuns let me stay on for a bit. If they were found out, they would have been in trouble, so when one day the letter came from Bill, enquiring if there was anyone who wanted to get married to a widower with two little girls, it seemed perfect. Even the nuns thought I was insane, but I agreed to meet him. And he seemed OK, very quiet but not mad or anything, even though he was much older than me. The idea of having two little daughters to love, well, that sealed the deal for me.'

'And how did you learn all of this if your mother died before you could meet her?' Nora asked.

'Sharif. My husband. He found me. Dolly spent her whole life looking for me, but she'd been told I was adopted and so contact was impossible. Dolly and Nadia, Sharif's mother, were best friends. Dolly was a kind of other mother to Sharif, and he promised her, on her deathbed, that he wouldn't give up. And he didn't, so here I am.'

'And he introduced you to Joe?' Nora asked.

'Well, Dolly had known Joe's brother Brian here in London; they were reunited after years and years completely by chance, and she'd told him the story of what had happened from her end—what their father had done to her, and to me. Brian wanted Dolly to contact Joe, but she refused. She said she didn't want to disrupt his life and too much time had passed.

'Later, I met Joe at Brian's funeral. We met, and instantly, I liked him. He knows the truth now, but he thinks he's my dad and so do I. He left it up to me, and I decided against a DNA test, because what good would it do? I can't bear the thought that the man I see as my father is actually my brother and my grandfather is my father. It's all too horrible. So as far as both of us is concerned, Joe is my dad, and we're leaving it at that.'

Carmel stopped speaking, and Nora just waited. The silence wasn't awkward; if anything, it was soothing.

'Our time is nearly up, but this week I'd like you to give some thought to this: Why are you not telling Sharif about wanting a child? Maybe do some of those guided meditations I gave you. Stillness can clarify our thoughts.'

Carmel nodded, putting on her jacket.

She had a lot to think about.

CHAPTER 37

The trip to Ireland was six days away, and Carmel was counting down with dread. She knew she was being ridiculous. It was just a holiday, she was a grown woman, and they weren't going anywhere near Birr or Bill or Julia. She needed to get a grip.

She'd slammed her computer shut yesterday when she heard Sharif's key in the lock because she'd been looking at pictures of newborn babies. She knew she should talk it out with him, but something was stopping her. Besides, he had so much to organise in order to get away. He would never pry; she'd have to tell him. He didn't ever interrogate her about the counselling, and at the beginning, she'd felt she should tell him how things were going with Nora. But over dinner the first night after Carmel started seeing her, he'd said,

'I know this therapy is a process, because when Jamilla died, I found it so hard—not just her loss, but the fact that I was a doctor who could help others but could do nothing for her. I just sat there, watching her fade away in front of my eyes. In the end, I went to speak to someone, a therapist, and it helped. I was against it at first—doctors are terrible patients—but in the end, my grief, depression, whatever you want to call it, was taking over my life. The man I saw was great, and he gave me good advice. He said not to talk to people about what happened there. Not to let the work that was done in the therapist's office spill out into my life, and he was right. Deal with it in there, say what you need to say, and then get on with your life. Sometimes when we are working through issues, we feel a need to share it with those around us and then, afterwards, regret it.

'In the months after Jamilla died, sometimes, I talked incessantly about her, then other times I didn't mention her name for weeks. It was weird. After a while, George explained that I needed to get things clear in my own head first, and so, at his suggestion, I told my parents that I would speak to them when the time was right. I asked them if they could just accept that I was dealing with it my own way and give me the space to do that. They understood, and though they were worried about me, they never pried. And, in due time, we got to talking about her again. I want you to have that same space, so I won't be badgering you to tell me how you're getting on. Talk to me, anytime you want, of course, but only when you decide.'

He was so understanding, so emotionally evolved, that sometimes he intimidated Carmel. He never lost his temper, or got frustrated or upset. He really was a very calm person, very mindful. But sometimes she wished he could be a bit more flawed. Immediately she thought it, she felt a pang of guilt. She'd had years and years of marriage to an emotionally stunted man, totally incapable of even the most perfunctory of human interaction, and now, here she was with Sharif, and she wished he was different. It wasn't even that she wanted him to be different—he was funny and charming and handsome and kind, everything you'd want in a husband—but she felt inadequate beside him, no matter how often he told her that in the eyes of the world they were equals, that only she saw all her hang-ups and imagined shortcomings.

With six days until they left for Ireland, Carmel was pottering about the apartment, taking a rare day off. Sharif was very busy at the clinic today, but he checked in by text whenever he got a moment. She'd gone out for sushi with Zane and Ivanka last night and woke at three in the morning vomiting. She thought the sushi had tasted off, but since she'd never had it before, she didn't want to appear gauche in front of her friends and ate it. Sharif gave her an injection to stop the nausea and left her with strict instructions to stay in bed and take it easy. Though she felt like death warmed up, he assured her it was a mild case of food poisoning—Ivanka and Zane were off with the same complaint.

She had stayed in bed for an hour, but a lifetime of early rising was ingrained, so eventually she got up.

She might as well pack her bag for the trip. She was a bit early, but she liked to be ready and, anyway, couldn't venture too far from the bathroom today. In the bottom of the wardrobe lay her little brown suitcase; it looked like the one Paddington Bear carried, Sharif had joked. The idea that she had fitted everything she owned in that just a year ago astounded her as she surveyed her walk-in wardrobe with the long shoe rack. She still didn't spend much, lots of things she picked up in charity shops or in the sales, but still her wardrobe was so much more diverse and glamorous than it used to be.

She was choosing which jumpers to bring—even though it was summer, the evenings got chilly—when the doorbell rang. Sharif was working, and anyway, he had a key and so did Nadia, though she never really called unannounced.

Carmel went to the door, her heart sinking as she saw the colourful bulk through the opaque glass of the door. She opened it with a fake smile on her face. This really was the last thing she needed.

'Zeinab, how nice to see you. Is Nadia not with you?' Carmel desperately looked behind Zeinab in the hope of seeing her mother-in-law. She'd never had to deal with Zeinab alone before, and she was nervous.

'No, she is not my keeper, Carmel. Can I not visit my nephew's house without a chaperon?' The way she pronounced Carmel's name seemed to leave out the middle *R*, sounding more like *Camel*. She was sure it was deliberate.

'Of… Of course… Please come in.' Carmel moved aside to allow Zeinab to enter. She swept imperially into the apartment, perfectly able-bodied despite the incessant complaints about her knees and her hip and her back that drove Nadia up the walls.

'This really is such a small place, considering Sharif owns this entire complex.' Zeinab glanced around their lovely home dismissively. 'Why does he live so modestly, do you think?'

'Er... Well, we like it here. And we don't need much space...' Carmel wished she could be more forceful and tell this old bat where to get off, but she didn't dare.

'Well, I expect that for you it must seem like a palace, after all you've been through?' The tone was sickly sweet, but the words cut Carmel.

She didn't need sympathy, and anyway, what Zeinab was offering wasn't sympathy—it was condescension.

'Actually, the house I grew up in was very large, lots of rooms, so this is nice and cosy.' She tried to inject some brightness into her voice. Zeinab reminded her of those predators she and Sharif had watched on Planet Earth on the BBC, David Attenborough explaining how they sat and waited, sensing fear and then pounced on their prey.

'Yes, an orphanage, Nadia said, and then you were sold into some kind of arranged Catholic marriage or something?'

Carmel swallowed down the lump of hurt. She was fairly sure Nadia would never have spoken about her like that. This was Zeinab twisting the knife, trying to belittle her.

'Well, it was a children's home, not an orphanage, and my first marriage wasn't arranged. It just didn't work out, that's all, and now... Well, now...' She had started well but faltered.

'Now you're happily installed here, married to my very wealthy nephew. How nice for you. It must be a relief to live so comfortably after years of uncertainty.' Zeinab smiled, but it never reached her eyes. She was eagle-eyed as her gaze rested on photographs and the few special items Carmel and Sharif had chosen to decorate their home. She went on, 'I was looking at the property pages this morning. There really are some lovely homes to be had around here. Not of the standard you'd find in Karachi—space is at such a premium here in London, so people have to forego the extensive grounds and so on that we enjoy in Pakistan—but very nice homes nonetheless.'

Carmel had no idea where this was going, but she was convinced it was going somewhere.

'Have you ever looked at those?' Zeinab asked, that smile again. It gave Carmel the shudders.

'Er... Well, I've seen some houses for sale when I go for a walk sometimes, but I can't say I've taken too much notice, to be honest.' Carmel tried to steer the conversation into less bewildering waters. 'Would you like a drink?'

She tried to quell another sudden wave of nausea. The injection Sharif had given her had stopped the vomiting, thankfully, but she still felt very queasy.

'Yes, tea.' Zeinab sat herself down on the sofa and took up the framed wedding photo on the side table. Carmel and Sharif were laughing in it; Zane had taken the picture on his phone the day they got married. Though they'd had an official photographer, and his album was really lovely, this was the photo they liked best. Carmel would always remember the moment it was taken. A very disgruntled Ivy, one of the cleaners at Aashna, had just returned from the ladies', where, she explained, the cast-iron guaranteed-to-have-no-spare-tyre slip she was wearing beneath her dress had rolled up from the bottom and down from the top and had been attempting for the entire wedding ceremony to cut her in half around the middle. Her descriptions of the struggle to get the cursed thing off in the bathroom had the entire table in stitches.

'I must say, I was surprised to hear Sharif had remarried, he so loved dear Jamilla,' Zeinab interrupted the happy memory. 'She was such a wonderful girl, an angel, I never thought he would get over it. Then I suppose one never truly recovers from the loss of a spouse. A love like they had, well, it only comes along once in a lifetime, if you're lucky.' She accepted the cup of tea from Carmel.

'He often talks about her,' Carmel said, trying to ignore the jibe. 'She sounded like a wonderful person. I know they were very happy together.'

'Oh, yes, she really was. She was a nurse, such a kind, caring girl, and her family are very well respected. Her uncle runs a lovely country club just outside Karachi, and her mother's people are very wealthy, property tycoons really you could say. I remember how she came to my house when I hurt my back years ago; oh, she was so knowledgeable, so gentle, but you just felt like she was so competent. I begged her to go back to Sharif once I was able to get around, but she insisted on staying until I was totally better. Oh, and my Tariq, he adored her. Well, everyone did really.'

'She went to care for you in Karachi?' Carmel tried not to sound incredulous. The idea that anyone would leave Sharif to spend time with this old bat mystified Carmel.

'Yes.' The normally verbose Zeinab was surprisingly tight-lipped. She gazed at Carmel, her dark eyes scheming, and then she spoke.

'She needed some time, after all she'd been through...' She sipped her chai.

'With the cancer?' Carmel asked, not out of curiosity as much as not wanting to appear unfeeling.

'No... Well, yes, among other things... Well, I'm sure Sharif has explained.' She smiled sweetly.

Carmel had no clue what she was going on about but was determined not to show her ignorance of such a huge part of Sharif's life.

'He's told me a lot about the life he and Jamilla shared. They were lucky to have known such love.' She didn't really know what else to say. She'd never felt threatened by his dead wife before now, not like she had with Bill and the huge wedding photo in the living room of his dear departed Gretta. Bill was not free, that was the fact. It seemed so obvious now, but she'd wasted all those years trying to get him to feel something for her. His rejection merely confirmed what she'd known all her life: that she was unlovable. She was trying so hard to foster feelings of compassion for her younger self. It wasn't that she was unadoptable–her grandfather had ensured nobody could adopt her. Likewise, Bill didn't reject her because of anything she was or wasn't—he'd just never gotten over losing Gretta. Carmel had to keep reminding herself of these facts.

Sharif, on the other hand, acknowledged that he and Jamilla had been good together but it was in the past. She was gone and they were here, and he was convinced she would want him to move on and be happy.

But Zeinab droned on. 'Yes. Everyone loved Jamilla. Especially Khalid, Sharif's father. Oh, he adored her, and she him. And of course, Nadia, Tariq and I, she had everyone under her spell. Now, tell me more about you. As I said, I was so surprised to hear Sharif was remarrying, but I suppose, men, they have needs, and Sharif is not the sort to just have a string of romances behind him. Still, there must have been something special about you?' Her tone suggested that Carmel being remarkable in any way was most unlikely.

Carmel resented this cross-examination, the feeling that she had to make the case for her and Sharif's marriage, and on top of that, she got the distinct impression there was something Sharif hadn't told her about him and Jamilla, something everyone else in the Khan family knew. They were normally so open and honest with each other, it hurt her to think there was something important he had kept from her.

'I don't know, really. We just met and sort of clicked, I suppose. He said I remind him of my mother, and he was very fond of her, she was almost like another mother to him...' That was definitely the wrong thing to say, judging by the look on Zeinab's face.

'Really? I thought she just worked for Nadia. I know she and Khalid gave Dolly—was that her name?—some support, financially, I mean, but I thought that was simply because she was a loyal employee of Nadia's business.'

Carmel gritted her teeth. Zeinab knew well the relationship between her mother and Sharif's family, but she was trying to unsettle Carmel.

'No, Nadia and my mother were partners in the dressmaking business, and she certainly was more to the Khan family than just that. She and Nadia were best friends, and she helped nurse Khalid in his final months. It was because she meant so much to him that Sharif found me. He promised her that he wouldn't stop looking.'

Zeinab seemed to be enjoying getting rise out of Carmel, as they say in Ireland. She barely suppressed a smirk.

'So, you are Dolly's daughter, and your father—I know you've met him—and his family? He was married to someone else?' Her brow furrowed dramatically. She was making it sound like Carmel's family was not only highly distasteful but also utterly confusing.

How dare she? Carmel was seething now. Normally, she was very open about her story—well, the part about her mother and father, anyway. Very few people knew her true story, the reason she was never adopted, and she did not care to enlighten them. She prayed Nadia hadn't inadvertently let something slip.

'Oh, Joe is wonderful. I love him dearly. Yes, after he and my mother parted ways, he married a lovely lady called June, and they had two children, Luke and Jennifer. You'll meet them. Sadly, June died a few years ago.'

'And does he live alone?'

Carmel was thrown by the question. Everything Zeinab said was heavily loaded, so this was a bit of a random enquiry. She wondered what was behind it. She longed to chuck the nosy old biddy out, but she was Sharif's aunt and Nadia's sister, so Carmel didn't dare.

'Er... Yes... Jennifer lives close by with her husband and little boy, and Luke has an apartment in the city. My sister Jennifer is a stay-at-home mum at the moment looking after my nephew Sean, and my brother Luke is a detective in the Irish police.' She felt the familiar surge of pride at saying the words 'my brother,' 'my sister.'

'How interesting that they would consider themselves your siblings though you were a stranger up until recently. It must take some adjusting, to suddenly find yourself at the centre of a big family when for so long you were alone?'

How did Zeinab manage to make everything she said sound mean, when those words from anyone else's lips wouldn't be seen as such? Carmel berated herself—she was being too sensitive. Zeinab was trying to rile her, and Carmel was damned if she would allow it.

'Yes, it is a bit different, but I'm loving it.' Carmel smiled serenely.

'And your father lives alone? Is he fit and healthy?'

'Yes, he's in great shape. He loves DIY and all of that, so he's always doing something.' Carmel glanced at the clock. Sharif wouldn't be back for ages, and she could think of no other way of ending this audience with Zeinab, but she wasn't going to spend her whole afternoon talking pointlessly with her.

'Well, when someone is fit and healthy, then it is fine, I suppose. I was never alone, thankfully. I always had Tariq, bless his soul. But now that I'm older and not as agile as I was, well, it is different. So many of my friends are lucky to have children to take care of them, but Tariq and I were never blessed with a family. It is a struggle to keep going, I can tell you.'

Nadia had told Carmel that Zeinab had all kinds of help in the house and that she got out and about all the time. She had a chauffeur, and a maid and a gardener—as they say in Ireland, there was no fear of her, but she was angling, no doubt about it.

'But don't you have a lot of staff, back in Karachi?' Carmel asked.

'Oh, yes, paid employees. Not the same as family, though. Nothing like family. In our culture, Carmel, care of the elders, respect for them, is very important. It is part of what we are, the way we take care of our older generations, visit them, spend time with them. Many of my friends now live with their children, or even nieces or nephews. Take my friend Amal, for example. She held out in her own house for as long as she could, of course, but in the end, her children were so upset at the thought of their elderly mother living alone that they insisted she come and stay with them. She was sad to leave her home, of course, but she is so lucky. I don't have anyone to do that for me. Nobody at all.' She sighed heavily.

Carmel fought back the urge to either panic or laugh. Was Zeinab seriously angling for an invitation to come and live here with her and Sharif? She must be off her rocker if she thought they'd agree.

'But, Zeinab, you're still a young woman. You're fit and healthy, and as you said, you have lots of friends. I know it is hard to cope without Tariq'—Carmel managed to make it sound sincere despite what she knew about the creepy man—'but if you can, try to see it as a transition phase in your life. You will need to grieve for all you have lost, but certainly it is not advisable to make any big changes in your life so soon after a bereavement.'

Zeinab gazed at her, weighing up how best to proceed.

'Yes, I am sure you are right.' Her tone could've cut glass. 'Now, I must go. Thank you for the chai.' And with remarkable agility for one supposed to be so infirm, she left, leaving Carmel standing in the middle of her kitchen wondering what on earth just happened.

CHAPTER 38

'Hi, Jen!' Carmel accepted a FaceTime call from her sister in Dublin the next day. She was back at work and feeling better, though not 100 percent yet, as she still had some cramps in her stomach. Ivanka was still off, and Zane was thrilled the impromptu food poisoning meant he'd lost five pounds. He was thin as a rail anyway but incredibly vain, so he was threatening to go back there again for another dose any time his impossibly skinny trousers felt tight. Carmel couldn't help but laugh, though she would never again darken the door of the Sushi Palace.

'Hi, is it a good time or are you busy?' Jennifer asked. She was always conscious that Carmel could be dealing with anything when she called. 'I've just got Sean down for a nap so I can talk in peace for five minutes!'

'No, it's great. Let me just get a coffee and I'll go into my office and we can have a proper chat.' She filled her cup from the fancy new coffee machine in reception, donated by the family of a grateful patient.

'Now,' she said, settling into her chair. 'Tell me all your news.'

Carmel had gotten used to the idea of Jen being pregnant again and felt fine speaking to her about it. That initial wave of longing seemed to have dulled to an ache, and she knew she could hide it successfully. If living as she did for the first forty years of her life had taught her anything, it was how to cover up her true feelings.

'Oh, I've no news really. My social life is zero these days, in bed by eight, dozing when Damien gets home and can take Sean for an hour, not cooking at all, you know yourself.' Jen's blooming complexion grinned at Carmel from the screen of her iPhone.

Carmel wished she did know herself but dismissed the thought immediately.

'Actually, Dad's on his way over here,' Jennifer said. 'We're going to put on an extension out the back. Dad reckons himself and Damien will be able to do it, with a bit of help from Luke, but I'm not sure. I'd rather get proper builders.' Jen chuckled. 'Y'know, the kind that are actually qualified?'

Carmel smiled. 'But think of the money you'll save, and Joe has done loads of that sort of thing before, hasn't he? I'm sure it will be gorgeous.' Carmel sipped her latte. 'What are you building, anyway?'

'Well, you'll see when you come over! I can't believe you haven't been here; it feels like you've been in the family forever. Anyway, yeah, we're building another bedroom. We're going to need it when this little one arrives.' Jen's smile said it all as she placed her hand on her belly. 'Apart from the fact that I need somewhere for my sister to stay when she comes to visit.'

Carmel nailed a smile to her face, ignoring the maelstrom of emotion churning inside her. 'Well, Joe is determined to get us over for the wedding and this big road trip he's planned, so I'll be there, all right. Now, tell me, how are you feeling? I've heard the first three months can often be the toughest?'

'Not too bad, actually. Exhausted, but I'm that way anyway running around after Sean all the time. He's got the energy of five kids, I swear. But all in all, I'm doing well. I hate coffee now—I was the same when I was expecting Sean. I can't even bear the smell of it, and I used to be a five-cup-a-day girl. But apart from a little nausea now and again, I'm grand.'

'I'll send you some of this amazing tea Sharif gets. I never had it before coming here, but he recommends it for people who feel a little nauseous after chemo. It really perks you up, but it's made just from flowers and roots or something. I know it's safe in pregnancy because he gave it to a patient's daughter who was pregnant, and she said she felt much better after it.'

'Thanks, sounds good. I'm just really happy, so all that small stuff doesn't matter really. We were waiting ages for Sean, I told you that. I didn't know if there was something wrong or what, but when I finally got pregnant after two years of trying, well, we weren't sure if we'd ever get lucky again. But it seems we hit the jackpot again, so we're over the moon.'

'Of course you are, it's wonderful news. Joe must be delighted at the prospect of another grandchild.'

'He was. He got kind of emotional, actually, which isn't like him. But I haven't told Luke yet, so don't say anything if you're talking to him. He's at some big drugs case in Madrid, an Interpol case involving loads of countries, but the culprits are Irish, wouldn't you know, so he's out there. I'll tell him when he gets back. He comes home most weekends and goes back out on Mondays.'

'Yeah, I wondered about that.' Carmel had spoken to Luke last Monday morning as he waited to board a flight back to Spain. 'Would it not be easier for him just to stay there?'

'Well, that's the other bit of news. Don't say I said it, I'm not even supposed to know, but our Lukie is seeing a girl and he seems to be very into it. She's the reason he's on a flight every Friday; otherwise, boy wonder would be chilling out with the tapas and the senoritas at the weekends in sunny Spain. But no, back he comes to rainy Dublin, sure as anything. He's being very cagey about it, though. Hasn't said a word to anyone, not even Dad, and he tells him everything.'

'So how do you know?' Carmel was intrigued and really hoped it was someone nice. Luke was such a sweet guy, she'd hate for anyone to hurt him. For all his messing and joking around, he was a sensitive soul.

'Well, because Dublin is a village really, and you can't do anything without the whole place knowing your business. Aisling works for

Aer Lingus, so she saw him in arrivals at the airport. Real romcom stuff—this girl was waiting for him at the gates, then running into his arms kinda thing. He didn't see Ais, so she let him off, but we were all wondering what he was up to. He's been very secretive of late. Sometimes he gets like that when he's on a big case, so we thought it was that, but no. Love is in the air, apparently.'

'Ah, I hope it works out for him. He hasn't had a serious girlfriend before, has he?'

'Oh, he did—God, what a tale of woe that was. She was Italian, gorgeous, tiny, all brown eyes and shiny hair and talking with her hands...' Jen rolled her eyes.

Carmel chuckled. 'I'm sensing some resentment there, Jen.'

'Yeah, well, wait till you hear. He was weak for her, stone mad about her, and she was a right little princess. Anyway, she went home to Verona for her mother's birthday or something. Luke was supposed to go but he had to work, so she went alone. They were together over a year, and he just idolised her, and anyway what does my lady do? Only send him a text—a text, can you believe it? To say she was staying in Italy, she had fallen in love with some Marco or Pietro or Franco or whatever, like in four days or something, and basically told poor Luke to send on her stuff, she wasn't coming back. He was gutted, absolutely devastated, and I wanted to rip her stupid Barbie doll head off of course. But anyway, it ended and that was that.'

'Oh no, poor Luke. That's awful.'

'Yeah, he was months getting over it. I'm half afraid this is another Italian, and that's why he's being so secretive. Or maybe he just doesn't want us all having opinions. It's one of the downsides of a big family, Carmel: everyone's an expert!'

Carmel laughed. 'I can't wait to meet everyone at the wedding.'

'Oh, you'll be like Kim Kardashian, you'll be photographed to death and everyone will want to hear your story from the horse's mouth. You've given the family no end of gossip fodder. I never really knew about your mam, thankfully Dad didn't go on about it, but now that you've reappeared in our lives it seems like everyone knew Dolly was the great love of his life.'

Carmel detected a sadness in her sister, and she was anxious to alleviate any misgivings. 'Joe's told me so often how much he loved your mam, Jen, genuinely loved her, not as a consolation prize or whatever. They had a genuinely great marriage. I'd hate to think me turning up was destroying the real memory of that. And even though I never got to meet my mother, I think she would have been very upset too if that happened. She knew your dad was happy with June, that's why she never went back.'

'Ah, I know that, it's a bit stupid, and I'm really happy we found you, so happy about that... But yeah, in a way, it does make me sad that everyone is going on about the thing my dad had with Dolly. Not to mention being forced to face the fact that my dad had a physical relationship with someone other than my mam. It's not something anyone likes to dwell on, I know, and we never had to until now, so yeah, it's not always easy. I mean they always say, 'Oh, but he had a great marriage with June too,' but almost like a side point or something. Luke and I got a bit odd with our aunt the other day when we met her and she started with it again...'

Carmel loved the honesty that existed between them. From the very first meeting with her sister, there had been no pretence. They both just said things as they felt them.

'I can imagine how hard that must be,' Carmel said gently. 'I wish I could do something, to stop it. I know that's not how Joe sees it anyway, and that's what really matters.'

'Yeah, exactly, we'll just have to stick together and put up with a bit of tongue wagging.'

'Always, I'm 100 percent behind you and Luke. You could have told me to buzz off and that you wanted nothing to do with me and nobody would've blamed you, but you didn't. I owe you both big time, so you'll always have my loyalty.'

Jen smiled, her eyes were suspiciously bright. 'Don't mind me, it's all the hormones. Damien says I'm mental these days, laughing one minute, crying the next. It's this little trickster in here I blame.' She placed her hand on her belly again.

'So, speaking of which, is it a boy or a girl, do you think?' Carmel asked.

Jen smiled. 'I don't honestly know, though either will be great. My mam used to say boys wreck your house and girls wreck your head, so either way destruction is in my future!'

'You must miss her, especially now,' Carmel said quietly.

'I do, so much. But, and I'm not just saying this, Carmel, I love having you as a sister. I know you don't have kids, but it's nice to have some woman in the family to talk to. Dad's great and everything, but he's my dad, y'know? And I think every time I mention the pregnancy, Luke changes the subject for fear I'm going to give him too much information on my internal workings.'

Carmel felt a flood of warmth engulf her. To go from nobody loving her to this new life full of family and friendship threatened to overwhelm her sometimes, but to hear Jen talk like this always soothed her troubled spirit.

They chatted about the impending arrival for a few more minutes, until Sean woke from his nap and Jen had to go.

Once she ended the call, Carmel sat in her chair and, try as she might, couldn't stop the tears. She was really happy for Jennifer, of course she was, but that didn't stop her feeling sad. She didn't know where this sudden longing for a child of her own was coming from, but now it seemed all-pervasive. She was becoming obsessed, constantly looking at babies in the park, in cafes, and imagining having one of her very own. She even bought some Johnson's baby powder the other day, just to imagine what having a baby would smell like. If anyone saw her, they'd think she'd lost her marbles.

Since the peculiar conversation with Zeinab, she'd suspected there was something Sharif hadn't told her. Zeinab was definitely stirring, though why, she didn't know yet. Probably just her fondness for causing dissension.

Carmel pulled herself together, fixed her face, and went about her business. She was going to have to talk to Sharif. Maybe they could go out to dinner later, have a chat uninterrupted. Between the new extension being built to the main building and the demands of the patients, it was hard to get quality time together, but she knew if she told him she wanted to talk, he'd organise cover. Still, she felt bad asking for his time at the moment; he didn't often take time off, and the preparation for his absence was very time-consuming. Patients and their families panicked when they heard Dr Khan wasn't going to be around for a few weeks, so he was anxious to help them build up trust with Dr Benedict Cruz and the locum team who were covering his holiday.

She could put it off, she supposed, but once they were in Ireland, the whole family would be there and it would be even harder to get time alone. She'd have to try to get some time with him before they left.

Part of her wanted to run scared from the conversation, but she had given too many years of her life in silence, not daring to have a point of view. Then Sharif had come and changed all of that. He would want her to speak her mind.

CHAPTER 39

'You look lovely.' Sharif smiled, his head to one side, admiring her as the waiter grinned and gave her the menu.

One of the many things she'd had to get used to when she and Sharif first got together were the compliments and how he didn't care who was listening when he gave them. She used to get embarrassed and wish he wouldn't, but she was getting used to it.

'Thanks. So do you.' She smiled, and it made him laugh.

'You always say that. I love it. Most women just accept the compliment, as if giving them is a one-way street, men to women. You don't do that.'

'I suppose there has to be some advantages to having an emotionally delayed, inexperienced wife?' She winked to take the self-pity from her words. 'I haven't a clue what's normal.'

'Well, don't ever change.'

They were at a lovely Thai place near Aashna, a place where they liked the food and the ambiance. Sharif had figured out quickly that very fancy places made Carmel feel on edge—she hated the sensation of being a VIP—so they tended to go more low-key with socialising. The Siam Orchid was lovely, and Carmel adored their fresh, spiced food. The staff knew them and were friendly without being overbearing, and just last year the grandmother of the family who owned it died peacefully and happily in Aashna, so they always made an extra special effort to make Sharif and Carmel feel welcome. The place was quite busy, and the general hubbub of chatter and low background music meant they could talk without being overheard.

After giving their orders for dinner, they ordered a bottle of red wine and were sipping in companionable silence when Sharif spoke again.

'So, what did you want to talk to me about? Anything in particular?'

Carmel put down her glass and swallowed. It was stupid to be nervous around him, but she was.

The food arrived, and it gave her a chance to gather her thoughts. Once all the dishes were on the table, Sharif raised his eyebrows questioningly.

'Well? Out with it.' He grinned.

'I... I don't know really where to start. I... I'd love to have a baby.'

There. It was out. She knew she should stop now, allow him to digest it, but she heard herself babble on.

'I know I'm probably too old, and you may not want to anyway, what with Aashna and everything, and even if we could, like, I have no experience of being in a family, let alone being a mother, and...then Zeinab said something...about you and Jamilla. She assumed you'd told me, but she wouldn't elaborate.'

Sharif leaned over and put his hand on hers. She stopped talking.

Something in him had changed. Gone was his twinkly smile, the roguish grin to be replaced by something else, something she couldn't read. He put his chopsticks down and sighed.

The silence was frightening. Maybe she shouldn't have said anything. She had no right to demand more, to pry into his past. If he wanted to tell her, if he wanted a child, he would have said so. The insecurities and fear raced around in her brain.

It wasn't like him to be speechless. He was always the one who soothed her, made her feel everything was going to be OK. Seeing the pain and confusion on his face now was so hard.

Eventually, he spoke, and even his voice sounded different.

'Carmel, I don't even know where to start.' He sighed again and took a sip of his wine. 'I haven't been honest with you. I should have been. I wanted to be so often, and even my mother asked me if I'd told you, but I just... I don't know... It was in the past, and I didn't want to go through it all again. We should have talked about this, about children and all of that, your hopes, your expectations, but to be honest I hoped it would just go away. I didn't want to deal with it. Too afraid, I suppose.'

He withdrew his hand, and it was as if he was pulling back from her. She cursed herself for bringing it up. Everything was fine, why did she have to go and ruin everything?

'It doesn't matter, you don't have to do anything Sharif,' she said, trying to turn the clock back. 'Forget I mentioned it...'

'No, Carmel, no. Secrets are bad. I should know that better than most; I've seen so many people when they're dying, regretting keeping secrets.'

He took a breath, and she was panicking. Had she ruined everything? Was he going to end it? She forced herself to be calm. Everything was going to be OK. He wouldn't leave her because she told him the truth. She knew he wouldn't.

'There is something,' he said. 'It's a sad story, but I should have told you before. I'm sorry.'

Carmel could hardly bear to see the distress on the face of the man she loved.

'I wish Zeinab had not said anything. I should have been the one to do that. But now that she has opened that can of worms, I want to tell you now.'

'OK,' she said quietly and placed her hand on the table, hoping he would take it once more.

He did, and then he began.

'Jamilla and I knew each other all our lives. You knew that. We grew up together, her family and mine emigrating from Pakistan at the same time. Though Zeinab likes to go on about Jamilla's family being wealthy, and one or two of them did do well, her parents were poor immigrants just like we were. And when we got married, well, it wasn't arranged, exactly. If either of us hadn't wanted it, then we could have pulled out. But both families were pleased. She was a nurse, and I was in my final year of medicine; we were happy.

'Despite lots of hints from our extended family, we decided to put off having a family until I finished my exams. She probably wanted to start trying to get pregnant right after we got married, but she waited because when we spoke about it, I felt we would have more money, be able to get a house suitable for a child, once I was actually working. Jamilla must have been more upset about it than I thought, because she told her mother. Then her father came and offered me money, to tide us over until I was earning a proper wage. And I... Well, I'm a proud man, and I refused—rudely, I must admit—and I got really cross with her. We fell out. I told her that what happened between us should stay between us and not involve her family. But that's not how Pakistani families work, I'm afraid.'

Carmel stared at the uneaten food in front of them, hoping the staff didn't interrupt their conversation to check everything was OK.

'So,' he went on, 'we fought, and there were tears and everything, but eventually I got my way and we waited. Then I got my first year as an intern, and I realised very early on that oncology was what I wanted to specialise in. It was a long road, with lots more study, and many more years of experience needed, but I felt I could do it. And so, again, I asked Jamilla to wait. I was working crazy hours, sixteen-and seventeen-hour days. I thought we had all the time in the world. She was working too, but she was happy as a staff nurse and had no aspirations for further study or career advancement. But she understood that I did. So she agreed to wait, but not before extracting a promise that we would have a family within five years, the time it would take me to finish my internship in internal medicine and get set up as a surgical resident. I agreed, and it seemed like everything was going to plan. She deflected all the nosy aunties with their questions about babies and was totally loyal to me.'

355

Carmel gave his hand a squeeze as he spoke. He glanced down at her hand and gave a weak smile. Though it clearly hurt him to tell the story, he kept going.

'Eventually, I qualified, and we stopped using contraception. Jamilla was pregnant quickly, and we were all over the moon. We'd moved to a little house with a garden, and while I still worked long hours, at least now I could support her and the baby financially so she could stay at home.'

He took a deep breath and then sipped his wine again.

'The early weeks of pregnancy were tough. She was exhausted all the time, she felt nauseous, and she'd feel full after just a mouthful or two of food. But we thought nothing of those symptoms. In fact, her mother and all the aunties were delighted—those were symptoms of a good, healthy pregnancy. So we weren't worried.

'But when we went for the first scan, I saw the tumour right away on the screen. Jamilla knew by my face that something was wrong. The radiographer and I exchanged a glance, and she left the room. I knew her well, because Jamilla was attending the hospital where I worked.' His voice cracked, and his breath was ragged.

'Jamilla turned and examined the screen. Of course, she was a nurse, and she could read the scan for herself. We were both fairly sure what we were looking at, though we had to have it confirmed. There was a slight chance it was just a cyst, but we both knew the more likely thing was much worse. She had ovarian cancer.

'We were referred that day to a colleague of mine, who told us that it was bad, about as bad as it could be, actually. The foetus was at thirteen weeks' gestation, and Jamilla would need immediate treatment. Usually cancer is only at stage one when found in pregnancy, and there are a number of options, but in her case, it was stage two. The cancer had spread into the fallopian tubes and the uterus, and so there was only one way to save her life, and that was to remove the womb completely, which of course meant terminating the pregnancy.'

Carmel could barely hear him, each word hurt him so much to say.

'Of course, as a doctor and her husband, no matter how horrible the prospect, I was in favour of that course. But she wanted to wait.

She wanted the baby so badly. There was a fighting chance of saving Jamilla's life, but time was against us. Both I and her consultant convinced her to make the hardest decision any woman could ever have to make. I know you might be thinking I should not have pressured her, it was her decision, but I just couldn't bear to lose her. Losing the baby was going to be horrific, but my darling girl, I just couldn't let her sacrifice herself like that. She finally agreed to the surgery, and it was the hardest day of our lives. I felt guilt, pain, fear... We clung to each other in the hours before she went to theatre, and I cursed myself for asking her to wait. If we'd gone ahead and had a family when she wanted to, maybe none of it would have happened. That thought has tortured me for my whole life, Carmel.'

She blinked back tears, all thoughts of eating forgotten.

'Afterwards, I lay beside my wife, held her in my arms, and cried with her for our lost baby.'

A tear ran down his cheek, and Carmel leaned over and wiped it away with her thumb. 'If it's too hard...' she began, barely able to speak herself.

'No, I'm fine.' He took a drink of water. 'Anyway, the operation was done. Afterwards, she grieved, and I worked. The more pain I felt, the angrier I was, the harder I worked. I tried to be there for Jamilla as much as I could; she was in constant treatment and almost full-time in the hospital. I would do my shift and then go to her room and sit with her. We even got a double bed put in her room so I could sleep there in the hospital with her.'

Carmel could hardly bear to see the pain etched on his face. She wanted him to stop, for his own sake, to go back to the smiling, jokey Sharif he'd been half an hour before, but it was impossible. He needed to finish.

'After the hysterectomy, she had chemotherapy, and once she was finished with that round of treatment, she went to Pakistan for a visit. She knew on some deep level that the treatment wasn't going to work long-term. I think she knew it from the start, actually. At that point, she was in good enough health and her spirits were high and she wanted to go home one last time. She loved Pakistan in a way that I don't really. I wanted to go with her, but she asked me not to. It broke my heart to let her go, but she went back with her parents and she wanted to spend the time with them on their own. They never said anything, but I know they blamed me as well for making her wait. They felt that if we'd had a family right away like normal people, then the cancer would have either never happened or been picked up at a very early stage. Jamilla loved her parents dearly, and she loved me too, but knowing how they felt about me was just going to add to her stress if I went. Very reluctantly, I let her go.

' She looked well, considering how sick she was. She didn't even lose her hair after that first round, not everyone does. We didn't tell anyone—only her parents and I knew about the cancer. She hated fuss, and if there's one thing an extended Pakistani family excel at, it is fuss. She said she wanted to keep things as normal as possible for as long as possible. So she went back, met up with all the family and all of that, and pretended everything was fine.'

'Oh, Sharif, I'm so sorry.' Carmel's heart was breaking for him. 'What a terrible story...'

He nodded sadly.

'They stayed there for a few weeks and then were due back for more treatment. She called me every day, telling me about all the places they visited, places from her childhood, and the people they caught up with. She was missing me, I know, but she was happy, too. And she knew the goodbyes to everyone in Karachi were forever.

'I worked day and night. I would come home from the hospital after a fifteen-hour shift and start researching alternative medicines. As a clinician, I would have dismissed almost all of that stuff when patients suggested it to me, but now it was my own wife, well, I'd try anything. I was exhausted, over-wrought and blinded with grief and pain.

'The tests when she came back were our worst nightmare: the chemo hadn't worked, the cancer had spread, and while the ovaries had been the primary, there were secondary tumours everywhere. They scheduled one more round of chemo, more to keep it at bay than cure it, but the cancer was so aggressive it was pointless. She was so sick, she lost her beautiful hair and just faded away in front of my eyes. Palliative care was all that was available. Back then, hospices were everything Aashna is not, all candles and whispers and people trying hard to make the environment peaceful. But Jamilla was too full of life for any of those places, so I took her home. We spent the last months together. We realised there was no time for anything but love. I took a leave of absence indefinitely, and the hospital were understanding. I looked after her, and we listened to music, watched films, slept, ate, everything together. She loved Elvis Presley, not really my thing, but I must have listened to "Can't Help Falling in Love" about a thousand times in those months.

'The day she died, she was actually brighter than she'd been for days, and we talked about my future. She told me to live after she was gone, not to just work all the time, but to actually get out and live life. That's what it's for. She wanted me to meet someone, to have a family, all of that. The next morning, a Tuesday, I'll never forget it—we'd been up late the night before watching a Bollywood thing—she loved them, in so many ways she was more Pakistani than I was—and she fell asleep in my arms. Normally, she woke early, needing pain meds, but that day I woke up and looked at my watch, Jamilla's head on my chest, and realised it was after ten. She'd died in her sleep. I lay there, for over an hour, holding her, not wanting to move, not able to face that day.

'But eventually, I got up and called the doctor. He came, and the whole thing after that is a blur. Relatives, friends, the funeral, food… It was like I was watching it all underwater or something. I couldn't even think of living the way she wanted me to, so I threw myself into creating Aashna. I didn't really fulfil her wishes until I met you.'

Carmel smiled weakly. 'You always said, when I thanked you for rescuing me, that I rescued you as well. Nadia says it, too, but I never understood how.'

'Well, now you do. I'm sorry I didn't tell you all of this before…'

'It's OK, I understand. It is so hard to talk about it, I can't imagine, and we kind of bury the past, don't we? But I'm glad you told me.'

'So when we never spoke about a family, I was relieved, I suppose.

359

I'm afraid of going back to that time in my life, afraid of you getting pregnant, that's the truth. I know its irrational. I of all people should understand that, but pregnancy can be complicated...'

'And I am over forty.' She smiled. 'It's OK, Sharif, you can say it.'

'I just couldn't bear to lose you, and I know you and Jamilla are two different people, totally different circumstances, all of that, and I hate even the sound of myself saying the words, but... I don't know, Carmel, the thought of it terrifies me.'

'We don't have to do anything you don't want.' She heard herself say the words but even to herself they sounded hollow. She felt for him—of course she did, what a horrible experience—but her overriding emotion was one of bitter disappointment. She would never be a mother.

Sharif nodded and squeezed her hand. The food was gone cold, but neither of them was hungry. Carmel stood and went to Punyaa, the owner.

'It's been a really hard day,' she said. 'Do you mind if we just settle up and go? It's nothing to do with the food, but we just can't tonight...' She took out her card to pay, but he waved her away.

'Of course, we will box it for you, heat it tomorrow. You and Dr Khan and everyone in Aashna do lot good. Sometime is hard,' he said in halting English. 'Do good for my mother. Please, no money, you go, good sleep, no money tonight.'

Within moments, the food was boxed up and handed to her in a paper bag.

She smiled. There really were such good people in the world.

'Thanks, Punyaa. I appreciate that. We'll see you soon.'

Sharif was outside on the pavement waiting for her. She linked her arm with his, and for the first time in her life, she felt like the strong one.

CHAPTER 40

'*L*et's take a day off.' Sharif was up on his elbow looking down into Carmel's sleepy face.

'What?' She struggled to wake up.

'Today, you and me, let's take a day off and just go somewhere.'

She opened her eyes, the events of last night slowly coming back to her. They'd walked home from the restaurant and gone straight to bed. And even though they were both exhausted, they'd made love, and afterwards, Sharif had cried, the first time she'd ever seen him do that. She'd held him in her arms until he fell asleep.

'But aren't the architect and engineer coming to go through the snag list with the builders today?' She hated to be the voice of reason, but they were going on holiday in four days and there was so much to be done.

'They are, but I asked Ammi to supervise it. They are more scared of her than me anyway. I just texted her, and she said it was fine. It will do Benedict good to have a day on his own in charge before we go away.' He smiled. 'What do you say?'

'Well, you're the boss, so I suppose if the boss tells me I have to take a day off...'

'Great.' He lay back down and drew her head onto his shoulder.

'Thanks for last night.' He spoke the words to the ceiling, suddenly serious, and she heard the rumble of them in his chest, along with the beating of his heart.

'No need. I love you, Sharif.' She kissed his neck and put her hand on his chest. 'How are you today?'

'Better. I should have told you the whole story ages ago, I just... Well, I couldn't. But you're right—we need to take out those buried feelings every now and then, no matter how painful, and take another look at them. I was so scared to even go back to those days, I buried it so deep. But now, I feel so much better having got it all out. I just wish it wasn't precipitated by Zeinab. But maybe if she wasn't stirring it up, you wouldn't have raised it and I would never have got the guts to tell you. Maybe I should be grateful to her.' He chuckled.

'Well, gratitude is fine, but not so much you let her move in with us, OK?' Carmel snuggled closer to him.

'Oh, did I not say? We're buying a huge mansion on St Andrews Park, nine bedrooms, loads of staff, dressing in black tie for dinner every evening, and Zeinab is coming with us. You're going to love it. Ow!' He yelped as she slapped him sharply.

'Not even as a joke, Sharif! I swear, I think she was deadly serious the other day.'

'Let me think, how would my life be improved by having my aunt move in with us? I'd be adored, but then I'm adored already. I'd be well fed, but I've got to like Irish cooking, so I don't need her for that. I get to curl up on the couch every evening in my pyjama bottoms with the most gorgeous woman on earth, and Zeinab would definitely not approve. And we get to make as much noise as we like together, whatever the activity, so again, I can't see Zeinab going big on that. So, on balance, there's nothing in it for either of us, therefore it won't be happening.'

'Promise?' Carmel wanted 100 percent assurance.

'Cross my heart and hope to die, I'd hate it, you'd hate it, Ammi would hate it, so, no, my love, it will never happen.' With a smile, he asked, 'So what will we do today?'

Carmel thought for a moment. 'Now, you can say no if you don't want to, but how about we bring some flowers to Jamilla's grave together? I've never been there, and I'd like to say a prayer and just to show her that you're OK and happy...'

She tried to quell the familiar feeling of panic that came whenever he was silent, the feeling that she had no right to make such an intrusion into his life.

'I'd love that.' His voice was barely a whisper. 'Thank you.'

The subject of her wanting a baby was like an elephant in the room. She felt like she should say something, tell him she didn't mind, but the thing was, she did mind. His fears were irrational. Jamilla was a different person, in a different place and time. But he was worried, and Carmel was older. A fleeting thought crossed her mind: maybe his saying he was worried about her was just an excuse, maybe he just didn't want to have a child with her because he didn't think she was up to it.

She went to get up, but he stopped her.

'I know we haven't talked about the reason you wanted to talk to me last night,' he said gently. 'It all became about me and the past and everything, and I know I mustn't have sounded very logical last night. We will talk about it, I promise. I just need some time. I'm sorry, Carmel, I want to be able to give you everything your heart desires, but this whole thing is so tangled up for me...'

Carmel felt a surge of hope. Maybe all was not lost.

'It's OK. We'll talk again. I get it, I swear I do. Life can seem overwhelming sometimes, and you need to take it in small chunks just to get through each day. You've been so patient and kind, and I'm sure all my insecurities and craziness have tested your patience, but you've given me the space and time to figure it out, so I'm going to do the same for you, OK?'

'I love you, Carmel Khan.' He held her in his arms, and she felt safe. Whatever happened, they would be fine.

After a light breakfast, they got up and on the road. As they drove, Sharif told her more about his life before she knew him, the things he and Jamilla had enjoyed, the experiences they had. Carmel felt she finally knew Jamilla more as a person than as just a girl who'd died.

All the stories, reminiscences and pain were unleashed, and Sharif talked and talked. She was happy just to listen and let him relive that part of his life.

As they sped along the motorway, she felt this new information had kind of balanced things up a bit. He wasn't perfect, he didn't get things right all the time, and he was a vulnerable, flawed human being like the rest of the world. He would have always said he was anyway, but Carmel realised she had put him on a pedestal of perfection that was hard to live up to. Now things felt a bit more even, and she felt herself growing a little more confidence. He needed her as much as she needed him. He always said as much, but she'd never believed it until now.

They came off the motorway and stopped to buy some flowers in a small garden centre. Carmel didn't consult Sharif but made her own selection.

The Muslim cemetery was part of a large inter-denominational one, and Sharif led her to Jamilla's grave. On it was a black marble headstone with a crescent moon and star and an inscription. Sharif explained that the inscription was in Urdu but read: *Jamilla Khan, 1971 – 2000. Beloved wife and daughter.*

Carmel laid a beautiful wreath of yellow rosebuds and baby's breath, because she remembered Nadia telling her Jamilla loved roses.

As they stood there at her grave, Sharif spoke quietly.

'Jamilla, this is Carmel. She's Dolly's daughter, who we searched so long to find. After you died, I could not keep my promise to live on. I'm sorry, but I just couldn't. But then, I met this wonderful person. I love Carmel and she loves me, and we are really happy together. Sleep well, my darling sweet girl.' He wiped his eye with the back of his hand, and Carmel linked her arm through his. When she spoke, her voice was husky with emotion.

'I'll look after him, Jamilla, I promise. We were both so lost, and now, we're finding peace at last. I hope you have, too, and your lovely little baby. Say hello to my mam if you ever see her. I know she looks after us, and I think you do too. Rest in peace, Jamilla.'

They stood together in silence for a few minutes, each lost in their own thoughts, and then they left, both feeling like something important had just happened.

They went for a pub lunch in a lovely place with a garden on a canal, and the sun was shining. A family were sitting beside them, the kids throwing bread to the ducks who paddled along the canal. Just as their food arrived, the mobile phone on the next table started ringing. The couple were at the water's edge with the kids, but the ring tone caused both Sharif and Carmel to smile amazedly. Elvis was crooning 'Can't Help Falling in Love' as the man dashed up from the canal bank to answer it.

'Our loved ones have a habit of doing that.' Carmel grinned. Her mother's song was 'Que Sera, Sera,' and she'd heard it coming from a pub the first night she met Sharif. And then on the first night she went out with Joe, an old lady used the phrase in a conversation with them. Carmel knew some people would say it was mere coincidence, but she knew it wasn't. Just as her mother communicated with her through a song, Jamilla was sending her blessing to them. She was sure of it, and she knew Sharif believed it too. He always said that nobody who had seen as many people die as he had could ever doubt the existence of life beyond the grave.

As they munched on delicious sandwiches and tea, Sharif seemed so much more relaxed.

'You look like you're on holiday already,' she observed.

'It's strange... I can't explain it, but I feel like a weight has been lifted, one I didn't even know I was carrying. I would have said last week that I was blissfully happy, and I was, but since we talked and after visiting Jamilla today, I don't know... I'm just glad we did it.'

'Me too.' She watched the mother hold the toddler's hand as she led him up from the canal bank to the table where their food had arrived.

'We can try if you want.' Sharif's words were gentle.

'We'd both have to want to, though,' she said, never taking her eyes off the family.

He put his hands on her shoulders and gently turned her to face him.

'I won't lie to you, Carmel. I've been thinking about this, and I could say nothing, just go along with it, but I'm going to be straight with you. Having a child isn't something I have a burning desire for, especially now, as I'm getting older. My only experience of fatherhood was so heartbreaking. I'm worried about you, and your health, and all of that. But I want you to be happy. More than anything, I want that. So if having a baby would make you happy, then I'm happy to give it a go.'

Carmel thought for a moment. Was that enough? That he'd do it for her but not because he really wanted a baby? She knew what it was to be an unwanted child, and while if she managed to get pregnant, she would want that child with all of her heart, what if Sharif didn't?

She knew that he would love the child, if she managed to have one, but what if he resented the baby for how it disrupted his life? What if he resented her? Was it better to leave well enough alone? They were happy, they wanted for nothing, and they lived fulfilled, satisfying days doing good in the world for people at the end of their lives. Did she have the right to bring a baby into all of that just because it was what she wanted?

She needed time to work this out. It had been such an emotional roller coaster these last few days; she needed time to process. She still didn't trust her own instincts, and even though she was getting better at it, she was unused to giving her emotions credit. Allowing herself to feel things without dismissing them as stupid was one of the exercises set by Nora. This was one of those times to practice it.

'Let's just see how it goes, OK?' She smiled. 'We won't do anything for now, and let's just go to Ireland and get that over with, and we'll talk again when we get home.'

'Of course, whatever you want.' Did she detect a hint of relief in his smile?

CHAPTER 41

*C*armel, Tim and Nadia were bundled into the back of Sharif's SUV as he and Zeinab took their seats in front. Zeinab had made to open the passenger door and Sharif was just about to shepherd her into the back, catching Carmel's eye as he did so, but Carmel gave a slight shake of her head. One thing she'd learned was to choose your battles wisely. Zeinab was going to be a trial, but they could not go to war on every tiny thing.

Already, there had been words when he saw the size of her suitcases.

'Zeinab, we are going to Ireland for ten days, not to the South Pole on an expedition. There's no way I can fit all of that in the car. You'll have to go through it and leave most of that stuff here.' He was firm, and Carmel heard the frustration in his voice.

Nadia and Tim were already in the car, their modest-sized baggage in the boot. Zeinab had looked traumatised, but Sharif was adamant so she emerged from the house twenty minutes later with still by far the biggest of all the cases—but at least there was only one of them.

'What on earth was in them, anyway?' Sharif asked as they pulled away from the kerb.

'Well, I don't know what it is like there, do I? I've never been somewhere so...well, somewhere so primitive. I was just trying to be prepared.' She looked like a scolded child in the front seat.

'Ha!' Sharif scoffed. 'Zeinab, that's so funny. You come from Pakistan to Ireland, and you think Ireland will be primitive? I guarantee you won't see the kinds of sights you would witness any day in Karachi. Extreme poverty, dangerous electricity wires, mayhem traffic, human life in all its rawness is to be seen in Karachi, and well you know it. We love it, of course we do, it's home and there is nowhere like it, but I think you'll be very pleasantly surprised at Ireland. It's very beautiful and totally first-world.'

Zeinab was fuming; she was well aware of the social divide between the haves and the have nots in her home country, but because she inhabited a beautiful home with lots of servants she tried to block the rest of it out. Sharif reminding her, especially in front of Tim and Carmel, was infuriating.

'I've been to India, Brian and I went there a few years ago,' Tim said, trying to mollify her. 'It's a marvellous place. The colours and the culture was fascinating.'

'India and Pakistan are two entirely different places,' she snapped. 'India is filthy and corrupt, and they are no better than they should be.' She then caught Sharif's eye, and his look told her to rein it in or she would not be happy with the consequences.

Carmel glanced at Nadia beside her. This was going to be a long trip, and they weren't even at the airport yet.

'So, Tim, tell us about County Mayo,' Nadia said, trying to restore peace. 'It is very different from Dublin, I believe?'

'To be honest, Nadia, I haven't been there for so long I doubt I'd recognise the place. I went online there a few days ago, to look at photos of the town I grew up in, Westport, and I was stunned. It looks so bright and colourful and full of prosperous businesses and lots of tourists milling about. It looks gorgeous, so I'm sure we'll all enjoy visiting, but it looks nothing like what it did fifty years ago, and that's the truth.'

'Well, nowhere does, I suppose,' Nadia said. 'The Karachi I grew up in is so different now, so much busier, so many more people, but time is a funny thing—it plays tricks on us. I'm really looking forward to this trip, though. Khalid and I came to Dublin once with Dolly, on one of her quests to find you, Carmel, but it was just going to fruitless meetings with religious orders and state officials, and we saw very little really. We had thought of spending a few days, but Dolly was so distraught at the lack of progress we just took her back to London. It was like that every time. She went over every year at least, sometimes twice a year, but never with any success. She would come back and lock herself in her little flat for a few days, and then she'd emerge ready to start again. She never gave up.'

'It is amazing how, with all the effort Dolly seems to have put in, she couldn't find you, Carmel,' Zeinab said, 'and then Sharif does some internet search and there you are, ready and waiting to be rescued like a princess in a tower.' She smiled beatifically.

Sharif interjected, a slight steel in his tone, 'The technology just wasn't there, I suppose. It was really a fluke. I found her through a Facebook group, and I'm not even on Facebook. It was set up when the late Dr Wayne Dyer came to speak at Aashna, and Carmel was a fan of his so she was on it. *IrishCarmel.* it was a total long shot that it was the same Carmel, but it was. I did some investigating, some research on her based on her Facebook posts, and hey, presto! It was wonderful.'

Everyone agreed how amazingly fortuitous the finding of Carmel had been, but Zeinab's mouth was set in a hard line. Carmel was convinced Zeinab saw her marriage to Sharif as the only obstacle to her living happily ever after with her nephew. She was totally deluded, but deluded or not, Carmel was, from Zeinab's perspective, a horrible Irish fly in the ointment.

The trip to the airport passed relatively calmly, and then Sharif and Tim fawned a bit over Zeinab, just to ease the whole thing through the security gates. The last thing anyone wanted was a scene. Sharif had heard about the wheelchair when she landed from Karachi, but she didn't request one this time, happy instead to have Tim and Sharif carry her luggage while Nadia and Carmel managed their own.

Last night, Nadia told Carmel about a stunt Zeinab had pulled a few years earlier. She had been telling her sister and everyone else, too, that she'd had heart trouble and had a pacemaker fitted. Everyone rallied round, and even though Khalid and Nadia were not inclined to, they visited her in Karachi. She really went to town on the convalescence, apparently unable to lift a finger. She had minions running all over the city getting her obscure treats, and she nearly drove everyone daft. Any time it was suggested that she do something herself, or she wasn't getting her own way, her 'heart' would start playing up. It turned out, several years later, when she was travelling to London, Tariq told the security staff at the airport that his wife had a pacemaker. They needed to see the paperwork to allow her to avoid the x-ray machine, and that's when the truth came out. There had been no heart surgery, no pacemaker—the whole thing was a fabrication to garner sympathy. Apparently, Tariq was fuming when he arrived and told Nadia, Khalid and Sharif the whole story, much to the embarrassment of his wife.

It had never been brought up since, but airport security was now a thorny issue. While Carmel could see Zeinab doing something that ridiculous, there was something very sad about it too. All she'd wanted was for her husband to pay her a bit of attention, but instead he told everyone the story, humiliating her. Carmel felt a pang of sympathy for her.

The whole procedure went as smoothly as it could go, and soon they found themselves sitting on the Aer Lingus plane to Dublin.

'Cead mile failte a dhaoine usaile, ar an turas seo go Baile Atha Cliath,' the glamorous air hostess began.

'What on earth is she saying?' Zeinab asked in a loud voice.

Carmel was seated beside her, and Tim on her other side.

'It's Irish, the Irish language. She's just welcoming everyone aboard,' Carmel explained.

'Oh, for goodness sake, everyone speaks English here. Why must we listen to that gobbledegook?'

'Fágamid siud mar atá sé.' Tim smiled as he spoke. Carmel's Irish was rusty, but she remembered what he meant: leave well enough alone. It was a well-used phrase in Irish. She realised that brushing up on her native language skills could be quite useful. Sharif and Nadia couldn't speak it, obviously, but the rest of the gang could, and more importantly, to Zeinab, it was gobbledegook. That could prove very handy indeed.

Carmel texted Joe, who was meeting them at the airport.

Just boarding now x

The wedding was in ten days' time, at the end of the trip, so once they landed they were taking to the open road in the minibus he had hired.

Brilliant. I'll leave in ten minutes so I'll be waiting for you all. Can't wait to see you pet, Dad xxx

She smiled. He always signed his texts *Dad*, even though she knew who they were from. It was like he wanted her to know how much finding her meant to him. She recalled the conversation they'd had last night, when she'd warned him just how difficult Zeinab could be. But he'd put her mind at rest.

'I'm well used to dealing with females of a certain age and disposition, I've been doing it all my life,' he said. 'Don't worry your head about it, my love. We'll manage Zeinab grand. She'll be eating out of my hand by tomorrow night, just you watch!'

Carmel had felt a little better after speaking to him, but she was still nervous. It was the first time she would meet her full extended family. Several McDaids had come over for Brian's funeral last year, but they didn't know at that stage who she really was, so this was going to be what Luke jokingly called the 'Carmel Launch.' And the last thing she wanted was mad old Zeinab upsetting anyone. She was so racist about Ireland already, based on zero experience of anyone or anything Irish, apart from Dolly.

Carmel knew whoever Sharif had married Zeinab probably wouldn't have approved of, but the fact that she was Dolly's daughter was certainly not helping. Zeinab was jealous of Dolly's relationship with Nadia, and any time Dolly was mentioned, Zeinab did this kind of irritating sniff. It drove Nadia mad. Carmel was dreading being associated with Zeinab in front of the McDaids. Joe's siblings remembered Dolly and were sure to want to talk about her. Carmel wanted so much to savour these titbits of information to further fill in her mental picture of her mother, but the thought of Zeinab sniffing disapprovingly every time the subject was raised was just mortifying.

Sharif had offered to stay right beside his aunt for the whole wedding to intervene before anything got too humiliating, but Carmel needed him at her side more. And Nadia seemed to exacerbate the situation unwittingly, Zeinab always trying to outdo her younger sister, reducing the normally able Nadia to a little mouse. Perhaps Tim could manage her? It was a lot to ask—she really was a tyrant in silks. She could be charm itself, or she could be a menace. The problem was she was so fickle, you never knew what you were going to get.

Carmel gazed appreciatively out the window as the horseshoe of Dublin Bay, ringed by the purple mountains, came into view. The countryside beyond the city was a patchwork of green, and the Irish Sea glittered azure as the cabin crew instructed everyone to prepare for landing. She wished she was sitting with Sharif, she needed his reassurance, but when she glanced across to where he was sitting with his mother, she found him looking over at her, smiling, and she relaxed. Everything was going to be OK.

She had not been back since the time she came to beg Bill to call off his horrible sister, who was trying to ruin Aashna and Sharif. Amazingly, she and Bill had talked more that day than in the seventeen years of marriage they endured before that. She had been dreading meeting him—things had ended so badly with her just running out and leaving him—but the conversation was actually very cathartic. He apologised for being a terrible husband, admitted that he still loved his first wife and that he should never have remarried, and said he understood why she left. All those years of being nothing more than a housekeeper, dusting the Waterford Crystal framed photo of him and Gretta on their wedding day, seemed to fade away that day and, with it, some of the pain of rejection. She'd wanted it to work, but she was so naive, thinking a girl raised in a children's home, without a family or a bean to her name, could just slot into Gretta's shoes and be Bill's wife and Niamh and Sinead's mother. It was never going to work.

Bill did as she asked, though, and Julia was called off. And, what's more, he signed all the divorce papers when the time came. Carmel didn't want a penny, or any bit of his precious farm, and that helped smooth things over. Still, she was surprised the morning she married Sharif to find a special delivery of a lovely Waterford Crystal frame from Bill, along with a card wishing them well and a note saying the frame was for their wedding picture. It was a sad life she had with him, but it ended as well as it could have.

She'd had no contact with him since that day. The divorce was handled by solicitors, she didn't even need to turn up, and so ended her association with Bill Sheehan, Birr, Co Offaly, and she thought with Ireland forever. And yet here she was, looking down on the land of her birth, preparing to meet her father's family. Life was very strange sometimes.

CHAPTER 42

*L*ooking down on the country that was her home for so long, Carmel saw Tim doing the same thing out of the corner of her eye. They were both going back, and though the circumstances were different, it was going to be a complicated trip for both of them. She hoped he'd be OK, that the legal business with the farm would go smoothly and nothing bad happened. He looked so distinguished, so tall and together looking, but she knew that inside he was in turmoil. Brian had been the stronger of the two in some respects, and Tim missed him immeasurably.

She caught his eye, and he smiled.

'Well, here goes. We'll stick together, Carmel, and we'll be grand.'

She would have liked to hold his hand as the plane touched down on Irish soil, but Zeinab was snoring loudly between them and they didn't dare wake her. They needn't have worried, as the slight jolt of touchdown roused her anyway, and she self-consciously dusted the crumbs from the two ham and cheese croissants she'd had on the plane from the front of her top.

'That was a nice easy landing,' she remarked. 'Sometimes they are so bumpy.'

'Oh, that's the Irish pilots, they are very well trained,' Tim quipped, winking at Carmel over Zeinab's stooped head as she bent to retrieve her unfeasibly huge handbag.

Sharif, with Tim's help, managed to gather all of the luggage, and soon they found themselves in the arrivals area smothered in hugs and kisses. Carmel beamed as she saw not just Joe, but Jennifer and baby Sean, Luke and some of the other McDaids she recognised from Brian's funeral. They had all made the trip to the airport to meet them.

'Welcome home, darling.' Joe grinned, embracing her warmly. All available hands grabbed suitcases as they made their way to the bus in the car park, the noisy chatter causing other travellers to look up in surprise.

'I got a sixteen-seater, so I thought we might all go for lunch. I've arranged a kind of buffet lunch, since we're so many at a hotel on the Galway road. This gang of relatives wanted to catch up with you before the wedding, so they'll come for lunch too, and we can strike off afterwards on the big adventure. How does that sound?'

'Wonderful.' Carmel smiled up at her dad as he walked with his arm protectively around her shoulders.

Her cousin Aisling was all chat, and Carmel asked her about the upcoming wedding.

'Ah sure, they all think I'm being a right bridezilla, but you know how it is. If I left it to anyone else, t'would be a total train crash, so if you want something done, do it yourself. My sister is taking the flower girls to get their shoes this morning, and there's going to be a standoff because my eldest niece doesn't want baby shoes, but I told Aoife just to put them in something that kind of matches, after that I don't care.'

Carmel grinned. 'So how many in the bridal party?'

Aisling caught her Uncle Joe's eye, and she playfully thumped him on the shoulder. 'Oi, you, what would you know about weddings? Keep your opinions to yourself.'

He chuckled. 'I never said a word.'

'You didn't have to.' Aisling rolled her eyes and turned back to Carmel.

'Well, there was to be ten bridemaids and seven flower girls, and then ten groomsmen, but we only have five little boys so we only have that many page boys, but then one of my bridemaids went off and got herself pregnant, which was very inconsiderate...' She deliberately spoke loudly enough to include Jennifer in the conversation.

'I had to take extreme measures to get out of wearing that horrific dress you picked out, honestly, I looked like a demented flamingo, all peach and feathers. So even though me and Damien don't want another kid, I had to do something.' Jen laughed.

Aisling looked mock outraged. 'Don't mind her, Carmel, she wouldn't know fashion if it came up and bit her on her ever-widening arse! She's a mammy these days, so it's all tracksuit pants and greasy hair.'

Carmel marvelled at the way the two girls hurled insults at each other in such a jovial way. They were almost the same age, and Carmel had often talked about Aisling with Jen. They were best friends as well as cousins, and everyone was thrilled for Aisling that she was finally having the wedding of her dreams despite the slagging she got from her uncles. Aisling had been engaged before, but her fiancée was killed in a road accident, and she took years to get over it. Her soon-to-be husband was a lovely guy and didn't mind a bit that the wedding was a match for Prince William and Kate Middleton's bash.

Joe chuckled, too, used to the two of them knocking sparks off each other.

Sharif was deep in conversation with Luke. Nadia and Tim were being escorted by presumably another cousin, while pushing Sean in his stroller. Only Zeinab seemed unaccompanied.

Carmel stopped and allowed her to catch up.

'Dad, this is Zeinab, Nadia's sister who is visiting from Pakistan. Zeinab, this is my dad, Joe McDaid.'

Joe stopped, released Carmel and gave Zeinab his full attention.

'Well, Zeinab, it's my pleasure to meet you. Carmel has been telling me all about you, and I want to say how sorry I was to hear about your husband's death. My own wife, June, died four years ago, and I miss her every day. All I can tell you is that it does get easier, but those early days were just a fog to be honest. We won't expect too much from you, and I hope the trip just helps you to get through these early days some kind of way.'

He offered her his arm to link, and she took it. Carmel watched in amazement as Zeinab seemed to be totally under his spell. Her cranky expression had changed to one of contentment, and she was basking in the glow of Joe's attention.

Living in England for a year, Carmel had forgotten some of the subtle differences between English people and Irish. In England, people were very conscious of the need for privacy, and nobody would dream of discussing someone's recent bereavement so openly, but in Ireland people were much more forthright. It was refreshing, but somewhat scary too, as she had no idea how Zeinab would react. She needn't have worried; the woman clearly was enthralled with Joe. Then Carmel remembered how Sharif always said Irish and Pakistani culture was similar in that way—people were quite forthright, and emotions were allowed.

'Thank you, Joe, it's a relief to speak to someone who understands how hard it is to lose a loved one,' Zeinab fawned with a saccharin smile. 'Tariq was my life, and I was his. We did everything together, and we were so united, life without him, well, it just seems so bleak...'

Carmel was glad Nadia was out of earshot. Zeinab spoke as if Nadia hadn't lost Khalid, and the way the lecherous Tariq was being eulogised after his demise was enough to drive poor Nadia up the walls. While Zeinab was playing the distraught widow, they knew the reality: Tariq had an apartment in the Central Business District of Karachi, hardly ever visiting his wife in the Clifton house.

The fact that Nadia knew that was one of the many reasons Zeinab resented her. She spun her tale of the devoted Tariq regardless to all and sundry, but she hated that Nadia knew the truth.

'Tell me, Joe, do you live alone?'

Here we go, thought Carmel.

'I do, Zeinab, but to be honest, I've such a huge family there's always someone on the doorstep or some place to be. And my daughter Jennifer, that's her over there with the dark hair, lives very nearby with her husband Damien and little Sean, and of course, there's another on the way so we'll all be kept very busy, I'm sure. And then my son, that's him'—he pointed with pride at Luke—'he lives in town, and I see him very often too, so I'm very lucky. After June died, I was inclined to stay at home, but they kind of made me get out and about, even when I didn't feel like it. And you know, 'twas the best thing for me. It doesn't do you any good, moping around the house, so I'm delighted you're here with us.'

'Well, thank you for inviting me. I was delighted when dear Sharif mentioned it. I've always wanted to visit Ireland, such a fascinating country, so rich in culture and language and everything. I can't wait to learn more about it, and I'm sure you're a wonderful teacher, Joe.'

Carmel couldn't believe her ears. Zeinab really was a piece of work. All that stuff about the Irish being backward and ungrateful and only speaking gobbledegook was out the window and suddenly Ireland was a cultural kingdom? The woman was something else. Now, she was squeezing Joe's arm and giggling up at him like a teenager.

Oh, great, Carmel thought. *Zeinab is flirting with my father.*

They boarded the bus, and Sharif sat beside Carmel.

'OK?' he asked, giving her hand a gentle squeeze. 'They love you; it's going to be fun.'

'I know, it is, I'm not nervous really, and amazingly, Zeinab seems to be behaving herself so far, so barring any unforeseen disasters it should all go fine.' She took a deep breath to steady herself.

'Don't worry about Zeinab. Between Ammi and Tim, they'll keep her on a tight leash, and anyway, as you say, she's behaving well. In fact, I think she has a thing for your father.'

'Did you notice that too? Oh my God, I hoped I was imagining it. I can't think of anything worse than Zeinab trying to get her claws into Joe. Do you think he noticed?'

'He's a man, and I know we are not always the most perceptive of creatures, but Zeinab isn't exactly subtle. She was practically salivating at the prospect!'

'Oh no, should we warn him?' Carmel didn't know whether to be amused or horrified. She was a little of both.

Sharif chuckled. 'I think Joe is a big boy. He'll manage Zeinab just fine. Now, let's go on this mad Irish adventure and enjoy ourselves, OK?'

'OK, let's do it.'

CHAPTER 43

*T*he lunch was a noisy, fun-filled affair, and everyone mingled and chatted happily. Carmel was introduced to yet more cousins, and they seemed to have taken the news that Joe had a daughter with another woman before he was married to June in their stride. She felt welcome and like she'd always known them. Her cousin Tadhg, Aisling's brother, even teased her about getting an English accent. There was no formality, it was just straight into laughing, talking and good-natured banter. It was amazing.

Several times she looked up from a conversation to find either Joe or Sharif watching her protectively, and she basked in the warm glow of their love. She thought of all those years in Trinity House, watching families on the street, or in the park where the care workers took them sometimes, and she remembered wondering if her cousins were among those children playing, or were those mothers and fathers holding their kids' hands on Grafton Street at Christmastime her aunts or uncles?

Maybe she passed these very people on the street and never knew her blood ran in their veins. She allowed herself to feel that loss— Nora was working hard with her to allow her to feel her emotions. The idea that this huge extended family of hers had lived in the same city as her all through her childhood but she never knew them made her immeasurably sad, but she tried to focus on the positive: the fact that it had all turned out OK in the end.

After a longer lunch than anyone anticipated, Joe finally herded everyone onto the bus. Nadia was glowing, possibly helped by the brandy Joe had insisted she try, and Zeinab was laughing happily while clinging like a limpet to Joe at every opportunity. Tim talked with Joe's brother Colm, and Carmel was so happy for him, to get to meet another of Brian's brothers and have him accept Tim for what he was to Brian. Joe had told the whole family, with Tim's permission, a few months ago that Brian was gay and Tim was his partner. The tenderness and respect they'd all showed to Tim since he arrived was heartwarming.

The bus was loaded, and everyone was buckled up when Joe slid into the driver seat and announced, 'Now, I'm not claiming to be an expert of anything, but I've been swotting up and I think I'm going to do OK as a tour guide. But you'll have to bear with me. If you have any questions, feel free to ask. If I don't know the answer, sure, I can make something up, all right?'

'And he will,' Luke teased from the back seat. 'We've been victims of his Irish tours since we were kids. I ended up failing history in the Leaving Cert because of all the claptrap he told us!'

Jennifer was sitting in front with Sean strapped into a car seat that Joe had made sure was safely installed. Damien and Luke had started out across the aisle from Jen and the baby, until Zeinab announced that she was very unused to busses so the front seat was the best place for her. Carmel suspected she just wanted to be behind Joe. Tim, Sharif and Carmel had taken their seats behind the others. The bus was big for their little group, but the extra space allowed them to spread out, and luckily, Joe had a bus driving licence—one of his many jobs back in the day, he explained.

They were just pulling out of the hotel car park when Luke jumped up and called, 'Stop, Dad, stop a sec.'

Bewildered, Joe opened the door to allow his son out. The group on the bus watched in bemusement as an ethereally beautiful, tall willowy girl with long dark hair threw herself into Luke's arms. She was absolutely stunning, all silky hair and toned abs, though she was dressed a little optimistically for Ireland, in teeny-tiny denim shorts showing off her slim, tanned legs that went on forever, and a tie-dyed t-shirt that said *Woodstock Forever* on top. Carmel guessed it was probably meant for ages five to six, because it barely covered the girl's rib cage. Her bare abdomen was adorned with a glittering belly button ring. She had a pull-along case beside her.

Luke, who seemed thrilled to see her, kissed her fully before grabbing the case with one hand—and her with the other—and helping her up the steps of the bus.

'Everyone, this is Carrie,' he announced. 'She wasn't sure if she'd make it, so I didn't say anything, but here she is!'

Carmel melted; he looked thrilled. But since nobody had even known about the existence of Carrie—though Jen had some inkling—the welcome was somewhat delayed.

Jen recovered first. 'So, you're joining us for the whole trip, Carrie?' she asked, and Carmel sensed the reticence in her voice, though her tone was friendly enough.

'Ya, like, I totally want to see, like, Ireland, and like the culture and stuff, like it's all so green and so historical, and I'm really psyched about the Wild Atlantic Way, so when Lukie said I could come, I was totally, like...psyched.' She smiled sweetly.

Sharif glanced at Carmel, and she suppressed a giggle.

'So, are you American?' Joe asked innocently.

She laughed, and everyone started. She sounded like a braying donkey. Her speaking voice was husky, seductive almost, but this laugh... It was straight off the stage.

'Like American from the U.S.?' she asked.

'Yes,' Jennifer said slowly. 'From the United States of America?'

'No, like, not really, like, but I watch a lot of vloggers? That's video bloggers, like on the internet? Y'know, stateside, but I'm not actually from there.' She smiled sweetly, glad she was able to explain the concept of the cyber world to these hopeless cases. She had that highly irritating habit young Irish people seemed to have developed of late, of upwardly inflecting every sentence so all statements sounded like questions.

Luke saw the direction this was taking and shuffled her into a seat, clearly delighted she'd made it.

Carmel caught Jen's eye and tried not to react. Carmel knew Jennifer was not amused. This girl hadn't made a great first impression with her fake American accent, condescending attitude and barely there clothing, and Jen worried about her brother, especially after last time. But Carmel just wanted Luke to be happy, and this Carrie seemed to put a very genuine smile on his face. If she was good to him, what difference did her accent make?

'Right. Sure, we'll get going so, I suppose.' Joe grinned as he sat back into the driver's seat.

'Joe, it is wonderful how you can drive such a big machine. How ever did you learn such a skill?' Zeinab was bordering on simpering, which made Nadia grit her teeth.

'She normally wouldn't deign to engage with a mere bus driver,' Sharif whispered in Carmel's ear. 'She must be smitten.'

'Your mother will strangle her if she doesn't go easy with the flirting,' Carmel whispered back with a grin. 'I don't know which is scarier: Zeinab being horrible or Zeinab being nice.'

'So, folks, I thought we'd begin our tour with a trip to New Grange. Now, I took Jen and Luke there as kids, but we haven't gone for ages, and it's all been developed, I believe, so it will be worth a visit. It's older than the pyramids, older than Stonehenge in England. An amazing place. It's a passage tomb, and it is huge. The stones used to build it were pulled from over a hundred miles away as the crow flies, and over five thousand years ago, that was no mean feat.'

'Use the mike, Dad, we can't hear you!' Luke yelled up from the back.

Joe squirmed a bit. 'Ah, I'd be like an eejit, and sure I'm not really a guide, I'm just telling ye a few bits that I know...'

"No, Joe, please, use the microphone.' Zeinab leaned forward and tapped Joe on the shoulder almost proprietarily. 'You have a lovely speaking voice, and it is so fascinating, it would be a shame if we couldn't all hear you properly.'

Carmel glanced at Nadia, who looked mortified. Something would have to be done, or poor old Nadia would crack up. Carmel resolved to have a chat with her when they stopped. Zeinab wasn't upsetting Joe in the slightest; he was well aware of her taking a shine to him, and if anything, he thought it was funny. But Nadia was clearly uncomfortable, and Zeinab wasn't exactly subtle.

Reluctantly, Joe pulled the gooseneck mike from its socket on the wall beside his head and put it in front of his mouth, testing it for sound.

'This is the end of the peace and quiet now, lads, Joe has amplification!' Damien joked, and everyone laughed. Everyone except Zeinab, who seemed to be taking umbrage on Joe's behalf.

'We are very lucky to have Joe to show us around, young man,' she said, her imperious tone cutting through the laughter. 'Perhaps you should have more respect for your elders.'

'Ah, he's only messing, Zeinab,' Joe jumped in quickly. 'I'm well able for him. Now, as I was saying...'

Damien gave a grin and gestured being slapped on the wrist. Luckily, Zeinab didn't see it.

'The lads that built this place were some engineers,' Joe went on. 'It's seventy-six meters wide and over twelve high, and was used to bury people, presumably the kings or whatever in that society. Anyway, it's a passage tomb, and over the entranceway is a thing that looks for all the world like a window, but they call it a roof box. And wait till you hear this: on the winter solstice, twenty-first of December, the passageway into the tomb is perfectly aligned with the rising sun, and the light shines in through the roof box, creeps along the passageway—and this passageway is sixty feet long, mind you—and then when the light gets all the way down, it floods the tomb chamber with light. It is absolutely incredible, and they had the technology to do this over five thousand years ago. There's a lottery you can enter to be there on the solstice, but they do a reconstruction when you visit, so we'll get to see that. It's not as good as the real thing, but t'will give us an idea.'

'It sounds incredible, Joe, how come we've never heard of it?' Sharif asked. 'I mean, in that everyone has heard of the pyramids, or Stonehenge?'

'Good question, Sharif. I don't really know, but I suppose it's not pushed as much as other sites maybe because of the damage being done just by condensation alone from people's breath? They mind it well, and they're strict about not bringing bags in that could brush off the walls and that, but to be honest, I think it's just another hidden Irish gem.'

'Do you remember being here, Luke, with Mam and Dad, and we had a picnic in the car because it was lashing rain?' Jen was reminiscing, but Carmel also got the impression she wanted her mother as part of the conversation. It was harder for Jen than Luke, she noticed. Jen missed her mother badly, and the arrival, albeit posthumously, of Dolly had threatened June's memory for a while. Or at least it had changed the narrative of how June was remembered. And aside from Dolly's memory and her relationship with Joe all those years ago, Jen was having a very hard time enduring Zeinab's attentions to her father now.

'Yeah, we all got soaked, and she had brought spare clothes for everyone except herself,' Luke said, chuckling at the memory. 'She had to wear Dad's old fishing gear, that was the only dry stuff in the boot of the car. She was complaining that she smelled like a trout.'

'Did she?' Carrie asked, her wide blue eyes innocent.

Luke did a double take. 'Did she what?'

'Smell like a trout? Like, does a trout smell? Maybe if he was dead, but then would he smell different to other fish who were also dead?'

Luke laughed heartily and gave her a hug. Carmel couldn't decide what to make of her, but her ditziness seemed to delight Luke. For such a smart guy, she seemed like an odd choice, but maybe there was more to her than meets the eye. They'd find out for sure after a few days on the bus anyway.

'It was a great day,' Jen went on. 'We went to New Grange and then to the Hill of Tara, and remember, Dad, you used to tell us all the stories about the old kings and queens and warriors long ago, and Mam used to be trying to get you to tone down the violence, but we loved it. The more gruesome the better. Fellas sliding around on the guts of their enemies, all that kind of thing.'

Carmel turned her head and blinked back tears. It amazed her how emotional she got about her own childhood these days, when, for years, she'd just accepted it as it was and it really didn't get to her. Sharif said she was thawing from the inside out and finally allowing herself to feel, and maybe he was right. Listening to Jen and Luke reminisce about picnics and day trips with their parents made her so sad. Maybe that was part of her longing to have a baby—so she could finally experience childhood properly.

Sharif placed his hand on hers, and she looked down at his brown skin, his manicured fingernails and his silver wedding ring. Though Sharif wasn't a practicing Muslim, the tradition states that men should not wear gold, so when they married, he chose a silver ring. Wedding rings are not part of Islam, but he said he wanted the world to know he was a married man. To this day, she remembered the feeling she got when he said that. For him, it was a casual remark, but for her, it meant so much that he not only wanted to marry her, but that he was proud of her and wanted everyone to know they were together. She leaned her head on his shoulder as they drove along.

CHAPTER 44

*T*im took photographs as they approached the massive tomb. It seemed to glisten in the afternoon sunlight. Luke and Carrie fell into step beside him.

'It's so sparkly, isn't it?' Carrie sighed happily.

'That's the quartzite in the stone,' Luke explained. 'That's how they know how far they brought the stones, because the nearest place to get quartzite is in the Dublin mountains, miles away. They think they rolled them on logs over land. I think that's how they did it, anyway, but maybe you know more about it, Tim?'

'I was never here before—sure, what am I saying?' Tim adjusted the lens on his camera. 'I was never anywhere in Ireland but Mayo—and Dublin, the day I got the boat to England.'

'But Carmel was telling me you travelled all over the world with Uncle Brian,' Luke protested.

Tim smiled at the memories. 'We certainly did. We've been all over Asia, Australia, Africa, the States... We even went to Antarctica one time on a boat, three weeks out of Ushuaia, Argentina. I was sick as a parrot the whole time, but it was worth it.'

'I'd love to hear about those trips sometime. We knew he travelled a lot, but to be honest, he was a bit cagey when you asked him about his travels. He was a great guy, but we learned not to pry, y'know?' Luke helped Carrie over some rough ground because the high-heeled wedges she was wearing were totally unsuitable for the terrain.

Tim sighed. 'It makes me sad to hear that, Luke. He wasn't naturally reticent, but he was always trying to protect me and so he had to hold back from all of you.'

'Protecting you from what?' Carrie asked.

Luke reddened a little; he obviously had not told her the story.

'Er... Well...' Luke stumbled. He was absolutely fine with Tim being gay, but it wasn't his story to tell.

'It's OK, Luke,' Tim said kindly. 'Brian, Luke's uncle, was my partner for fifty years. But before he and I got together, I was married and had kids. It's complicated.' He shrugged.

'And are your kids here?' Carrie asked.

'No, they live in England, but I don't see them, to be honest. They aren't comfortable around me.'

'Just because you're gay?' Carrie was flabbergasted.

'Yes. I believe that's the reason.' Tim bent down to get a better angle of the tomb.

'That's crazy,' Carrie said. 'You should so say something. I mean, look how the Kardashians took the news about Bruce Jenner becoming Caitlin, like they were totally fine about it, and he actually looks good as a woman. You should just ask them straight out if they're homophobic. Like, it might be totes awks for, like, ten seconds, but then they'd probably have been cool. And if they're not, well, then it's their loss, right? Like, I get that things were different in the olden days. But they don't know what they're missing. I don't really know you yet, but I think you're lovely, and I'd say Brian must have been crazy about you 'cause you are like really fit, for an old guy. Like Sean Connery kinda, y'know? Being gay is just so cool right now—my personal trainer, Darryl–he's so ripped, I mean, it's just awesome—but anyway, he's got this Puerto Rican boyfriend who is a dog counsellor. Well, he specialises in poodles actually, they suffer a lot from anxiety, but anyway, he's like really old, forty or something, and his mum and him go shopping together and everything. Your kids are losing out if they won't have you in their lives. But look at this gang you've got here. Like, all of Lukie's family seem like they totally want you in their crew so, like, let people go who don't want to know you. As Taylor Swift says, "Haters gonna hate."'

'Well, that is probably the most sensible take I've ever heard on the subject, Carrie,' Tim replied without a trace of sarcasm. 'And you know what? You're dead right.'

Carrie went to examine some 'neat little flowers' and was busy making a Snapchat story as Tim and Luke stood gazing at the ancient edifice.

'She's a bit quirky...' Luke said with a grin.

'There's more to Miss Carrie than meets the eye, Luke. I can see why you like her.' Tim was anxious to put the younger man at ease.

'I really like her, and I know she can come across a bit daft, but honestly, she's great, and so loyal and decent and honest. And she might come across a bit... I dunno... But she is really wise about things. She gives me great advice. I trust her, y'know? I'm not seeing her that long, and I'm away during the week, so I only see her at the weekends really, and we don't know each other that well, but I really like her. Jen can't stand her, though. I know by the face of her. I just want them to give her a chance.'

'Look, I'm no expert, but I have been around forever, so here's my tuppence worth if you want to hear it?'

Luke smiled. 'Go on.'

'She seems like a really nice girl, certainly no malice in her, and she is beautiful looking, even I can see that.' He chuckled. 'The others might think she's a bit off the wall, but they'll be kind, and once they see what she's really about they'll see why you like her so much. Trust her. I think she'll surprise you.'

'If my sister doesn't choke her first. She's protective of me even if I don't need it.' Luke shrugged.

Jen appeared then at his shoulder. Damian and Sean were slowly making their way up since the toddler was insisting on walking himself rather than sitting in the stroller, which would have been so much faster.

'I'll probably try to choke who, might I ask?' She held her hand up to her eyes to shield the strong evening sun.

Luke glanced in Carrie's direction and gave a nod of his head.

'Ah, I see.' Jen nodded sagely.

'Well, I don't know what to say to you, little brother. You've picked some beauties in your time, but this one takes the biscuit. Like, is she actually that thick or is it an act or what?'

Tim saw Luke bristle. Sure, Carrie did come across as a bit of an airhead, but he wasn't happy with his sister slagging her off so harshly.

'And you're brain of Ireland, are you? Don't be such a cow, Jen. She's a nice girl, and what did she ever do to you? She's trying to be nice, why can't you do the same?'

Jennifer reeled at the quick turnabout. She was hurt but lashed out at Luke. 'Well, we all know what part of your anatomy has been doing the thinking lately. She's a muppet and you know it, Luke, and I can't believe you're inflicting her on us for the whole trip. You never even asked Dad if she could come along.'

Luke knew about his sister's quick temper, and she was well and truly riled now.

'It's none of my business, I know...'

The siblings both turned their gazes to Tim, who worried he was sticking his nose in where it wasn't wanted. But he did remember that Irish families were more expressive than British ones. English people valued the stiff upper lip, being stoic and all of that, where the Irish tended to say what they felt.

'But I don't think you two want to fall out?' he ventured. 'This is an emotional trip for all of us, in different ways, so maybe we need to try to, I don't know, be a bit more understanding. Look, what do I know? Nothing, except that you two love each other and this is a silly argument. So my advice is to just let it go, and we'll all enjoy ourselves.'

They both stood in silence.

'I will if she will.' Luke gazed at a spot over Jen's head.

'Fine, it's your funeral.' Jen sighed, and Tim shot her a warning glance. 'Fine, fine, I'll play nice. Just watch—we'll be totes, like, besties.' She nudged her brother to show she was just fooling around.

'Thanks.' He gave her a quick hug.

The group assembled at the entrance to the tomb, and a local guide told them the stories of the people long, long ago who lived and died there. This was the heart of Ireland, very close to the Hill of Tara, where the high kings lived 'in the olden times,' as Carrie might have put it.

Carmel found herself feeling pride as Sharif, Nadia and even Zeinab were blown away by the place. This was her country, and even though she'd never been anywhere except Dublin and Birr, she was beginning to feel the beginnings, at least, of national pride in her country.

And at least Zeinab wasn't complaining. Quite the opposite, actually; everything was splendid as she sycophantically sucked up to Joe.

The rest of the day passed wonderfully as the sun shone on the lush green fields and stone walls. In the evening, Joe took them by Clonmacnoise, a gorgeous monastic settlement from the 7th century on the banks of the River Shannon, the longest in Ireland.

'I knew Ireland was beautiful, everyone says so, but honestly, it is breathtaking,' Nadia remarked as she and Carmel sat on a dry stone wall watching the late evening sun set behind the huge round tower of Clonmacnoise, bathing the entire place in its buttery glow. Tim was taking more photos, and Luke and Carrie were messing around in the old church, laughing. Jen and Damien had gone to the cafe to get a snack for Sean, and Zeinab looked like she was holding court with Sharif and Joe.

'It is, and to be honest, I had no idea,' Carmel admitted. 'I can't believe I lived here for forty years and had no inkling it was like this. I mean, I could have come, I suppose, or found out about it on the internet or something, but I just never did. I feel like a very poor ambassador.' She smiled.

'Well, Joe is doing a great job,' Nadia assured her. 'I don't know how he manoeuvres that big bus around those tiny roads, not to mention all he knows about the country. He's better than any professional tour guide, I'm sure. And he's gone to so much trouble.'

'I know, he's amazing, isn't he? And everyone is getting along so well. I was kind of dreading it, to be honest, but so far so good.' Carmel was trying to bring the conversation around to Nadia and Zeinab. She knew Nadia would enjoy the holiday so much more if Zeinab wasn't getting on her nerves so much.

'Well, everyone but my sister,' Nadia grumbled. 'I know, I'm trying not to let her get to me, but the way she's fawning over Joe, I just want to throttle her.'

Carmel wondered just for a moment if there wasn't more to the story. Initially, when Joe and Nadia had met, Carmel thought there might have been a spark between them, but she'd dismissed it. They did get along very well, though, and liked a lot of the same things, but they seemed happy to be friendly. Nadia had no contact with him except when Carmel was there, she was sure of that. But she was starting to think that maybe Nadia's frustration wasn't just embarrassment at the obviousness of her sister's flirting but also maybe a little tinge of jealousy? Joe was lovely to everyone, and he had a way of making whoever he was talking to feel like they were the most important person on earth, including Zeinab.

'But at least it means she's on her best behaviour, right? She doesn't want Joe to think badly of her, so she's being extra nice. That can only be a good thing, can't it?' Carmel's eyes searched her mother-in-law's face.

Nadia sighed. 'I suppose so.' She gazed downwards as she spoke, not looking at Carmel. 'I'm just... I don't know. This is a big thing for you, to come back here, to connect with your family. And for Tim, as well, and I just wish she wasn't here. I know it makes me sound so mean and nasty, and as you say, at least she's not being rude, but the way she is with Joe, it's embarrassing.'

Carmel wondered if she should dig a little deeper. She'd lived a whole life of never sticking her nose into anyone else's business, but she felt close to Nadia. Not just as mother- and daughter-in-law, but woman to woman.

'I don't think Zeinab is his type,' Carmel said gently. 'He'll just be nice to her for our sakes, and humour her, but it's not like anything is going to happen between them.'

Nadia looked up, her brown eyes searching Carmel's face.

'Do you like him?' The words were out before Carmel even knew it.

Nadia grew flustered and reddened. 'It's not that. She's just so irritating. I just wish she could act normally.' She glanced around. 'We'd better get back, it's getting late and we need to get to the hotel.'

Carmel let it go, but something about the way Nadia had deflected the question made her think. The whole thing would be 'a bit Jeremy Kyle,' as her friend Zane was prone to say, referring to the trashy reality TV show where people found out about the paternity of their children or revealed affairs on live television. Her dad and Sharif's mother getting together might look a bit odd, but if life taught Carmel anything, it was that you needed to seize opportunities for happiness and love wherever and whenever they came along. If Nadia liked Joe and he felt the same, why shouldn't they enjoy a relationship? It would certainly explain Nadia's reaction to Zeinab's flirting.

Joe was single and had been since June died. He was a good-looking man, Carmel could see that, fit and well-built, and he was a charmer, no doubt about it, but not in a sleazy way. He was just a great laugh, and he saw the bright side of everything. The way he'd immediately embraced her and took her into his life as his daughter was a testament to the kind of man he was.

And Nadia was like a mother to her, as much as she was to Sharif. She and Dolly had been so close, they talked about almost everything, and shared so much, it was as if Nadia could bring Dolly alive for her daughter and she did, sometimes in glorious Technicolor. By all accounts, Dolly was larger than life, full of energy and mischief. Nobody but Nadia, Khalid and Sharif knew the heartache that lay beneath the jovial exterior.

If a relationship between Nadia and Joe was something they both wanted, then Carmel was going to do her best to make sure it came about.

CHAPTER 45

Over coffee and after a delicious dinner in the hotel with the whole group, Sharif whispered in her ear, 'A nightcap in our room?'

She loved that while he was a sociable man and chatted easily with everyone, his favourite thing to do was spend time alone with her.

'Absolutely,' she whispered back.

They made their excuses and left the gang to it. Zeinab had been monopolising Joe all evening, and Nadia was doing her best to ignore it. She sat beside Jennifer and Damien and heard all about their plans for the extension and the new baby.

Sharif had bought a lovely bottle of gin in duty-free, and he arranged ice, lemon and tonic to be sent to the room. He made them both a drink while Carmel removed her makeup and slipped into her pyjamas.

Handing her the gin and tonic, he tucked a stray hair behind her ear. 'I miss you. It feels like there's always people around. I'm glad to have you all to myself for once.'

She put her drink down, placed his beside it, and wrapped her arms around his waist.

The old version of her would never have taken the initiative, but she was getting bolder with Sharif. The revelations of the reality of his marriage to Jamilla, and the fact that he had made mistakes, that he wasn't the perfect person she thought he was, had made them closer. He did need her, she was finally coming to accept, as much as she needed him. It evened things out somehow.

Going up on her toes, she drew his lips to hers and kissed him deeply.

'I miss you too,' she whispered, taking his hand and leading him to the bed. As usual, their lovemaking was passionate and tender, and afterwards, they lay in each other's arms, chatting. They would talk again about the future, but for now they had decided just to enjoy the holiday and deal with it when they got home.

'So Zeinab seems to be behaving better than we hoped,' he remarked.

'Well, she's on her best behaviour for my dad, I think.'

'Really? I knew she was flirting to annoy my mother, but do you really think she likes him that way?' Sharif asked.

Carmel smiled. For a smart man he could be very unobservant sometimes, especially on matters like this. 'Definitely. She's trying to impress him; she fancies the pants off him.'

Sharif laughed. 'Really?' he repeated. 'I suppose that would explain it. Has he any interest, do you think?'

'I doubt it. I can't see her being his type, really. Besides...' Carmel paused. As far as she was aware, Nadia had never had another relationship after Khalid died. She wondered how Sharif would take to the idea of Nadia and Joe. Regardless, she decided to come clean. He loved his mother and would want her to be happy, and anyway, she might need his help.

'Besides what?' he prompted.

'I think Zeinab may not be the only woman with her eye on him.'

'I'm not surprised. He's a great fellow. I'm sure plenty of ladies would be delighted to have Joe on their arm. But I don't think he's seeing anyone, is he?'

'Not now, no. I don't think he has since June died, and that was a few years ago now. I asked him before, and he just said he was kept

395

busy with the family and his properties and all of that. But if the right woman came along, I think maybe he would consider it.'

'But you don't think my cantankerous, snobbish aunt is the right woman?' Sharif chuckled.

'No, I don't, but maybe your sweet, kind mother is.' Carmel paused, trying to gauge his reaction.

'What? Really? Joe likes Ammi? Are you sure?' Sharif seemed astounded.

'No, I'm not even half sure, but I think she likes him. I think that's why Zeinab flirting her head off is driving Nadia bonkers.'

'Well, they do get on well,' Sharif agreed, 'and they seem to have a laugh together when they meet. But do they see each other outside of us?'

'No, I don't think they ever have. Joe would be afraid we wouldn't approve, and Nadia probably the same. So I was thinking we could test the waters, so to speak, and if there was a bit of something, we could give it a little nudge. What do you think?'

Sharif sighed. 'I don't know. I mean, sure, I really like Joe, but, well, I never really thought of Ammi like that. She and my father had such a good marriage, and being an only child, well, after he died, it was just the two of us. I'm not opposed to the idea, I don't think, I just need to try to wrap my head around it, you know? And there may not be anything anyway...'

She knew he was thinking aloud, so she didn't interrupt.

'Has she said anything to you?' Sharif asked.

'No, not directly, but we were talking today, and she was just venting about how crazy-making Zeinab was, and I asked her, and she got all flustered and embarrassed, and denied it of course. But there was something, I just know there was.'

'Well, should I ask her?' Sharif wondered.

'No, let's just sound Joe out first. If I can ever prize Zeinab away from him. Maybe you could distract her some time tomorrow, and I'll get Joe on my own.'

'Sure, I'll take her to a gift shop or something, flash the cash. She'll love that.'

They lay in silence, and Carmel cuddled up to him. Just as she was falling asleep, he spoke again.

'I know we said we'd wait, talk about it later, but I just want you to know that you are the most important person in my life and I want you to have everything you want. I know I didn't sound too enthusiastic about the prospect of having a child. It's nothing to do with you, I just have such sad memories and such guilt about making Jamilla wait and all that turned out to mean. But I want you to know that if you want to try for a baby, then so do I. You'd be such a wonderful mother, I know you would.'

Sometimes, without warning, tears came unbidden to Carmel. She never remembered crying as a child, or even in the years with Bill, but since she'd moved to England, she was prone to tears. It embarrassed her, but Sharif was always telling her that it was just her thawing out —years of frozen emotions finally being given some space to be.

He didn't say anything, just held her until she could reply. She leaned up on one elbow and looked down into his face.

'I don't know if you'll understand this, but I want to have a baby, to have someone to love. I love you so much, and Nadia and Joe and now Jen and Luke and everything, putting so much love in a life that had absolutely none, but it's not enough. I can't explain it, but the desire to hold a baby of my own in my arms, to hear someone call me Mammy, calling you Daddy, to have a person of our very own, my own flesh and blood, it's... It's so overwhelming sometimes its scares me. When I heard Jen talking about going on picnics with Joe and June, or just things Zane or Ivanka would say about when they were kids, I realised I had no childhood. Not really. I don't have any real happy memories, and maybe I want to relive childhood through my own child, I don't know. I never felt this, not once with Bill, but now it's all I think about. I know the odds are against me—I'm forty-one, and I don't even know if my reproductive system works properly —but I—'

He drew her tightly to his chest. His strong arms around her stopped her disintegrating. 'I know. I understand. Let's go for it, OK? We won't know until we try.'

'You really want to? Not just to keep me happy but for you as well?' she asked, her voice barely audible.

'I really do,' he whispered, and she knew he meant it. She would stop taking the pill immediately.

* * *

SHARIF WAS true to his word, and the following afternoon as they explored the colourful, arty city of Galway, he insisted on taking his aunt to get a souvenir in a very expensive-looking gift store. For once, she wasn't thrilled about spending time with her nephew, as she had attached herself like glue to Joe, but Sharif wasn't taking no for an answer.

Carmel had asked Joe quietly at breakfast if they could have some time together, just the two of them, during the day, so he gave Luke directions to the cathedral, and the Claddagh and the Spanish Arch, and made arrangements to meet everyone for fish and chips and a pint in McDonagh's in a few hours' time.

Jen had stayed in the hotel for a rest. While she was feeling good, her energy levels were not what they normally were, so she was happy just to relax there. She promised she'd join them for dinner. Damien was so great with Sean, Carmel wondered if Sharif would be as hands-on. She immediately chided herself for the thought; she wasn't even pregnant yet, and it most likely would never happen, so it wasn't doing her any good at all speculating on the nonexistent future baby. Time enough for that if she did actually manage to conceive.

Joe put his arm around her shoulders as they strolled down Shop Street licking 99s. She'd protested that she didn't need an ice cream, they'd had scones with jam and cream and coffee before the group broke up, but Joe insisted.

'I never bought you a 99 as a kid, so you'll have to eat forty odd years of them now.'

As the woman in the shop had swirled the thick, soft-serve ice cream onto the cone and stuck a chocolate flake in it, Carmel had been transported back to a time when she was around seven or eight. She'd had a bad tooth and was taken to the dentist to have it pulled.

'No more 99s or chewy toffees for you, young lady,' the dentist had remarked jokingly once he'd pulled the offending tooth.

'What's a 99?' she'd asked.

The dentist and his nurse had looked embarrassed. They'd forgotten she was a child of Trinity House and were talking to her like she was a normal kid.

'It's an ice cream on a cone with a chocolate flake in it,' the nurse had explained. Then the dentist put his hand in his pocket and pulled out a five-pound note, thrusting it at Carmel.

'Not too many now, but an odd 99 won't do you any harm,' he'd said gruffly.

She'd put the money in her pocket and when she got back to Trinity House she hid it in the base of a box each child was given for their personal belongings. She never spent it. It was the only present she'd ever gotten as a kid.

She considered telling Joe the story now, but she hated to see the sadness in his face when she recounted bits of her life as a child, so she said nothing.

They chatted easily as they walked along, stopping every so often at shop windows to look inside. The streets were busy with locals and tourists alike, and buskers vied for attention. Music was everywhere, and children played and dogs barked and all seemed right with the world.

As they passed one shop, Joe lifted up Carmel's right hand and inspected it.

'Good,' he announced before leading her into a shop.

'What?' she asked, giggling.

It was a jewellery shop, selling many variations on one product: the Claddagh ring.

Carmel gazed at the array of rings on display. Each had the same basic but intricate design in varying metals and with different stones inset.

'The hands are holding a heart, on top of which is a crown,' the shop assistant began her explanation.

'We know,' Joe said gently. 'We're Irish.' He smiled to take the sting out of his words. 'The hands symbolise friendship, the crown is for loyalty, and the heart is for love.' He spoke directly to Carmel. 'Pick one. I want to buy it for you.'

'You don't need to do that—'

He held a hand out to stop her objections and spoke quietly, out of earshot of the staff and other customers. 'You are my daughter, and I hope we'll always be friends. You will have my loyalty to the day I die. And, well...' He stopped at the love part, suddenly shy. 'Please, let me do this.'

'OK. Thanks.' She kissed him on the cheek, and he gave her a squeeze.

They walked to the counter. 'Can you show us the best ones, please? I want to get my daughter here a really nice ring.'

The assistant didn't need to be told twice. She hastily extracted a tray.

'These are white gold, platinum and gold, set with diamonds, sapphires and emeralds.'

They had no prices, and Carmel began to panic. 'I like the ones over there...' She pointed to the cheaper varieties on open display.

'You're having one of these.' Joe was adamant.

'But they are probably so expensive,' she whispered. 'Honestly, the other ones are just the same and—'

Joe grinned and picked out a gold ring, inset with an emerald, and slipped it on her finger.

'You must wear it with the heart facing in. It tells the world you're spoken for. I think Sharif would rather that.' He winked. 'Though, I often thought of getting one for myself, facing it out, to see if there were any bites from gorgeous women!' He laughed. 'Do you like it?'

Carmel looked at it, the emerald sparking as she moved her hand. She loved not just the ring, but everything it symbolised. It was an old wedding ring, traditional to the Claddagh village outside of Galway, and its intricate design was uniquely Irish. Friendship, love, and loyalty, absent for so long, and now in her life in abundance. It was a symbol of her new life.

'I love it.' She smiled, trying not to allow her emotions to bubble over again. She took it off, and the lady polished it up and went to put it in a box.

'I'd like to wear it now, if that's all right?' Carmel said.

'Of course.' The woman smiled and handed the ring back to her. She slipped it on the ring finger of her right hand.

She smiled. 'Thanks, Dad.'

'You're very welcome, my love. Now outside the door with you till I settle up with this lady.' And he whooshed her outside.

CHAPTER 46

*S*he stood outside, her back to the wall of the shop, and turned her face to the sun, closing her eyes. The street musicians, families and groups of teenagers milled around, and all the chatter settled easily in her ears. She was perfectly content. The talk with Sharif last night had lifted her spirits, and knowing they were both on the same page filled her with happiness. She was wondering if she should raise the subject of Nadia with Joe when she was startled by a voice.

'Carmel? Is it you?'

She snapped her eyes open, and her mouth went instantly dry. She felt as if someone had punched her in the stomach.

'N-Niamh... Oh, hi. H-How are you?' Carmel could hardly speak.

Bill's daughter was standing in front of her, large as life, exuding indignation and righteous fury from every pore. Carmel hadn't seen her in over two years, but she looked the same. Perfectly highlighted blond bob, Michael Kors handbag, designer clothes head to toe, and a bit too much makeup for a day out in the city. She'd gained weight since Carmel last saw her, and she was wearing very tight leather trousers and a low-cut top. It wasn't flattering. Niamh and Sinead were now in their early thirties, but this outfit was for a much younger, slimmer woman.

'How am I? Well, I might ask you the same question. Not to mention what are you doing here? I thought you'd hightailed it off to London to be with some Indian or something?' The tone was simultaneously accusatory and dismissive, and Carmel had forgotten that was how people used to speak to her.

'I'm fine, thanks, fine. Er... Yes, I live in London now...' She wished she could be more articulate, but seeing Niamh out of the blue had rattled her.

As she was about to try again, Joe emerged from the shop. 'Are we right?' he asked, not realising she was in conversation with Niamh.

'He's not Indian,' Niamh accused, glancing Joe up and down, her nose wrinkled in distaste.

'Sorry...' Joe stopped, realising this woman was addressing Carmel. 'Who are you?'

'Who am I? Oh, well you might ask, don't mind me. I'm Niamh Sheehan-Condon, just her ex-husband's daughter. You know, the one she abandoned to go off with some Indian, some refugee off the internet or something. Though you're no more an Indian than I am, so he obviously didn't last long.' She snorted, delighted to have caught Carmel out, as she saw it.

Joe seemed to almost get taller and broader, standing slightly in front of Carmel. 'You have the wrong end of the stick there, Niamh Sheehan-Condon,' Joe said, smirking slightly at the affectation of a double-barrelled name. 'I'm Joe McDaid, Carmel's father.'

'What? Oh, I've heard it all now. Her *father*? You are in your eye her father. Sure, she's out of a laundry, or an orphanage or something. Her mother was an unmarried mother, and she was left to the nuns and the tax-payer to rear. You're no more her father than the pope.' She turned to Carmel. 'You might have conned poor Daddy, and now you've this eejit running around after you like a fool, but I'm wise to you, lady, always have been. How dare you come back here, swanning around Ireland with another of your fancy men? Thank God my poor father isn't here. He could do without running into you after everything you put him through.'

Joe put his arm around Carmel, who was trying to formulate a response but failing. His voice when he spoke was one Carmel had never heard before, dark and threatening. 'My daughter has every right to go wherever she likes in her own country. And, the day she left that miserable farm was the day her life began. She *is* my daughter, my blood runs in her veins, and I will never allow you, or any member of your pathetic family, to hurt her ever again. And, her husband is from Pakistan, not India, you ignorant woman, and he is a wonderful man who loves her as she deserves to be loved, not treated like some kind of unpaid maid for your emotionally stunted father. Now, I suggest you take yourself off and leave us alone, or I'll have you arrested for harassment. Your *poor Daddy*, as you call him, made Carmel's life hell along with that auld wagon of a sister of his, and you seem to have followed in the same path. But no more. You have nothing to do with Carmel, or any other member of our family, so take your lardy arse off now and don't bother us again, do you hear me?'

Carmel smiled involuntarily. Joe sticking up for her, her dad, fighting her corner, felt so great. She didn't know where it came from, but the sight of Niamh, so outraged she couldn't actually speak, struck her as so funny.

'How dare you laugh at me, you little tramp?' Niamh hissed, leaning forward, spittle escaping her Botoxed, scarlet lips. Just as she was about to continue, a tall, harassed-looking man intervened.

'Niamh, I've been looking everywhere for you...' He noticed Carmel. 'Oh... Carmel? How are you?'

'Hi, I'm fine, thanks.' Carmel smiled weakly at Niamh's long-suffering husband. Theirs was the wedding she had hoped to be involved with in some way. She'd even applied for a passport in case Niamh invited her to go wedding dress shopping abroad, but Niamh had taken Julia instead. Cillian was always a nice lad, though. He'd spoken kindly and politely to Carmel on the few occasions they met. What he was doing with the dreadful Niamh was anyone's guess.

'Cillian, if I were you, I'd take her out of here before she finds herself up in court for harassment.' Joe was stern. 'Come on, Carmel, the rest of the family will be wondering where we've got to.'

He led Carmel away down the street, leaving Niamh seething and snapping at poor Cillian.

Joe led her into a bright, sunny pub and, without asking what she wanted, ordered her a brandy. She caught a glimpse of her reflection in the mirror behind the bar; she was snow-white.

She said nothing but took the drink and allowed Joe to bring her to a corner table. He'd got a pint for himself and took a long draught before saying anything.

She sipped the brandy. It was so strong but warming. She realised she was trembling. 'I'm sorry,' she began. 'I should have—'

Joe leaned over and took her hand. 'You have absolutely nothing to apologise for. That woman is a poisonous bitch, and she needed putting in her place. I was glad I got to do it. Who the hell does she think she is? I've never hit anyone, least of all a woman, in my whole life, but that was the closest I ever came.' Carmel had never seen him so angry.

'I thought by avoiding Birr I'd manage to avoid all the Sheehans, but I forgot Cillian is from Galway,' she said. 'They must have been here visiting his family or something. I had my eyes closed, leaning against the shop, the sun on my face. It was lovely. I would never have done that before, I'd have felt foolish, and if Bill heard I was going around Birr leaning against walls with my eyes closed he'd have probably had me committed to the county home.'

From nowhere, Carmel felt the urge to giggle, a combination of relief and entertainment at the idea of her sleeping against shops in Birr—and the image of Bill's perplexed outrage at such mental behaviour. It made her laugh so hard the tears came down her cheeks, and she shook with laughter.

Joe watched in amazement as she laughed at the hilarity of the image, but it was infectious and soon he joined in. Within moments, the two of them were almost in convulsions, wiping their eyes and barely able to catch their breath. Two German tourists looked on in bemusement, and the barman who was wiping glasses nearby grinned.

Eventually, the laughter subsided.

'Oh, Joe, I feel better. I don't think I've ever laughed like that before, but that image just tickled me. Everyone back there in Birr, full of opinions on everyone else's business, and me just sleeping up against walls... Julia and Bill would need to be sedated to cope with it.' She wiped her eye once more.

'Well, I'm glad you can see the funny side, pet, even if you have a quirky sense of humour.' He winked and took another drink from his pint of Guinness.

'Look, what can they do to me at this stage? Nothing. And poor old Cillian. I always liked him; he's a grand lad.'

'He seemed OK, for the one second I saw him. He's got his work cut out dealing with that one, though. She's a lighting wagon, as my mother used to say.'

'Oh, he does. I remember their wedding. Nothing was good enough, like, the money they spent, well, she spent, it was obscene. And Bill signing cheques away for everything, he never saw any wrong in them, and to be honest, they both grew up very spoiled. Sinead—that's the other girl, Niamh's twin—is a bit nicer, but neither of them really bothered much with me. Julia was in their ear, though, since they were tiny, so they were predisposed to hating me. And then, when I left Bill, well, that was the icing on the cake, as they saw it. I never had a relationship with them so there was nothing to lose. So I don't actually know why Niamh was so angry...' Carmel was surprising herself that she could be so reflective and calm about it.

'Well, as you say, small town, gossip, she probably feels that you disgraced her father or something. But there's no excuse for the way she spoke to you. None at all. And I'm glad I got the chance to tell her to her face.'

Carmel looked at Joe, the face she had come to love so much and said, 'When I was small, I remember this nun in the primary school, she was horrible. Some of them were nice, but this one, she was really mean. Anyway, at the time, kids got free milk in school, but I hate milk, always have—and it drives my asthma crazy. Sharif says it's often the case with asthmatics; dairy exacerbates breathing problems sometimes, so people who suffer from that tend to shy away naturally from milk and things. Anyway, I asked one of the care workers, not a nun, one of the lay people who worked in Trinity House, to write a note for me to the nun to say I didn't have to drink the milk. So, the next day, I was terrified, but I handed her the note, signed by the care worker. Another girl in the class, Julie Murphy, also had a note from her dad saying more or less the same thing. Well, the nun went mad, almost inflated in front of me—and she was huge to begin with. I was only a skinny little eight-year-old, and she went mental. Slapped me and Julie with a meter stick and made us stand up for the whole day, no lunch allowed or anything, for having the cheek to ask not to have milk. We were just changing over from feet to meters in those days, so each class had a meter stick, but she used it for slapping the kids.

'Well, Julie went home and told her dad, and the next day he came down and knocked on the classroom door. It was a big timber door with lots of small panes on the top half, solid wood on the bottom. She didn't open the door, just continued on with the lesson, but held her hand up to the timber bit on the side of the glass to stop him opening it. We were terrified and fascinated at the same time, chanting our eight times tables or whatever, wondering what was going to happen next.

'Well, she's calling out the tables, and next thing, he wraps his fist in his jumper and smashes his hand through the glass pane, grabbing her by the veil and tugging it off her. We never saw a nun's head before, they were always covered, so we were just gazing, horrified and terrified and thrilled all at the same time. He dragged her head close to his and through the door said, "If you ever touch my daughter again, it will be the last thing you ever do, you dried up auld Mickey dodger." He left and we all sat there, not knowing what to do. The nun just pulled herself together and carried on as if nothing had happened, but she never so much as looked sideways at Julie Murphy for the whole year after that. I remember that night, lying in bed wishing I had a dad to stand up for me like that. And today, my wish came true.'

Instantly, just like with Sharif, Carmel regretted telling the story.

But she and Nora had discussed it often, and they'd come to the conclusion that Carmel would have to tell the stories of her childhood, even if it upset Sharif or Joe, because it was the only way of being true to herself. Still, it was hard to see the pain in Joe's face.

'I wish I could have gone down there, I wish I could have protected you, loved you, I wish things had been so different.' Joe's voice was choked with emotion.

'I know you do, and so do I, but I didn't tell you that story to make you sad. I told you because I want you to know it's never too late. Sure, I could have done with parents when I was small. Things would have been so different. But then, it was Dolly led me to Sharif, and then to you, so who knows? Maybe it was for the best. It seems much worse in hindsight, I know it does, and compared to the childhood Jen and Luke had, well, it's like chalk and cheese. But I'm OK. I'm more than OK, I'm happy. I'm getting stronger every day, and having Sharif and Nadia and all of you, well, like I said, it's a dream come true.'

CHAPTER 47

When everyone met for fish and chips in the big pub on Shop Street, Galway's main thoroughfare, the cacophony of voices was almost deafening. There was a huge group of young people, some of them carrying instrument cases, on one big table and the entire McDaid clan on the other. Jen had strolled in to meet them, and she looked rested. Sharif and Zeinab had yet to appear.

Luke and Carrie were busy telling everyone about how they'd ended up at an African drumming class in the park.

'It was so...like, OMG, like healing or something?' That upward inflection again. 'Lukie and me are going to buy some and go busking on Grafton Street when we go home, aren't we, Lukie?' She was sitting on his lap, her arms around his neck, nuzzling him.

He grinned. 'Er... We'll see...'

'I can just see the Garda Commissioner being over the moon about that, a member of the vice squad drumming away on the street for spare change.' Joe winked and nudged Carmel, who was sitting beside him. 'Just the image the Gardai are looking for.'

'Leave him alone,' Carmel chided. 'I'd love to try drumming. It's supposed to be very good for you.' She wanted to support her brother, who was getting it from everywhere. Jen and Damien were constantly teasing him, and now Joe as well.

'Thanks, Carmel. It's nice to know at least one member of my family isn't picking on me 24/7.' Luke sighed in mock despair.

'Where's Sharif?' Carrie asked.

'Still shopping with Zeinab. He promised to buy her a souvenir.' Carmel grinned and moved to make space between her and Joe as Nadia returned from the ladies'. Carrie and Luke were on the other side of her father, and Tim was across the table, so whenever Zeinab did arrive, she wouldn't be able to monopolise Joe.

With all the business of meeting Niamh, Carmel had never gotten to raise the issue of Nadia with Joe. Instead, she was just going to observe. She deliberately made chat with Tim, Jen and Damien, Sean conked out in the buggy beside them, leaving Joe and Nadia to talk.

Tim was telling everyone a very funny story about something that happened to him and Brian in Indonesia, and Carrie was very busy nuzzling and kissing Luke, who seemed to have no objections. Every time Carmel glanced over, Joe and Nadia were deep in chat, and they seemed perfectly happy in each other's company.

The food arrived just as Sharif and Zeinab entered the bar laden down with bags. Sharif's face lit up when he saw Carmel, and she pushed over on the bench to make room for him to sit beside her.

He filched one of her chips. 'God, I'm starving. I thought I'd never get her out of the bloody shop.' Then he murmured in her ear, 'I missed you.'

A young waitress with lots of tattoos and piercings and multi-coloured dreadlocks passed Zeinab by, despite her gesticulating wildly to attract the young woman's attention. The girl instead stopped beside Sharif.

It was something Carmel noticed and she often teased him about, how female waitstaff were so attentive. He was gorgeous, of course that was why. Even girls much too young for him could see that. Carmel could see the admiration in this girl's eyes as she took the order. He did look particularly sexy today in a burgundy shirt, open at the neck, and petrol-coloured jeans that hugged him in all the right places.

'Carmel, you look like a fox in a chicken coup, gazing at him like that,' Jen whispered to her as Sharif discussed wine with the girl. 'Not that I blame you, of course.'

Carmel reddened. 'I wasn't... I was just...'

'Just admiring your gorgeous man, I know. As I said, nobody would blame you.' Jen winked and turned her attention back to what Tim was saying just before they were all distracted by a commotion at the other end of the table.

Zeinab was trying to insert her rather ample bottom into a space between Joe and Luke, despite there being a perfectly good chair on the other side of the table. When it became evident that she simply wouldn't fit, she almost barked, 'Oh, for goodness sake, Nadia, you know I need to have my back to the wall! I can't sit outside, I've told you that so often, but you never listen. Look, you come out here and sit on this chair, and I'll go in your seat by the wall.'

Nadia was about to leave her seat, despite the fact that her food had already arrived, when Joe piped up, 'Look, my grub hasn't come out yet, so why don't you take my seat, Zeinab, here beside Nadia, and I'll sit out there with Tim?' Before Zeinab could think up any other reason, it was all done and a very disgruntled Zeinab found herself beside her sister, far away from the object of her desires.

Jen tucked in with gusto. 'I'd love a beer,' she grumbled as Damien ordered another pint. 'Don't ever let me hear you saying the "we're pregnant" remark. If *we* were pregnant, we would both be on the fizzy water.'

'I know,' Damien said. 'I'll make it up to you when the spare arrives...'

'The what?' Sharif asked.

'The spare, that's what we're calling him. Like, y'know, the way the royals have an heir and a spare? Well, we already have the heir, so this one's the spare.' Damien winked surreptitiously, knowing the effect his words would have on Jennifer.

411

She glared at him. 'That's what *you're* calling him, or her—it might be a girl, you know.'

'Joking... I'm joking, my darling... I know how crap it is, feeling sick and knackered tired all the time. And you're being such a trooper, I mean it, I'm so proud of you.' He gave her a kiss, and her frostiness melted.

The fish was smoked cod, and in the thin beer batter with a tartar dip, it just melted in the mouth. The chips were cut from real potatoes and smothered in salt and vinegar. It was delicious. Sharif finished his huge portion and then started on what was left of Carmel's. She wondered where he put it all. He ate so much but never gained weight.

'So, Joe, what's on the agenda for tomorrow?' Nadia asked.

'Well, tomorrow and tomorrow night and possibly the next day, we'll be in the glorious county of Mayo,' he announced extravagantly.

'Where we're hoping I won't be run out of town,' Tim added wryly.

'Well,' Zeinab said, 'I must say, if we were in Pakistan, a man who lived such a lifestyle...'

Only Carmel and Carrie heard her. All the others were busy laughing at Sean, who had spread ketchup all over the table surface. But she wasn't done. Carmel was horrified. What was she about to say? She couldn't let the others hear.

'Isn't it so funny how they named a place after a sauce?' Carrie piped up loudly.

Everyone turned to her, bemused.

'What?' Jen was perplexed, and even Luke's brow was furrowed.

'Mayo, like, it's totally random, right? Like there's nowhere called Ketchup or Mustard, is there, Lukie?' She smiled innocently.

Joe stifled a smirk. 'Well, Carrie, pet, I think the name comes more from the Irish word,*Maigh Eo*, and when the British changed the place names, they didn't really consider what it meant, just what it sounded like. So that's why we have such funny-sounding place names. In Irish they make perfect sense.' Joe's smile was kind so as not to humiliate her.

'Oh, I see,' Carrie said and gave her attention to her meal, but not before giving Carmel an almost imperceptible wink.

Carmel exhaled. Carrie had really saved them acute embarrassment there. Zeinab was about to launch into her 'gay is a lifestyle' rant. She'd treated Carmel and Nadia to it one afternoon after meeting the outrageously camp Zane, and they had been horrified. Of course, Zane had ramped it up for Zeinab. He'd explained to Carmel once that being gay in his West Indian culture was still very much frowned upon, and he'd endured terrible bullying as a kid, so now he was out and proud and to hell with anyone who objected.

But Zane was only one side of the story. Tim was quite another. He was gentle and quiet, and Carmel would have been mortified if Zeinab had said anything hurtful to him.

Zeinab shifted uncomfortably in her seat, and Carmel shot her what she hoped was a clear warning. She'd known the older woman still was having trouble accepting Tim. One evening before the trip, she'd asked why Tim didn't just take anti-gay drugs or get hypnotised to get him 'back to normal.' She'd then gone on to explain that he'd probably never met the right woman and got nervous so he resorted to his own gender out of fear. And, according to her, there were no gay Pakistani men.

Nadia had been beside herself with worry that Zeinab would say something along those lines to Tim, so Sharif had to sit her down before leaving and warn her not to say anything rude. She still looked on him with undisguised suspicion and mistrust, but she'd acted OK up to now—until the potential situation Carrie had so deftly averted. In fact, Carrie had jumped in just in time. Tim was right about her— she might appear ditzy, but she was one smart cookie.

'Ah now, Tim,' Joe said, anxious to get the conversation away from condiments and back to the plan for the next few days. 'I know it must seem strange after all these years, but try not to be too worried about it. You have a fairly formidable posse behind you, so nobody will be running you anywhere, and anyway, I'm sure it will all go grand.' He patted Tim gently on the back and turned to address the rest of the group. 'So, Tim will attend to his affairs, and the rest of us will go on a bit of a skite. There's the most marvellous sea stack out at Downpatrick, then I want to show you the Ceide Fields—the first evidence of farming in Ireland, it goes back into pre-historic times—and some dolmens and ring forts, and I thought we might walk or even cycle a bit of the Greenway. They've turned a lot of the old railway lines into cycle paths, and there's a gorgeous one from Westport, Tim's hometown, so I thought we might do that?'

There was general agreement, except for Zeinab, who looked nothing short of appalled at the prospect of cycling anywhere. The chat continued over the meal, and soon the crowd began to disperse. Jen and Damien took little Sean home, and Carrie almost dragged Luke out the door, so anxious was she to get him alone. Zeinab, Nadia and Joe took a taxi, even though it wasn't far and a lovely night, because Zeinab said she simply couldn't walk. They offered to have Tim join them, but he said he'd prefer to walk, so once they'd settled up the bill, Sharif, Carmel and Tim began the walk back to the hotel.

They could hear the *ting ting* of sails and rigging as they strolled along the quayside in Galway. Even though it was almost eleven at night, it was only dusk, and when Sharif remarked on it, Tim replied,

'Yes, I'd forgotten that about Ireland. In the summertime, it never really gets dark. It goes kind of dusky around midnight, but by three or four in the morning, it's bright again. The day I left, it was in the middle of June, and I remember walking to Westport town, the farm was about seven miles outside, and even though it was two or three in the morning, it was quite light. I never imagined I'd come back, and yet here I am, a lifetime later, so much done.' It was hard to tell if he was wistful or just sad.

'How do you feel about tomorrow?' Carmel asked. She felt kind of united with Tim by the isolation of their early lives. That's why she'd been the one to break the news to him that Brian was dead. Not to mention the fact that Dolly had confided the whole story of Carmel's conception and birth to Brian and Tim years before. Brian and Tim had been there for her as she told the whole sorry tale and again, along with Nadia, Khalid and Sharif, to pick up the pieces every time Dolly returned to London after yet another fruitless search for her daughter in Ireland. When Carmel attended Brian's funeral, the first time she met any of the McDaids, they'd had no idea she was Joe's daughter or that Tim was Brian's life partner. They stood together in the crematorium that day, and afterwards, Tim had cried in her arms at the loss of his one true love.

The family knew the whole story now, of course, about both Carmel and Tim, but for so long they were both outside looking in at life. They were connected in empathy.

'How do I feel?' Tim repeated. 'The truth? Sick to my stomach. I don't know why. It's ridiculous. Everyone I knew is dead and gone, it's just a scrap of land and a few forms. But I don't know... It feels so...so bloody sad, I suppose.'

Carmel linked her arm with his as they walked. He was easily a foot taller than her, straight as an arrow. As always, his snow-white hair was neatly brushed back off his high forehead. In his herringbone Crombie coat and felt trilby hat, he looked almost like some off-duty duke or lord swanning about. Nothing about his demeanour gave away the inner turmoil Carmel knew he felt. They were both good at hiding what was really going on. She just hoped she hadn't done the wrong thing in convincing him to come here.

'It's bound to be emotional, and you're still raw after Brian,' she said. 'You should just take the day as it comes and accept that you are going to feel something. It's not just any other day, and if you get a bit upset, then that's fine. You don't have to put a brave face on things if you don't feel it.'

Tim chuckled. 'Ah, yes, little miss self-help. How right you are.'

'I mean it,' she insisted. 'I know my life was a train crash for so long, but I didn't go around the bend because of self-help books. Wayne Dyer, Deepak Chopra, Sharon Salzburg—they were my friends, they kept me from tipping over the edge. I know some of it sounds like old claptrap, but most of it makes perfect sense.'

'I know, and you're right,' Tim conceded. 'I'm only joking with you. I want to thank you both, actually. Carmel, you, especially, for convincing me to come along, for being with me on this trip. I would have definitely cried off if it wasn't for you.'

Sharif patted the older man's back. 'Sometimes you need your friends, simple as that. We all do. Carmel is right, you know, just allow yourself to feel whatever you feel tomorrow. Don't try to mask it or bury it. We're all going through things all the time. Everyone has a story—you know that better than most—so live your story. Sure, it was sad, and your parents missed out on so much by not having you in their lives, but you might find that going there tomorrow gives you some peace, some closure, as our American friends say.'

'Maybe.' Tim seemed lost in another world.

'So, what's the situation with the farm now, do you know?' Carmel asked.

'It was leased to a local family. When my father died, my mother let the neighbours farm it for a small fee. She wrote to me, just telling me he was dead and the arrangements she had made. I sent a mass card, and that was that. Then, when she died, well, the neighbours wrote to me asking if the arrangement could continue, so I said it could. I had no interest in the place.

'The house is empty; it was just closed up after my mother died and left there. I don't have a clue what shape it's in, close to derelict, I would imagine, though. The son-in-law of the man we used to rent to wants to buy the land, so I'll sell it to him, and sure, if he wants the house as well, he can have it. I don't even need the money, but he seems anxious that it be in his own name, not rented land, so I might as well do the right thing and do the deal. It's something to do with European grants for farmers, don't ask me what. He The auctioneer started explaining in a letter, but to be honest, it wasn't long after Brian died, and I couldn't concentrate so I just tuned out.'

'Well, I'm sure it will all go fine,' Carmel assured him. 'Are you going to meet him there?'

'That's the plan. I'm seeing him and his wife at the farm tomorrow at three, with Jim Daly, the local auctioneer. I'm not sure about him, to be honest with you. He seems a bit, I don't know, a bit greedy or something. He suggested a figure, but I think it's too much. They're a young couple with a family, the farm came to her, and she married this lad, and they're trying to make a go of it. If they had my land with their own, they stand some kind of chance of making a decent living.

'Daly reckons we can get six thousand an acre, and there's about a hundred acres there. Some of it is bog and a bit under forestry, but mostly it's good grazing land. But I can't see how two young farmers from County Mayo can raise that kind of money. They're terrified it will go on the market and then they're snookered forever, but I won't do that to them. I'll meet them tomorrow and weigh the situation up, and if at all possible, I'll do a deal with them. As I said, I have no need of the money, and my children have made themselves very clear that they want nothing to do with me or my estate, so all that's left is for me to try to do right by these young people at least. Maybe some good can come of the place after all these years.'

'You're a good man, Tim. But be careful.' Carmel felt so protective of him. She would hate to see him taken advantage of. 'I have first-hand experience of Irish farmers and land and all that means. They'll do anything for it. Then, most people are nothing like my ex-husband, so maybe they're nice and it would be a good thing to give them a break. Just be careful anyway.'

Sharif grinned. 'Carmel, this man was a banker all his career, I think he's a fairly good judge of character at this stage.'

'Well, it's certainly taught me to look beneath the surface anyway,' Tim said.

As they approached the hotel, Carmel and Sharif went to say good night, but Tim looked like he had something else to say.

'Tim?' Carmel prompted.

'Ah, it's nothing. Good night, you two, and thanks for another lovely day. See you both in the morning.' He went to go to his room on the opposite side of the lobby to theirs when Carmel urged Sharif to go on without her and ran after Tim.

'What were you going to say?' she asked as he went to put his key in the door to his room.

He smiled. 'You're a perceptive woman, Carmel Khan, do you know that? All those years of just listening and saying nothing. Look, it doesn't matter, I...'

417

'Do you want me to come with you tomorrow? If you do, I'm happy to.'

'It's stupid, I know. I don't know why I'm being like this. It's just a bloody bit of land. But...'

'It's not stupid. It's hard to go back. I can't imagine trying to set foot in Birr ever again, or Trinity House. I know our lives took different paths, Tim, but we have a lot in common, not really fitting into the world or something. The others don't get it the way we do. So, will I come tomorrow?'

'Are you sure?' Tim asked. 'Joe had such a tempting itinerary planned, I feel bad dragging you away from it. And this is your homecoming trip after all...'

'The places Joe is taking everyone tomorrow have been there for centuries; they'll wait. Tim, I had an empty, lonely life for forty years, and now, I have family and friends and people who actually want me around, not just putting up with me. Nobody ever needed me before, and it feels so good to be needed. I'm not saying you need me tomorrow, but if it would make it a bit easier on you if I was there, well, that would mean as much to me as to you.'

'Thanks, Carmel. If you're sure, then I'd feel so much better with you beside me.'

'It's a date.' She grinned and went up on her tiptoes to kiss his cheek. 'Good night, Tim. I'll be right beside you, and if you ask him to be, so will Brian.'

'I'll certainly ask him. I talk to him every night. Sounds mad, I know, but I do.'

'I talk to Dolly too, and I never even met her, so we can be basket cases together.' She chuckled as she left him and went to join Sharif.

CHAPTER 48

The next day, the group took off in the bus, leaving Carmel and Tim to sort everything out. Sharif was, as usual, wonderfully supportive, delighted Carmel was accompanying Tim and telling her she would be a great help to him. The way he encouraged her in everything never ceased to amaze her. He not only protected her, but he thought there was nothing she couldn't do and urged her to go boldly at life, taking chances and trying new things.

'Will we rent a car?' Carmel asked over a late breakfast. 'That way we can travel on our own and come and go as we like. The hotel reception have a sign saying they will arrange it. I checked earlier, and we can pick it up here and drop it off at the hotel we're staying at tomorrow.'

'Well, I haven't driven since I had my knee replaced last year,' Tim admitted. 'There's no need when we are right on the tube. So I'd be less than confident, to be honest.'

'Well, I'll drive. I have my licence, so it should be fine. What do you think?'

'I think you are my guardian angel, Mrs Khan, that's what I think. Let's do it. The farm is about seven miles outside of Westport, so having our own transport would be so much better than trying to get taxis or lifts or whatever. But I insist on paying, OK?'

'Fair enough.' She held her hands up in surrender. 'I've never driven in Ireland, but if I can navigate London then I can surely manage rural Mayo, right?' She smiled. 'Just to be safe, though, let's get good insurance.'

The car was organised in very quick time, and Carmel felt a little surge of pride as she handed over her driving licence and Tim's credit card. She would have loved to travel back in time and show that timid child in Trinity House and then that subjugated woman in a lonely farmhouse just how far she would come.

'If you just take a seat in the lobby there, someone will bring the car over to the front door. They'll come to find you when it's here, Mrs Khan,' the charming young hotel receptionist explained. 'Can I get you some coffee or tea while you wait?'

Carmel looked at Tim. 'We're not long finished our breakfast, but we never say no to a cup of tea, so yes, please, that would be lovely.'

They sat in companionable silence. Carmel sensed Tim was happier not to have to talk, so she read the paper and he just sat, in quiet contemplation, sipping his tea. Within twenty minutes, the car arrived, and Carmel had butterflies as the young man who delivered it handed her the keys. He showed her how everything worked in about five seconds flat and immediately was on his mobile phone, deep in some vital conversation with someone called Macca about a part for a motorbike. It didn't look like he was coming back, so they sat in and Carmel nervously edged the car out of the hotel car park.

'We're about an hour and a half from Westport, according to this,' she said, poking at the sat nav. When she figured out how to work it, she followed the directions out of the city of Galway.

Tim seemed to have relaxed a little now they were actually on their way, and they chatted easily on the trip. After a few minutes, she'd gotten the hang of the car and was driving confidently. The time flew by as they marvelled at the gorgeous rolling hills, the ruins dotted everywhere, and the bustling towns they passed through. As they approached their destination, she saw lots of signs for Westport House.

'What's that?' she asked. 'A hotel or something?'

'Well, no, though I think now there are holiday places to stay in the grounds or a camping site or something. It was the home of the Browne family—they held the title Marquis of Sligo—but it's owned by someone else now. The Brownes made all their money in slave trading between Europe and Jamaica, so it's got a murky past. The house itself was just opening to the public when I left, but my father was often up there, on various matters to do with land. I went with him once or twice as a boy; it's an incredible house, beautiful. It's also got a connection to Granuaile the pirate queen of Connaught. Her great-granddaughter married in there. There are some great stories about her pirating on the high seas, feared by everyone. Apparently, she met Queen Elizabeth the First, and the queen couldn't speak Irish and Grainne couldn't speak English, so they conversed in Latin.'

'Wow! That sounds like a fascinating place. Maybe we'll get time to visit tomorrow. If not, we'll just have to come back sometime.' Carmel indicated to turn down the main street.

'Well, you've changed your tune,' Tim teased. 'I thought this was a one-off trip, never to be repeated?'

'OK, I admit it, I'm having more fun than I anticipated,' Carmel conceded.

'Even crazy ex-step-daughters aside?' Tim asked. She'd told him and Sharif about the encounter with Niamh, and both of them had congratulated Joe on how he handled it.

'Even that,' she agreed.

The main street of Westport was a hive of activity. The shops were all painted different bright colours, and the goods for sale were many and varied, from Asian street food vendors to traditional crafts. There were antique shops, jewellers, sweet shops, cafes, pubs and restaurants to suit every taste. People chatted on street corners, families strolled by licking ice creams, and nobody seemed in a hurry. A traditional band were playing outside a pub, and children were dancing wildly to the music while their parents had a drink in the sun.

421

Tim was agog.

'A bit different to how you remember it?' Carmel asked gently as they drove slowly down the street, their progress impeded by the nonchalantly jaywalking Irish.

'You could say that.' Tim gazed in amazement at his hometown. 'Look at that.' He called out the storefronts as they passed: 'Turkish barbers, Polish shops, a yoga studio... I wouldn't recognise the place, and yet, some parts look the same. Clew Bay, the river, Westport House, even some of the buildings. But it all seems so vibrant now, so colourful and full of life. I remember it being drab, cold, the street covered in horse dung—nothing like this.'

'We're a bit early.' Carmel checked the clock on the dashboard. 'Will we get out, have a wander round?'

'Let's do that.' Tim was still mesmerised by the transformation.

They passed a very enjoyable hour wandering up and down the streets and poking about in the shops, and Carmel bought Sharif a pair of cufflinks in an antique shop run by a very charming young man who seemed to have tattooed every inch of his skin. The cufflinks had a Celtic design on them, and she knew Sharif would love them. He often wore double-cuff shirts so he had many different pairs of cufflinks already, but he loved getting presents and she loved giving them to him. She enjoyed seeing how his eyes lit up with delight even if it was just one of his favourite cakes from the local bakery or a book from a charity shop.

Soon, it was time to make their way to the farm. Tim's sense of dread had dissipated since last night, but now that the return to his home place was imminent, he went quiet again. Carmel could see the anxiety behind his eyes.

She tapped the townland Tim gave her into the sat nav and eased the car out into the slow-moving traffic once more.

He didn't speak, so neither did she. He needed to compose himself, and the silence wasn't awkward as Carmel deftly manoeuvred the car around the twisty roads. As they turned off the main road and drove up a hill, there was a fine two-storey farmhouse on the left, and the sat nav indicated that it was their destination. The hedging all around the house was neatly kept, and the house itself didn't look derelict—quite the opposite. It looked as if it had been recently painted brilliant white, and the windows gleamed, reflecting the afternoon sun.

'Is that it?' Carmel asked, surprised. She'd been expecting some tumbledown ruin, overgrown and neglected.

'Yes... I think so. Well, I know it is, but it looks much better than it did when I lived here. It's not like I expected.'

They pulled into a neat farmyard, where a newish looking tractor was parked up in one corner and stables lined one side. Right in the middle of the yard was a cherry-red BMW convertible. *What an impractical car for Irish weather*, Carmel thought. It was such a flashy, showy car, she wondered who on earth would own such a vehicle.

Tim and Carmel got out, and immediately they were spotted by a middle-aged man who ran over to greet them. He wore a shiny suit and a pink shirt with a really garish tie. Carmel deduced immediately that he was the owner of the convertible. She thought the welcome he gave them, as he pumped Tim's hand, a little too effusive to be genuine, and she didn't like his lecherous gaze and his nudge-nudge remark to Tim along the lines of, 'Life in the old dog yet, eh?' His boomy laugh was also very off-putting.

Tim made the introductions. 'Carmel, this is Jim Daly, the auction-eer, and Jim, this is a friend of mine, Carmel Khan.' Carmel didn't imagine the slight emphasis on the word friend, but Jim was too thick to grasp it.

'Carmel!' he said, leaning in to kiss her cheek and placing a hand on her waist. He smelled strongly of aftershave. He was paunchy, and his hair had a peculiar plum sheen to it. She'd seen old lads in Birr dying their hair jet-black when they were in their seventies, fooling no one of course, but this dark purple colour was a new one on her— and certainly a colour never found in nature. Jim clearly saw himself as a bit of a hit with the ladies, and the double entendres just kept coming.

'So, Tim, as I was saying on the phone, this is good land, and a fertile farm is better than a fertile woman, I always say, and if you've no plans to settle down here yourself, however tempting the company...' He winked at Carmel, and she deliberately remained stoney-faced. It put him off his stride. 'Yes, well...eh... If you're not staying around then I think we should look for 500,000 for the farm, and if they want the house, and I think they will, we'll bring it up to 700,000 for the whole shebang. They're getting a good deal at that, and they can't afford not to take it because they'll be surrounded if they let it go to someone else. You see, this farm almost encircles theirs, so we have them by the short and curlies.' Jim beamed, delighted with himself.

Before Tim could respond, a couple Carmel judged to be in their thirties entered the yard.

'Ah, here we are now, Tim, and Carmel of course, this is Catriona and David Lynch.' Jim was enjoying being the Master of Ceremonies. 'They have the neighbouring fa—'

'I know exactly who you are,' Tim cut across him. 'We've corresponded, and I knew your mam and dad, Catriona. My condolences on his passing.'

The woman smiled and shook Tim's hand. She was dressed for farming in jeans, boots and a dark-green fleece. She had a pleasant, open face, and her brown hair was tied up in a ponytail. 'Thanks, Mr O'Flaherty. Mam got your mass card, and she really appreciated it.'

'Call me Tim, please. And how is she, your mother?' Tim asked.

'Ah, Tim, she's OK, but she's in the county home now. She has senile dementia, so she has good days and bad days, you know? Most of the time she's content enough, though.'

'I'm sorry to hear that. Your parents were much younger than me, but I knew the family of course when I was growing up.' Tim turned to her husband. 'And you're a native of Westport as well, I believe, David?'

'I am.' He was tall and balding and very quietly spoken, also dressed for farming. They were an unremarkable-looking couple, but they seemed very genuine and Carmel liked them. They were worried, she could tell. Their whole livelihood depended on what happened here today.

'My family, the Lynches, are farming in this parish for six or seven generations at least. My older brother has the family farm now, out at Scarteen Cross, so myself and Catriona are farming here.'

'And you have children too?' Carmel asked, though Jim seemed anxious to get on with the negotiations, clicking his pen and jingling change in his pocket.

'We have. A boy of eight called Jack and a little girl, Katie, she's three, so we've our hands full. We have a German au pair at the moment helping us to look after them because we're making silage and we need to stay at it for as long as the weather holds.' Carmel loved his soft West-of-Ireland accent.

'It sounds like you're busy so,' she said with a grin.

CHAPTER 49

'So maybe we could have a look inside the house and have a chat in there? You are interested in buying both the farm and the house, I take it?' Jim was practically salivating at the thought of the easy commission he was about to make.

'If you don't mind, Jim, I'd rather stay out here for now,' Tim interrupted. 'I haven't been in there for many decades, so if I go in there...I'd like to go alone.' He glanced up at the gable end of the farmhouse. Carmel was surprised how assertive he was being; he always seemed so mild-mannered. But it was clear he didn't like Jim Daly any more than she did. She had only ever known Tim in retirement, but she could see in the way he was dealing with the obnoxious Jim how he'd risen through the ranks in the bank during his career. There was a quiet confidence and determination to him, and something about his demeanour brooked no argument. It was a side to him she had not seen before.

Jim was chastened, but he was determined to keep his commission on track. He was the kind of guy who had probably been bragging to all and sundry about the killing he was about to make. He wasn't going to have it snatched from him now.

'Right, well, OK so. Well, David, and Catriona as well of course,' he added her in as an afterthought, 'as you know, this is a fine farm of land, excellent road frontage, and well drained. As good grazing as you'll get anywhere in the county, and the house is in great shape, from the outside anyway.' There was that boomy laugh again that was really getting on Carmel's nerves.

'It's fine inside too. We go in every week, open the windows in summer and air it out, and in the winter, we keep a heater on.' Catriona was matter-of-fact.

Tim was perplexed. 'You've been doing that since when?'

She looked surprised at his reaction. 'Well, since always. When your father died, Dad used to look in on your mother, check she was OK, do odd jobs around the house, take care of the garden, that kind of thing, and then when she died, he just kind of kept on doing it. So I suppose, when we took over the farm, when Daddy died, we took that on as well.'

'So your family have been taking care of this place for years?'

'Yes, well, since before I was born,' Catriona said. 'Your parents were very good to us, and then your mam renting us the land for very cheap for so long, and then you doing the same, it was the least we could do. Our families have been good neighbours for generations.'

'Well, times change, and we must all move on, I suppose.' Jim did not like the direction this conversation was taking. 'Now, Tim here is living the high life over in London, so he's happy to sell this property, but only at the right price, of course—'

Tim silenced him. 'Jim, I'm sorry for dragging you out here, but I think we can manage this ourselves. It seems like my family and Catriona's have had many happy years of peaceful co-existence and co-operation, so we'll continue that. That means, unfortunately, we have no need of your no doubt excellent negotiating skills. Thank you, though, and of course I'll settle up with you for your time to date. If you just send me a bill for hours worked, land registry searches, that sort of thing, if you carried them out?' Tim smiled innocently, and Carmel had to stifle a giggle.

Jim puffed up like a bullfrog. 'Well, this is not advisable at all, Mr

O'Flaherty. You could seriously jeopardise your position. If I could just have a quiet word...' Jim felt his commission slipping away.

'There's no need, I assure you. My position is fine, and as I said, we'll take it from here.'

'But... But legally...' Jim was grasping at straws.

'Oh, don't worry on that front,' Tim assured him. 'My solicitor will ensure that whatever we decide today will be all signed sealed and delivered properly, but I appreciate your concern, Jim. It's so nice to know people care.'

Jim had been given his marching orders in no uncertain terms, and he knew it.

'On your own head,' he muttered as he almost stomped back to his ridiculous red car. It began to spit rain as he drove away, and he had to stop again and struggle to get the roof to close. Realising they were all watching in amusement, he got back in with the top still down and drove off, the rain soaking his purple hair.

'Would you both like to come up to our house, have a cup of tea?' Catriona asked.

Tim smiled. 'That would be lovely.'

As they made their way back to the car, David said, 'We can actually walk. It's only a few minutes through the field, but it's three miles around by car. If ye don't mind a bit of drizzle.'

'Not a bit,' Carmel laughed. 'We're Irish and well used to the rain.' They chatted easily as they went through a wooden gate around the back of the farm house. But as they turned a corner, Tim stopped, stock-still.

Carmel put her hand on his arm as he stood and stared.

'This...' His voice was hoarse... 'Who did this?'

The garden behind the house was a riot of wild flowers, every imaginable colour and size, and the entire thing was surrounded by a beautiful dry stone wall. Right in the middle of the garden was a stone seat and a sundial. Carmel thought it was like an oasis of paradise in the patchwork quilt of green farmland that stretched down to the Atlantic.

'Oh, the wild flower garden?' Catriona asked. 'That's been there for years and years. We don't do much to it, to be honest; it kind of flowers every year itself. We mow it at the end of the season, and let the seeds fall out and then gather up the clippings. That's what my father did anyway. Your mam loved it, but it was your dad that really minded it apparently. 'Twas he built the stone wall around it and added in the seat. I remember my father telling me how he offered to help, but your dad said no, he'd do it himself. Every night, after a full day farming, he'd be out there, fixing the wall or making the sundial. I don't remember him, he died when I was young, but my parents spoke of him often. Your mam loved it too, and right up to the time she died, she'd ask Kathleen, that's the home help, but sure you know that, 'twas you paid for her to be here, to push her out to the garden in her wheelchair. I remember my uncle visiting once and remarking how it was out of character for the O'Flahertys to have such a thing. They weren't given to that kind of frivolity, I suppose, but they just loved the place.'

Catriona's chatting covered up Tim's shock, and Carmel linked his arm through hers as they walked. He was a deeply private man, and she knew he wouldn't want them to know the origins of the garden. To spare him, Carmel prattled away with Catriona and David about life on the farm and their children until they arrived to a new house.

'Oh, I was expecting another farmhouse!' Carmel remarked as she took in the new-looking brightly painted dormer bungalow.

'Well, we built this when David and I got married. Mam and Dad were still living in the home place. We have their place rented out now, to our au pair and her boyfriend, actually. He's Dutch, and he makes knives. They're happy as Larry there. The place needs modernising, really, but they're kind of alternative so they like having no central heating and stuff like that.' Catriona grinned.

Their kitchen was warm and bright, the big fridge covered in drawings done by the kids.

'Are Jack and Katie here?' Carmel asked. Tim was yet to speak. The discovery of the wild flower garden that he'd planted all those years ago had shaken him to his core.

'No, they're at a camp. It's a community-run thing for the kids of the area; they go to the playground and down to the beach. Kristiana, that's the au pair, is with them. Now, can I get you tea or coffee?'

'Tea please.' Carmel gazed around the sunny room. Toys were stacked in one corner, a pair of tiny shoes under the table, small bright-coloured coats hanging on a hook near the back door. The normal stuff of family life was strewn around—Disney character lunchboxes, colouring pencils. It wasn't chaotic or dirty, just a real working home. To anyone else, it would not have been remarkable, a similar scene represented all over the world in homes where small children were loved and cared for, but Carmel realised she'd never been anywhere like it in her life. Bill didn't encourage friendships with people her own age in Birr, and as a kid, she wasn't allowed to go to anyone's house to play. Not that she was ever asked, but she often wondered what family houses looked like. And now she knew.

'Tim? What can I get you?' Catriona broke through his reverie.

'Oh, I'm sorry, what a lovely home you have. Tea would be great, thanks.' He seemed distracted, and Carmel wondered if they shouldn't leave the deal for another day.

When David went to answer the phone, and Catriona went out to the pantry to get something, Carmel whispered, 'We can do this another day, if you'd prefer?'

Tim patted her hand. 'No... I'm fine... It's just a lot to process, the garden. I just don't know whether to be happy or sad. I'm both, I think...'

Catriona came back with some scones, butter and jam and placed them on the table, moving a stack of colouring books. 'Sorry about the mess. It's like shovelling snow when it's still snowing trying to tidy up after my pair.' She was doing her best to make space on the table.

'Please, don't apologise. It's lovely. I would have loved to have grown up somewhere like here.' The words were out before Carmel realised she'd said them. She didn't often discuss her past, and never with strangers. She reddened in embarrassment, frantically trying to figure out a way to divert the conversation.

Catriona looked at her for a moment and seemed to understand her discomfort. 'I know sure. They have so much now.' David came back in then. 'Everything OK?' Catriona asked him.

He nodded.

'So, Catriona and David, I've been thinking,' Tim began. 'And do you mind if I ask you a personal question? It's only in relation to what we're going to do.'

'Of course.' It was Catriona who spoke.

'How are you both, financially speaking?' The words hung in the air.

Carmel felt she should excuse herself. This was their private business. But to do so now would be rude.

The young couple looked at each other, words unspoken passing between them.

'We're fine,' David began.

'We're really struggling.' Catriona's voice was louder.

'Cat—'

'No, David, we might as well tell him the truth. Look, Tim, we came down today, and our plan was to ask you to do us a deal. I know the place is worth six hundred thousand, more probably, but we just haven't got that kind of money. Jim Daly has been saying to people that the place would be up for auction soon, and we'll be almost totally surrounded if someone buys it. We're doing OK, on the bit that we have. But we're into organic farming, and producing ethically sound food is much more expensive than the alternative. Our chickens are free range, the cows are grass fed most of the year, and what we'd love to do is set up an open farm—you know for families to visit, and maybe have a farm shop selling our produce and a cafe. We run the local farmer's market in Westport, and we've a great little co-op running, but we are stuck in that we can only produce so much on the land that we have. We can't really afford your farm, that's the truth, but we can't afford to let anyone else have it either. We went to the bank, and they can't—or won't—lend us that much...certainly nothing like six hundred thousand.'

Tim glanced at Carmel, and she knew he was checking in with her:

do they seem genuine? She thought they were, and she guessed Tim did as well.

'So you don't want to buy it?' Tim asked.

'Well, we do, as in, we can't let anyone else buy it, but now is not ideal for us, Catriona is right.' David sounded tired. Carmel imagined them night after night sitting at this kitchen table going over the figures, trying to find a way to save their livelihoods, and her heart went out to them.

'But I thought it was something to do with grants from the EU?' Tim was gentle but probing.

'No, we just said that to Daly.' David cut a scone in half and buttered it. 'He's such a blabbermouth, everyone in the place would know our business if you told him. Nobody with any sense tells him anything.'

'I can well imagine that's the case all right.' Tim thought for a minute. 'OK, how about this? I could just say let's keep going with the rent, but I'm not a spring chicken, and when I die, you'll be faced with the same problem. Worse, actually, because I don't have anyone to leave it to so I was considering leaving whatever I have to charity.'

Carmel knew how hard this was for him, denying the existence of his children, but it was their doing, not his.

'So here is my proposal: I give you the farm, the house, the whole lot. It's either you two or a charity, and the way I see it, you are just as deserving as any other cause. Or, if necessary for legal reasons, I'll sell it to you for a euro or something, and I might come back now and again, for as long as I'm able. I know I didn't want to go into the house today, and maybe I will some other time, but seeing the garden, knowing the place is taken care of... I didn't think it would affect me so much, but it has, and I realise that this place is a part of me, even after all these years. The fact that your family cared for it means more than I can say.'

CHAPTER 50

*C*atriona and David were speechless. The silence hung heavily between them all.

'But... But, Tim, we can't do that.' Catriona was struggling to articulate. 'This is your land, your family's land, and no matter what the situation, we have to pay you for it...'

Tim leaned over and put his hand on hers. 'Please, I'm quite sure this is what I want to do. I'm quite wealthy, I own my own house, and I have everything I need. I've travelled all over the world, and now that I'm getting on in life, my needs are fewer. You're young, just starting out in life, and I like the sound of what you're doing—the farmer's market and sustainable farming and all of that. Brian, that was my partner, he died last year, was a great gardener, he'd love that idea as well. So, consider it a donation, whatever you want to call it.'

He saw the confusion on their faces—Brian was his partner?

'It's a long, sad story, but in a nutshell, I'm gay, that's why my father threw me out. I got married and had a family, but for obvious reasons it didn't work out. And then, luckily, I met Carmel's uncle, Brian, and we were together for many years. I want to do this. My children are grown up and don't want anything to do with me. Your family looked after my parents, and seeing that flower garden today...

I planted that with my friend Kitty Lynch the summer before I was sent away. I thought my father hated me, hated what I was, and my mother never really connected with me either once I left. So I lived all my life thinking they never cared about me. But they did care. They looked after that garden, and that must mean something.' Tears shone in the old man's eyes.

'Hang on a minute,' David said. 'Your friend Kitty Lynch, how old would she be now?'

'Same age as me, I suppose, maybe a bit younger? Mid to late eighties. Why?'

'Because I think your Kitty Lynch is my grandaunt. She lived here all her life. Her nephew Donal is my dad. She's the only Kitty Lynch in the parish, to my knowledge.'

'And is she still alive?' Tim asked. This day was proving more and more amazing.

'Oh, indeed she is, hale and hearty. She's a bit of a character, never married or anything, but she's been all over the world. She lived in America for years and then in South Africa. I can take you to meet her if you like?'

'If she is the same Kitty, I'd like that very much,' Tim said quietly. 'I owe her an apology, and it's long overdue.'

There was a moment of silence, and then Tim perked up again.

'Now back to the deal! Are we on? I'll instruct the local solicitor here to draw up all the necessary paperwork. You two can take care of the fees for that and any other technical things that need to be done, but as far as I'm concerned, it's all yours.'

Catriona's eyes filled up with tears. 'I can't believe it. Are you certain this is what you want to do? It seems too much, and I don't want you to feel like we pressured you and regret it afterwards. And, I mean, what about your family? I know they've said they don't want it, but when they hear you've given it away to strangers, they'll be furious, surely?'

'Catriona, David, listen to me,' Tim said seriously. 'My children don't even know this place exists. Their mother made sure that they have no sense of being half-Irish, so you need have no worries on that score. Nothing about Ireland, Mayo, or me holds even the slightest interest for them. As for me regretting it, I don't do regrets, I just don't. Life is for living, and I'm grateful to be in a position where I might be able to make a real difference to someone. So please just accept it. Will you?' He gazed from her face to his.

David stood up, walked around to the side of the table where Tim sat, and stretched out his hand. 'Thank you very much, Tim. My family will always be in your debt. And if we can ever do anything for you, anything at all, then please just get in touch. And that garden will always be looked after. I promise.'

Tim shook his hand, and Catriona joined them and kissed Tim's cheek. 'Thank you, Tim. You don't know what this means to us.'

Tim put his arms around both of them, and Carmel had to wipe away a tear.

They drove in the hired car behind Catriona and David on the way back into Westport. They were taking Tim to meet Kitty again.

'How do you feel now?' Carmel asked.

'Oh, Carmel, I don't know. Honestly, I don't. Seeing the wild flower garden stirred up so many emotions in me. Like, he tended that so lovingly, for so long, they both did, and that touches me deeply, but then it's such a bloody waste! If they did love me still, why couldn't they put pen to paper and write to me? They knew how to contact me. I wrote to them, sent Christmas cards and all of that, I gave them an address they could contact me at—a priest, actually, he was very good to me. I waited and waited for a reply, but nothing ever came. It was as if I was dead. And now I find out they looked after my garden, I can't help but think they saw it as tending a grave, except I was alive and desperately wanting their love. Those first months in London were the worst of my life. I honestly thought about suicide so often. Nobody wanted me; I felt I was alone in the world.'

'I can imagine what meeting Brian must have felt like,' Carmel said, 'someone to love, to feel accepted by. Though the circumstances were different, I do understand, Tim, I really do. I felt like you for so long— unloved, unlovable.'

'I know you understand. And even Marjorie, I mean, it wasn't a perfect marriage obviously, but she made me feel wanted. And I was so low, so vulnerable, I suppose, I grabbed her with both hands—figuratively, if not literally.' He gave a sad little smile. 'She deserved better.'

'Not better, Tim, just different. Try to think of it this way: because of her marriage to you, she has children she dotes on, and grandchildren too, so I'm sure she doesn't regret being married to you from that point of view. It's incredibly sad that your kids feel the way they do, but you've tried, often, and nothing is budging so it's time to let it go. Marjorie deserved to be married to a man who could love her, that's true, but you did not deserve to be frozen out of your children's lives, so she's not without blame here either.'

'You're right, I suppose,' Tim admitted reluctantly.

'I think when it comes to the pain of the past, we just need to take it out, look at it, not bury it or anything, but then relegate it to where it belongs: in the past. All we have is now, this moment, and regrets and recriminations serve nobody. Not Marjorie, not your parents, not Charles and Rosemary, and most definitely not you. You did your best, and you've kept your promise to Marjorie all these years at huge personal cost to you and, in some ways, to Brian, so it's time to stop beating yourself up about it.'

He sighed. 'I'm thinking a lot about Brian today. I wish he was here with me, though he would be saying exactly what you're saying, I'm sure. He was so strong, so good at dealing with people. I left all of that to him. He used to laugh, saying I could be the nice English gentleman while he got to play the rough Paddy.'

'I don't know, you managed to put the run on that creep Jim Daly fairly well.' Carmel grinned.

'He was awful, wasn't he?'

'Dreadful,' she agreed. 'I never saw hair that colour before.'

'And that car. Good lord, what was he thinking?'

'Not much, but men like him really do believe they are God's gift to women, poor deluded eejit.' She giggled, and Tim joined in. It helped to lighten the mood.

'So, what will you say to Kitty, if it is the same one?' Carmel asked, carefully following David and Catriona as they drove effortlessly along the winding country roads. The road was only really the width of one vehicle, and the hedgerows grew high on both sides. She really hoped they didn't meet a tractor or something. She was getting more confident as a driver, but earlier on, she'd had the trauma of reversing under the gaze of some sixteen-year-old smoking a cigarette while driving a huge combine harvester. She'd managed it, but thinking about it was something that made her come out in a cold sweat. She'd seen it all around the roads of Birr, when she would sit in the back as Bill and Julia sat in the front seats on the way to and from mass. Sometimes the farm machinery was only inches from them as they edged past on the narrow country roads.

'I'll apologise first anyway,' Tim decided. 'I just left, and we were such good friends. I never contacted her again. Those early months in London, I wrote to her, oh, maybe fifty times, but every letter ended up in the bin. I was afraid she'd heard about the incident with Noel in the barn and was disgusted. Things were so different then. There was no understanding whatsoever. And I was worried she really thought we were the makings of a match. She was just another name to put on the list of people I'd let down, so I never got the guts to make contact. Then I met Marjorie, and the one time I mentioned Kitty, she went silent on me for a week, so I never brought her name up again.'

'Isn't it odd that she never married, like? In those times, it just was what people did. Love, compatibility, political alignment, and all the things people seem to worry about now in relationships didn't feature really. People just got married, usually to someone local, and stayed married and raised their families. I can never decide who had it easier? Like, their life expectations were so low, but there was a contentment in that. Our life expectations, in our generation, are so high. By reading magazines, you'd be convinced every relationship is doomed nowadays, if you're not reading the same newspaper, eating the same paleo, sugar-free diet, and swinging from the chandeliers every night of the week.'

Tim laughed out loud. 'Carmel, you're a tonic, honestly, thanks so much for coming today. I couldn't have managed without you. You're a great friend, just like Dolly was. I remember one time, when Brian was in the hospital, and there was a problem with my mobile—I don't know, it's all a bit Double Dutch to me, Wi-Fi and hop spots and cellular data, it's like these kids in the phone shop are speaking another language. Anyway, it wasn't working, and I tried dealing with them but got nowhere, so Dolly grabs me and the phone one day and steams into the Vodafone shop, raises all colours of holy hell, and makes a total show of us. I was mortified, but in the end, they fixed it. She was a lion, honest to God; she was so loyal. And even though she and Brian didn't agree with her decision to say nothing to Joe about her and about you, we were friends with her. And, oh, did they have some scraps about it, full-on screaming and fighting, but they were cut from the same cloth, well able to stand their ground. They were reared in the same place, where people wore their hearts on their sleeves, and if you had a difference of opinion it often ended with a punch. But it never changed how she felt about us. She loved us, and we loved her. Sometimes, I just can't believe that, now, here is her daughter, being just as good a friend to me.'

Carmel loved these stories about her mother. It was as if with each little tale—from Sharif, Tim, Nadia, people in Aashna—another bit of the huge painting that was her mother's life got coloured in. It was wonderful. She basked in the glow of being needed, as well; there was nothing like the feeling that you're really helping someone you care about.

Ahead, David and Catriona were slowing down as they approached the town of Westport. They indicated right up a hill and turned into a lovely development of smallish houses encircling a green area bordered with marigolds. In the centre of the green was a huge rose bed, where a profusion of white roses bloomed.

'It's like the Irish flag,' Carmel remarked as they admired it, 'the green, white and orange.'

They parked up and got out. A plaque on the wall of the first house told them this was called St Gerald's Crescent and was an assisted living community for the elderly inhabitants of Westport.

David and Catriona led them up a little path to one of the houses and knocked on the cardinal-red door.

THE CARMEL SHEEHAN STORY

It was opened quickly, and a tiny woman stood there. She couldn't have been more than four-foot-ten, her thinning silver hair tied back in a bun.

She gazed past her grandnephew and his wife, straight to Tim. She just stood for a long moment, taking him in.

'I don't know whether to hug you or murder you,' were her first words.

'I probably deserve the latter, but I would love the former.' Tim grinned..

'Do you hear him and his plumy English accent!' Kitty laughed. 'Come in here to me, Tim O'Flaherty, till I get a good look at you. Come in let ye...'

David and Catriona exchanged a glance. 'We'll leave ye to it, Auntie Kitty,' David said. 'We've to pick the lads up from the summer camp. But enjoy the visit, and sure I'll give you a ring later on.'

'Right so, thanks for finding him.' She patted David on the arm.

'Oh, 'twas he found us, and what's more, he's giving us the farm.' Catriona couldn't contain her excitement. 'He's like a guardian angel.'

'Is he now? Well, isn't that something?' Kitty grinned and bade goodbye to the young couple as she ushered Carmel and Tim into a little sitting room.

CHAPTER 51

'So, who have I here, besides my long lost friend?' Kitty enquired.

'This is Carmel Khan,' Tim said. 'She's a friend of mine from London. Well, actually, she's Irish as well, but we met in London. We're over here on a kind of a trip around in a bus with Carmel's family and her husband, so I tagged along.'

'Well, thank God for that,' Kitty said. 'I thought you were like one of those old men who lose the run of themselves and want to have a young one on their arm, fooling nobody of course. So, you're giving my nephew and his wife your farm? Sit down, sit down, let ye.'

Carmel settled into an armchair with white lace-trimmed anti-macassars on the back and arms. The huge three-piece suite of furniture seemed to take up most of the floor space in the small room. The fireplace was cleaned out for the summer, the grate filled with pinecones painted silver, and the whole effect was cosy and welcoming. The entire room seemed to be stuffed with ornaments and photos of a variety of children, weddings, first communions. There was a delicious smell.

'I'll make ye a cup of tea now in a minute,' Kitty said, 'and I've a cake in the oven. It won't be long.'

'It smells amazing,' Carmel said. 'You have such a lovely home.'

'It's nice all right. The council build these for all the old fogies like myself. They're small, but it does me. I can do a bit of gardening outside, and I potter away. I'm able to get down to the shops and everything, so I'm very lucky, and sure the family are great.'

'We were admiring the display with the marigolds and roses as we came in,' Tim said, never taking his eyes off Kitty. The years had done their work, but she was still the same no-nonsense personality.

'Well, I was doing it myself, with an old fella over beyond in number seven, but it got too much for us, the weeding and that. So my other nephew, Paudie, he works for the county council, so he organised to send up some fellas every week. They're on community service for blackguarding around the town, drunk and disorderly and the like, and the judge here says a bit of hard work is what they need and they'll have no more energy for acting the clown around the place. So that's who takes care of the donkey work now, and I tell them what to do.'

'I bet you do.' Tim chuckled, and Kitty joined in.

'Ah sure, they're grand lads. I bring them in for tea and a bit of cake after, and sure one fella says to me that he never ate home-baked cake before. Imagine that? But sure, the mothers and fathers get everything in the auld supermarket these days, too busy for baking. I won't go there, though, no; then, I get everything I need in the local shops. Sure, 'tis only a few pence dearer, and you're supporting your own. That big German supermarket they have now out the Galway road, sure that's not doing much for Westport, is it?'

'If more people thought like you, Kitty, the towns would be in better shape, no doubt about it,' Tim agreed. 'There is a corner shop at the end of my road. Three generations of a family, the Patels, and he has the same problem. They opened a Tesco Metro on the high street, and the people flocked to it. Poor Sanjay, the grandson of the original owner, doesn't know how long more he can keep going.'

'Things were simpler in our day,' Kitty said. 'People went to the butcher for meat, and the greengrocer for the fruit and vegetables, and there was a newspaper shop and a sweet shop everywhere. It's all bundled into one now, the price of progress, I suppose. So, where do we start?'

Her question caught Tim unawares, but her blue eyes bored into his. She might've been old, but she was sharp as a tack.

'Well...' He smiled. 'It has certainly been a long time...'

'Well, we haven't either of us much to go to the end, so we better get cracking,' Kitty said matter-of-factly. 'Why did you leave without a word? I went up to your house the next day, and a few days afterwards, but they just said you were gone and you weren't coming back and that was that. I got the impression they hated talking about it. My own family, too, were just bewildered, and of course I had all the pitying glances for a few months afterwards.'

Tim leaned forward in his chair and took Kitty's hands. 'I'm so sorry. I wrote so many letters to you, but I couldn't post them.' He took a deep breath. 'The reason I left was my father found me in the barn with Noel Togher. Kitty, I'm a homosexual.'

Carmel was kind of shocked, to hear him use that word. She was used to him being gay, and Brian and Zane; in fact, she was surprised at how many gay people there were in the world. But that word, *homosexual*, seemed so clinical or something.

'I'll go and make the tea if you like, Kitty?' Carmel suggested. She wanted to give them some space.

'Do, girleen, 'tis all out in the kitchen.'

Kitty gazed at Tim and then down to where their hands were intertwined. 'I knew that, even then. But I thought we loved each other, we could have shielded each other, and I suppose I thought it might still work. You should have contacted me, Tim.'

'I know I should have, and I'm sorry. But I'm so glad we didn't marry. You deserved someone who could love you properly. A proper relationship with children and everything.' Tim was trying to make her understand. 'I didn't know much back then, but I knew I could only bring you pain.'

'You're right about one thing: you didn't know much back then. If you did, you would've known that men are not my thing. I suppose that never occurred to you?'

Kitty watched his face as he processed her own bombshell.

'What?' he said, disbelieving. 'Are you telling me—'

'Yes, I'm a lesbian. But at least when we were young, though people in Westport might have been disgusted by you, they knew what you were existed. Girls who were attracted to other girls was unheard of back then. I felt like the only one in the whole world. With you, at least, I felt a bit normal.'

'Oh, Kitty, I can't believe it.' Tim smiled sadly. 'If only I'd known, we could have run away together.'

'Oh, once you left, there was nothing keeping me here, so when I got the chance to go to America, I took it. A local girl, Marie Donnelly, do you remember her? Well, she got work with her brothers in New York, and she came home on holidays and she invited me to go back with her, so I did. I spent twenty-four years in New York—Brooklyn. I loved it. I met Georgie Harper there, a beautiful black girl from Tennessee, and we were together for eighteen glorious years, until she was in a horrible car accident coming home from the shelter. She set up homeless shelters for women and girls. She died of her injuries three weeks after the crash, and I thought I'd die too. I swear, I remember thinking that no human could withstand that much pain. But I did. Every street corner, every bar, every cafe reminded me of Georgie, and I couldn't bear it in Brooklyn for another second, so I left New York and never went back. An opportunity came up in South Africa, so I went there.' She sighed. 'You're not the only one with secrets, Tim.'

'Kitty...I had no idea. I mean, all these years I was afraid I'd broken your heart, too.'

'Haha! D'ya hear him?' She found that idea very funny. 'A broken heart by Tim O'Flaherty, no indeed. You never broke my heart, Tim. My heart was broken only once, when I lost my Georgie. You only have that kind of love once in a lifetime.' She shook her head sadly. 'How did life treat you, after you left here?'

Tim told her the whole story—those first awful months, Marjorie, the children, and finally, Brian.

'And how long is he dead now?' Kitty asked.

'Just over a year. People say it gets easier, but I'm not there yet,' Tim admitted sadly.

'Well, would you look at us, two young freaks of nature, and we couldn't even admit it to each other. Do you know what I think, Tim? I think your father did you a great favour by throwing you out. Imagine if he never caught you? Or he did and never said anything? You'd be up there still, a lonely old bachelor farmer, never having known the joy of children or a love like you had with your Brian. Yes, then, 'twas the best thing he ever did for you.'

'I'm not sure that was his motivation, but you're probably right,' Tim agreed. 'We'll never know now, though, will we?'

He told her about the wild flower garden, and she was silent when he finished.

After a moment, she said, 'I met him one Christmas Eve, your father. He was coming out of Hannigan's below, and he had a few drinks on him. He wasn't much of a drinker, I'd say, but he was drunk that evening. 'Twas the first Christmas after you left. Anyway, I was going home after picking up a few things for the Christmas dinner for my mother, when he stopped me. I was shocked, first at the state of him, and second because he'd given me very short shrift when I called after you left.

'Anyway, he said something to me. He said: "If you see him, tell him..." And then he stopped. 'Twas as if he just couldn't say the words but what he wanted to say was kind, not harsh. He waited for a second. He was a bit unsteady on his feet. He said, "Tell him I'll mind the garden for him." Sure, I never saw you again from that day to this, so I couldn't tell you anything, but he missed you. I'm sure of it, and sure it near killed your poor mother. She'd sit over on St Teresa's side of the church, all alone on a weekday, and she'd cry. She got a mass said for you every year on your birthday and on the anniversary of the day you left. 'Twas you she was crying for, her only child.'

Tim was hardly aware of the tears that ran down his cheeks as Kitty described his parents. That part of his head and heart had been locked away for so long, he'd buried the pain so deeply, that it came as a shock to have it resurface.

'I wish...' Tim managed through his tears. 'I just wish they...'

'Sure, Tim, if wishes were horses, beggars would ride,' Kitty said gently. 'There's no point to wishing now. But you should know they never forgot you, never stopped missing you. That's really why your father got so close to Catriona's family. They were the family he had lost, I suppose. You did a good thing giving herself and David the land. You'll really make a mighty difference to them, and they were very good to your parents. What goes around comes around, as they say, the wheel is always turning.'

On and on they talked about old school friends, about Georgie and Brian, about all the changes to Westport since they were young.

'What made you come back?' Tim asked, curious.

'Well, I had a great few years in Cape Town. I loved it there. I had little bakery and a café, and I made great friends. Even though the time I was there was difficult—apartheid was still in full force—when Mandela came to power, he changed everything. Really, everything. I was so fortunate to live there in those years. He drew together a nation that was so divided it was impossible to see how they could ever pull in the same direction. He was a remarkable man. But, in the end, I was getting older, the body wasn't what it once was, and I wanted to be near my family. My brothers were always close with me, if they weren't with each other, and I visited home often so I knew all the kids and everything.'

'And did they know about you? About Georgie?' Tim was gentle.

'Well, I keep a photo of her beside my bed, and I talk to her every night, but they've never asked and I never say who she was. I think they do know, but the idea of an auld wan like me having relations with anyone is enough to put you off your dinner, so acknowledging my being a lesbian would probably finish them off completely. It's not a problem for me or for them, so we just leave it be. Now, let's have that tea. I don't know where your friend has got to.'

Tim's mobile phone beeped, and he took it out of the pocket of his coat.

I've gone to meet the others at the hotel. I let myself out the back door. Think you need time alone with K. Talk later C xx

'Carmel let herself out,' Tim said as he went to join Kitty in the kitchen. 'She probably felt a bit in the way what with us banging on about the Dark Ages.' The cake was out of the oven. Carmel must have taken it out before she left, otherwise it would have burned to a crisp by now.

Kitty stood there in front of him, and suddenly they were not two old people, almost ninety years gone, but a boy and a girl, so afraid of the world they'd been born into, where nobody would accept what they were. Tim took a step across the tiny room and wrapped his arms around her, holding her close.

'We did OK, Kit. Despite it all, we did OK. And here we are, together again for the final act.'

CHAPTER 52

Carmel was delighted to see the bus in the car park of the hotel. She missed Sharif and longed to tell him about the day's events.

As she walked into the hotel, she was almost knocked down by a sea of purple silk that turned out to be Zeinab, and by the looks of things, she was in high dudgeon.

'Zeinab, is everything OK?' Carmel asked as the woman barrelled past her.

'Oh, Carmel, no, everything is not OK. Nothing like it, in fact. I simply cannot stay one more moment, not another second. I'll take a taxi to the airport this minute and return to Karachi. Have my things sent on from London.' She seemed to be both upset and furious simultaneously.

'Look, whatever's happened, I'm sure we can sort it out,' Carmel said placatingly. 'Why don't we just go for a walk, just around the block, and compose ourselves, and you can tell me what the problem is?' She knew she sounded like someone dealing with a recalcitrant five-year-old, but honestly, that was how Zeinab behaved sometimes.

'No, there is nothing anyone can do. Nothing at all.' Zeinab was attracting attention from the people sitting at the tables outside the hotel having a drink.

'Why is that lady in the funny dress screaming and crying, Mammy?' asked a little girl in a high-pitched voice. 'Did she cut her knee?'

A red-faced mother tried to distract the little girl, but the child was not for deviating from this very interesting floor show. The mother mumbled something and tried to get the child to eat some of her sandwich, but the little voice rang out again. 'She looks like Princess Jasmine from Aladdin, except way wrinklier and fatter, doesn't she, Mammy? Maybe she's Princess Jasmine's granny?'

The group gathered at the next table were trying to stifle giggles as Zeinab turned on the child.

'Where I come from, children are trained not to be rude to their elders. I see no such efforts are made here.' Her eyes flashed dangerously.

'I'm so sorry,' the mortified mother said, her face burning. 'She's only three, and she doesn't know—'

'She needs a good spanking,' Zeinab cut in. 'That would teach her how to behave. If she was mine, I can tell you—'

'What's going on here?' Just as Zeinab was warming to her theme, a tall man in his thirties emerged with a tray, taking in his embarrassed wife and his daughter, who was now crying behind her mother.

'I was saying,' Zeinab replied in her overbearing way, 'that if that child was mine, she would find herself properly chastised for rudeness.'

The man placed the tray on the table and lifted his little daughter into his arms. 'Well, she's not yours, so you can mind your own business. Now, Lily, did you say something to upset this lady?'

'No, Daddy, I just said she looked like Princess Jasmine's granny,' the girl said quietly through sobs.

'And that's all?'

The little girl nodded, and the man glanced at his wife for confirmation. She nodded, too.

'And that's what has you advocating assault on my little girl, is it?'

the man demanded of Zeinab. 'Yerra, you'd want to cop on to yourself, going around taking umbrage at nothing. She's only a child; she didn't mean any harm. And anyway, you're not exactly a spring chicken, are you? Go on away now, you mad old bat, and don't be annoying us.'

This exchange now seemed to have gathered even more spectators, and Zeinab was the focus of everyone's attentions. Carmel didn't know what to do. She stood by as Zeinab marched back into the hotel without another word.

'I'm so sorry.' Carmel was mortified. 'She's...well, I'm just really sorry.' There was no way to defend or explain.

'Ah sure t'wasn't your fault.' The man smiled, and Carmel turned gratefully away.

Carmel got the key of their room and let herself in. Sharif was stretched on the bed reading.

'Hey, you're back, great.' He leapt up and went to kiss her. He took one look at her face and immediately asked, 'What's up? Has something happened?'

She told him about the business downstairs with Zeinab, and he burst out laughing.

'Dead right, too. If someone was telling me to beat my child, they'd get the same response. I can just imagine her face, and her indignant stomp off. Just let her cool down. It was probably nothing. She was driving my mother insane today, fawning over Joe. It was a bit much, to be honest, and I apologised to him when we got back, but you know Joe. He pretended he didn't notice. Maybe Ammi had a word with Zeinab—that's probably it—and she didn't like it.'

'Right, well, she was threatening to leave, go to the airport, straight back to Pakistan.' Carmel was still worried.

'She won't, believe me. She won't do anything of the kind. She's just looking for attention and to paint herself as the victim. Ignoring her is the only way to deal with it. Now, how did it go on the farm?'

'Fine,' Carmel said, still uneasy. 'Great, actually. We had a lovely day. But, Sharif, can we go for a walk? I feel like I need some air.' The encounter with Zeinab had really upset her. She wasn't used to dealing with conflict. In Trinity, everything had been calm, because it was such a transactional relationship between the kids and the staff—no emotion involved. And then with Bill, it was years of just nothing, no fights, no arguments, but no conversation, no connection, either. But she was learning, listening to her friends in Aashna talking about falling out with sisters or brothers, or having blazing rows with friends, and she was beginning to realise that it was a part of caring about someone. Emotions can run high and spill out as anger just as much as joy and love. This was obvious to most people, but again, she found herself trying to figure out normal interpersonal relationships.

'Of course,' Sharif said.

She smiled and slipped her hand into his.

They walked up to the grounds of Westport House, and it was spectacular. Huge thickets of rhododendron and hydrangea blossomed everywhere, and flower beds provided riots of colour. There was a river running through the grounds, and they walked and talked for two hours. She told him all about Catriona and David, and about Tim meeting Kitty again after all these years. She told him about sitting in the kitchen with the kids' stuff all around and how lovely it all was. He didn't flinch at the mention of children, as he had done up to now—or maybe she imagined it, but he seemed happy to discuss it. They came back to the incident with Zeinab, and he promised he'd find her once they got back and check she was OK.

'So, how was your day?' Carmel asked as he helped her over a huge log.

'Wonderful,' he said, smiling. 'Just amazing scenery. The sea stack is incredible. It's this huge column, I think it's about a hundred and seventy feet high, just off the coast. It used to be connected, and then there was a storm that broke the land bridge so they had to get people off with ropes. Joe told us the legend about it, that when St Patrick was converting everyone to Christianity, the local chieftain wouldn't go along with the new religion so Patrick struck the ground with his crozier and the land split in half, creating the sea stack and leaving the doubting chieftain alone on the rock. I'm not sure how true that is, but the place really is remarkable. You can see all the different colours of the layers of rock; I've never seen anything like it. And the sea beneath, foaming as it crashes, all the colours of turquoise, blue, green, azure. Honestly, I was blown away, literally and figuratively.

'Then we went to the Ceide Fields. It's a farm, the first evidence of farming in Ireland, five and a half thousand years ago. It's hard to get your head around it. And the life there was fairly sophisticated. I'd never seen a bog before, fascinating. Then we went to Killala, a gorgeous little village with loads of ruins and an old monastery, and we had some lunch there. We really had a great time.'

'I'm glad. So what was Zeinab doing that drove Nadia more mental than usual?'

'Oh, she was just being herself really. She sees admiring another culture as somehow disloyal or something, so every time the rest of us were in awe, she'd pipe up with "Well, there's much better than that in Pakistan" kind of thing. It drove Ammi mad, so she openly refuted her by saying she never saw a sea stack or a bog or a pint of Guinness in Pakistan and would she please just give us all a break?

'Well, that went down like a lead balloon, as you can imagine. So, Zeinab, knowing how much it drives Ammi crazy, turned up the dial on the flirting with Joe. She was making out like she couldn't walk on the rough terrain so had to hold his arm all the time; then, when we were having lunch, she was offering him bites of her food. She even had her hand on his leg at one stage. Anyway, Ammi had enough, and when we got back, she told me she was going to have it out with Zeinab, tell her she was embarrassing us by her behaviour and warn her to stop immediately or else.' Sharif grinned, he clearly found the whole thing very amusing.

But it only made Carmel uncomfortable. 'Or else what?'

'Well, I don't exactly know, but she wasn't taking any prisoners. I probably should have gone, but I decided to stay out of it.'

'Well, I think I walked right into the tail end of that particular chat,' Carmel said with a grimace.

'Don't worry. It'll be fine. They get on each other's nerves, that's all.'

Carmel wanted to fight Nadia's corner. It wasn't fair to say they

451

were both to blame. Nadia was lovely and normal and reasonable, and Zeinab was a self-serving lunatic. Carmel said as much to Sharif.

'I know,' he said calmly, 'but she'll be going back to Karachi after this trip, and we won't have to see her for years.'

'Unless she decides to stay and shack up with her favourite nephew.'

'She won't, don't worry,' Sharif assured her. 'And even if she tried, her favourite nephew has a scary Irish wife so that's not going to fly. It's all going to be fine. Now, we better start heading back. We're eating in the hotel tonight, and the table is booked for eight, and it's seven now.'

* * *

DINNER WAS ANOTHER LOUD AFFAIR, with Carrie entertaining everyone with a story about her and her sister in a Botox clinic. Even though she came across as a bit vacuous, there was something wise and endearing about her, Carmel thought. And she was crazy about Luke, so that was good enough for Carmel. Jen was even warming to her a little bit, especially as it turned out she was like a toddler whisperer with Sean. He, like his uncle, was mesmerised by her, and she seemed happy to play with him for hours.

'She took him to the pool this evening, let me have a spa treatment,' Jen whispered to Carmel. 'I was terrified she'd let him drown and insisted Luke went too, but apparently, she spent the whole time with him, playing away. I think my son is as besotted as my brother.'

'It certainly looks that way,' Carmel whispered back as both Sean and Luke gazed adoringly at Carrie as she explained just how badly wrong Botox can go if the therapist is in the middle of a text fight with her boyfriend. Apparently, the boyfriend had been at a stag party the night before, and the girl hadn't heard from him all day, and all his friends were being very cagey.

The upshot of the whole thing was the boyfriend was supposed to be doing a couples' photo shoot with their cats that day, and he'd accidentally found himself on a lorry heading out of Dublin Port for

Poland. The therapist's frustration resulted in the client, who happened to be Carrie's sister, leaving the salon with a permanent expression of panicked disbelief. Carrie did a wicked impression of her sister at every social gathering for the next three months, with her eyebrows practically in her hairline and her eyes unnaturally wide.

Nadia and Joe wiped their eyes as the story was further embellished by Carrie, clearly a raconteur extraordinaire. She recounted the conversation in a flat Dublin accent, nothing like the mid-Atlantic drawl with the upward inflection she normally used. It turns out she was a brilliant mimic.

She had the whole table in stitches by the end.

'I suppose, like, being in the whole medical thing you totally, like, hate the idea of cosmetic surgery, Sharif?' she asked, her blue eyes innocent. Carmel suspected they may have misjudged Carrie; she wasn't as dumb as she let on.

'I suppose you might think that, Carrie, but in fact, I don't think like that. I think we get one body, and it is an amazing piece of engineering, and if you take care of it, it may last you for a long time and stay in good working order. But equally, if you don't, then that's your choice. Some people like to be vegan, don't drink or smoke, take lots of exercise, and they might live to a hundred, or they might get cancer at twenty-five. Equally, you can abuse some bodies, and they keep on going regardless. Look at Keith Richards.' The whole table laughed. 'I'm in the whole medical thing, as you put it'—he grinned—'at the end of life, when people are dying. And I'm not sure that being very good, no meat, no booze, no Botox, is actually the way to go. In Aashna, we let people do whatever they want. We all have choices, and as Dolly was fond of saying, none of us is getting out of here alive.'

'Well, I think that calls for another bottle of red.' Joe called the waiter. 'We're all going to die anyway, so we might as well live while we can.'

'I totally agree, Joe,' Zeinab said, the first thing she'd said all evening. She'd barely acknowledged Carmel and totally ignored Nadia.

Joe, relieved that her dark mood was lifting at long last, was happy to jolly her along. 'Sure, I know you don't usually, but could I tempt you to a small glass of Malbec from sunny Argentina? It's lovely, so it is, no more than yourself.' He was determined to charm her.

'Well, Joe, if you think I should, then maybe I will. I'm not used to drinking, mind you, so you'll have to catch me if I fall.' She gave one of her tinkly laughs, the ones that drove Nadia insane.

'Oh, there's plenty strong men to lift you if you need it, Zeinab, but I promise it won't come to that. One glass, and we'll have you tucked up in bed.'

'Joe McDaid, I hope you mean alone,' Zeinab tittered. 'I'm a respectable lady.' Carmel noticed that Nadia was gritting her teeth and focusing on her dinner. Nobody else noticed the flirting, really, or they were so used to it now they just ignored her.

Apparently, Joe decided the safest course was to turn to speak to Carmel. 'So, pet, how did it all go today with Tim?'

Just as she was about to reply, Zeinab nearly climbed into Carmel's lap to involve herself in the conversation. It was too much for Nadia.

'Please, Zeinab,' she interrupted, 'perhaps we'll let Joe and Carmel have some time?' Her brown eyes pleaded with her sister to just be normal, but Zeinab was having none of it.

'I'm quite sure Joe is perfectly capable of deciding who he would like to spend time with, Nadia. He does not need you like some kind of human Rottweiler.' Zeinab's voice carried over the hubbub of conversation, and the chat at the table stopped for everyone watch the exchange between the sisters.

Joe, mortified, tried to smooth things over. 'Ah now, ladies, I'm sure we can—'

'No, Joe, please,' Zeinab interrupted. 'I'm sorry if my friendship embarrasses you. I was merely trying to blend in with the lovely friendly Irish ways. Clearly, my sister here thinks otherwise. She denies me a little comfort even in the aftermath of losing my darling Tariq. But some sisters are like that. It is hard to accept, but it is how it is.'

'Zeinab, please,' Sharif tried to intervene. 'Ammi didn't mean anything like that. Let's just all enjoy our dinner—'

'No, Sharif, it must be said. When Khalid died, oh, how she mourned. Going about like a wet week for ages. But yours and Khalid's marriage was so good, so perfect, wasn't it, Nadia?'

Nadia sighed wearily. 'Zeinab, I don't see what that has to do with anything.'

'Zeinab,' Sharif tried again as everyone else looked down at their plates. 'Let's not do this—'

'Sharif, let your mother speak,' Zeinab went on. 'Let her tell us how heartbroken she was, how much sympathy she got from everyone, but when the same thing happens to me, no such consideration. There you are looking so innocent and reasonable, poor Nadia putting up with her sister, isn't she a saint? Don't think I haven't seen the looks, the eye rolling, the martyred expression you have given to Carmel and Sharif behind my back. I'm not blind, you know.'

'Tariq and Khalid were nothing alike,' Nadia said gently. 'Our marriages were totally different. And of course I feel for you, I just... Look, let's discuss this another time.'

Carmel had never seen Nadia so upset. She was shaking, so embarrassed in front of all the McDaids.

'Another time?' Zeinab snapped. 'Why not now? You can give us all some tips on how to have the perfect marriage. She laughed bitterly. 'Oh, yes, the perfect Khalid, the wonderful Khalid, not the same Khalid Khan who had an affair with Shanti Chutani, is it? The girl who was told by your precious Khalid to pack her bags and was sent back to Karachi in disgrace after he used her and then rejected her, making sure his silly wife never found out? She never got to tell her story in London, but you know Karachi, Nadia, gossip spreads like wildfire. I had the whole story within days of Shanti's return. So, to protect my little sister, I confronted him the next time I met him, and you know what he says? It was nothing, a brief affair that meant nothing, and then he begged me not to tell you. So I didn't, out of kindness to you and to his memory. But I see now you are not worthy of such kindness.'

Carmel wanted to run up and wrap her arms around Nadia. Darling, kind Nadia, who'd loved one man her whole life.

'I don't believe you,' Nadia said quietly and stood up, pushing her chair back. Sharif was there, right beside her, and he put his arm around his mother.

'It's not true, Sharif.' She was trying to reassure him, like he was a little boy again, but something on his face stopped her in her tracks. 'It's not... Is it?'

'Come on, Ammi, let's go.' He led her away from the table, and Carmel wanted to follow but Joe put his hand on her knee.

'Maybe give them a second love,' he whispered.

He was right. She loved them both so much, but this was a conversation they needed to have alone.

'So, are we having desserts?' Zeinab asked cheerfully, as if nothing had happened.

CHAPTER 53

*T*he rest of the group finished dinner quickly and made their excuses. Carmel sat with Joe and Zeinab once Luke and Carrie, and Jen, Damien and Sean were gone. Tim had yet to appear, but he was probably still reminiscing with Kitty.

'Should we go to the bar? I think there's music tonight,' Zeinab said brightly, still pretending it was all perfectly normal.

'No, Zeinab,' Joe said. 'I won't anyway, not tonight. And I think Carmel here is in need of a rest too. It's been a long day.'

Though Carmel had known Joe for only a short time in the great scheme of life, she felt connected to him and was getting good at reading his signals. He was clearly disappointed that the future of the trip was now in jeopardy, given what had gone on between Nadia and Zeinab. And the fact that she showed no remorse or even awareness of the hurt her words had caused was not helping.

'Let me buy you one drink, please, as a thank you for organising this lovely holiday.' Zeinab was wheedling now, and it made Carmel cringe.

'I won't,' Joe said, firm, 'and to be entirely honest with you, Zeinab, I think you should find your sister and try to put right some of the damage done here tonight. I'm not claiming to know anything about it, and I don't really know you or your family, but Nadia seems to me to be a very kind person who never has anything but good to say about people. And she was badly hurt this evening.' He stopped short of blaming Zeinab for the hurt caused, but the implication was clear.

'But, Joe, you don't understand,' Zeinab insisted. 'She comes across like that, all sweetness, but she isn't really like that. She—'

'I don't want to get involved,' he interrupted her. 'It's between the two of you to sort it out, but I do know this: we never know when the people we love will be taken from us, anyone, anytime, anyplace. So we shouldn't squander those relationships. Nadia is a good person, as are you, I'm sure, and though we all have our hang-ups and faults, every single one of us, if you don't make things right with her, you'll regret it. That is a fact. Now, Carmel, will we go for a short walk? I feel like I haven't seen you all day.'

'That would be lovely,' Carmel responded. She almost felt sorry for Zeinab sitting alone at the dinner table, but she couldn't think of anything kind to say, so she said nothing.

Joe exhaled heavily as they left the hotel grounds. 'Well, that was unexpected.'

Carmel linked her arm through his as they walked down the main street of Westport, still a hive of activity.

'Is it true, would you say?' he asked.

Carmel thought for a moment. Sharif had revealed the affair to her in confidence ages ago. His father made a confession to him before he died, and Sharif had been so angry, but it was Dolly who talked him down. She told him how sometimes the truth was overrated, and if he had come clean to Nadia all those years ago, she would have left him, and Sharif would have come from a broken home. Nadia and Khalid genuinely had a great marriage, but he'd made one stupid mistake and decided to bear the guilt alone in order to not destroy his family. Eventually, Sharif calmed down and saw it the way Dolly did. But he'd had no idea that Zeinab knew.

Still, there wasn't much point in keeping the secret now, not after Zeinab had blabbed the whole thing out over dinner. And Joe was very discreet anyway. So Carmel decided to tell him the truth.

'Yes. It is.' She explained what Sharif had told her, and Joe listened without interrupting.

'Poor Nadia,' he said, when Carmel was finished. 'That's awful for her. The man is dead, so she can't have it out with him, but now the memories are gone too. She'll see everything they had through this lens now. It's not fair.'

'No, it isn't,' Carmel agreed. 'I love Nadia. I feel like we should have stopped Zeinab, but Sharif had no idea she even knew the story. And when she's on a roll, there's no stopping her anyway. It was horrible for Nadia to find out, but to find out like that, in front of everyone... I don't know. What makes someone be so cruel? To their own sister? I would have loved a sister growing up, and now that I have one, I can't imagine ever hurting Jen like that, or her me.'

Joe put his arm around her shoulders and hugged her close to him. 'I love that you and Jennifer really feel like sisters. And thanks for smoothing the Carrie situation, too. I know Jen was savage when she met her, and I know Carrie comes across a bit ditzy, but Luke is stone mad about her, and she makes him happy, so what's the harm? Jen is over protective of him, always has been, but seeing you be nice to her and keeping the whole thing going changed her. The old Jen would have been farting fire, as my mam would have said, God rest her.'

Carmel pealed with laughter. 'Farting fire, I love that.'

'Seriously, though, having you in the family, it's just brilliant. I'm so delighted. And you hear how, often, when people find their birth families, it doesn't work out. But with us it really has, don't you think?'

Carmel smiled at his need for reassurance.

'It's worked out better than anyone could ever have imagined.' She squeezed his arm. He was so strong, but there was a vulnerability to him that she loved. She thought about it as they walked along in companionable silence.

He came to visit them in London every two months or so, stayed with them, and they all enjoyed it. She called him *Dad* now more than *Joe*, but she never actually said the words 'I love you' to him. But she did love him. He'd never said it, either; the closest he'd come was the

459

day he bought her the Claddagh ring. Though, she was in no doubt about how happy he was to have her in his life.

She wondered now should she say it. Sharif had been the first person to ever say those words to her, ever in her whole life. And, while her friends bandied the words around in a jokey way—like *Much as I love you, we're not seeing that film again* type of way—she'd never said it first to anyone.

The old familiar feelings of insecurity and worry bubbled to the surface again. What if she made a fool of herself? What if he was embarrassed and didn't know what to say? Should she wait for him to say it first?

She took a deep breath. She was going to have to take responsibility for herself and her emotions. Own them, as Nora was fond of saying. Instead of dismissing all her emotions and thought, she was supposed to try to give them airtime. *You're allowed to have feelings*, she told herself.

'Dad?' she began.

'Yes, pet?' he asked, turning his head.

'I love you.'

He let her go and turned towards her, saying nothing. She wondered why he didn't respond until she saw the tears. Joe was a big, tough Irish man, of a certain age, not given to crying fits, so she got a bit of a fright until she realised they were tears of joy.

He said nothing but drew her into a hug.

Eventually, his lips in her hair, he managed to croak, 'I love you too, sweetheart, more than you'll ever know. I wanted to tell you, so often, but I knew you had to come to me, not the other way round. I'd have waited forever, but I'm so glad I don't have to.'

She realised then that she was crying too. 'What are we like?' she managed, when Joe gave her his handkerchief to blow her nose. 'Everyone passing will think we're mental.' People were milling about, all caught up in their own lives.

'Sure, in my case they'd probably be right.' He grinned.

They strolled back as the clock on the top of the main street rang eleven. She texted Sharif.

Is Nadia OK? Will I come back to the room? Can stay in another room if needs be? Xxx

He texted back a few moments later.

She's asleep. I had some mild sedatives in my bag so I gave her two. I'll meet you in the bar in twenty minutes, OK? xxx

As they entered the lobby, they spotted Zeinab sitting on one of the huge overstuffed sofas dotted around the reception area.

Joe glanced over, and Carmel put her hand on his arm. 'I'll talk to her,' she whispered, and Joe nodded.

'I'll be in my room if you need me.' He kissed her cheek and left.

Carmel felt the familiar butterflies as she approached Zeinab. Anything could happen.

'Hi, Zeinab,' she said quietly. 'Can I join you?'

The older woman looked up and locked eyes with Carmel. 'I can't imagine why you'd want to, but yes, sit down.' She sounded exhausted.

'How are you?' Carmel asked.

Zeinab stared straight ahead and eventually sighed. 'I don't know, Carmel. I honestly don't know. I feel...empty inside. I should probably feel something, some remorse for telling Nadia about Khalid's affair, and for...well, for everything really, but I just feel hollow.' Her voice was a monotone, not her usual animated self.

Carmel said nothing but just sat beside her.

'I suppose you and Sharif and everyone hates me now?' She shrugged. 'Of course you do. I'm a terrible, wicked woman. Hurting my sister like that, humiliating her. I deserve your contempt.'

Carmel wasn't sure if this was another of her attempts to garner pity, if she was waiting for everyone to rush over and say, *No, don't be ridiculous, it was nothing.* But she didn't think so. There was a resignation in her voice that Carmel had never heard before.

'I don't think contempt is what we feel, but we are confused. Nadia didn't deserve that. Why did you do it?'

Zeinab turned and looked at Carmel. 'You have lived a long time. It was a long life before you met my nephew, observing, watching, listening. It gives you a certain, I don't know, a sort of stillness, a serenity.'

Carmel didn't know how to take that; it sounded like a compliment, but she couldn't be sure.

Zeinab went on. 'Why did I do it?' She paused and gave a sad little smile. 'Because I hate her. There. I hate my only sister.'

'Why?' Carmel asked, trying to keep the shock from her voice.

Zeinab waved her jewelled hand dismissively. 'Oh, for so many reasons. Our parents loved her more, she was prettier, better at school. She married for love, to someone who loved and respected her, despite what I revealed. He loved her to the day he died, and he was eaten up by guilt but didn't want her or Sharif to suffer for his mistake. Khalid was such a good man.' She sighed, her thoughts straying to the past.

'But you loved Tariq. You're always telling us how good he was...'

Zeinab's harsh laugh rent the air in the quiet lobby. 'Good? Oh, he was good all right. Good at making money, good at having affairs, good at never coming home. Yes, he was excellent at all of those things.'

Carmel had heard as much from Nadia, but it was a shock to hear Zeinab be so candid. 'So because your marriage was a bad one, you wanted to hurt Nadia?'

One part of Carmel felt she had no right to pry, but they were here now, and maybe she could get Zeinab to see how hurtful she had been, and maybe set about fixing the relationship.

Zeinab leaned her head back against the cushions and closed her eyes. As she did, Sharif came out of the lift. Carmel spotted him but shooed him away with her hand. He looked perplexed for a moment but took in the scene and nodded, indicating he was going to the bar.

Zeinab sighed, a sigh of pure weariness that seemed to come from her toes.

'I suppose so. She had everything—the nice life in London, a husband and son who adored the ground she walked on, even a meaningful career. And Dolly, your mother, she and Nadia were so close, and I knew your mother couldn't stand me. Whenever we would visit, I'd see them, the knowing glances, the sympathetic smiles. "Poor you, stuck with your stupid sister again." She chose Dolly over me every time. And, of course, she couldn't stand Tariq. She should have been respectful to him because he was my husband, but she wasn't.'

'Where Tariq was concerned, she had her reasons, Zeinab,' Carmel said. 'It wasn't based on nothing.' She was anxious the conversation stayed in the realm of reality, not some sad narrative of Zeinab's where everyone was mean to her and she didn't deserve any of it.

'She said that to you?' Zeinab snapped her head around to face Carmel once more.

'Yes, she did,' Carmel said honestly. 'She didn't like him because she thought you were worth so much more. She disliked him because he wasn't a good husband to you. Her aversion to him was because she loved you. She knew you married him because it was what your family wanted, and that she was the lucky one who got to defy their wishes because they already had one daughter in a good match, as they saw it. You marrying Tariq set her free. That's how she saw it. And then to see him treat you badly, it upset her. She wanted to be close to you. My mother and Nadia were friends, sure, but there is room for more love in a person's heart. There's always room for more.'

Zeinab smiled. 'For one who hasn't known much love, you seem to believe in it.' The words weren't harsh, just bemused.

'Maybe it's because of that. It's true I never had anyone love me, not for the first forty years of my life—except my mother, and I never got to meet her. But now that I do, I can see how precious it is. It's why I can't understand how someone who has a sister could choose to reject them. I know Nadia wasn't without fault in this. And if you felt left out or whatever when you visited before, then that was wrong too. But what you did tonight was so cruel. And I think you know it too. I don't know if there's any way back for you two, but I really hope there is. And if there is a way you can make it up to her, I think you should try.'

Zeinab rested her body back against the couch again and nodded slowly. 'I'm not a nice person, Carmel. I used to be. I was a kind child. But I don't know, something along the way, I...I just changed, and I don't like who I've become.'

463

There was a cheerless acceptance in her voice.

'Zeinab, people change,' Carmel assured her. 'I'm not the same person I was two years ago. I was afraid of everyone and everything, and I was living out a life of drudgery because I thought that was all I deserved. Then I met Sharif, and everything changed. You've a perception of your life, and maybe some of it is right. Maybe your parents did love Nadia more, she *did* have a great marriage with Khalid, and Tariq treated you badly. Believe me, Zeinab, I know how undermining a toxic relationship can be. But, the point is, Tariq is gone, and you are your own person with your own path to follow. Did you meet Oscar, the yoga teacher at Aashna?'

Zeinab shook her head.

'Well, he used to be an investment banker, making tons of money,' Carmel explained, 'but so miserable—drinking, being a crap husband and father. He had a breakdown and trashed the house, terrified his wife and kids. But look at him now. He's calm and happy. He has a great relationship with his kids and even with his ex. It was hard work earning their trust again, but he stuck at it, and now they love him. People can change, but you have to want to change.

'Maybe get some sleep and see if you can talk to Nadia tomorrow. She's sleeping in our room now, and we'll leave her there. Sharif and I will sleep in Nadia's room. But in the morning, I'll go up to her and see if she'll see you.' Carmel wanted to pin down a plan rather than leave it up in the air. Zeinab could well return to her awful self once the guilt wore off, but if there was a plan, maybe she would follow through with it.

'Very well.' Zeinab dragged herself up and gathered her things. 'Good night, Carmel.'

'Good night, Zeinab.'

As she went to walk away, Zeinab turned back, suddenly looking very old. 'And thank you.'

'You're welcome.' Carmel gave the older woman a smile as she stood and watched her walk slowly towards the lift.

CHAPTER 54

$\mathcal{C}$armel entered the bar, which was still buzzing with people. Sharif was sitting with two gin and tonics, reading a medical journal. She sat beside him.

'I got you one. I imagine you'll need it after that.' He gave her the drink, which she sipped gratefully.

'Thanks.' She exhaled fully. 'What a day.'

'What happened with Zeinab? That conversation looked pretty intense.'

'Well, I think she regrets what she did to your mum, but she's just so...I don't know...like her life has been kind of empty, and she feels like it's OK to be mean or something. But she's full of guilt and shame and self-loathing. She feels like Nadia got everything and she got nothing out of life. It's just hard to connect with her.'

Sharif sighed. 'I just can't believe she would do that to Ammi, you know? She is devastated, really heartbroken. It's so hard to watch.'

Carmel put the glass down and tried to process that last fifteen minutes. 'Well, as I said, she knows that what she did was horribly cruel. And she admits she was jealous of your mother and that her marriage to Tariq was terrible. She was more open and honest than I've ever seen her. She seems to think she's an awful person, and I think she wants to apologise to Nadia but is not expecting her forgiveness. I told her to leave it until the morning, that Nadia's sleeping now, so we'll see. How is she?'

'If she does forgive her, it's going to take time,' Sharif said. 'I've never seen her so crushed, even when he died. It's like every memory is tainted or something, and she's angry with me, too, for knowing and not saying it. I tried telling her—I explained all about going to Dolly when I wanted to hit him I was so angry, and how she talked about the truth being overrated. I tried to say what Dolly would say if she were here. That my father loved her and only her his entire life and that he made one stupid mistake and regretted it instantly. It wasn't an affair as Zeinab made out. It was a onetime thing. He regretted it immediately, and he was torn apart with guilt and shame.'

Carmel sighed and held his hand. 'Let's just see how things go in the morning. Honestly, this feels like the longest day in history. It's been a roller coaster.' She leaned against him, and he put his arm around her while she told him about the exchange between herself and Joe.

'Well, the situation with Ammi and Zeinab might be broken permanently,' Sharif said, 'but for Tim and that young couple and his friend Kitty, it's a happy-ever-after, so the day wasn't a total washout. I'm so glad you and Joe are getting even closer. We don't stop needing our parents just because we grow up. I have that with my mother, as you know… Or at least I did.'

'She'll forgive you, Sharif, of course she will. But she's hurting, and we have to give her time.'

He sighed. 'When I was starting out, in Aashna—actually, even before that—it was Ammi who always backed me. She was there beside me and Jamilla, when Jamilla got sick, and when we had to end our baby's life, she was there. When Jamilla died, it was Ammi I called. And then, setting up Aashna, she has always been there, right by my side. Such loyalty is rare in life, even from blood relatives. And now she thinks I betrayed her. My father did. That is a fact. But she believes I should have told her. Maybe she's right. She's been so steadfast, so dedicated to my happiness and success, and now, well, now, everything is different.'

Carmel heard the desolation in his voice and longed to help, but there was nothing she could do.

'I think I'll take her back home tomorrow. Is that OK? I don't think she can keep going with the trip now, after everything. Can you understand that?'

Carmel felt a panic. Was he leaving her? She forced herself to be calm. 'Well, I'll go with you. I don't want to leave you to do that on your own, and I—'

He turned and faced her, holding both her hands in his. 'My darling girl, please don't do that. I know how much you were looking forward to this wedding and how Joe can't wait to show you off to everyone. This is a really big thing for you, and I do wish I could be in two places at once, but Ammi needs me now. And you'll have Joe and Luke and Jen and everyone, while she only has me. I was so low after Jamilla died, she didn't leave my side for weeks, making me eat, talking, not talking, just being this constant strong presence. And having that helped me get through those first horrific months. I can't let her down now, even if she's angry with me. She needs me. I know you might feel a bit intimidated facing that gang on your own, but you won't be on your own, my love. You'll have your family, the ones who will love you as much as I do. I've been thinking about it, and this is the only thing that makes sense, so I'll take Ammi home tomorrow.'

He glanced at his watch. 'Actually, we should probably go in a couple of hours and try to get to Shannon in time for the first flight back to London. Zeinab can stay here, or go back to Pakistan or... Well, to be honest, I don't care what she does. But you go on to the wedding as planned, and then you can fly home to me when it's all over and you've met your family.'

His chocolate-brown eyes were pleading with her to understand and give in, but she dreaded the thought of him leaving her. She knew she was being pathetic, and of course she had Joe and everyone, but Sharif was her rock. Still, she would have to do it, let him be with Nadia. His mother needed him more right now.

'Of course, come back with me if you really want to,' he said, trying again. 'I'm not laying down the law here, I know better than that.' He grinned. 'But I believe it would be best for you and I really think you'd regret it if you missed out on the chance to meet your whole family.'

'It's fine, Sharif, and you're right. I should stay. Joe would be so disappointed if I left, and Nadia really does need you. OK, I'm a big girl.' She smiled weakly. 'I can do this. The wedding is on Saturday, so that's the day after tomorrow, and I'll fly home either Sunday or Monday.'

They went to bed in Nadia's room, and Sharif booked himself and his mother on the first flight back to London. Eventually, they fell asleep, entwined in each other's arms. She woke when his alarm went off, though the room was still in darkness.

'Go back to sleep, my love,' he whispered. 'I'll call you later, when we're back at Aashna. I'm just going to get Ammi.'

He kissed her gently and tucked her in. He dressed quickly, and as all his things were in the other room, he was ready to leave in a matter of moments. They'd packed Nadia's things the night before, so he just needed to bring her suitcase with him. He rubbed Carmel's head and bent over her to kiss her goodbye.

'I love you,' she murmured.

'I love you too,' he replied.

She must have drifted back to sleep, because when she woke an hour later, it took her a moment to remember where she was.

She lay there, in the dark. The distant sounds of occasional traffic and the odd muffled conversation from the car park behind the hotel was all she could hear. She pulled the blanket up to her chin, and soon she wasn't forty-one, she was seven or eight again, in her small iron bed in Trinity House. A memory returned, of a nun, Sister Bridget, who had been very kind. She played with the children and showed exceptional warmth; all the kids loved her. One day, Carmel had made her a card at school. It was coming up to Mother's Day, and all the other children were making Mother's Day cards, so she decided to make one for Sister Bridget. She was so proud of it—it had a blue butterfly on the front, and inside she had written in her best writing: *To Sister Bridget, happy mother's day, love Carmel.*

She didn't let any of the girls in her class see it, because she didn't want to have to explain. But it felt so good to have someone to make a card for.

When she'd gotten back to Trinity, there'd been no sign of Sister Bridget, and when she asked Mother Patrick, the Reverend Mother who ran Trinity, where she was, she got a curt, 'Sister Bridget has gone to another convent. She won't be coming back.'

Carmel couldn't believe Sister Bridget would go without saying a word. Just leave. She was heartbroken, and she scrunched up the card she had taken such care to make and cried tears silently into her pillow.

As an adult, she'd once asked what had ever become of Sister Bridget, and one of the care workers who had been there the longest said that poor old Sister Bridget suffered from her nerves. She'd apparently imagined some kind of relationship between her and Father Delaney, who said mass in Trinity once a week, so she had to be moved for her own sake, before she disgraced herself and the entire congregation.

That was the last time Carmel had experienced such an acute sense of loss. She had loved and been let down, and she'd vowed at age eight never to get that close to anyone again. It was a promise easy to keep all those years—nobody ever tried to get close to her. But Sharif, he changed all that.

She knew she was being ridiculous—it was only a few days, and she'd survived for over forty years on her own before she met him—but she could not shake the bereft feeling she felt in his absence. She got up and dressed and went back to their room. It was still early, and the others probably weren't up yet.

All of her things were where she'd left them, but all of Sharif's stuff was gone. She sat on the bed, took the pillow from his side and held it to her face. It still smelled faintly of him, the woody, spicy scent he always wore. She held it close and allowed the tears to come.

469

CHAPTER 55

*C*armel was trying and failing to read a book when the sound of gentle tapping came on her bedroom door.

'Who is it?' she asked through the door, suddenly nervous.

'It's Zeinab.' Her voice was uncertain.

The very last person on earth Carmel wanted to see was Zeinab. But she'd have to open the door.

Zeinab stood there, looking positively dowdy compared to usual. Gone were all the jewels and the heavy makeup, and her hair didn't even have its usual sparkly clips. She wore a plain dark plum-coloured *shalwar kameez*.

'Carmel, I'm sorry to come so early, but I just wanted to—'

'Zeinab,' Carmel stopped her. 'I'm sorry, but they're gone. Both Sharif and Nadia, back to London. They left early this morning.'

Zeinab must have heard the despair in her voice. 'I'm sorry.'

'Yeah, me too.' Carmel couldn't summon up the strength to be anything but blunt.

'Is everything OK between you and them, you and Sharif?' Zeinab took in the empty room, Carmel's bloodshot eyes.

'Yes, fine, but I decided I wanted to stay and go to my cousin's wedding. My dad has gone to lots of trouble for us to be here, so it wouldn't have been fair on him if I just took off. But Nadia couldn't face it, not after everything.'

'This is all my fault, isn't it?' Zeinab spoke quietly.

Carmel didn't answer.

'So what should I do now?' the other woman asked.

'I have no idea, not one,' Carmel responded wearily. Last night, Zeinab had seemed so despondent, and she still was, but not to the same extent. And anyway, the more Carmel thought about it, the more appalled she was at what Zeinab had done.

'Does Joe know they are gone? Should we tell him?'

Carmel thought she detected a bit of enthusiasm in Zeinab's voice. Surely, she wasn't still trying to have a crack at her father, after everything? The woman was incorrigible.

'*We* won't tell him anything, Zeinab. If *anyone* is going to speak to *my* father about this situation, it is me.'

'But what should I do? I'm at a loss...' Zeinab wanted Carmel to solve her problems and salve her conscience, and Carmel was in no position to do either of those things.

'That's up to you, Zeinab. I don't know what you should do, to be honest, but I do know that Nadia doesn't want to see you, so if you do go back to London, perhaps make arrangements to collect your things from her house through Sharif or something. Maybe going back to Pakistan is the best option, for now, anyway?'

'Well, I don't want to miss the wedding. I mean, Joe did invite me, and it would be so rude—'

Thankfully, they were interrupted by Carmel's phone ringing. 'Sorry, Zeinab, I've to take this...'

She managed to hustle the old woman out the door and gratefully shut it after her.

'HI, Jen,' she answered the phone.

'Hi, Carmel, are you all OK?' Jen sounded hesitant. 'I wanted to call last night, just to check, but I didn't know...'

'I'm fine, Jen. Well, fine is probably a bit strong, but I'm all right. Sharif and Nadia are gone back to London...' She filled Jen in on the rest of the night's events, and her sister was supportive and sympathetic.

'I'm so glad you're staying for the wedding, though, I really am. Don't worry, you won't be on your own for a second. We move as a pack, us McDaids.' Jen was joking, but she seemed to sense Carmel's anxiety at facing the whole family without Sharif by her side. She ended the call arranging to meet Jen for breakfast in an hour. She was going to get Joe and Luke to come, too, but just the four of them. So they could have breakfast together as a family.

She texted Sharif, knowing he wouldn't even be landed yet.

Have a safe flight. I love you and Nadia.

She pressed send and threw the phone on the bed. As it landed, it pinged. A text.

She grabbed the phone but saw it was only from Zane.

Alrite luvburdz? Out clubbin' Ivanka is to blame.#deadbodytomo #workinhospicejoke Miss yo' sweet lil'Irish face. Zxxx

Normally, she loved to get his messages—he always cheered her up —but not now. He always called her and Sharif *luvburdz*. It was kind of an in-joke after he planned their engagement party last year, threatening to have a hundred white doves delivered.

Suddenly, the room seemed to be closing in on her. She needed some air. She pulled on some tracksuit bottoms and a t-shirt, slipped into her trainers, and let herself out. The streets of Westport were almost deserted. There was the odd milk truck or delivery van, but the tourists had not yet surfaced after the revelry the night before.

She walked fast, almost trying to run away from her own thoughts swirling frantically round her head. She tried to rationalise the feelings of abandonment and the frustration with herself at feeling so frightened and alone. She had her family here, she'd lived without Sharif for forty years, and now she was distraught at spending a few days away from him. It was stupid. She knew it. But Nora was teaching her that her reactions were informed by her experiences. Her fear of abandonment, her fear of being alone all stemmed from her childhood.

Round and round the thoughts went, and she was getting more

and more frustrated with herself. In the pocket of her hoodie, she found her earphones. She liked to listen to podcasts when she walked at home, so she stuck them in her ears. She scrolled to her podcasts and selected a Wayne Dyer one. His lovely voice always soothed her, and he seemed to always know the right thing to say.

She was engrossed in her phone so she never saw the broken pavement, or the van that was going too fast, too close to the kerb.

* * *

SHARIF'S PHONE FLASHED 'INCOMING CALL' as he waited at the carousel at Heathrow. His mother had hardly said a word since they left Ireland, except to ask why Carmel wasn't coming back with them. He explained that she'd be back in a few days, that she was going to go to the wedding—he never mentioned her speaking to Zeinab—and that everything was going to be OK. She was still a little sedated, and for that, he was grateful.

'Hello,' he answered his phone.

'Sharif? It's Tim.'

'Oh, hi, Tim, em... My mother and I are actually back in Lon—'

'I know,' Tim interrupted. 'Zeinab said. I'm sorry to have to tell you this, but there's been an accident.'

'What happened?'

'It's Carmel. She's been knocked down by a van. The young fool driving it was out late and drove to work early this morning, he was over the limit. Carmel is in Galway Hospital. She was taken from the scene by ambulance.'

Sharif felt sick; blood pounded in his ears. 'How is she?' Is she badly hurt?'

'I don't know, Sharif. Joe and Luke are following the ambulance in the hire car. I actually came on the accident. I stayed at my friend's house last night and was walking back to the hotel early this morning. She must have gone out for a walk or a run or something. She was wearing sports clothes, anyway. The paramedics wouldn't let me go with her, and the guards wanted to talk to me as well, get her details and all of that. That's how I know the driver was drunk.'

Sharif swallowed. 'Was she conscious?'

'I don't think so, Sharif.' Tim sounded so upset. 'I'm sorry.'

'And was she injured—I mean—could you see any external injuries?'

There was a pause.

'There seemed to be a lot of blood. I'm sorry, Sharif. I'll go to the hospital now. Jen and Damien are coming, too. I'll ring again when I know more.'

'I'm on my way back, Tim. I'll get the next flight hopefully.'

Shaking, Sharif went over to where his mother was standing.

'Ammi, Carmel's had an accident. She's been knocked down. Tim just called. She's in an ambulance on the way to hospital, and he said she wasn't conscious and there was a lot of blood.' He was trying to stop the panic rising up in him.

'Come on, get to the desk and get a flight back.' The news seemed to have jolted Nadia out of her trance-like state. 'Move, Sharif, come on.' She grabbed him by the arm and pulled him to the Aer Lingus desk.

They explained the situation, and the woman on the desk was very understanding but told them the flight was fully booked and the next available flight wasn't until seven that evening.

'But you can go on standby, and if someone cancels—'

'Not good enough,' Nadia muttered and left the desk, headed to the security queue.

'Is anyone flying to Shannon?' she yelled on the top of her voice. People stopped and stared at this tiny Asian woman asking over and over for people flying to Shannon. Eventually, a young couple said they were.

Nadia stood before them. 'If you let me and my son take your seats, I will give you a thousand pounds in cash right this minute. I will go to the cash point over there and draw it out and hand it over. All you need to do is come with me to the Aer Lingus desk and tell them we are taking your seats. It's an absolute emergency, my daughter-in-law in critically ill in hospital, and we need to get to her.'

The couple looked at each other. The boy wasn't keen, but the girl, said, 'It's fine. We can stay another night.'

'Marvellous.' Nadia led them to the Aer Lingus desk, and Sharif went to the cash point. They handed over the money.

The change of name was done, and Sharif and Nadia had to run to make the flight, their luggage presumably still circling the belt in the arrivals hall.

Nadia took total charge as Sharif tried over and over to contact the hospital. Carmel was in Accident and Emergency so was not yet on the hospital system, he was told. Eventually, he managed to get through to the Emergency Department.

'A and E, Moira speaking.'

'Hello, my name is Dr Sharif Khan. My wife Carmel Khan was admitted in the past hour, a road accident?' He tried to keep the panic and frustration out of his voice. He knew firsthand the level of pressure staff in emergency medicine were under, and he also knew adding to it wasn't going to get him very far.

'OK, let me check. Please hold.'

Some horrible tinny music played while he waited. He began to think she'd forgotten about him, but he continued to hold as his mother showed both passports and they boarded the plane. She found their seats, and he still waited. The music was on a loop, and he felt the ridiculous tune drilling into his brain.

'Sir, you'll need to end your call.' The stewardess tapped his shoulder. 'We are about to take off.' She was about fifty, and despite a lot of makeup, she still looked like a bulldog chewing a wasp, so Sharif didn't defy her. He had seen people removed from flights for security infractions in the opinion of the cabin crew, so he couldn't take a chance. 'Now, sir,' she added, with a steely glare.

Reluctantly, he pressed end. It was an hour and ten minutes to Shannon, and the cabin crew were just going through the security demonstration. He glanced at his watch. *9.15.* They'd be there by

10.30, rent a car, and he could be in Galway an hour later if he put the boot down. But what if he was too late?

He couldn't allow himself to think like that. She was going to be OK. She had to be OK.

Nadia leaned over and put her hand on his as they took off, back to Ireland.

He looked at her. 'I should never have left her. If I—'

'Sharif, stop this now. We must pray that our darling girl is all right. Nothing else matters.'

'But if I hadn't left her—she didn't want to stay alone...'

'Why?'

Sharif ran his hands through his silver hair. 'I talked her into staying for the wedding. She wanted to come with us. What will I do, Ammi, what if she dies? I can't go through it again. She might die—she might be dead already...'

Nadia had only ever seen Sharif like this once before, when Jamilla had died. She knew it was hard for him, he was so worried, but he needed to calm down.

'Stop that now. Sharif Khan, you need to pull yourself together. Your wife needs you, and we'll find out how she is the moment the plane touches down. But for now, we will just pray to Allah to keep her safe.'

For the first time in his adult life, Sharif prayed. He asked Allah to keep Carmel safe. He didn't know who or what, if anything, he was speaking to—Allah, God, Buddha, the Universe, something, nothing, some power other than himself, something stronger than him, some force to keep her alive.

He shook his head when the same stewardess offered him tea or coffee; he couldn't swallow anything. After what felt like an interminable hour, the captain announced to the cabin crew that they should take their seats for landing, and the lights to indicate no more walking in the cabin came on. Sharif wondered if he could get a signal on his phone as they came into land, he decided to risk it, despite the clear instruction not to switch it on until the plane had landed. He didn't care what the Aer Lingus woman thought—he took out his phone and switched it on. *Searching for network* flashed up on the screen.

He pressed several buttons in frustration. Still searching for network. They disembarked, and as they hustled their way through the crowd to get to the immigration desk, he was so glad of his British passport. His mother had one, too, which spared them the added wait of travelling through the much longer Non-EU queue they would have had to endure on their Pakistani passports.

Ping. A text.

Welcome to Ireland...

Sharif rejected the text, and two more, both offering competitive rates for roaming. He rejected them instantly. Then one from Joe.

At hospital now. No news.

And one from Tim.

Carmel in ER. Team with her. She's alive but no other update.

Sharif showed it to Nadia, too relieved to speak. Then he found Joe's number in his phone and rang it.

It was answered on the first ring. 'Sharif, it's Jen.'

'How is she?'

'Dad is just gone off with someone now. We're waiting for him to come back. I'm not supposed to have the phone on here. One sec, I'll go outside and ring you back. Where are you?'

'At the airport, I'm just renting a car now. Call me as soon as you can.' He hung up and relayed what she'd said to Nadia.

Nadia dealt with the car hire, shoving things to sign at him, taking his driving licence and credit card out of his wallet, nudging him to enter the pin. Eventually, it was all done. Sharif just stared at the phone, waiting for Jen to call back.

He knew the protocol well. If a doctor had good news to deliver, he or she was usually happy do it in front of the gathered family or friends. If it was bad news, they took the next of kin aside.

He couldn't bear to go further down that line of thought. Why wasn't Jen ringing back? He tried Tim.

It rang out. He hung up, frustrated.

Then the phone rang. Joe.

'Sharif, it's Joe.' His tone was terse. 'Tell me.'

'She's going to be OK.'

Relief flooded his body. He felt tears of relief well up in his eyes.

'I... I'm just so relieved. I'm on the way. How bad are her injuries? Tim said there was a lot of blood. What happened?

There was a long pause, and then he heard Joe's voice.

'She was out walking or running or something when she was knocked down by a van. She did lose a lot of blood, but the ambulance arrived quickly. They're taking her to theatre now to set the broken bones in her arm and leg. She had a fracture to her skull, as well, but they think it's not too serious. No internal bleeding as far as they can see, but she'll have a scan when she goes down to theatre.' Joe's voice had softened.

'OK. Is she even a little aware?' Sharif asked.

'I haven't seen her, just spoke to the head of the assessment team, and that's all he told me. They're fairly sure there's nothing internally, and her vital signs are strong.'

'Well, if you get the chance to see her, can you ring me? I want to speak to her, even just for a second.'

'OK, I will. Drive safely. Oh, Sharif, is Nadia with you?'

'Yes. Do you want to speak to her?'

Joe hesitated. 'Ah no, I'll see you both in a bit.'

CHAPTER 56

$\mathcal{J}$en, Damien, Zeinab, Tim and Joe all sat in the hospital canteen sipping drinks they didn't want. Luke and Carrie were gone back to the hotel to get some of Carmel's things. She'd been in surgery for two hours now, and there was no word. The nurse had told them to go off and get a coffee and she'd call them when Carmel was back from theatre.

Luckily, an old college friend of Jen's was married to a Galway man and they lived there now, so she offered to mind Sean. She had a little girl of more or less the same age, so he went off happily.

When Sharif and Nadia arrived to the Emergency Department, They went in search of the rest of the family and guessed the café.

As they entered the café, the others stood up. Seeing the whole family there made Sharif even more worried. If it was just a broken arm, surely, they would have gone home.

Zeinab kept her distance, and neither Sharif nor Nadia acknowledged her.

Nadia went straight to Joe, who drew her into his arms for a hug. Seeing her seemed to melt his stoic exterior. 'My poor girl. Hasn't she had enough crap to deal with already? I'm glad you're here,' he mumbled, so only Nadia could hear.

'Yes, well, Sharif had to come back. We should never have—'

'I'm glad he's back too, obviously,' Joe interrupted her, glancing to see Sharif in chat with Jen, Tim and Damien. 'He is of course who she'll want to see, but...' He looked around to verify—Zeinab had gone to the ladies'. 'But I'm glad you're back,' he said.

She looked up at him. He wasn't letting her go.

'I'm glad to be back, tooWhat's the latest?' Nadia asked.

Just as he was about to tell her what he knew, his phone rang. 'Hello, Joe McDaid.' The others all turned to watch him. 'Right, great,' he said into the phone. Then there was a pause. 'Yes, he just arrived... Sure... Right. Thanks.'

They all stared at him, faces expectant, as he hung up.

'She's back and seems OK,' he said. 'The doctors want to see you, Sharif. The rest of us are to wait here, and they'll let us know when we can see her. She's in Recovery. Follow along the green tile, and it's signposted, the nurse said.'

Sharif didn't need to be told twice and virtually bolted out of the canteen. He passed medical staff of all varieties and saw nothing. Normally, he was very interested in hospitals and how different places did things, but now all he wanted was to see Carmel. He found Recovery easily and gave his name at the reception desk.

'She's in cubicle four, second on the left. The curtains are pulled, but you can just go in.'

He found her spot and heard voices coming from the other side of the curtains. So often in his life he'd been the one the family were quizzing, needing information, some good news. It felt strange to be on this side of it again.

He parted the curtains, and there she was. Her blonde hair was matted with blood, her face bruised. Her arm was in a plaster cast from wrist to shoulder, and her leg was covered by a metal cage to keep the blankets off it. All the injuries seemed to be on the right side.

'I'm Sharif Khan, Carmel's husband,' he introduced himself to the very young-looking African doctors consulting at Carmel's bedside.

'Hello, Dr Khan, oncology?' the shorter of the two said with a smile. 'Carmel's aunt mentioned it.'

'Yes, that's right. How is she?' The last thing on his mind was Zeinab. He could just picture it: *My nephew is an oncologist you know!* Guaranteed to annoy the medical staff treating their patient. They would do their best if her husband was a binman or a plasterer either.

'She's OK. Mild linear open fracture to the skull, but neurosurgery had a look at the x-ray and are confident painkillers will do, no need for their involvement. There's no evidence of cognitive impairment. There's a fracture to the ulna, distal, and a tibia fracture as well.'

'Is that it?' Sharif asked.

'Yes, she's been fully scanned,' the doctor told him, 'though it would have been better to know about the pregnancy before the MRI. But your wife was unresponsive in the ambulance. She woke up briefly in the A&E pre-theatre, but we sedated her. Thankfully, baby seems to have survived the jolt, and the heartbeat is good and strong.'

Sharif sat down on the seat beside Carmel's head.

'I didn't know, we... I don't think Carmel knew either...' He was trying to sound coherent. 'We were trying, but...'

'Well, it's a dramatic way to find out all right, I suppose.' The taller doctor chuckled. 'Yes, she's about six weeks, so its early days, but everything looks fine. Congratulations.'

When they left, Sharif just sat watching Carmel.

She was pregnant. He was going to be a father.

An hour ago, he was afraid he might lose her, and now, here she was, growing their child inside her poor broken body. Six weeks. He knew she was on the pill, but he was trying to think back. Then he remembered the bout of food poisoning—vomiting and diarrhoea could render the contraceptive pill ineffective. That must have been it. He was sure she had no idea. She would have said.

He rubbed the uninjured side of her head, brushing her hair back off her forehead. The injury to her skull meant the skin was broken, dark blood congealing around her ear. The bruising was extensive; she was going to be very sore for a few weeks, and there would have to be physio to get the range of movement back in her wrist and ankle. But she was alive.

He kissed her head and held her hand. With his free hand, he texted Joe.

She's still sedated. Set her wrist and leg and stitched up her head. The bruising is extensive but she's ok. Only one visitor today but come on your own and I'll sneak you in for a second?

Almost immediately, the response came.

On my way

Joe appeared at her bedside ten minutes later, and he held one of her hands while Sharif held the other.

'She'll probably be out of it for another hour or so,' Sharif spoke quietly.

'Maybe I'll let the others get back. We were to check out and move on today, but now we're probably best off staying put till we know what the situation is.'

'You should all continue, of course,' Sharif insisted. 'Carmel is going to be fine. I'll be with her. You should all go.'

'I don't know, we'll see, Sharif. The way things are with your mother and Zeinab is another thing. Nadia has had enough upset. I don't want any more. But Zeinab has been very nice, trying to be helpful and all of that. I think she is really sorry.'

Sharif sighed. 'Nearly losing my wife this morning puts everything into perspective. What Zeinab did was cruel and hurtful, but, I should know this better than most, we never get enough time, we all leave too soon, and there's not a moment to waste on anger or bitterness. If my mother accepts her apology, we'll leave it at that. But it's up to Ammi.'

They sat in companionable silence as Carmel rested on. She'd get a fright when she woke up, but the injury was all superficial, Sharif could tell. *It will take a few months, but she'll be fine.* He watched her. How would she take the pregnancy news? He imagined she would be thrilled. He hadn't really allowed himself to think about it much, his overriding emotion being relief that she was OK.

'If I hadn't gone off like that...' If he'd stayed, she would have been in bed with him, not running around Westport.

Joe sighed. 'Did you ever hear the phrase, *if wishes were horses, beggars would ride?* You were looking out for your mam. Nobody could have predicted this.'

Sharif nodded.

'Now, I'd better get back to the others, though, to be honest I'd rather stay here, just to be 100 percent sure. But you'll look after her, I suppose, and poor old Nadia will need a bit of back up.' Joe rose from his seat and bent to kiss Carmel's head gently. 'I'll be back later on, pet, and Sharif is staying here. You'll be fine, darling, don't you worry. We're all looking after you.'

Sharif stood.

'Let me know when she wakes, OK?'

'I will. And thanks for taking care of my mother. She's very fragile right now.'

Joe smiled. 'I know, and she got an awful blow, but she's a tough old bird your mam. She'll be fine.'

Sharif chuckled. 'I'm not sure she'd be happy to be described as a tough old bird.'

'Ah, Nadia knows I'm only joking. Sure, I'm fierce fond of her.' Joe felt in his pockets for his keys. As he turned to go, Sharif heard himself say,

'Are you?'

'Am I what?' Joe replied.

'Fond of Ammi?' Sharif looked directly at his father-in-law.

Joe coloured slightly, uncomfortable with the turn the conversation had taken. 'Well, I...'

'All I'm saying,' Sharif interrupted, 'is if you do like her, as more than a friend, Carmel and I are happy for you.' Suddenly life was so precious, every single minute, because you never knew what was around the corner. 'And I think Ammi might feel the same way,' he added. 'If you don't, no harm done, and we won't talk about this again. But I just wanted to give you a bit of an edge. We men so rarely have that when dealing with the fairer sex, don't we?'

Joe blustered. 'Well, I don't know about that... Sure, we're a bit old for all of that stuff now and ... Well, sure... Anyway, I better get going, and you'll give me a shout when Carmel wakes, right?'

'Of course.' Sharif smiled and went back to his wife. After an hour of just sitting there, his thoughts racing, trying to rationalise the last few days, Carmel's consultant appeared on his rounds.

'Good afternoon. I'm Donnacha O'Halloran. Your wife is under my care.'

Sharif stood and shook his hand. 'Sharif Khan. Thanks for all you have done for her. If you hadn't worked so quickly to stem the bleeding...'

'Well, it was the paramedic really. She was in bad shape coming in to us, but if it weren't for them, she'd be a lot worse. The nurse on duty tells me you're an oncologist?' He checked the chart hanging on the end of Carmel's bed as they spoke.

'Yes, I—well, we actually, Carmel and I and my mother—run a hospice in London.'

The doctor checked Carmel's vital signs and her IV line. He briefly gave Sharif the update of her progress, and as he did, Carmel's eyelids fluttered.

They both turned, and Sharif went straight to her.

'Sha... Sharif,' she managed, her voice raspy.

He held a Styrofoam cup of water to her dry lips, and she sipped and swallowed. Her eyes closed again.

'It's fine, Carmel, I'm here. Just go back to sleep. I'll be here when you wake up.'

CHAPTER 57

The other doctor left, and Sharif just held her hand. Over the next twenty minutes, she regained consciousness.

Eventually, she made another attempt to speak.

'My head hurts. What happened to me?'

'You were knocked down, my love, but the ambulance came quickly and you're going to be fine,' he soothed. 'A bit sore, but apart from a broken arm and a broken leg, you're OK.'

'Everything hurts,' she croaked.

'I know, my love. You got a few nasty cuts and bruises, so that's why you feel so sore, but now you're awake we can get your meds regulated to manage the pain.'

'OK.' She sighed and seemed content to drift back to sleep.

As she dozed, half in and half out of consciousness, Sharif texted Joe.

She's awake and talking, but very tired. If you're coming back I'd say give her another hour at least.

Joe messaged back instantly.

What a relief. See you later.

The next time Carmel woke, Sharif called the nurse, who administered some painkillers, and within twenty minutes, Carmel was much more alert and seemed comfortable enough.

'Carmel, I'm so sorry,' Sharif said. 'I should not have gone off like that. I feel so guilty. This is my fault...' He knew he shouldn't be laying this heavy stuff on her so soon after her surgery, but he needed her to know how sorry he was.

'It's OK,' she whispered and swallowed. He offered her some more water, and she smiled weakly.

'I love you. So much. When I thought it was worse, Carmel, I...' His voice cracked.

'You won't get rid of me that easy.' She smiled again and added, 'Can you help me sit up a bit? My back is sore.'

'Of course.' He lifted her gently, making sure her leg wasn't dragged, and though she winced in pain, she relaxed back against the cushions. She put her hand to her face.

'My face feels all...I don't know...puffy or something.'

He gently removed her hand from the worst of the bruising. 'I know, and you have a bit of bruising and swelling to your face, but it will go down in a few weeks. You'll look a bit colourful for a while though.' He smiled and kissed her palm as he placed her hand back beside her hip.

'Oh God, do I look desperate?' she groaned.

'You look gorgeous, and what's more, you look alive. At this moment in time, that is all that matters to me.'

She grimaced. 'I don't feel very gorgeous, I can tell you.'

He was sure she didn't know about the baby. She would have asked about it first if she did. 'Carmel.'

He paused, and she turned her head slowly, the pain registering on her face. 'What?'

'When they brought you in, they did a scan to check for internal injuries, and in the course of that, they discovered something.'

What bit of colour she'd had drained from her face. She swallowed and winced.

'Tell me. Don't drag it out, just say it. Is it bad?'

'No.' He smiled. 'it's very good. You're pregnant, six weeks roughly, and the baby is fine. Heartbeat is strong, and the accident didn't do any damage to him or her.'

Carmel said nothing. She just stared at him.

'Are you OK? This is great, isn't it?'

She nodded. Her good hand went to her abdomen and rested there. 'Are they sure? That everything is OK?' Tears slid from her eyes. Could what he was telling her possibly be true?

'Yes, everything is fine. Our little prince or princess is cosy and happy in there.' He placed his hand on top of hers.

'And you're happy? Like really, not just saying it because you think it's what I want?'

Sharif held her good hand in both of his and leaned close to her, his face only inches from hers.

'I'm going to be honest. I wasn't sure, even when I said we'd try. I was partly doing it to please you. If you'd said you never wanted kids, then that would have suited me fine. But now, knowing our son or daughter exists, Carmel...' He swallowed, trying to get the words out. 'All the time you were sedated, I just sat here, knowing, imagining what he or she will be like, what they'll look like, sound like. What it will feel like to have someone call me Abba...'

'Like the Swedish pop group?' She chuckled but stopped instantly —it hurt to laugh.

He grinned. 'No, it's Urdu for Da-'

'I know, you eejit, I'm only messing.' She smiled on her good side then sighed. 'I can't believe it. We're going to have a baby. I'm going to be a mammy, like some person is going to call me that. Mammy and Abba. The poor kid will be culturally confused.'

'We can send them to an Islamic school taught through Irish maybe?'

She laughed. 'Stop. You can't make me laugh!' She groaned again. 'I feel like I've gone ten rounds with Mike Tyson. Every bit of me hurts.'

'OK. Misery and tragedy from now on, I promise.'

'Stop it I said!' She tried not to laugh.

'OK... OK. I don't want Dr O'Halloran throwing me out for

distressing his patient. Are you sleepy? Will I let you rest? I can just sit here, and you sleep if you want to.'

'No, I don't feel sleepy. Sore and a bit groggy still, but I've slept enough. Can we talk about the baby? I just can't believe it. I never thought for a second that it could really happen for me. Having someone of my own, like, I know I have you and Joe and all the family, but a baby, my own child...' She was still trying to make it a reality in her head.

'Do you think it's a boy or a girl?' Sharif asked.

'A girl.' Her answer was instant and definite.

'You sound sure.'

'I don't know why, but I do, I think it's a girl. What will we call her?'

'Isn't it obvious? There's only one name our daughter could have.'

'Dolly Khan. I like it.'

Sharif leaned over and gently kissed her abdomen. 'Hello in there, little Dolly. This is your abba, and I love you already, so very much. So be a good little girl and grow healthy and strong, and your mammy and I will be waiting to meet you next spring.'

Carmel rubbed his head with her good hand as he spoke to their baby. 'How... I'm amazed. I was taking the pill until recently...'

'I think that dodgy sushi is what we have to thank. You were throwing up for days, and that interrupts the effectiveness of any drugs in the system.'

Moments later, the porter arrived with a senior staff nurse.

'We're going to take you to the ward now, Carmel. You'll be with us for a few days, just till we can be sure everything is healing properly, OK?' The nurse was already preparing the bed for transport.

'I don't think I can get up...' Carmel started to panic.

'No, we won't be getting you up at all,' the nurse explained. 'We'll wheel the bed up and leave you in it. Now, if your husband could just move out of my way?' She remarked pointedly. He stepped into the corner of the small room made a face behind her back, which made Carmel giggle.

Thankfully, a private room was available, and she was soon settled in.

'Is my phone dead?' Carmel asked.

'I'm afraid so, but I'll get you a new one just as soon as I can.'

'No, it's OK, I just wanted to text Jen to maybe get some of my things, pyjamas, toothbrush, stuff like that.' She leaned back on the pillows again. The effort of moving exhausted her.

'Don't worry, she's already on it,' Sharif told her. 'I'm sure they're on the way back here now.' He could see her eyelids drooping once more. 'Go to sleep now, and I'll just wait here, OK?'

'OK...' And within a moment, she was asleep again.

Relief flooded Sharif's mind and body. It felt like he'd been on a knife edge for months. Was that business with Zeinab only last night? It felt like a lifetime ago. Carmel was OK, and they were having a baby.

He dozed in the hard chair and only woke when he felt a hand on his shoulder.

'Ammi.' He woke to find Nadia and Joe in the room. Nadia was carrying Carmel's smaller suitcase.

'How is she?' Nadia asked, her face registering shock at how battered Carmel looked.

'It looks worse than it is,' Sharif assured her. 'She's going to be fine. A fractured skull, ulna and tibia, a deep gash on her head... She has some dissolving stitches there, and some soft tissue damage to her face and chest. But nothing she won't recover from with love and care.'

'Oh, Sharif, thank goodness she is alive. I...'

Tears welled in Nadia's eyes for the first time since they'd heard the news.

Carmel's eyes opened. 'Hi, guys,' she said weakly.

'Hello, my darling girl, it's so good to see you awake.' Joe held her hand and kissed her forehead.

Carmel saw Nadia was crying. 'Ah, Nadia, I'm grand...honestly... I'll be fine.'

Sharif was about to put his arm around his mother, to comfort her, but he noticed Joe got there first. He also noticed how his mother relaxed into the man's embrace. Surely, Joe hadn't taken him at his word that quickly.

His face must have registered some confusion.

'Are we missing something here?' Carmel asked straight out, trying not to smile.

Joe looked from Sharif to Carmel and then down at Nadia.

'Well, I suppose we have to come clean sometime.'

adia looked sheepish, but she explained. 'Darling Sharif, Joe told me what you said this morning, and I'm sorry for not being honest earlier, but we were worried how you and Carmel would take it. Jennifer and Luke too, but... Joe and I, well, we have been seeing each other a bit...'

Joe helped her out, his arm still firmly around her. 'We liked each other for ages, since the very start, if I'm honest, and we've gone out to dinner a few times. We talk on the phone most days, but as Nadia said, it was a bit weird. Not the dates, they were lovely, but just the whole setup. And so we thought maybe it would be better to be friends and that, but, eh... Well, we didn't manage that so well. So when you said what you said this morning, Sharif, that you and Carmel had discussed it, and that ye were OK with it...'

'Joe came back and told me,' Nadia continued for him. 'And, well, I hope you meant it and that you spoke for Carmel too?'

'So you two have been together for ages? Is that what you're telling us?' Carmel was stunned. They were a pair of dark horses.

'But how could we not know?' Sharif was equally perplexed. 'Whenever you come over Joe, you stay with us, and Ammi, you've only been away for those weekends on the yoga retreats... Ammi, those were yoga retreats, weren't they?' Sharif seemed genuinely shocked.

This time, Joe and Nadia really did look like teenagers caught getting amorous on the couch by early returning parents.

'I don't know, Sharif, the elderly of today, there's no dealing with them,' Carmel teased. 'Sex mad. I blame the kids myself, or maybe it's the vitamins they all take now. Has them like goats in spring.'

'Stop that talk you! Respect you elders!' Joe chuckled but then grew serious, worried. 'Are you sure ye are OK, though, seriously?'

'Of course we are, you silly man! We're thrilled for both of you. And now we can all go on one of those trashy shows on daytime telly now—*Long-Lost Irish Dad in Romp with Paki Mother-in-Law*. I can just see the headlines.' She giggled again and immediately winced with pain.

'Hey, less of the romping images if you don't mind, please.' Sharif shuddered with mock horror. 'That's my mother we're talking about, and she does not romp.'

'Indeed,' Joe said sincerely. 'She's a perfect lady, and she means a lot to me.'

'Does anyone else know?' Carmel was fascinated at how they kept it secret for so long. Nadia had been going to so-called yoga retreats for months.

'Zeinab,' Nadia revealed.

It was the first time her name had come up since the accident.

Carmel and Sharif waited for an explanation, and Nadia began, 'When we went back to the hotel, I decided she and I needed to talk. So we went for a long walk, and she apologised for the way she'd blurted out about Khalid's affair. I was so hurt, but I realised my hurt was at him, not her. I could have found out anywhere in Karachi on any of the occasions when Khalid and I went back. I'm sure some of our Pakistani friends in London knew, even enjoyed pitying me as the grieving widow, clueless as to what my husband had done.

'After talking to Sharif, who got his wisdom from our darling

Dolly, I have come around to how they saw it. It was one mistake a long time ago. Khalid loved me and Sharif. I know he did. But he made a mistake, and rather than destroy three lives, he bore the guilt and shame himself and allowed me and his son a life of carefree happiness. He was not a selfish man, and his memory is still in my heart. Nothing will ever change that. So, I told her why it annoyed me so much to see her flirting with Joe. I was jealous, simple as that. I... I had—*have*—feelings for him, and she touching him and trying to ingratiate herself just annoyed me. I wasn't kind. Her marriage to Tariq was a bad one, and she admits it now. I think she is tired, tired of always pretending, always having to look down on others in order to elevate herself.'

Sharif was glad his mother and aunt had patched things up, but he wasn't convinced of his aunt's ability to change. 'I hope you haven't said she can live here or anything, though, have you?'

Nadia smiled. 'I said I forgave her, Sharif. I didn't say I had entirely taken leave of my senses. Of course not. She could drive the Dalai Lama insane. No, she's going back to Karachi next week, just like she planned.'

Sharif sighed with relief. Carmel grabbed his hand, her glance questioning. He nodded slightly.

'Well, since we are in the business of revelations,' she said and paused. 'I'm pregnant.'

It was Nadia and Joe's turn to be shocked.

They gently hugged Carmel and nearly squeezed the life out of Sharif. The delight in the room was palpable. Tears of joy coursed down Nadia's cheeks as she hugged her son and held her daughter-in-law's hand.

Joe texted Jen and Luke, who had come with him and were down in the lobby waiting for the all-clear to come up to see Carmel. As his son and daughter entered, he blurted everything out, explaining the scenes of jubilation they met in what should have been a sickroom.

Everyone was talking at once, and Jen and Luke seemed amazed but pleased at both pieces of news.

Joe McDaid stood back and surveyed the various parts of his life, unfolding in ways he could never have imagined. His two daughters, both expecting babies of their own, deep in excited chat about how their children would be cousins. And his son and son-in-law teasing Nadia about the secret romance. He began to sing, at first quietly, but eventually so everyone could hear.

'When I was just a little girl, I asked my mother, what will I be? Will I be handsome, will I be rich? Here's what she said to me.'

By the time he got to the chorus, they were all singing along gently.

'Que sera, sera, whatever will be, will be. The future's not ours to see, que sera, sera.'

THE END

Thank you for reading the Carmel Sheehan Series, I really hope you enjoyed it. If you would like to leave a review on Amazon, https://www.amazon.com/Jean-Grainger/e/B00BFUM5N4 that would be wonderful, and I would really appreciate it.

To hear more about new book releases or special offers, just go to my website www.jeangrainger.com and sign up for my mailing list. When you do that you will receive a free full length novel.

I love hearing from readers, so if you want to drop me a line, you can reach me at jean@jeangrainger.com

This series really was a labour of love for me. So many people in our country, and around the world, ended up in state care over the last century in particular, and their experiences are often only coming to light now, decades later.

While Carmel is a work of fiction, her story of feeling less than, her whole life is a common one.

I am so grateful, that I get to do what I do, and none of it would be possible without you, the readers, who continue to support and encourage me every day, so I thank you.

Jean Grainger,
Cork, Ireland. September 27, 2018

Made in the USA
Columbia, SC
07 December 2020

26649766R00300